A BAD END

A BAD END

FERNANDO ROYUELA

Translated from the Spanish by
Peter Bush

Hispabooks Publishing, S. L.
Madrid, Spain
www.hispabooks.com

Copyright © 2000 by Fernando Royuela
Originally published in Spain as *La mala muerte* by Alfaguara, 2000
First published in English by Hispabooks, 2016
English translation copyright © by Peter Bush
Copy-editing by Cecilia Ross
Design © simonpates - www.patesy.com
Cover image: *La muerte tocando guitarra*, Fernando Botero, watercolor,
    164 x 119 cm, Ca. 1980, Colección de Arte del Banco de la República

ISBN 978-84-943658-9-8 (trade paperback)
ISBN 978-84-944262-0-9 (ebook)
Legal Deposit: M-2211-2016

Esta obra ha sido publicada con una subvención
del Ministerio de Educación, Cultura y Deporte de España

For Pote Huerta, to the poison of literature

... and let us reflect,
how when the drama persists and the false sorrow
turns true in our hearts,
that nothing can be done, that the end
we fear is imminent,
that, naturally, our adventure will end,
as it must, as it is written,
as it inevitably must.

Ángel González
Entr'acte

ONE

I've known an endless string of bastards in my lifetime and not wished a single one a bad end. I won't make you an exception. Human beings roam this world blissfully unaware of the tragedy that's lurking around the corner. Some invent gods to help soften the pain, others, meanwhile, seek out the immediacy of pleasure to keep the inevitable at bay, but all are finally measured by the yardstick of death. I'd been warned about my fate, but I never thought it would happen the way it did.

I know why you've come, but I'm good. Till now I'd never faced up to the implacable advance of nonexistence, and that's why your presence belittles rather than terrifies me. I now realize that from the very beginning my life had pointed to our meeting, that my steps were doomed to reach this moment, that I couldn't possibly escape my fate, however ridiculously hard I tried, that nobody, not even those I have loved, will ever be able to mourn my departure. I know you have come to relish the spectacle of my death, I've seen that in your rust-veined eyes, in your grisly fascination, but I no longer fear the end. People say that at the moment of death, scenes from one's life dizzily return like the stills of a film. They say that once you have seen them, consciousness shuts down. That may be true, and right now I may be witnessing the accelerated passage of memories of a blurred past. The likenesses of the faces of the dead underline the continued presence of the spirit and can help the living unpick the conundrums posed by awareness of their finite nature. That will be where I will overcome. Nothing else matters; it's idle chatter and conjecture.

I know you're here to seek diversion in the staging of my death and that it's futile to invoke pity, tenderness, or compassion. I also know you don't harbor any bad faith or hatred and that you only hope to use me to satisfy your curiosity before the inexorable finale. So be it; here you find me wide open, like a book you've just picked up: my every hour its pages, my memories the reason to read, my extinction the final full stop.

I've known a variety of bastards in my lifetime and not wished a single one a bad end. My brother Tranquilino, however, copped it badly. A goods train did away with his first-born rights. It happened one drought-ridden July. He was so happy he'd just made it to fifteen, then, before he realized what hit him, the engine had crushed his forehead. His brain spurted and trickled along the sleepers, where the ants had a field day. Ants store supplies up to guarantee a trouble-free winter, forward planners that they are, and then die just like crickets, that being the wretched lot of nature. My brother Tranquilino enjoyed burning them. He'd chop the heads off a whole box of matches in the entrance to an anthill and set fire to them. Enthralled, he'd watch the chitin burn up, endlessly delighted by the hellish smell scorched lives give off, until the smoke evaporated up his nostrils and his slaver ran out. He was polishing off the town's anthills one by one until that train engine stripped away his life with a hollow thud that echoed beneath the interminable sky of La Mancha.

My brother Tranquilino was so blissfully simpleminded, he was unaware everyone awaits the final transit Providence has assigned, and though some people who insist that they are free might disagree, that's how it is, like it or not. Everyone is welcome to his self-deceit, to his measly cowardice. In the end, it makes no odds. It's in man's nature to rebel against his fate, but he will die anyway. The ants snacked on my brother's brain, but they were only doing what ants have to do. It could have been worse, though it wasn't. Events unravel as they do and not as one would wish. I'm a good case in point—a dwarf from topknot to toe, tiny hands, bandy legs, flat head, a real freak of nature, though respected now thanks to the deference endowed by the tinkle of cash. My mother burst into tears the instant she saw me emerge from her womb. It was nighttime, and she went into labor suddenly and hard. She cried first because of the pain and then out of sorrow. My head tore the flesh yoking the female anus and vagina. The vet later let it be known that she howled like a mountain wolf that's been shot to pieces. When my mother gazed at me, she saw at once how deformed I was. "This one's not come out right, either, has it, Don Gregorio?" Still dangling me by my ankles, the vet simply nodded and wiped the beads of sweat from his forehead. She asked him to break my neck, but the vet benignly ignored her request, cleaned off the slime with lukewarm water, and dressed me in the dusty-pink bodice my mother had bought from a tinker as part of the first outfit for the baby girl she was hoping to give birth to. "He looks better now," he replied, while my mother sobbed, her heart distressed by the spectacle of the male dwarf—not female baby—she'd engendered. Otherwise, she'd have called me María. María, and not Gregorio, after the vet who'd brought me into the world.

Life has always loomed large over us dwarves. Some take to it like a fish to water despite their diminished state and are even happy, while others tramp along the shores of existence like dogs driven wild by urban detritus, licking the sores of their own resentment, tempered by the terrible lash of indifference, as they tumble and stumble toward their tombs.

The gift of violence is usually placed in the clutches of the despairing, the dispossessed, and the demented, but in the end all are done to death by the same bludgeons they use to kill. My brother was a natural bastard; I mean, it was in his blood. His brain was sweet licorice the ants didn't appreciate. The train engine sent the poor fellow flying when he was crossing the line on his way to the miniscule orchard my father owned by the cemetery wall. I reckon that man was never my father. More than likely my brother's, but mine, no way. My father must have been some random bastard who happened to shoot his seed and genetic shortcomings into my mother's womb. Perhaps one of those truck drivers on their way to Valencia who stopped for lunch at El Paquito's, on the outskirts of town, on the far side of the highway. My mother worked there. She cooked stews, washed up, looked after the bar, and did a little bit of the other when she felt like it or they paid for the opportunity. She could be a touch flirty and whorish, like so many women who'd just suffered in their young flesh the shortages brought on by the war. They say she met her husband on the way to the coast when they were being evacuated from Madrid, at a toilet stop in the village made by the Red Aid convoy in which she was traveling. She was a busty sixteen and grabbed him when he appeared over the riverbank where she was crouching, emptying her bladder over a wall reduced to rubble. That was her piece of luck; only two trucks in that convoy made it to Valencia. The other four were blown up by a hail of mortar fire that descended from Franco's heavens.

At El Paquito's the truck drivers could eat beans and pig's ear and then have a nap, alone or with my mother, in the spare room on the mezzanine, away from the blistering sun, their stomachs stirred by digestive gases. I reckon the man who sowed the seed of my life must have possessed a rotten set of chromosomes and belonged to the subsoil of the species, otherwise I can't explain my ravaged face, my ruin of a body propped up by the most grotesque of cornerstones. At the time, my putative father was very ill with tuberculosis, so much so that he passed on a mere three weeks after I was born. He coughed up a gob of sputum, threw up a piece of lung, and collapsed on the sweat-soaked pillow where he'd been resting his enfeebled body. Before he died it's very likely he saw the awesome breasts of the angel of death up by the ceiling, because his eyes bulged wide open when he stared into that flaking void of plaster. My mother wasn't a bit put out by her husband's demise. She was too busy with her cleaning chores and wayward acts, and besides, widowhood granted her moral sovereignty over her own acts. As we all know, the flesh is weak, and hers, being no exception, got lumpier and bumpier. El Paquito's was her base. I hardly saw her. She left me in an esparto-grass basket, diaper cloths carelessly knotted around my middle, and come noon went off to deal with the meat stews, pleased to be rid of the sight of me and eager to toil. "Take a look at him now and then and clear the flies off, so they don't lay their eggs on him," she bid my brother, who nodded back. There I was, in the suntrap of the kitchen floor, stewing in my own soft shit from her first milk, which I champed and gorged on when it was on offer, lest she steal it from me for some traveling salesman still fond of sucking tit. In my heart of hearts is lodged hunger immemorial, the immemorial hunger of Spain. My huge appetite or the insect-like way I clung to her nipples scared my mother, and with every mouthful she gave me, she became more convinced she'd engendered a satanic beast that should have been strangled the minute it poked its bonce into this world. Her milk tasted of angel water perfumed with civet, of savory, nutritious tears, and even of anisette cream, so no wonder I hung rabidly to her glorious breasts and no human brawn existed capable of decoupling me.

My monstrous appetite terrified my mother, and I expect she thought I was going to suck her guts out, because she'd go spare and pinch my nostrils so I gasped for breath, opened my mouth, and dropped from her nipple. She didn't love me. That was fair enough, but at the time, I lacked the acumen to grasp why. Her husband threw a coughing fit simply watching my birth and was struck speechless. I tell you, he died three weeks later. A third gob of spit complete with a blood clot stuck in his soft palate like a posthumous stalactite of snot.

By now, my real father must be offering up his flesh to the worms if that's what Providence decreed. I never met him. I never knew who he was, and that dearth of knowledge was the little I had in common with my mother. She effortlessly turned her back on me to devote herself diligently to El Paquito's clientele. She perfected her beans with pig's ear and became a dab hand at preparing other dishes from La Mancha, like greasy fried breadcrumbs, and bacon soup, which swamps the stomach and thickens the intellect. She took great pains waiting on tables, polishing saucepans, and making and unmaking beds, whether drowsy after a relaxing siesta or in a vinous, nighttime haze. She was a real boon to the owner, a yokel from Motilla del Palancar whose business she eventually propped up with the loot deriving from her servile habits.

The milk she gave me tasted of velvety petals, hidden juices, and still seems warm in memories driven by the white venom of nostalgia. If I clung to her and bit her, it was because I sensed that the next ration might be a long way off or might never come at all. I didn't do so out of spite, I assure you, but from hunger, that hunger that I tell you is part and parcel of me. A man is the hunger he has suffered—whatever the hunger, whoever the man. My brother Tranquilino watched me suckle with the high hopes that flush the faces of fools and sully their looks with a crystalline flow of dribble. The poor lad met his end in the first flower of life, when he was on the threshold of youth, with his semen just beginning to seep. A goods train rolled him over. Bits of his brain fed ants over a whole winter, those same ants he brutally set light to and morbidly watched squirm in the fire, spark in the flames, and in the process perfume his nostrils with the acrid smell of their scorching holocaust. He'd now be sixty-one if he'd not been splattered through the air when he crossed the track on his way to our orchard by the cemetery wall. Of course, there are more horrific deaths, but that was the one my brother copped, and there's no changing that now.

Though your presence in this house fills me with anxious foreboding, it confirms my decision to believe in nothing and accept that destiny is irrevocable and beyond my control. I guessed your intentions the moment I saw your nose peer around the corner, the moment I felt your fascinated fingers exploring the slopes of my deformities and stroking the pages of my soul. There's no need to reveal why you've come; it's obvious from your eyes, your silences, the almost invisible, secret way you strive to listen to me. I sensed the end was nigh, I was at least forewarned, but I never imagined it would be such a hole-in-the-corner affair.

You've come not knowing what brings you or what kind of place this is. I'll tell you. You are in my house, we arrived almost at the same time, you from God knows where, and I from attending my last supper. Providence decided I should finally accept the invitation to the charity Christmas dinner the Meredith Brothers Foundation traditionally puts on year after year, so that's where I've just been. Public figures currently in the limelight love to attend this banquet, celebrated politicians, fashionable actors, preening intellectuals, wealthy entrepreneurs, and socialites in general, all fond of seeing their photos in the glossies. I sent the organization the generous gift it was so kind as to seek from me, and in exchange they desired my presence; you can imagine how people perform to the gallery on these charity evenings: everything is stagey, flashing smiles, and designer vanity. I've barely had time to take off my tie, shower, and pour out that glass of scotch to relax my muscles while waiting for Ms. Dixon to arrive; I'm sure you will have seen her in the media.

When they first make my acquaintance, it's quite usual for people to be wary, mainly the result of their own limitations when it comes to having different kinds of folk than themselves in conversation rather than from any repulsion I might actually be generating. I'm used to that. The fact one is a dwarf means one's already frail frame must develop an extra layer of thick skin. First they can't think what to say, then they tense their muscles, some are rude, but in the end most manage to make a huge effort and produce a couple of polite sentences or clichés: "It's a wonderful night"; "I imagined you were older"; "It's a real honor to shake your hand." Then they clam up, move away, and sink into self-justification of their own shortcomings. Tonight was no different. To my right at the dining table it was all smiles and eyes trying not to look my way, behind, the waiters ignored me except when they served me, with all due attention. Opposite me, the mayor held forth endlessly, addressing nobody in particular. When his eyes met mine, a pleasant, understanding smile blossomed on his cheeks. To my left, however, Commissioner Dixon seemed to be warming to a much riskier gambit, more suited to a lunatic or imbecile than a woman of her standing. However unlikely it might seem, Belinda Dixon, the European commissioner, had been coming on to me quite outrageously throughout the dinner, and I naturally found that rather worrying. Look at me, so old and deformed, yet sparking a woman's desire! No doubt she wanted to use me to act out some kind of unsatisfied perversion. In truth, I felt only pity for her at first. I thought she was a woman in turmoil, someone who was quite unbalanced and capable of committing any act of madness while preserving that smile on her lips. I've always been attracted by extreme personalities, especially those lodged in powerful bodies. Gradually, nevertheless, I'd begun to realize that her presence in that place was no mere coincidence. That it all formed part of a premeditated scenario. Everything had been thought through: her words, her gestures, her risqué comments. I jotted my address on a scrap of paper, and she assured me she'd back out of a previous after-dinner commitment and rush, as soon as humanly possible, to indulge herself in my delightful company. I came home as quickly as I could, and here I am, waiting. When I heard you arrive, I assumed you must be her, that she'd most likely slipped in through the servants' entrance which the maid had opened to take out the trash; I'd heard the roar of the truck and concluded that must be it, but the moment I saw you appear, I finally realized what it was all about.

Throughout my life I've repeatedly reflected on the sardonic nature of Providence's intrusions into my affairs but never concluded it was mere entertainment—a trumped-up novel or wretched fable. I get it now—your presence in my house, tonight's dinner, the youth I wasted among wild beasts . . . I had been forewarned, Providence made sure of that, but only today did I realize that this is how the end would come, and by extension I now wonder whether all other mortals will have to experience something similar one day. It would be so amusing if everybody, you for starters, were to end up in the same situation and at the moment of death the erratic nature of your condition were revealed in the same contemptible way as is happening now to me. Nowadays it seems nonsensical to look to a transcendent beyond and forget the logic of the thinking that governs the social mechanisms of daily life, but in my case it hasn't helped that I've hung on to life, or struggled against it in the disproportionate way you can perhaps imagine. In the end, effort and determination achieve nothing.

One could legitimately surmise I'm feeling desperate, or at least nervous, or perhaps terrified by the looming void, but you see, it's nothing of the sort. My brother Tranquilino was never scared by the crimes he committed; he was one of those bastards without a conscience. He enjoyed hurting me, but never did so in bad faith. The ants, at least, made the most of his brains—poor critters, always hunting for food. My brother used to behead matches at the tiny entrances to anthills and set fire to them. An orangey flash suddenly exploded, filled his nostrils with the scent from the combustion, and he'd take a deep breath and relax. A holocaust for the poor critters, of the three- to four-hundred-degree variety. Then they took their revenge and snacked on the ideas rotting in his encephalic mass. Much good it would do them. Therein lies the greatness of biology, in the futile struggle for survival. Fate amuses itself at our expense and in our faces, and though its belly laughs aren't necessarily counterproductive, they sometimes inflict real pain. That decision spits out the misery of the day-to-day grind and airs humanity's deepest fears. It's quite another matter if it's done with contempt and ignoring one's own contradictions; that's when it ceases to be curative and acquires the sharpness of a blade.

Now nobody calls me a dwarf, at least not to my face. They used to. That was a living death—dwarf, fetch this, dwarf, do that, dwarf, come here, dwarf, go there, piece of shit dwarf, if you don't hurry up, I'll kick you in the face and that will teach you what's what—but all that frightful behavior is a thing of the past, and now people greet me respectfully and congratulate me on my saint's day almost obsequiously. The world goes round and round, the world changes, and all that remains is the hypocrisy of those who take part in each year. If you could pray, I'd be grateful if you would say a prayer in memory of my brother. A train engine clattered into him when he was on an errand for my mother to get a basketful of tomatoes from our plot next to the cemetery wall. It wasn't a great death, but it could have been worse. Just imagine if he'd fallen down a well and drowned after desperately trying to clamber up the slimy walls, pulse racing, hysteria mounting, his life slipping away squish-squish on a dark, wet slide to death. Pray a God save you, if you know how, or a Credo, if it's easier. He used to watch me suckling with hatred in his eyes, and my mother would tell him to beat it, but he took no notice and stayed there, still and silent, feet glued to the kitchen floor, watching me suck the marrow from my mother's soul, the little she had left after all that romping with truck drivers.

It once hailed mollusks in La Mancha. It was the morning when my brother Tranquilino decided to put my crib under the pole of the chicken coop. I was sleeping inside, in the liquid shit in my diapers. He often did that until I learned to walk around the age of one, but that was the only day when mollusks hailed down on La Mancha's dry lands of dung, bitterness, and death. They were as large as a man's fist, and their shells clattered hard on the village roofs. People ran to save their skulls, and the odd animal's back was broken.

I have other defects apart from being a dwarf; I am moved, for example, by poetry and when reading it lose all will to persevere in this world. It's something inevitable that comes from when I fell in love as a child. It could have been worse. It can always be worse. I could have been hooked on invoking the Devil on moonless nights, deranged on barren heaths, chanting evil ditties, and leaping around as one does—*Oh Prince of Darkness, oh wisest, most beautiful of angels, God deceived by fortune and denied all praise, take pity on me in my wretchedness*—but it was not to be. Things are as they are and not as one dreams, wishes, or wants; besides, the Devil would have profited little from my company. My brother Tranquilino put me under the chicken coop post and left me there to help while away his time. He loved watching my body being whitewashed by the hen's excrement, marveling perhaps at the sheer quantity of their crinkly shit. At the time, there was no television, and village life was monotonous. I can't say it wasn't equally so in cities, but I only speak of what I know and hold my peace about what I don't. I understood nothing or next-to-nothing about that moisture falling from heaven like angels' snow and was resigned to my impotence, perhaps crying the occasional futile tear and learning very early and painfully that there are times when it's better to keep one's mouth shut than seek pity from others. When my weary mother made it back from El Paquito's and saw me whitewashed from head to toe, she bellowed at my brother like a woman gone mental, and if she was quick enough to grab him, she'd give him a good leathering, not because he hadn't looked after me but because she now had to do overtime cleaning me up. However, it was a different story that day, and not because it had hailed mollusks in La Mancha, as it did, but because my evil-minded brother

23

decided to behead his matches into my navel. His finger scoured out a hollow in the hen shit, and when he'd made a proper hole, he beheaded three boxes and set fire to them with a mischievous glint in his eye. A cloud of phosphorus rose up the coop post from the center of my belly as I howled my head off in pain. Surprised by the flash, the hens flew up in a flurry of frenzied feathers like archangels under blasphemous attack. If I'd known how, I'd have turned on my front to try to put out the flames in my midriff, but I was only a newly born dwarf, and my worldly knowledge was limited to the instinct to suckle, so I burned, and would have burned to death if my brother hadn't had the sense to foresee the consequences of his mischief and made use of the cure closest to hand. When the flames were so fierce they were about to spread to my reed crib, he undid his fly and peed on me. His spurting liquid washed coolly over my body like holy water. He urinated copiously from my top nut to my pedal extremities, thus dowsing the flames with an opportune shower of uric acid. The misfortune didn't spread, and the fire was put out immediately. I was left with a cavernous gully in my stomach, as if I'd been hit by a tiny mortar bomb or a miniature *falla* effigy from the San José fiestas had been set alight in my navel. I still have the scar. It's not half what it was, but just take a look and you'll get an idea of his dangerous deed. Time erases everything except for hatred and the desire for revenge. It has stopped rankling, but my memory still feels sore when a storm is due. Time heals everything except for the amputation of our extremities and the huge desire for revenge that nests in the mind like freezing birds waiting for their sharp claws to revive.

Being peed on triggers a mysterious sense of well-being that, depending on the situation, can even prompt sexual arousal.

The psychic aberrations wrought by sex have always caused a furor. Anyone who has traveled the world will attest to that. Things are what they are, and it is pointless trying to kick against the pricks. Fire frightens animals, puts their nerves on edge, and they flee in panic down the first path they find, even if it means leaving strips of flesh on thorn bushes or blinding themselves in their flight and hurtling down a ravine like animal Icaruses. Panic must have curdled my brother's urine in his bladder, because the flood that hit me was as hard as wrought iron, so much so that to prevent me from burning, he damaged my weak, cartilaginous bones, as they necessarily were so soon after my birth. The mollusk downpour preoccupied the village for a couple of days, and nobody worried about me, not even the vet. Except my mother when she came back the next morning from El Paquito's. She saw my feverish cheeks and realized my navel had been burnt; she was kind enough to treat it with a poultice of olive oil, dung, and rosemary flower honey. If she hadn't, I'd probably have snuffed it. Burning to death *is* a bad end. My brother never did that again; obviously he took fright. From then on he stuck to anthills, and that kept him busy and amused for the rest of his life, until that train rolled into him and he was spattered to high heaven. The poor fellow didn't die happy, but at least he never suffered. The annals don't register any deluge of mollusks that day in La Mancha, but the storm did catch Algimiro Calatrava, the Scarface of the Chorrero mill, in wasteland, and it smashed his face in. He tried to shield himself with his hands, but the storm blasted away and it was hopeless. Ten minutes longer and he'd have met his end, as well. He'd lost consciousness when they found him. There were villagers who cooked the shellfish with onions or steamed them, and even said how tasty, though that's hardly surprising from people living in the backcountry, with yokel brains, skin turned leathery by the blistering sun, and palates reared on chewy bacon. Algimiro Calatrava cursed the heavens because of that incident that almost blinded him. "I shit on that bastard God that dropped those creatures on me. I hope the Jews spit blood on him," they say he kept saying. Everyone squares their accounts with fate as best they can. Some even defy it with fists held high, but in the end fate wins out and sours their good fortune. We like to waste our energies on senseless acts, and now you see the result, we simply meet our end when our time is judged to be up.

Some people I've dealt with have led me to intuit that the impulse driving some men to create or procreate is a kind of sublimation in their own flesh of the life-generating power of the divine. On the other hand, I'd rather think that the drive they possess is only the neurotic expression of an inability to see life from the perspectives of common sense and normality. To recreate scenes in painting or imagine the lives of others in a novel has to be a form of macabre amusement that ought to turn against those practitioners in the guise of a proper social rebuff. The specter of Faith Oxen revealed to me when she appeared in my London hotel room that she'd read to the end of my life in fate's grimy pages. A splendid statement coming from a ghost. She didn't say whether she's read yours as well. If people's lives were written in advance, they'd simply leap across all ethical boundaries in a mayhem of the flesh, and nobody could blame them for behavior not of their choosing. It's an attractive idea, at least worthy of inclusion in a fable, although I can tell you that using the horrors experienced by human beings to spin out a yarn reveals a remarkable lack of scruples.

Portrait painting, novel writing, and film making are, for the most part, despicable acts and should be treated with contempt and the full rigor of the law.

My brother Tranquilino might well have liked to paint portraits, though possibly not. He died young and didn't have the chance to paint a picture or taste a pizza *capricciosa*, let alone a *quattro formaggi*—they weren't the rage at the time. A train robbed him of his life one bright morning while swallows mewled hungrily above the overhead power lines. My brother might have been happy writing novels or making films, though possibly not. Who can say? The poor fellow met an early death, but at least he had the opportunity to taste mollusks. Raw, but still. A train rolled over his life on a morning when the swallows were swooping and whistling hungrily above the posts by the railroad track. Perhaps they were the very same dark, hungry swallows that returned to hang their nests from that balcony year after year, though not the ones that learned to hate our names because of the countless pebbles we catapulted their way. Apart from being a dwarf, I am unlucky enough to find poetry moving, and please do hear me out without getting offended, and I hope nobody will start malevolently misinterpreting my words.

When the civil war finished, a school was built in the poplar grove on the village outskirts. It had a huge green-painted entrance door that was bolted to the ground by a crossbeam the children jumped over when they were going in or out. *Grupo Escolar Ledesma Ramos* was painted on the façade in letters that stood to attention straight out of a calligraphy of victory. I didn't attend very much, the master said I'd be better off with the animals in the fields than learning trigonometry, and besides, if I did put in an appearance, the other children only greeted me with a round of kicks. "Shall we boot him to bits?" they shouted, and right away their toecaps lofted me sky high. My brother also joined in the chase. His kicks hurt most, not because they came from his feet, but because he put the most energy into his onslaught. I clearly rankled him even though I was a dwarf.

I'd sometimes hide behind the wasteland by the threshing ground and spy on the children when they started playing soccer after school with rusty cans or round rocks wrapped in rags. That way, their kicks didn't harm me anymore. In those days, municipal sports stadiums didn't exist. Nor, for that matter, did sports newspapers, the ones that produce such enigmatic headlines, particularly for a non-believer like myself whose only sport in life has been the marathon of scraping by. If I left my hideout and strained to watch them having fun, they'd aim the ball at my head rather than the goalmouth and score when they hit me. The religion of the leather ball rules the West. Its disciples are dazzled by sumptuous opulence, they eye the fortunes in play, hoping a crumb might fall from some corner and bolster their own lives. Childish dreams that awake to disappointment or grief. I never owned a proper ball, though I was sometimes used as one. I tell you, I still remember what those pitiless taps felt like, I still remember those kicks, soft, pitying kicks, or kicks packed with flat-footed glee, kicks that hurt in the depths of your soul, as if those nether parts *were* your soul, or, vice versa, your soul were that leather object.

Those brutes bashed me whenever they felt like it, so I stopped going to school, and rather than educating myself on all that boasting about the conquest of Granada or the heroics of Guzmán el Bueno, I shut myself in the stable with a book

I'd taken from the school and which, with determination and the help of Providence, I soon learned to read: the *Rhymes of Gustavo Adolfo*. That's where I began to adore poetry, to be moved while I hid from the madding world and enjoyed incognito the frothy flow of his verse, a dwarf alone among animal droppings.

In the pages of that book, I found consolation for a deformity I began to see would forever be the butt of others' anger. There I succeeded in tasting melancholy's iron-flecked charm—*Floating silk of haze and mist, twisting ribbon of foaming white* ... —and as a climax to my absurd childhood, I went and fell in love.

The Civil Guards' barracks sported a *Todo por la patria* on the façade that looked down on the Plaza del Caudillo. Endless pots of geraniums, enameled with the red and yellow of the national flag, gave a fly-blown flourish to their authority. Gossip had it that Sergeant Ceballos was a coward as well as a bastard. Gossip from the camp of the defeated, naturally. People also said that during one of the attacks launched by the Nationalists on the Teruel front to cross the Tagus, Sergeant Ceballos shot his lieutenant in the back so the latter couldn't give the order to advance into the enemy fire that was buzzing with shrapnel released from mortars on the other side of the river, from the direction of Cuenca. Then he shot himself in the foot to a frightful hullaballoo, which all earned him— surprise, surprise—a medal for his valor in battle, awarded by none other than General Mansilla y Gutiérrez de Tejares. "With brave men like yourself, victories come shining bright; may a peerless morning star always guide your glistening brow at dawn along the path of pride at having served your country with the glorious courage of a soldier who marks the flag with his blood and craves only the unrivaled badge of being called Spanish—*viva Franco, arriba España*."

Sergeant Ceballos was one of those bastards exalted by the pomp of their uniform, I mean, a man greased by power. Nevertheless, he had two virtues: the length and color of his moustache, which was wondrous to behold in its wine-soaked glory when he took it for a nighttime stroll around the village bars, and the daughter he sired. "Hey, dwarf, come and clean my shoes with that pesky tongue of yours and then shine them on your mother's hairy twat."

Sergeant Ceballos was a decorated war hero and voiced his desires with the bellicosity his rank merited. Everyone nodded and acquiesced; otherwise, apart from me and his booze, his only entertainment was sniffing out hares in the hills, shotgun on shoulder, or disemboweling birds when practicing his aim. "If I catch you, dwarf, I'll shave every hair off that pear-shaped skull of yours, you bonehead"; and when he saw me skedaddle, he'd guffaw, in that gruff, croaky voice he coaxed out of his larynx. I wasn't really worried by his attitude, or by the cruel way he insulted my handicap, or if his boot caught me when I was slow on the uptake; at the end of the day, he possessed an authority conferred by the triumph of arms, which, in those days was sacred. I could have put up with all of that—his stamping on me, his slaps, his huge contempt— but not his insistence that I should keep well away from his daughter, his intolerable view that I shouldn't see her or talk to her.

Sergeant Ceballos was a bastard invested with the right of might, though that didn't spare him from a bad end. I fled from his path the moment I spotted him in the village, not because he was going to humiliate me with insults or aim hurtful barbs at my dignity, though that was bad enough, but because he was the father of little Margarita, the love of my life at the time, and because his mere presence drove me crazy and forced me to wonder angrily how a repulsive idiot like him could have sired such an angel. Little Margarita had the whitest skin, long eyelashes, and an aroma of flaky pastry that trailed in the air behind her, as if her tresses were scented with cake-shop essence. In the afternoon, I stationed myself by the ruined wall where the women used to pee when they walked back from doing their washing in the river (that same wall where my mother first bumped into my father), waited for her to leave school, and then followed her back to the barracks, bathed in the feminine smells wafting from her springtime. "Clear off, titch, can't you see we want a piss? Everyday it's the same, clear off, beat it to the hills with the goats and maybe they'll shit on you," they groused, gathering up their skirts at the speed demanded of them by their bladders.

Sergeant Ceballos had sternly warned me to leave his daughter alone, and he never missed an opportunity to scour my sensitive feelings with his threats. "If I catch you hovering around her, I'll cut them off, if you have any, and stick them straight up your ass." I had no choice but to ignore him; my heart dictated to me without an ounce of sense, and I could only wish for him death, a fine death that he never met. I was sure of one thing, if coming into this world was worth the candle, it was only to admire beautiful little Margarita.

Love between children is raw and painful, perhaps that's why it is the truest, the one that most issues from the soul. Little Margarita would never have kissed me; she'd rather have been deflowered by a toad. Conversely, I'd have given the rest of my life to taste her lips just once, to drink from them with mine, to wallow in the double cream of her cheeks and bedeck myself in the pollen of her love. When I was older, I felt something similar, though in a more prosaic, not to say indecorous, fashion. That was with Juana, though people called her "Blondie."

The lowering sky creaked like an old beam on the point of collapse when little Margarita left school at midday. She was the only light. She scattered her smiles and wore a mystery about her chest that my eyes devoured. The air tasted hard in her footsteps and jammed my lungs, as my short legs felt a real strain keeping up with her nimble pace, not to mention the way she was punishing my heart. I crouched behind the crumbling wall by the riverbank, just before school ended, and counted the minutes. You could still see bullet holes, like small niches in the flaking stone—orifices left by the executions ordered by Franco's troops when they entered the village like wild animals in May of '36 scattering death sentences like confetti. "Clear off, dwarf, for God's sake, we're going to have a piss," the women shouted bad temperedly as they walked up from the river where they'd been washing clothes, their brows streaming with sweat and bundles of sheets still wetting their hips like dripping clouds. Startled by their bawls, I leapt up on my short shanks and ran hell-for-leather to hide somewhere else, dead quiet, behind a dry, half-rotten elm tree split by lightning, behind the mule trough, or in the shadowy arches on the plaza, dead quiet, waiting for little Margarita to slice deep into my disquiet with her sharp-bladed footsteps. I've always found it fun to take refuge away from people and, protected by my solitude, to scrutinize the world without being seen myself. I don't deny this may be a consequence of my handicap; you see how I'm the first to acknowledge my defects in public: a dwarf, a grizzly temper, a liking for poetry, and all the rest I've yet to recount.

The teacher didn't want to see me anywhere near the school. He said my ugly looks distracted the pupils and that I stopped them from learning what they needed to become pillars of society; in other words, he reckoned I was a freak of nature, and if painters had been around now like the Goyas or Velázquezes of yore, I might have at least served as a model for the monsters they wanted to paint, but as there weren't, I was no use at all. My brother Tranquilino did go to school. He'd rest his bonce on the window and engross himself in the spectacle of the storks flying to and fro from the belfry, while he picked his nose out of pure boredom. He'd have just loved to burn their nests with them inside, but a train killed him before he reached an age to be able to carry out such a lofty deed. Iron wheels carried him off one morning when he was on an errand to pick tomatoes from our plot of land by the cemetery. He met a really bad end; he was smashed and shredded.

The teacher was a fuddy-duddy who was proud of the Latin he'd memorized in his youth and now, on the last straight of his career, grimly hissed at his pupils. "*Dulce et decorum est pro patria mori sed omnia vulnerant postuma necat*, as Brutus said when he enacted his parricide, meaning, in plain language, that penitence always accompanies sin," and he'd slaver over his witless wit. Then, at home, he purged his aches and pains by revisiting the glories of Hernán Cortés as recounted by Bernal Díaz del Castillo or wallowing in the historical melodramas penned by Juan Eugenio Hartzenbusch.

I thieved a book from the school, the *Rhymes* by Gustavo Adolfo. The teacher didn't notice then, but he did once catch me reading it behind the pissing wall. It was evident that he'd gone out to nose around the piss after ordering his pupils to copy out five hundred times *José Antonio enlightened the fatherland with his wisdom and sowed the dawn of Spain with his blood.* "Who the hell taught you to read? Let me have a look; this isn't your book, you've stolen it. You're a thief as well as a freak," he rasped angrily, no doubt because our unexpected encounter had highlighted his own perversions. "People who read poetry aren't real men. Besides, those who read Bécquer tempt those who *are* with love's silly notions. You never will be a man, that's patently obvious, but at least have an animal's dignity and don't aspire to feelings that are inappropriate to your nature." I didn't understand what he meant. I simply snatched my book from his hands and ran off. Poor fellow. He met a bad end, the end that awaits all those men who like to wallow in their loneliness, a cold and miserable death that dragged out over two winters.

I've always liked to escape from people, to shelter out of the way, to gaze at whatever without being seen, and darn the gaping holes in the cloth of reality with the eager thread of my thoughts. Reading was one way, but not the only one; fasting and masturbation also brought their grain of wisdom. Ninety years ago, Gustavo Adolfo had puked the aesthetics of melancholy all over his *Rhymes*. Now I picked up the baton and replaced him in the amorous anxiety stakes with my utopian adoration of little Margarita. I would seek out a pigsty, a stable, a dung heap, and in its darkest corner sink into a mire of sighs and self-pity, a smooth-cheeked innocent, unaware that it was, in fact, animal excrement. *Over your breast you bow a brow so melancholy, to me you're like a snapped Madonna lily.* Gradually, quite unawares, I was inching up the slippery steps that, irrevocably, sluice into the bewilderment of love. With each poem I read, little Margarita Ceballos's mother-of-pearl face increasingly seemed to belong to the deity of bliss, the one whose kisses could redeem me from my original defects. I wasn't any less despicable than I am now, but I was trying to squeeze heaven dry with that blessed meekness that brings submission to the weak and destiny to fools; that was the stuff my dreams were made of. Experience is the great saboteur, time the spoiler, and at the end of the road, there's only that sediment of unease that settles after the orgasm with which Providence conceives us. I was sired by one bastard of a tramp who stopped at El Paquito's to relieve three things at once: his bladder, his belly, and his knob; then he disappeared whence he came, on his way to the east coast, to load boxes of fish that finished up as mildewed merchandise in Madrid.

Sergeant Ceballos used to say my mother was a bitch in heat who'd let herself be licked clean for a plate of fly-ridden meat. Sergeant Ceballos was one of those bastards in uniform, though it didn't stop him from meeting a bad end. The thick, wine-soaked moustache that bristled threateningly from his nostrils couldn't save him when his time came, what's more, it contributed to his suffering, because the three gypsy grasshoppers who did him to death used them to string him up from the fruit tree where he atoned for his sins, a maverick apple tree hidden in the mayor's pear orchard; and then people reckon gypsies don't have bright ideas. The grocer, whose concubine was Blondie, experienced a similar *contretemps* years later that taught him a lesson for leaking positions to the Sandinista army. Sergeant Ceballos was knifed simply because he brought it upon himself. If he hadn't raced after them in their orgy of thievery in the orchard, surely nothing untoward would have happened, but he had to swagger in his fine uniform and take two potshots at the gypsies. He must have been plastered on plonk, otherwise he'd never have dared challenge them. They held nice masses for him, full of candles and Madonna lilies, though they did nothing to resurrect him, and little Margarita became an orphan, juicy and ripe like the mayor's pears, which her father gave his life to save. They'd loaded up three quarters of the cart when tragedy struck. It was nighttime, the stars were scintillating on the lime deposits in and around the river, and the blades of their knives were exhilarated by that explosion of light. He shot twice. It's very likely he pulled the trigger four times, but the men in the village said only two actually fired. The gypsies weren't frightened; on the contrary, they went for him, pummeled the back of his neck, punched him in the stomach, buckled him over, threw him to the ground, and sunk their knives into his guts, then strung him up, still alive, by his moustache from the maverick apple tree that happened to be at hand. *That* was their bright idea. They could have bashed his skull in or ruthlessly cut through his jugular, but things being what they are and not what we might like them to be, the gypsies strung Sergeant Ceballos up one silvery night after entertaining him with a display of knives, as if they'd just escaped from a poem by Federico. His cheeks turned to rigor mortis leather; the next morning they glistened with hoar frost. The following week the gypsy grasshoppers were caught trying to cross the border into Portugal and were all garroted, first because it was the current fashion and second because that was the judges' sentence, but by the time they meted out their punishment, Sergeant Ceballos lay half-rotten in the village cemetery, the welcoming little cemetery by the orchard where my brother was heading to pick tomatoes the day the train rolled him over.

Previously, priests were the only ones privy to the details of the stories their parishioners were so good as to tell them in the secrecy of the confessional. When they'd heard them, they imposed some form of penitence and absolved them with a two-fingered gesture. Today, nobody listens. I only had to see you to realize that you'd come to carry out the designs of Providence, that you were here to terminate my life. Providence has its cruel side, and facilitating my meeting with the European commissioner tonight is redolent with unforgiveable sarcasm. These are strange times, and not even you can escape the turmoil, peculiar times when everyone is a prophet in his own land. Sergeant Ceballos, with his dark-purple moustache, his veteran's honor and cheap swagger, could never have adapted to them. It was just as well he died when he did. By the time they found him that morning, one of the knots stringing him up by his moustache had worked loose and his corpse was swinging with a macabre tick-tock. Magpies, those birds of ill omen, were croaking on his shoulder, and now and then they stuck their beaks into his ear-holes to savor the wax. Smaller beasties and native insects skated over the pool of frozen blood on his shadow. The men from the village scared them off with their cries. "They've hung the sergeant by his moustache, they've hung the sergeant by his moustache, his belly is slit and one eye is dangling down his cheek!" He was a fresh corpse that swaggered no more. I ran over to have a look. They didn't let the boys get close, but they weren't that worried about me. Naturally, swaying on one end of his moustache, his guts hanging out, it hardly seemed possible that not so long ago he'd taught me a lesson that had cracked my skull and ravaged my soul.

As so often, I was stationed at the pissing wall, waiting for the bell to ring at the end of the school day so I could lap up little Margarita's footsteps. I remember how I was trembling more than usual that day, perhaps because I so wanted to recite to her at the top of my voice, out in the open, some of Gustavo Adolfo's lines that perfectly captured my feelings: *I know the reason for your sighs; I know the source of your secret sweet lethargy.* When she walked out, I hopped after her down a street called Caídos de la División Azul to the village plaza, a shabby plaza with a drinking trough for mules in its center that pretended to be a fountain. Little Margarita occasionally turned around to look at me, perhaps shocked by the way I stumbled along, far too clumsily that day, or perhaps worried my proximity might do her some physical harm. She glanced back on the sly and sped up. The harshness in her angry eyes was no doubt reflected in the balloons of spit bubbling from my mouth because the slope was so steep. Gustavo Adolfo was simmering in my brain, but my panting and puffing led her to misread my intentions. By what strange, untimely means do feelings flood our bodies? How could I fall in love with that flesh-and-blood monster? The discharge from such sweet charms is evil, and it's best to steer clear. However, being such a dullard and coward, I sank into that sticky mire like a fly in honey a bear's about to eat, flickering with desire and ready to die. Little Margarita flashed a devious grin in my direction when she saw her father in the plaza heading toward me. The lines I should have declaimed clotted in my throat at the sight of him. "Why are you slavering after my daughter, dwarf? Didn't I tell you not even to whiff her? Come here, you titchy critter, and let me teach you what's what." I didn't have time to say that I was only hoping to recite a few lines of poetry I'd been learning by heart, because he grabbed me by the gizzard, lifted me up level with his eyes, and after impregnating my nose with the stink from his breath or tickling it with the scimitar of his moustache, he hurled me at the mule trough, and so unluckily that I cracked my skull on the water spout. "If I find you within five miles of my daughter, dwarf, I'll cut them off, you little bugger, I've told you that more than once, and I won't tell you again," threatened Sergeant Ceballos, full of himself and shaking my snot off his uniform with a grimace of disgust. Scared to death, skull cracked, the water red with my blood, I made a supreme effort to remain dignified, so as to at least impress little Margarita, but the pain was such that I couldn't contain myself, and I started blubbering. Tears of unrequited love, of hurt pride, of battered dignity streamed down there in the presence of deadpan little Margarita. I even wept blood. That was the only time I ever did. In other circumstances I've wept bile, semen, and even whisky, but I've never again shed a tear of blood. I cried so much, it all got mixed up with the water, and the whites of the eyes of the mules that drank there over the next few days were striated with blood. Seen from a trough, the world seems large and alien. Little Margarita smiled a sick rabbit smile, laughed at my peculiar baptism, and had no pity or compassion for me in that state. The clapper in my brain banged against my skull, and humiliation coursed through my veins until it swamped my heart. I stayed there awhile, broken and bewildered; dogs came to sniff out the extent of the damage, which was considerable even though I was only a dwarf, and showed me their weary tongues as if trying to deaden my pain with the balsam of their saliva or at best taste my humors and thus satiate their own appetites.

Sergeant Ceballos was a coward of the old school, a man who was ill served by his own limitations and only lost his temper with weaklings, but think on this, in the end he got it wrong and paid for his arrogance with his life. He was probably drunk when he caught the gypsies stealing pears, if not, there's no accounting for his deed, or perhaps he just underestimated the race; that night he received his just desserts in stab wounds. He met a bad end, though it could have been worse if the wolves had come and gorged on his corpse, still clad in the Civil Guard uniform, as indeed it was, but that was not to be. Things happen the way they do, and not as people might want them to. My forehead emerged badly from the lesson he taught me, and learning Gustavo Adolfo's poetry by heart did me no good. The pain went deep, and though it flowered from my head, its shoots actually sprang from my soul. I left the trough battered and limp and walked to my mother's house with my head split open. Despite the pain, I kept imagining a thousand kinds of revenge that were all quite fantastic and impossible. It's incredible what the human mind can spawn. Over the years I have learned to classify my emotions; initially I was helped by the regular kicks that came my way, but later, particularly after the designs of Providence led me to the ranks of the great and the good, I met with scorn the smiles of hypocrites, faced out with aloofness the mellifluous tones of flatterers, ranted with anger against the pettiness of the wretched, and sought revenge to soothe wounds that hadn't healed and were still sore. "Whatever can have become of little Margarita?" I wondered one night a long ways off from my childhood when malt whisky was clouding my memory with nostalgia's tawny gold. Could she still be living in the village, or might she have moved off to a dormitory town where she now lived a life of disillusion in the barren wastes of menopause? Would she still remember the disabled dwarf who never had the courage to love her after that? Without giving it too much thought, I decided to clear up my doubts and contract the services of a detective agency to investigate where she'd holed up. I was curious to find out what the rough edges of time had done to my childhood's most sublime desire, ineffable dreams that turn to ash when you wake up an adult, ash or mud, because the stuff of dreams is unstable and can be lethal, out of necessity. The detective they sent, a skinny, cadaverous fellow seemingly reared on lettuce leaves, didn't flinch when I revealed his task: "I want you to find little Margarita Ceballos." And he didn't hesitate to charge me an exorbitant fee when he found her in Ciudad Real in a matter of days. As far as ordinary folk are concerned, dwarves are excrescences that must have sprouted like warts on an old woman's face, and they cannot conceive how we can fall in love. Money, nevertheless, puts everything right. In his report, he wrote that little Margarita Ceballos had been driven into impoverished widowhood by the unpaid fines handed out to her cabdriver husband and now ran a tiny haberdashery where the most sold items were extraordinary knickers for fat women and bras like saucepans. Hers was a simple life, and she misspent the scant earnings from her shop on slot machines in bars or the Eldorado Bingo Palace, a haunt suitable for pensioners chastened by necessity. I jettisoned all the commitments in my diary, told my chauffeur in confidence of my destination, and arrived the following day. I'd not been to Ciudad Real for many years, probably since the last time I performed there with the Stéfano circus in '66, and the city seemed as anodyne as so many others across that Spain I visited

42

in my youth, led by the hand of Stéfano di Battista. We reached
the address in the report. I got out of the car and went over to
the haberdashery. Before deciding to go inside, I took a look
in the window. Through glass covered in squashed flies, I
glimpsed a messy array of unfashionable lace and lingerie that
hung from two racks that had faded in the yellow sun. Her
back to me, on a ladder, little Margarita was putting boxes of
stockings on metal shelves, and wasn't I astonished when I
registered the big-bang of her hips expanding before my eyes
and what one might dub a Taj Mahal of a bum, gross buttocks,
an extraordinary mass of flesh, such was the effect the passage
of time had inflicted on my childhood love. After my initial
shock, I started to laugh and heave with guffaws that blocked
my windpipe. I opted not to go in. I would plot something
that would adequately respond to my plans for her. Death,
perhaps.

Time imprints its grotesque round on individuals—a
molecular weight of seconds that accumulates into hours and
distorts bodies. An advantage of being born a dwarf is that
one takes one's deformities in one's stride; one isn't forced to
complain when they appear at different growth stages. If little
Margarita had been stricter with her food, she might never
have become so fat, but then again she might have. Providence
makes its decisions in advance, and nobody, not even lunatics,
can reverse them. Over the years I have learned to anticipate
its diktats at every second and recognize its voice amid the
sighs of despair and poverty and even the fanfares of opulence,
and please believe me if I say my will has always yielded to
its designs. The deadly dust of resignation gradually settles on
life's long, tortuous road, and nobody escapes the erosion of
the flesh.

Faith clouds the intellect, stymies critical thought, and brings on death, although you might retort *what is death when one dies for faith?* They tell the followers of Mohammed that if they die defending their faith, they will go to paradise. Sergeant Ceballos proclaimed his faith in his uniform, and look how he ended up, a paltry piece of flesh disemboweled at dawn by a flurry of stabs from a couple of rag-and-bone men. He must have been plastered on plonk. I shall never forget the way he looked at me in the trough, at once a bully and a coward. My blood streaked the water crimson, and the whites of the eyes of the mules that drank there turned ruby red, as if they were two blood clots rather than two pupils. Little Margarita begged her father to dunk my head under so she'd never have to look at it again, but he paid no heed and simply reiterated his threat: "If I find you within five miles of her, I'll neuter you."

I extricated myself from the trough as best I could; it wasn't easy, it had a high parapet, and the strength had gone from my arms. I walked to my mother's house, instinctively searching for relief like an injured dog wanting to be licked. I walked past my brother Tranquilino, who was lurking in the shadows of the poplar grove and about to practice with his slingshot by shooting a pebble in my direction, a slingshot he'd cleverly fashioned from a forked hazelnut branch so he could kill storks in flight. The poor fellow had the decency to abstain when he saw the blood streaming from me as if I were the carved wooden ecce homo statue they promenade in Holy Week amid heavy wax candles and pointed hoods. I should have said *ecce homunculus*, but Latin is a dead language useful only for deciphering the brief lives of the tenants of tombs. "Did they thrash you, Gregorito?" he asked when he saw me. "Fuck, you're covered in blood," and without more ado, off he went to kill birds or incinerate ants or waste the little life that was left to him on trivial pursuits before the train rolled over him, crash, bang, like a bevy of nightmares dissipated by the dawn.

My mother lived in a large, down-at-heel house. Everywhere was littered with piles of useless junk, survivors from bygone uses and days, from times that might have been happy. The entrance was a shadowy alcove off which staircases led to the kitchen and bedrooms. On the ground floor, right-hand side, the door to the stable was open, a gloomy spot that reeked of the lingering stench of guts even though there were no animals. A handful of hens clucking out of tradition still lived there, bereft of company and perching on posts. The rest was pure absence. Mules, donkeys, sheep, and pigs had left their mark on the walls, and aromas from their butchered fates hung visibly between shards of light that seeped through a large window crucified by a wrought-iron grill. The remains of a small hutch still stood in one corner; my mother's father-in-law had built it with wire and wood to house rabbits and hares, wild creatures that capered in the fields before the starving adversaries of '36 cleaned them out tooth and nail as they were shooting left and right in these lands God once threw up. "God doesn't exist," intoned my brother Tranquilino with the conviction of a fool. "God doesn't exist, mother told me so," then he walked off quite full of himself, jumping hysterically and kicking the air like a donkey. That midday when Sergeant Ceballos taught me a lesson on the trough in the plaza, I'd probably have rather sought refuge and relief in those shadowy stables and the melancholy of Gustavo Adolfo's *Rhymes*. Grief best and most bitterly wallows in its own impotence when in solitude. I would have done so with pleasure, perhaps for the last time, but my head was on fire, and spilt blood was quick to dowse my desires with its outrageous hues, so I decided to go up to the kitchen and wait for my mother. I laid down on the bench we kept next to the pantry wall. My thoughts were buzzing like a legion of flies gorging on the honey of my ideas. I spent the whole afternoon there and a good part of that night, with no food or drink, restless and queasy, until my mother returned from El Paquito's. Perhaps my raging temperature gave me a few hours' sleep; perhaps I dreamt of a lake of rose petals where little Margarita swam naked in my presence, unperturbed by my dwarfish deformities; perhaps I dreamt little Margarita shamelessly abandoned the florid water where she'd performed fantastic pirouettes and showed me firm extremities that I eyed eagerly, loving the way the water ran off her belly, until she was completely out of the pool and I gazed in terror at the disgusting dimensions of a male sex nestling in her groin like an elephant's hairy trunk. Dreams may—or may not be—meaningless. Dreams are unforeseen happenings that often torture us with their tangible unreality. Perhaps they are faint anticipations of death, horrific samples of the void that pursues us daily until we sink into it forever. When I woke up, a puddle of blood had spread next to my cheeks. I heard my mother's footsteps on the stairs. Her face was wan and pale from the unhealthy fug in El Paquito's, and the rest of her body had been battered by the horizontal nature of her toiling. She walked over and placed her hand on my forehead, and do believe me if I say that despite the life I've endured, I still treasure that gesture amongst my loveliest memories; at the end of the day, a mother will always be a mother, and however much she tries to hide it, however monstrous her son may be, instinct will always seep through her pores like milk from the tit. My mother sat on the bench, lifted my head up, and rested it on the warm pillow of her calf. Her body smelt limp, of molten metal and intimate juices. Then she caressed my face with a tenderness she'd never previously shown. "What's happened to you, Gregorio?" she asked, and before I could reply, her lips deposited on my forehead the crumbs of a kiss that had perhaps belonged to someone else. I burst into tears. A waterfall of self-pity hit my eyes, the sobs mingling with my blood in a fusion of fluids that might have been mistaken for a rite of compassion had some Gothic painter accurately portrayed it. *The Crystalline And Red Of Their Bodies* might have been the title of such a work had it been depicted in the classic style of descents—my cross my mother's crossed legs, and me, a dwarf Christ just emerged from the passion. "Sergeant Ceballos hurled me at the trough and my head hit the spout. He called you a bitch." Rage ravaged my mother, the rage of impotence that grates on the edge of the teeth. She got up and started washing the gash with cold sink water. Then she disinfected it with a dash of cognac that didn't burn but rather soothed the searing flesh. "I expect you were chasing his daughter," she said reproachfully. "You're so stupid. Can't you see a dwarf can never beat a bastard like him? Don't aim so high, my son, and be happy if they're not kicking you or throwing stones at you. Keep clear of people. People are evil. People only want to let off steam and for others not to get on their nerves. There's no pity in this life, my son, just remember that. Let's see whether this knock teaches you a lesson and you act more sensibly from now on, because you're going to have to start learning. I mean, you were born a dwarf. You could have been born a hen or a lizard, but, you know, God willed you to be born as you were born, and the best a dwarf can do is to avoid other people or entertain them." "I only wanted to recite a poem to little Margarita," I retorted, "a pretty one about love and swallows I'd learned by heart. I didn't do anything wrong, and the Sergeant just walloped me." "You're a silly titch, that's what you are; reciting poems to a Civil Guard's daughter, you know, is a crime in itself. Listen, Gregorio, love doesn't exist, let alone the love you find in poems—you just learn your lesson. Love is just feeling a strong urge to fuck. Do you know what fucking is, or are you even thicker than you look? Come on, don't act like such a simpleton; take from life the little you can, while you can."

I shut up, dumbfounded. My mother had never spoken to me like that before. And never did so again, not even the day she sold me to pudgy Di Battista. She took the same bottle of cognac she'd used to disinfect my gash, filled a glass to the brim, and put it between my lips. "Drink this, you'll soon see how it will relieve you inside and love's sorrows will disappear." I did just that, and sure enough, they left me, never to return.

A kick in the face knocked little Santomás's teeth out when he was in his teens. It happened when he was trying to explode a Chinese firecracker up a mule's rear, the kind that come wrapped in starry paper and sound off like little farts. Little Santomás brought that upon himself. It could have been worse. It could have severed his head with its iron shoe or smashed his guts in with a sly kick, but things happened as I described them and not as I'd have wished, so little Santomás simply lost his teeth. "Ay, ay, ay!" he cried, bleeding from the mouth, "it's bashed my face in, ay, ay, ay, it's really bashed in." Little Santomás bawled his way through the village until they stopped his hysterics and dulled the pain with beeswax. Little Santomás was a bastard from the polite, self-righteous classes, the sort that let ladies pass first only because they want to rate their butts from behind and then went to church on Sundays, strutting their stuff with the faith of their elders because they thought they were better than everyone else. Poor fellow, he met a bad end even though he was toothless. It happened in Rome. He burnt up in a passenger plane, but that happened much later, on the eve of the admiral's assassination, and by that time, I wasn't around in the village.

Little Santomás, you should know, was baptized and had taken his first communion. Don Vicente the priest let him commune after asking him only if he believed in God or committed sins of the flesh. "Yes, padre, I believe, yes, padre, I sin, but only with my own flesh, because I can't with other people's, otherwise I would, but I repent for my nature and my heart grieves and I intend to make amends, and I want to go to heaven rather than hell, because my father says the reds who executed my uncle Amancio are burning in hell, and I don't want to burn alongside that rabble."

As I said, a kick knocked out little Santomás's teeth when he was in his teens; my brother Tranquilino was there, they weren't on bad terms. He put a Chinese firecracker up a mule's rear and—bang!—was kicked in the teeth. The poor fellow didn't want to burn in hell but burnt up in a passenger plane, on a Pan Am Boeing in which he'd flown to Rome to hear Paul the Sixth say mass; it happened the day before Admiral Luis Carrero Blanco was flung through the air as if hobgoblins were pulling his hair. It was when the singer Camilo Sesto was jumpstarting his career (*I shall always fall in love with people who don't love me*), and it was cold in Madrid, a butcher's cold that froze the marrow of your bones. He met a bad end. My brother Tranquilino enjoyed the episode and laughed till he dropped. They weren't on bad terms, but they weren't on good terms, either. Little Santomás used to call him a bastard, but only on the basis of hearsay; he didn't really know what the word meant.

I also longed to take my first communion. I told my mother, who told me to speak to Don Vicente. "Go and see the priest, and if he gives you his blessing, so much the better." Don

Vicente was a bastard with a threadbare soutane and greasy baldpate who did his best to avoid me. His fingers were as thin as asparagus tips and his nails so grimy they looked like a barren plot pecked over by magpies. His habit stank of anisette, and leprous deceit marked his thin cheeks a deathly pale. I was wrong to talk to him, but at the time I was fascinated by the spectacle of the liturgy. Don Vicente grabbed one ear and lifted me level with the buttons on his chest. "You runt, you want to take communion, when you're not even baptized? How can an abortion spawned in sin ever take communion? Off with you to the fields to chew rats, and may the Lord be merciful and forgive you for coming into this world." Upset by his harangue when I was expecting sympathy, I couldn't think how to react, and taken aback by the nasty turn of events, I blurted into his face, "I shit on the host, you bastard," rather timidly, though articulating my words well. "You are arrogant like all your ilk, you wretched dwarf. Leave the house of God this minute, and don't ever profane it again with your filth. Clear off you, titchy bugger." The priest spoke with the bloodshot eyes of the demented, and his saliva-soaked words spluttered out. I stumbled, hobbled out of there, deeply unhappy, but with the rich scent of vengeance in my nostrils. I would wait for the right moment and show that priest how far its splendor could reach.

My life is a wasteland; every flower I touch sheds its petals; on my ill-omened path, someone keeps sowing evil I will then reap. For one reason or another, poetry has always been a haven for my spirit, a sacred, inviolable place where beauty and solitude meld in a sublime hypostasis of feeling. Man has many other shelters, but none as perfect as poetry. From its clandestine shelter I have wrought my plans and woven my sticky webs of dreams. Poetry is the language which Providence uses to scatter its whims: . . . *someone keeps sowing evil I will then reap.* Those lines inspired the mechanism for my revenge and gave me the drive and energy to inflict it.

Darkness is always propitious when it comes to profanation. I waited until the evening before the first communion for children who'd reached the required age. The village was sunk in silence or in contrition. Only the distant red lights from El Paquito's showed any signs of life. I prowled around the church like a wild animal until 3:00 a.m. I checked the priest was sleeping deeply in the adjacent rectory and waited for the dogs to exhaust their ration of barks. Then I walked over to a wall, jumped on a stump, broke a sacristy window with a stone, and slipped inside. Nobody saw me, nobody heard me, nobody smelled me. Up on the tiles, cats were still meowing, relishing the tail end of their suppers. I entered the room. Darkness ruled, and the shadows were accomplices to the defiance throbbing in my heart. I tiptoed. I could have contained that fierce, vengeful desire burning within me. I could have bit my tongue when Don Vicente slapped my face so superciliously, I didn't have to insult him the way I did, I could have backed down and borne my suffering in the stagnant silence of my consciousness, but Providence sometimes forces man to face his destiny, and then he has no choice but to grasp the blistering embers of fate and perhaps extinguish them with a big, lunatic gob of spit or any other fluid that happens to flow from deep within him, and that's just what I did. The night was as dark as a soul that dies unconfessed. The following May morning would dawn with Mary's innocence, and the village children would take their first communion. I crossed the sacristy, a vile little room that smelled of cinctures and chasubles suppurating with the stink of time, and then into the church, before banging into the sculpture of Saint Roch, who was sleeping cloaked in oily lamp light; it was funereal and cosmic, his infamous dog that lost its tail in the nursery rhyme barking at the moon. My silent footsteps echoed off the ashlars of the walls and thundered around the sinewy barrel of the vault. It was like entering the grave of a pope and whiffing his decomposing carcass.

I felt the massive echo from the darkness resonate in my eardrums while a spiral of damp lined my nostrils with the reverential fear generated by the presence of the sacred or the dead. I was a mere child who hitherto had never dared complain about his fate. I was scared, but determined; an inner strength directed my footsteps, acted as my will. I reached the altar, drenched in sweat. My temples were on fire. The cross of Christ filled the place with the grand spectacle of torture. Polychrome wood pitted with crimson sores, his pale body leaked bloodcurdling spume through its ribs. Christ's head lolled to one side, and because his gaze was fixed on an area of the floor, his presence didn't deter me, quite the contrary; though a dwarf, I found comfort in that friendly exchange from one death mask to another and grew in strength at the sight of his fake performance—a scrap of wood and a scrap of flesh in a midnight encounter. "God doesn't exist, mother told me so," I parroted my brother's words. Ineffable bliss suddenly flooded my mind. It was the same euphoria I experienced when my mother gave me that medicinal cognac; I was drunk on revenge. The key was in the tabernacle lock. The chalice was inside. An unfolded silk veil lay on top of it in a display of seamless asepsis. I grabbed the chalice, and I put it on the floor under the altar. With one swipe I removed the veil. Inside, a pile of hosts awaited the next day's communion, the gleeful communion of the children who would feel for the first time the body of Christ on their tongues, an unleavened body of bread that would gradually slip between their teeth like an ancient rite or a pinch of salt. Without a second thought, I pulled down my trousers and, right there, crouching over the chalice, started to empty my bowels. As I remember it, I heard a cock crow three times, or more likely it was my mother's early-morning cock-a-doodle-do proclaiming her return from El Paquito's. When I'd relieved my guts, I put the alb back and placed it in the tabernacle, gleaming and apparently immaculate, though profaned within by the steaming blasphemy of my defecation. The stench began impregnating the stole when I locked up. It was a peculiar stench I'd never experienced before. Perhaps it had its origins in the oxidizing of the wheat by my excrement, perhaps it came straight from the pigsty of hell. I'd given myself a fright. I'd often hear men voice empty blasphemies threatening what I'd just done, but I'd never thought the feeling one experienced after actually doing it would be one of such astonishing defiance. I touched nothing, I waved my hands in the air, and, after dispersing the evidence of my presence, I fled the way I'd come—Christ's cross, the barreled vault, Saint Roch with his doggy-woggy who'd dropped his tail, the broken sacristy window, and the retreating night sky the only witnesses to the insalubrious nature of my mischief.

I was born a dwarf, as you see me now, my legs tucked under my body, my arms that barely reach my hands, and my hands squeezed against my shoulders like little wings with fingers. I was born a dwarf, but a human being is not measured by size or by degree of beauty, but by the quantity of cash he handles; the greater the amount of cash, the bigger the size, naturally. There are no dwarves when money is at stake. I was born a dwarf, but it could have been even worse, because I could have been born a pig to be slaughtered or even a worm used for bait, one that dies half on the hook and half in the fish's mouth. Things are what they are, and little or nothing can be done to go against their nature. Only the very brave are occasionally courageous enough to defy their destiny. The mad sometimes try, but their attempts have no merit.

Even toothless, little Santomás was radiant with joy on that Sunday morning when he was preparing for his first communion. His grandmother had been to Valencia to buy him a sailor's suit with blue braids and a lanyard of cord plaited from gold thread that snaked across his chest and slipped into his jacket pocket in appropriate military style. He was toothless. I couldn't take first communion and never even acceded to the grace of baptism; in terms of Roman Catholic orthodoxy, when I died, I would go to hell. Pitiful beliefs.

Little Santomás was one of those stuck-up bastards that rejoice in an unctuous blind faith in themselves, yet I expect it's for that reason he experienced a death lit up by flames. The children were so looking forward to receiving the communion wafer that May Sunday, and, in comparison, I'd have been happy, too, if Don Vicente hadn't gone and refused me the sacrament. I shouldn't have bothered to tell him what I wanted, I should have anticipated his contempt, but only Providence is prescient, and sometimes our ears are deaf.

A bright sun shone that day, a pure kind of sun, the sort that fills men with hope. In the front pews, in their Sunday best, the children were anxiously waiting for the ceremony to begin. They exchanged sly smiles that spoke of the happiness in their hearts. The packed church was heaving. Coughs, clearing of throats, sweat galore, exalted hymns all fused and defined a kind of unity of destiny in the very provisional nature of those times. I peered fearfully around the corner of the doorway and waited for the drama to unfold. Through the legs of the multitude standing in front of me, I could barely see the central aisle and the altar at the end of it. Don Vicente was wearing a threadbare liturgical chasuble topped by a glorious red stole, as befitted the first Sunday in May. A beam of light illuminated his face, and seen from afar in such garb, he looked to me like a scarecrow of the faith. Christ's cross emphasized the authority of law with its heavy-duty pay-off. Crucified Christ was still looking at the floor. His attitude had hardly changed since the previous night. A man walked into the church and stamped on me, as he hadn't seen me. "Get out of here, titch," he whispered loudly, manhandling me out of the way. Four old biddies in black, wrinkled their faces and their veils, turned around in unison and spat reproachful, saliva-free glances in my direction. Shamed by the huge guilt of having been born so repulsively into this world, I had no choice but to draw in my ears and hide behind a confessional, out of the way in a corner of the triforium, that was begrimed by the dust of sins. I could hardly see what was happening, but I clearly heard the big buzz, like a whoosh from hell, that swept out of the tabernacle when Don Vicente opened the door for the moment of the hypostasis. He must have noted some peculiar smell, because he leaned his head to one side before opening it, perhaps wanting to locate the source of those mephitic gases. The children at the communion stood and gaped at the bluebottles that swarmed

56

out, glinting like Satan's hemorrhoids, hovering in repugnant clusters above their shocked faces. That unspeakable plague immediately filled the vault, and people started clamoring in disgust. The critters comprising that transubstantiation formed a veritable multitude, milling in their thousands, so many, in fact, that their fluttering wings made the walls tremble and cracked the glass in the windows. The insects pirouetted up and down as if craving the sinful stuff the congregation harbored a-plenty in their consciences. It was as if they wanted to be part of the communion, and to die in mouths, which, of course, is what happened in those that didn't shut in time. Many children crunched them and said they tasted juicy, like cakes soaked in wine or water sweetened with honey. People fled, panic stricken. Some jumped over me, others trampled on me, and all, quite unawares, sorely damaged my spine and brought great suffering upon me. When the church had emptied out, those insects that had blossomed in the matter deposited by my guts, as if by spontaneous combustion, began to return whence they'd perhaps come and disappeared en masse into the blue sky. Only a few were left perching on Saint Roch's doggy, wound around his tail, thus supplying him with a new, longer wagger, for heaven knows what prosthetic purpose.

Life is an ineffable mystery, with so much baffling arcana. Those of us who are conscious can at least say that, and indeed have the moral duty to do so and to seek out, perhaps in the wonders of existence, the traces of an originating divinity. Gustavo Adolfo indicated as much in the sickly flowers of these lines: *As long as science fails to discover the wellsprings of life, and in sea or heaven an abyss that resists reason resides, as long as humanity advances but knows not where it flies, as long as mysteries haunt mankind, there will be poetry!*"

Little Santomás was a bastard of the illustrious, nose-in-the-air kind and crushingly able to inflict pain on the helpless. A mule kicked out his teeth when he was in his teens. It struck him because he stuck a firecracker up its anal sphincter, one of the Chinese sort, with a lengthy fuse greased with gunpowder, that were always going off in village fiestas when we were children—the Feast of the Assumption, Michaelmas, May Day, and all those. The mule's kick landed unluckily for him and cleft his palate. Little Santomás was sent flying when the firecracker went off and spattered shit everywhere. The animal was clearly constipated. Firecrackers are usually harmless, but depending on where and how they are placed, they can do a lot of damage, though bombs do more. A bomb sent One-Eyed Slim and Inspector Esteruelas off along the road to hell. It sucked the blood from their veins. That was in Madrid, in '78. Providence mercifully ensured I wasn't at the site of the carnage; I now know why. Slim said I should go, to keep him company, but I didn't feel like meeting Esteruelas again. At the time, I was begging on the steps of the church of Our Lady of the Immaculate Conception, right opposite the cafeteria where the artifact exploded. It was part of my commitments to

One-Eyed. The Grupos Revolucionarios Antifascistas Primero de Octubre claimed responsibility for the attack. At that time, murders were often carried out in order to destabilize the transition process, but I shall tell you later how much I was involved in such thunder and lightning.

If Don Vicente had lived to a ripe old age, he'd never have stomached those turbulent times, and his heart would have burst in his chest just as the mule's kick smashed up the face of little Santomás. He believed in divine justice, in a universe hierarchically ordered by an almighty creator, in the enemies of the faith, in the daily presence of the Devil in people's lives, and in Machaquito anisette. "Clear off, you titchy bugger," he shouted the day I went to ask to receive the sacrament he should have been sensible and granted; he'd have saved himself the embarrassment of having to go and explain what happened to his higher-ups. Don Vicente was a bastard whose life gradually went sour on him. The Bishop of Albacete called him to account, and he had no choice but to tell him the facts. From then on, he could only see messengers of darkness and try to avoid going to the lavatory. "The sticky vagina of the whore of Babylon has descended upon us with a stench of coriander and a stink of cashews!" he preached on Sundays and obligatory holy days. "Repent and believe in the Gospels!" He went mad. They exiled him to the diocese of Calahorra and he went mad, or perhaps he was mad already. The church had to be exorcized. Incense was burnt in every chapel, and Hail Maries, Credos, and Our Fathers were prayed; it was a lovely ceremony that revealed enormous contrition. The whole village joined the procession, everyone carried a candle, the women were veiled, the men resplendent in clean shirts and ties, and the children silent, respectful, and extremely reverential. Little Margarita was there clutching her black prayer book, as was the worthy, if toothless, Santomás, and others who kept their distance from me, and even my own brother Tranquilino, whose eyes were bewitched by the flames of so many flickering candles. I saw them parade by from the top of a steep slope on the outskirts of the village. The enigma behind their lamentations was sealed in my belly like a secret encrypted in the designs of Providence. These times are contradictory, they are times for the end of time. The world often pretends to be what it isn't, and everyday reason tends to see through its fantasies, but in the end the mystery of life has to be fathomed by each and every individual, and each should extract the baggage that suits them. In any case, after all that nonsense, confusion, and idiocy spread by word of mouth in the village over the business of the bluebottles, I realized that rather than clinging to someone else's dogma, one should find what matters in one's own inner self, the stuff one learns from life itself, the real master when it comes to teaching lessons with a magisterial cane.

That year, the rebel army finished off the last centers of resistance, and Fulgencio Batista, the dictator, rather than facing defeat like a man, had no qualms about fleeing his country. That year, Federico Martín Bahamontes won the Tour de France and proudly walked onto the podium in the Parc des Princes as if his victory had been a minor feat. My mother was still beautiful, and with a lingering coquettish knack she kneaded her body with the Tokalón cream she told the truck drivers to buy in Madrid. "We've been married for six years, and my husband still dotes on me. He often says I'm as pretty as I was during our honeymoon. He goes too far, of course . . . but he's quite right. When I admire my skin, I see the years go by without taking their toll, ever since I've been caring for my skin with Tokalón cream. This is what I do at night. I apply nutritious Tokalón cream, and it tones my skin while I sleep. A light application of Tokalón day cream in the morning, and my skin is well protected for the whole day and stays white, clean, and soft," said the advertisement for the concoction. For a few coins, my mother let the lusting hands of truck drivers wander over her on their short pleasure breaks at El Paquito's. She didn't overcharge, or give discounts. The establishment docked her for the use of the bed and took a commission, more than half her rate, all told, so the money she took home from frigging and cooking was no astonishing amount. "Mother, give me two pesetas for a pencil," I'd beg her. "Don't bother me, and use your tongue for a paintbrush," and I'd leave not having put two words together on the blank sheet. I sometimes did so in my head, and lines came out very much in Gustavo Adolfo's style, but they quickly slopped down the drain of oblivion and may still be swimming in the sinkholes of my memory, next to my last impressions of childhood in that village. Damned village. I would soon have to leave and never return.

It was around the feast of Saint Blaise when the storks flew back, and around Michaelmas when the musicians, an orchestra full of beat-up instruments, made their appearance and provided the village fiestas with their soundtrack. They came in a van that was ready for the junkyard, battered as it was by merciless, nonstop rumbling over the rugged fatherland. The musicians lodged in beds hired out by Aurelia La Cacharra, the owner of the bar in the plaza, and they set up the platform with their collection of instruments and sheet music next to the town hall, right in front of the rusty cross where the names of the village lads who'd died for God and Spain figured under the runny letters of the name of José Antonio, weathering the storm of oblivion. His honor the mayor also allowed a few fairground stalls, to add to the festive spirit: shooting galleries primed with leather balls stuffed full of sand whose fate was to be hurled at dummies dressed up as the enemy; *churro* stands shrouded in steam; and modest bingo stalls where people played for transistor radios, cookware sets, and luridly dyed propylene sponges. The orchestra played until half past midnight, and then, after the final flourishes of the national anthem, the grand finale to all that gaiety, with its da-dee-da, dee-da-dee, the bandsmen left to down a few glasses of anisette to the good health of La Cacharra, who invited them as men, musicians, and clients. "Maestro, you can really play," she'd say, coming on to the man with baton, "you're a fancy, filigree musician, and you should have studied in the Spanish infantry music school and not wasted your time playing all these raucous boleros in villages." "Well, you know, my dear, I don't know what to say. Light music is my thing—Antonio Machín and Doménico Modugno," and he started humming the tune to *Perfidy*, oblivious to La Cacharra's real intentions. Nonetheless, once glasses had been raised and spirits lifted, the musicians decided to pay a visit to El Paquito's, where they all played their oompah-oompah symphonies on my mother, the ones best blown with mouth aligned to the thighs of the instrument. I've never been too keen on music, let alone the light kind. It brings back bad memories from that Michaelmas feast night that God should damn. I got my just desserts, that's for sure, but it smelled so sweet, and I lost it—muscatel grapes, a recent storm, and clean beds—I couldn't stop myself, and I lost it. It was the scent of disaster, sweet and juicy like the early delights of adolescence. At most, music drowns my heart in nostalgia. A maddening itch runs through me when it zings into my earholes. Music is the larynx of angels—of those in hell. Damned music, always perforating the organs of the rational mind.

People were dancing boleros in the plaza—"*Clock, don't mark the hour, my life is at an end*"—*cumbias*, mambos, and Gypsy *paso dobles*. Lightbulbs were casting festive sparks on men's shoulders like electric flakes of dandruff, and dotting the women's long tresses with pinheads of light. I was watching the dance, hidden under the orchestra platform beneath the patched canvas covering the iron supports. I'd yet to acquire that need to parade my deformities on the dance floor to earn my bread, as would later be the case. Fiestas don't want misfortune, they keep the grotesque out of sight and frighten off the monstrous with guffaws of laughter. I was banned from dancing. Juan Felipe, the village idiot, bounced up and down without taking his feet off the ground, like a coiled spring of flesh dangling a thread of green spittle in time with the music. People generally pitied him and threw him crusts soaked in wine; that was his good fortune. The poor idiot. Between bounces he laughed in my direction, and his smile gave my hideout away. Poor idiot. From time to time, the lads went over and dropped bits of cabbage leaf on the back of his neck, and he laughed at their bit of fun in exchange for Saci sweets. "Don't look this way, you idiot," I whispered softly, signaling to him to clear off, but he was stubbornly intent on keeping an eye on me. If he gave away my hiding place, the lads would most likely beat me with sticks for a spot of fresh entertainment, so I decided to throw a stone at him, and my aim was so brilliant I cracked the center of his forehead. Juan Felipe the idiot fell to the ground in front of the orchestra like a sack of invertebrate flesh and blood. The musicians carried on playing, and nobody registered what I'd done. My deed boosted my courage, which was just what I needed. The shadows shielded me. I had successfully done the deed, and the shadows shielded me. Providence upped my valor. They rushed the idiot Juan Felipe off on their shoulders so the doctor could examine his latest gift, and on a high, I decided once again to shape my destiny.

Soppily swaying her hips, little Margarita was dancing boleros on little Santomás's arm. I was closely observing their movements from my shadowy shelter, and with every step they took, I heartily wished they would die. I shut my eyes tight, as if the pressure from my eyelids might make my dreams come true, but the second I opened them, there they were still leaning into each other as much as decorum and respect would allow. "Dance, dance and be damned," I winged those words their way and laughed my head off at the worm-eaten smoothness of their corpses floating in the lava storming my imagination. The gash opened by Sergeant Ceballos the day I approached his daughter with lines from Gustavo Adolfo had healed by now. Subsequently I'd kept my distance as instructed, scrupulously so, as fear warranted. Far off and over time, my adolescent feelings had transformed into ones that were less spurious and hence lustier, a lust illuminated by the phallus thrusting like a lighthouse of flesh between my legs. Now I was only interested in that girl for the primary matter of her body. I was only attracted by her elemental female smell, her circular hips, the curve of her buttocks, the extraordinary slopes of her breasts, so many magnets to my eyes. So much pampered softness within hands' reach! I wanted to be swept up and buried in the prairie of her skin now carpeted by down as fresh as filaments of sun at daybreak. I wanted to explore that uncharted ecosystem and descend to the bubbling spring of her Nile with the morbid rapture of a great explorer. I wanted to enter her caverns of flesh and discover unimaginable treasures, make them mine, spread myself therein. The night sounded beautiful, the orchestra was melting the wax in my ears with an interminable repertoire of songs that were horrible when played, and even worse when sung. Everything was ripe for me to go into action, which is what I did. Tired of dancing, little Margarita had sat down on a stone bench to seek refuge in the gossip of other girls. Busty and bosomy, they were all amorous intrigue. Away from his little beauty, little Santomás was exercising his virility, shying at the dummies in the shooting gallery. A gang of youths joined him, all tainted by impure, adolescent thoughts, all on the brink of infamy. "Tonight I'm going to lay Juani, just look at those red-hot cheeks of hers!" I emerged from my hideaway, my mind made up. The glowing bulbs highlighted my movements, but the way my aim had struck that idiot Juan Felipe on the forehead filled me with courage, and I felt I was flying across the plaza. In fact, my bandy legs were tripping clumsily toward the girls, and that was what they could see: an approaching dwarf, a deformed creature cutting a path between the legs of the dancers, narrowly escaping being squashed. "Look, it's Gregorito, I reckon he's coming over." "That eyesore wouldn't dare, my father's threatened him, and he'll pickle him if he comes within a yard of me." When girls get their periods, their hearts coarsen and they become puking brats ready to vent their ire on the most hallowed feelings of men. It's a law of life. "Just look at that pole poking from his pants, it must be like a donkey's, he's a disgusting dwarf, if he comes any nearer, I'll scream." A hop, skip and a jump, and I landed in front of the girls. They were grinning viciously. I didn't open my mouth; I didn't have the extra ounce of strength that required. I simply stretched my arm out as far as I could and pinched little Margarita's right breast, swiftly, quickly, like a driver honking before he crashes. She slumped off the bench and let out a hysterical, piercing shriek. "Aah, aah! The dwarf touched me, that dirty little dwarf touched me!"

After doing the evil deed, I scampered off to nowhere in particular. My hand still cherished a memory of cotton, the indelible feel of her flesh, you might say I would remain grasping a warm lark's feather forever and ever. I ran off while, alerted by little Margarita's shrill cries, people chased after me. "Get the dwarf, get the dwarf!" barked the bitch. I looked behind me as I ran and saw a huddle around her. Almost all of them were waving their arms as they scoured the pitch-black night, scrutinizing the terrain beyond the fairground lights where I was pounding away fast. Panic coursed through my body like poison. Where could I go, where could I hide? They were bound to catch me anyway, my runt's legs weren't up to a proper escape. I was doomed to be punished, there was no possible chance of remission. Nobody would help me, not even in my dreams. Well, they could smash me to smithereens; I'd be happy enough to take the lovely memory of a woman's breast to the grave. So ran my thoughts, black as the grief awaiting me, not the barren grief of Federico's ballad, but a hefty one delivered by fists and bludgeons; murky thoughts that translated into a wish to see the lot of them in the grave, their bodies dismembered, their parts decimated by insects' bloodthirsty jaws.

I thought of heading for El Paquito's and had got halfway there when a posse of youths caught me in a waste ground in an oak wood. The pack pursued me, armed to the teeth with clubs, sticks, and iron bars, and little Santomás was the leader, you could see that by the way he stared at me. Little Santomás was one of those bastards who wholeheartedly believe in their own strength, but he came to a bad end. His gums attracted flies, which he chewed with the limp squish of the toothless, and that's why he was endlessly spitting. "Grab him by the scruff of the neck, don't let him get away," he whelped, enjoying giving out orders. Running had exhausted me, and I couldn't have cared a fig about my fate. They held up me by my hair, and little Santomás, without saying a word, aimed a gob of spit my way and blinded me in one eye. They tied my hands to the trunk of an oak tree and ripped my shirt off so my back was bared to their lashes. They pulled the rope tight around my wrists, reducing the circulation of blood to a dribble, and then twice kicked me hard against the tree. The moon splashed its silver over my torso, and the metallic singsong of crickets seemed to be applauding the show. Little Santomás took his belt off and, before he started hitting, ran the leather over my skin, perhaps investigating the sinews of my anatomy. Then the lashes began, and my flesh oozed the bloody liquid of pain. Amused by their cruel extension of the fair, my captors laughed whenever I shuddered and joked at every new turn. "His skin is in tatters, he looks like a skinned goat." I felt my consciousness fading, I sensed death edging nearer with every lash, but Providence intervened, not willing my days to be over so soon. They say it's the archangel Saint Michael who at the final, supreme moment takes newly lost souls to their destinies in eternity. It was his feast night. The air smelled of grapes, and perhaps it *was* the archangel who prevented my soul from becoming painfully detached. It's a fact that I saw him appear on a hill, silhouetted against fleeting shadows. Suddenly the lashes stopped hurting, and a feeling of well-being flooded my consciousness. "Hit him harder, he looks as if he's recovering, hit him so he learns that dogs don't lick women—crack, crack, crack." My blood painted the night with rubies. The substance of my life crystallized into precious stone. Angels don't exist. Angels don't exercise their wings any less than archangels, let alone rush in with flaming swords of vengeance. That night, Algimiro Calatrava, Scarface from the Chorrero mill, was the one who saved my life. Walking back from the mill and pissed as a newt, he'd slumped down by the crags of Salobral, just at the top where the road slopes around. Scarface lived by himself, with fifteen lame dogs he fed on green vegetables to curb their wild habits. So many vegetables inside so many dogs led to flatulence, and the stink in his mill was renowned, and nobody went near for fear of fainting. The mollusks had caught Scarface in the middle of wasteland that day when they hailed down, and they shattered his face. He couldn't protect himself and was left disfigured for life. Solitude helped him become resigned to his misfortune, and the dogs sufficed for the little warmth he had left to give. He expertly ground the wheat he brought to the mill, was a skilled miller, and the flour he produced was as fine as the ash of a cremated corpse. "What do you think you're doing to the dwarf?"

asked the apparition from the top of the mound. "Let him go, or I'll bash your heads in." His eyes flashed with their own light on his ugly face, like carbuncles from hell. He was a fearsome sight to behold. The youths were terrified and shut up until they smelled who he was. "They're whipping my skin off in strips," I moaned faintly. "He squeezed the breasts of the sergeant's daughter; we're giving him his just desserts," retorted little Santomás, trying to justify the punishment he was inflicting, but rather than doing that, he fanned the scent of justice driving Scarface and unleashed a torrent of rage. "You gang of wankers, you always pick on the weak; I'm going to give you hyenas what *you* deserve." The corners of his lips were foaming as he advanced on the cowering youths, and trying to create the suitable ambience to stoke their fear, I began to moan faintly for no justifiable reason. Annoyed by that interruption, little Santomás brought down one last lash with all the might in his muscles and then was the first to beat it in order to dodge the rocks that Scarface started hurling. The rest of the youths followed him and vanished into the crevices of the night, on their way to the village, like animals terrified by flames.

Poetry doesn't fantasize. Poetry puts the seal on man's tragedy, his impossible struggle against the fate that awaits him. The specter of Faith Oven was quick to reveal the fate Providence had reserved for me, but she stammered, and it was difficult to follow the threads of her thoughts. I failed to understand the vague meaning of her words, but over time I've come to realize what was happening; consequently, when I saw her, I didn't doubt for a single moment that her presence signaled my destruction. Fools, dogs, and poets are the best at divining other worlds; some bay at the moon, others slaver, and the last rhyme non sequiturs nobody heeds or cares about.

Sometimes poetry turns into a balsam, at others into a sting that sends the venom of the species deeper into the wound until it is infested and putrefies. Showered by a snowstorm of flour, the body's wounds quickly close. The fine dust of flour mingles with the blood, making a thick balsam that immediately sets over the skin. Sores heal swiftly, and within seconds not a trace of the hurt remains. However, if the flour is made from chaff or has been poorly sieved, the result changes, and the ointment, rather than being a cure, hastens death. This is what Algimiro Calatrava, Scarface from the Chorrero mill, told me as he healed my back from the lashes. When the pack of youngsters had fled, he came over, untied me, and carried me in his arms to the mill. On the way, my head cleared uneasily. When we arrived, he ripped off the tattered remains of my shirt and lay me on my back on a mound of pure, white flour that was like a mixture of grated angel wing and cloud dust. For a moment the flour heightened the pain in my wounds, but then its soft touch quickly relieved my suffering, and I felt as if I were levitating on a real cushion of well-being. My every muscle exquisitely relaxed. Calm pervaded my thoughts, and the most benign of smiles whirled and curled from my mouth. "Squeezing a woman's breasts when she's not in heat is a bad business and brings only trouble. You must catch them on the right day," Scarface advised me as he pretended to test the air with his nostrils. "You know, if you feel like it, and you can't hold off, you should rub yourself off," he continued. "Listen to me. You just rub yourself off and don't tell a soul. I've lived here by myself for the last thirty-three years. Thirty-three, Christ's age. Thirty-three years rubbing off, and I'm still in one piece. Women's breasts rot in a flash, and it's no fun fondling rot. Boy, get this straight, don't be misled by females' bosoms. Female flesh is unhealthy, and a bad session can leave a bad taste in the mouth for the duration. I've not touched one in thirty-three years, and look how well I've stood the test of time just rubbing myself off. Crikey, they've skinned you alive, kid. Your back's a real mess. This is what comes from wanting to taste the flesh of another. Do as I do, and keep clear of women. Rub yourself off, it's healthier, and you won't catch any of those VDs that're going around. You're old enough to rub yourself off. Has anybody taught you how?" and there and then, the Scarface of the mill unbuttoned his fly to reveal the huge mushroom of his scrotum then started masturbating slowly right in front of my eyes, and pleasured longingly with each stroke, accelerating faster and stronger, his mind misted by a joyful throb until sperm snow-stormed the mound of flour where I was lain.

Over the next few weeks, the village savored soft, delicious bread richly spliced with our physiological spice.

TWO

Pudgy Di Battista was a posh bastard fallen on hard times; circuses didn't make money anymore. Pudgy Di Battista treated his raging blood pressure by diluting his cognac with dashes of Carabaña mineral water. High blood pressure threatens the obese, and the second they drop their guard, it bursts their veins. "Carabaña water—high blood pressure, laxative, gallbladder infections, different dosages. Dilute three spoonfuls of Carabaña water in a cup of chamomile or lime tea and take on an empty stomach. It reduces blood pressure and drains the gallbladder." The impact was immediate, and you wanted to defecate on the spot. They don't make it anymore. It's today's world: less chewy and more plastic. Perhaps bowels move better now; what can I tell you of the inner workings of my business? Pudgy Di Battista added Carabaña water to his first morning shot of cognac. Then he'd have an urgent need and rush to a chamber pot he kept under the bed next to a few other items of personal hygiene.

"A stick can trick the hicks from Carabaña," my brother used to sing, before a train engine throttled the voice in his throat. He was on his way to pick tomatoes from a tiny plot my mother owned next to the cemetery, well fertilized by the bodies of its unburied tenants. He met a bad end but didn't complain. They don't necessarily have to be from Carabaña. A stick can trick any hick, a long, willowy one, say, the sort used to thwack a lion's back when it's starving and opening its jaws to snaffle the first thing in sight, a hunk of meat, a tamer's forearm, or a monkey wrench. It's a circus thing. Wild animals, clowns, trapeze artists, the filth in the wings, the picturesque poverty you glimpse behind the big top. "Hey, Gregorio," my mother said one day, "grab this lion-taming stick and off you go with this gentleman who'll show you the world and make a man of you." Pudgy Di Battista grabbed my hand. He grasped it in limp, boiled-fish fashion and told me to kiss my mother because I wouldn't be seeing her for a long time. And the truth is I never saw her again.

What was my life going to be like from then on? A set of futile queries buzzed around my brain, a desolate scenario that quickly took shape in a caravan, trapezes, transhumance, and hollow clownish laughter.

The red and crimson canvas of the Stéfano circus big top was erected on the village threshing ground in lovely spring weather. Children bawled cheerily. High spirits spread through the air like a fleeting firework display. Di Battista's megaphone van drove around the streets broadcasting the wonders of the show. "Come, old folks and kids, young gents and ladies, come and be thrilled by beautiful Doris's balancing act on the trapeze, come and laugh at the Culí-Culá brothers' clowning. Come and wonder at the wild animals from the Atlas Mountains that can split a man in two with one swipe of a paw. Buy your tickets now for the three once-in-a-lifetime performances of the Stéfano circus before it leaves for its triumphal tour of Europe and the United States of

America. Big show, tonight at six. Half-price for babies at the breast and army conscripts."

The children's chatter in the wake of the van sounded like bees humming. All that blather seemed so exotic. Bliss blossomed on skin toughened by the harsh country breezes, fierce frosts, and itches from eczema brought on by poor personal hygiene. Bliss feeds itself and only needs a sugar lump or the plain taste of a bread roll to find expression in a child's smile. The circus was a fabled paradise in children's dreams, tangible proof that apart from pain and hard grind, there was room for fantasy.

I performed under various names. They called me "Gregorio the Great." They also put "Goyo the Dwarf" on the posters for a time. I spent sixteen, almost seventeen years in pudgy Di Battista's company, doing the rounds of the Spanish circuit. Sixteen interminable years in which I learnt to measure the miserliness of Lady Luck and the happenstance of Providence. I was there until I escaped, when the company went bankrupt and collapsed. A pity about Di Battista, he met a bad end, his guts burnt to a cinder, and he didn't ask for any pity.

Pudgy Di Battista was a posh bastard fallen on hard times; circuses weren't making money anymore—too much food for the animals, too much worn out equipment, too many wages from so few box-office takings. Pudgy Di Battista waxed flabby fat, and sweat beaded his brow the whole year through. His flesh looked like remolding, and however hard he tried to lose weight, it always reverted to its original gravitational pull. A universe of pap you could say, of pap and cognac. The poor bugger. He wasn't spared a bad end, either. He was desperate. Delirious, he kept saying that the

Virgin of Fátima had appeared to him, until finally one day he glugged a bottle of bleach for breakfast, and that washed his gripes away.

The more devastating the exit, the worthier it seems. Not that it's much consolation now with you opposite, but it's true enough that surprise factors can help gild the vulgar pill. The second I saw you, I knew why you'd come. I recognized it in the changed expression in your eyes, the glint in your gaze, and the scornful way you abstained from answering any of my questions. Tonight, over the course of supper, my body trembled from head to toe several times, but I blamed that on European Commissioner Belinda Dixon's obscene advances. In our concern for the minutiae of everyday life, we never stop to think how one supper may perhaps be our last, yet, as you see, everything can come to that.

I don't know whether to call the fact we were served cocks' combs as an entrée astonishing or simply odd. My fellow guests gaped in amazement, not crediting the plate that had been placed before them. Bragging in the upbeat tone of his own election posters, the mayor insisted they were really a kind of mushroom cooked in court bouillon; concretely, oyster mushrooms, he added. Someone to my right reckoned, however, that they were bamboo shoots, a delicious, typically Cantonese dish. Some people seize the first opportunity to display a would-be cosmopolitanism that sets them apart from the rest of us mortals; it's unavoidable, they're born that way. Others argued they were slices of porterhouse steak marinated in aspic, but it was left to Commissioner Dixon to reveal the secret without the help of the maître d'. "They are cocks' combs," she remarked, looking horrified, "cocks' combs in bread crumbs." I tried them out of curiosity. They were slippery on the tongue and fell apart like communion wafers. In fact, I quite liked them and downed several glasses of wine so I could squeeze even more taste out for my discerning palate. So you see, that was my last supper. I'd like to know how to pray and commend myself to a Supreme Being in which my individual consciousness could be extended after the final call, but I'm afraid that's impossible in my case. Prayers relax and comfort, but never change what has to be. At the time, what had to be was my forced exit from that village.

My mother was left alone in this world, and I was hitched up to the Stéfano circus like a chattel, trailer, or wild animal and thus fated to roam the land, with no points of reference, no roots, like a nomad driven by the need to survive on his wits or other people's unsavory charity. My mother was left alone in this world, her only livelihood an old whore's. She stayed on at El Paquito's dispatching truckers for a few years until grief polished her off. If any doctor had examined her, he'd have diagnosed cancer, but grief was what really killed her. Deep grief she never aired and which gradually wore down her insides. I never saw her again. I didn't miss her, either, and didn't have much cause to do so, to tell the truth, but that hardly matters now that she is asleep for the duration, where moss and grass open the flower of her skull with their deft fingers. My mother never knew any Lorca to write poems to her. Nor did she have a decent death, though hers was perhaps better than the one meted out to Federico. He could really write. I will always revere his poems; they were my refuge among the wild animals.

The day after I was sold, the Stéfano circus upped the stakes on their show of dreams and forever abandoned the village where I was born. I left behind a truncated childhood spoilt by beatings, knocks, and emotional disorders that brought a variety of aftermaths. I left behind unhappy times, full of dubious illusions and sickly fantasies where I'd learned to wallow in the clandestine kind of life granted by the knowledge I was different, immune to insults, with head held high beneath a crown of sorrow. Stuck in the caravan Gurruchaga was steering, amid a heap of motley items, I peered out of a type of porthole that opened wide to the world and saw the glittering lights of El Paquito's receding into the distance. It was early morning, and dawn was exploding with flights of swooping swifts. The caravan smelled of muck, but a different, smellier muck, if that's possible, not as strong, but more tangible—more real, like the new life awaiting me.

The Stefáno circus was a startling place. Everything made this country yokel gasp and brought slaver bubbling to my lips—the dense aromas in the big top, the spectacular sight of bears, lions, and tigers, the fetid charms of their roars, the junk in the covered wagons, the pervasive sense of the provisional; everything was new and surprising, and yet something malign lurked in that hotchpotch. A circus is truly a sanctuary of the grotesque. The oddest things you can imagine can happen at any moment—a bouquet of flowers, clumsy high-wiring leading to death, a crime of passion, a loud guffaw that becomes a premonition of disaster. A circus is the realm of the impossible, the home of ambiguity, and the last frontier of reason.

The grotesque triggers people's belly laughter and relaxes their guts. Depending on how and when, deformity sometimes

80

comes up trumps. The public took its time finding me funny but finally did, you bet it did, my survival hung on their laughs. I soon began to miss the cutting wind that brought me round of a morning in the village and the monotonous pace at which things happened without variation, like the little figures appearing on those mechanical clocks the exact moment the hour is struck. The circus offered another view of reality, one that wasn't more agreeable or less tragic, another dimension of existence hard to understand from the outside. The circus was a grazing ground for monsters, a field fertilized for the nurture of eccentricities I would soon have to harvest. There I learnt to distinguish the pettiness of bodies from the goodness of souls, and the pettiness of souls from the goodness of bodies, there I suffered life's derision in my own flesh and experienced the intense satisfaction that comes with the knowledge that one is not yet dead; it was there I became a man.

Gurru, the shit man, was Chinese, or Basque, or from nowhere in particular. People's manners are generally decided by the social cream in the milk they suckled. This hit you between the eyes in the circus. Gurruchaga's mission in life was to muck out the animal cages and get food for the inmates. A demanding task in times of shortages like those it was our bad luck to experience. He was equipped with a spade for digging ditches, except that rather than sticking it into the rock-hard soil of Spain, he stuck it into the soft fecal matter in the cages.

Pudgy Di Battista diluted his cognac with Carabaña mineral water. A few drops of water in all that alcohol did little to help his blood pressure, but he kept pouring them in, perhaps to be at one with his conscience. It was quite usual to

81

watch him giving out orders that got confused as he slurred, and the result was an unintelligible juggling act one needed patience to unravel: "Vedi thatta fella dil capello colore shit? Youlla aiutarle cun ze cleanin' di cages," and thus he assigned me to the charge of Gurruchaga.

Elephants spread their legs before peeing, raise their trunks, relax their bladders, and release a cascade of urine on the ground as if a thick spurt of amber were streaming from the well of their insides. Pudgy Di Battista gave me over to that prickly individual whose face glistened with the grease of defeat. He wasn't at all amused by this ward Di Battista had foisted upon him, and he welcomed me churlishly. His first decision was to take me to the elephants and shove me in among them. "Give them a drink," he growled, "there's a bucket." Terrified they might trample me to pulp, I filled it with water and put it within reach of one. An elephant, whose truncated tusks had degenerated into worm-eaten stumps, grunted as it stretched out its trunk and put the end in the bucket. It halfheartedly sipped, savored the water in its mouth, then spat it out at top speed into my face, complete with thick globules of snot like the swollen bodies of lampreys. Gurru erupted into a hiccupping laugh he almost choked on. "Look, kid," he recriminated, "you must give elephants water before they start digesting, or else it gives them stomachache and they puke up. You've got a lot to learn, and the first thing to do is to learn to look after yourself among so many animals. If you do whatever you're told to without giving it a bit of thought yourself, you'll have a rough ride around here."

What most impressed me about that first conversation was that he called me "kid," rather than *dwarf, crud, cripple,* or something equally nice.

Gurruchaga could guess an animal's ailments by the smell of its droppings. "Look, kid, the tiger has got a chesty cough, can't you smell his shit's a bit moldy?" The organoleptic qualities of excrement are vital when it comes to diagnosing diseases. He crouched over their deposits as if he were testing the sound of the planet's gravitational pull, and when he was right over them, he flared his nostrils, took a deep breath until he filled his lungs with the stink. Then he clicked his tongue and announced his diagnosis. "This monkey's in heat big time; we must sort that." The smell and even the taste of excrement were, as far as he was concerned, an infinite source of information; where experience couldn't take him, the tip of his nose did.

When it was belt-tightening time, Gurru fed the animals on their own fecal matter, which he camouflaged with chunks of stray animals that Providence was good enough to send our way: dogs, rats, cats, or sheep cast from their flock, which we'd occasionally bump into and were a wonderful find in that sense. It cost a fortune to feed the circus animals, and Di Battista's resources were always minimal, so Gurruchaga went to all kinds of lengths to find them victuals. Dog was what there was mostly. Carnivores are keen on canine flesh, and it's easy to find. We'd have to be very unlucky not to come across a stray dog on the road and be able to stun it to death with a surprise blow to the head. Gurruchaga was in charge of the operation, and I helped him as much as my natural clumsiness allowed. Any sacrifice was better than letting our animals starve. Di Battista would never have forgiven that and would have betrayed him to the military courts. Gurruchaga knew as much; he had a past to hide. "Hey, Goyito, try this—this elephant's got cirrhosis of the liver, his shit tastes of ethane," and the elephant took note and died after a week of protracted agony, the moans you could hear all over the circus finally did everyone's mind in.

Despite the privations and the penury, the Stéfano circus was a happy processionary caterpillar, roaming Spain in pursuit of the good weather factor. In summer we penetrated northern backwaters, in autumn we did the southeast coast, in winter we visited the villages and towns of Extremadura and Andalusia, and in springtime we flowered on the Meseta. I always traveled with Gurruchaga, stuck in his caravan next to the pile of junk that made up his baggage in life. I helped him clean the cages, see to the hygiene of the animals, and procure their fodder. I gradually adapted to the work. I thought anything was better than having to appear in the ring and keep the spectators happy. I took great care of the cages and washed out all the excrement, so they shone spick and span like newly polished altars. I was a diligent worker, and nobody bothered me. Gurruchaga watched me handle the spade in amazement. I didn't do at all badly considering I was a dwarf, I put my heart into it, my heart and my sweat. Initially I was afraid of the animals and waited for them to enter the ring before seriously tackling their cages, but they immediately got used to my presence, and I worked in them and they didn't bat an eyelid except when they were sick and undernourished. "Whistle the Spanish national anthem for that tiger or it'll stick a paw into you," Gurru advised if he saw me in any danger, and I whistled away as cocksure as anything. Gurruchaga was a prickly character who hardly spoke to anyone. On the other hand, he began to take a shine to me. In honor of his nickname, he spent the whole day up to his neck in muck, and flies buzzed around his temples even when he was cooking. "Shit is life, kid. In the war, I shit my pants the first time I went into battle, and it saved my skin," he confessed one night after a relaxing cup of coffee. "We were in Belchite, and Franco held a hilltop vantage point. When the people in my brigade whiffed what my panic had produced, they ran away from me, and their reward was to get shot to pieces by the Fascists when they saw them move. I stayed still and was fine. That saved me. The rest was pure butchery. Their machine-gun nests rat-a-tatted death for a couple of hours. Our tanks couldn't find a way through, and we lost the position. The battalion was wasted, but I saved my skin thanks to that shit. Just remember this, and never scorn even the most disgusting filth. Shit is life; it saved mine."

Apart from his canary-colored hair, Gurruchaga had the loveliest hands when it came to cooking our grub. He never washed them, and perhaps that's why his meals were always incredibly tasty. When we erected our installations in the places we were going to perform, he was responsible for two main tasks: the organization of all the tackle for our encampment, and procuring food for the animals, even for the lot of us, if circumstances required. The general norm established by repeated practice was for one family from all the circus families to see to the cooking of one meal that should be for everyone who felt like partaking. The Montinis, for example, the high-wire acrobats, offered macaroni without chorizo, the Gutiérrezes, the jugglers, cooked mountains of rice with a wonderful aroma, and the Gambero-Gamboas liked to pickle whatever they got their hands on. Gurruchaga provided the raw materials for the dishes, even though he was only occasionally called upon to prepare our pittance. If he cooked, the wherewithal of his meals could scale unheard visual heights, often verging on works of art in terms of shape, color, and texture. The taste was something else, and opinions tended to differ or even be hostile, so he was rarely allowed to be chef. We who've so often been starving to death have always been fascinated by the paraphernalia of cooking, perhaps because our stomachs have long memories when it comes to the hungry years. On the threshold between late childhood and early adolescence, I went from bread and dripping, perhaps sprinkled with sugar, to Gurruchaga's grandiloquent offerings, and that made me realize I'd grown up. The content made the difference; my stomach began to expand and channel substance to my head. Nonetheless, it wasn't all delicious delights. Food shortages and lack of ingredients meant there were days when we were reduced to bread and water. These were the last of the hungry years, with a hefty sting in their tail, when welfare and development had yet to hit Spanish hearths. That's why when juicy fodder was on offer, we filled our bellies fit to burst for fear of what tomorrow might bring, and it ended up looking like a wedding feast for beggars. "Hey, kid, how come you were born a dwarf?" Gurru would ask while he was stirring a pot of lentils and pig snout and other nice porcine offal. "Why do you dwarves have elongated heads?" he kept on with his queries. "You dwarves are oddballs. You seem made differently, but in the end you do everything the same as the rest of us, and you're probably even bigger cusses." I ignored his insidious chatter and shut my mouth, so I didn't swallow more flies than would strictly come with the food. "You dwarves should be governing Spain and not Franco. With those big heads of yours, I bet you'd work out a better future for us," and he chewed and chewed until he regurgitated his gastric juices out of the dry flaking corners of his lips.

We reached Córdoba on a morning white with almond blossom that smelled of the high seas. The mineral structure of the mosque glittered against the indigo sky, like a silhouette of the past plucked from a fairy-tale twilight. The Stéfano circus camped its caravans on the other side of the Guadalquivir, on an esplanade opposite the Calahorra Tower, next to some ruined mills. Gurruchaga was happy, which was quite unusual for him. He smiled broadly, like a young kid. The air reached us from the river with a scent of toads, and we all quivered and shivered differently; ours was an intense desire to live life to the full. These were the lethargic early sixties, and the threadbare curtain of misfortune was beginning to fall in tatters on the Spanish spectacle of starving cadavers. The first sparks of hope and tangible signs of economic well-being were evident in the way people behaved, although the real takeoff had yet to come. The military were shuffling offstage, and technocrats were taking over the reins of that pompous, freedom-killing, single-voiced nation whose fate, by the grace of God, was still shaped by a Caudillo. Nonetheless, Córdoba dawned that day half Roman, half Moorish, oblivious to the jiggery-pokery of the Movement, swirling with archangels and swallows, Saint Raphaels and Caliphs, the phantoms of tradition or legend.

The city's raucous trade was resuming. Carts of fruit and vegetables were crossing Julius Caesar's bridge, coming from the orchards in Almiriya and turning up the streets to the Plaza de la Corredera, where traders set up their stalls very early. It was the Thursday market, and hens shrieked in their

87

cages, waiting to be scalded in stewpots. It was a resplendent Thursday market, and the aroma of cold meat and sausages wafted through the air on the briny Andalusian breeze— pork loins toughened by the rising temperature, sparkling saffron juices trickling from chorizos, a rich aroma of brawns spreading across a decorous backcloth of strings of garlic, bunches of carnations, and earthenware jars full of green olives. That spot was a delight to the senses. Everything was on display and up for sale. Amid so much color and so many spicy, piquant smells, Gurruchaga's eyes lit up with the single desire to cook a local dish. "Have you ever tried Cordoban *salmorejo?*" he asked, enthused. "I don't have a clue what that is," I replied. "And what about oxtail? Have you ever tried oxtail?"

At the dinner organized by the Meredith Brothers Foundation from which I've just returned, they'd given us breaded cocks' combs and not oxtail or Cordoban *salmorejo.* They were wafer thin and dissolved on the tongue like communion wafers. As I wasn't really hungry, I hardly took a bite of the other courses, which may have been interpreted as grossly impolite, given my prestige in this country's food industry. Nothing could be further from the truth. I'd had enough with the cocks' combs and the wine to notice what was happening. During the entire soirée, the commissioner had done nothing but rub in my face how efficient the anti-hemorrhoid cream was that she was now applying to her intimate problem, so much so that she challenged me to take a look at the outcome. I had no desire to go against her wishes and jotted my address on a piece of paper with a request for her to come when the dinner was over. She smiled as she read my note and gave me a gleeful glance that flickered morosely.

Politicians are unpredictable. Women are voluble. Providence wiles away its hours on such sarcastic ploys.

That day, I was coming back with Gurruchaga from doing the job we'd been assigned. We'd bought a sack of tomatoes from some gypsies, and they were in such a bad state they were a wondrous sight, all together fermenting like a bunch gone to rot. I stumbled on behind. I was wearing six oxtails twisted around my neck like a necklace of meat—hot skins, the plumes of their tails sluicing down my back and trailing across the ground behind me. Gurru had got them at a bargain price from a sharecropper working on a farm. They were already giving off a stink that betrayed their vintage. I used all my strength to keep them aloft, but their weight and my short stature made it impossible, and they snaked behind me, furrowing the dust on my footprints. When we were crossing Caesar's bridge, now almost back at the circus, a few hooligans who'd been staring at that great event began to taunt us with insults and barbed jokes. It was obvious they thought it very funny to see a dwarf wrapped in oxtails sweating his guts out. "'Ey, a dwarf wi' six tails," they screamed and laughed. "'Ey, cop that, a dwarf bugger who's escaped from the circus." "'Ey, you dwarf bugger, where's yer off to with all 'em tails?" they kept shouting as they circled us. Gurruchaga suddenly turned around and gesticulated frantically at them to clear off. "Leave us in peace, you bastards, off you go and do something to keep your whore mothers happy." They didn't like his riposte one bit, and their scabby tempers became more frayed by the second. "All those fat cocks yer've 'ad stuck up yer asshole must 'ave made a big mess, right, yer little faggot?" they jibed, as they aimed kicks at our sack of tomatoes. "I'd bet yer'd giv'us a butchers if we giv'yer a peseta." He kept walking, deadpan, trying to ignore them, deeply sunk in that hermetic silence of his. To avoid a confrontation, he looked into the distance, at the indigo sky spreading before us like a defining display of nature. Gurruchaga knew about insults, beatings, and bullying. Memories of such were open sores in his flesh. They came within an ace of executing him after the shortest of trials when he fell into the hands of the National Army, right at the end of the civil war. Providence was charitable enough to ensure the military didn't discover what company he'd kept before their uprising, and he was only given a life sentence: forced labor in the Valley of the Fallen. I only found out about these circumstances years later, after General Franco had died, I suppose because of a similar intervention by Providence that spared him from execution. It was then I discovered he'd managed to escape from the Valley with three other prisoners, they were being hunted down, and by a freak of destiny he fell into the hands of Di Battista, who offered him silence and shelter in return for hard work and no pay. He was trying to bury himself in the circus when I turned up. *Red* and *fag* were words that had long since lost all meaning as far as he was concerned. Gurruchaga nurtured an open wound in his heart, an abyss in his soul he avoided hurling himself down at the cost of constant self-denial. "Yer've got yeller skin, chicken yeller, yer fag, bet yer paint yerself, so the big machos chase yer ass." We kept walking, dodging the insults and kicks they threw our way, trying to intimidate us. Once we'd crossed the bridge and were close to the first caravans of the Stefáno circus, fed up and sweaty as we were, the worst was yet to come. One of the youths, no doubt the cockiest of the lot, grabbed one of my oxtails and started whipping me. Bastards are always deciding to lash me, I can't think why. Human beings are complex, and the mentality of such bastards is so tortuous as to be unfathomable. He lashed me twice hard in the face with that leathery tail. The little bone at the end almost gouged one of my eyes out. I shouted, and the wretch started to lash me even harder simply out of the pleasure he got from seeing me squirm. He lashed me another five times, until Gurruchaga, stirred by my grief, threw the sack of tomatoes to the ground and then, without more ado, chucked himself at the youth big time, and head-butted him. That spread-eagled him on the ground, where he started punching him in the stomach with clenched fists in an attack of unbridled brutality I'd never seen from him before, to the point that crimson blood started bubbling from his victim's mouth. When the rest of them saw Gurruchaga the caveman in action, they shot off back over the bridge like frightened rats, toward the vicinity of the Mosque, in search of shelter in those narrow streets. "Let him be, or you'll kill him," I shouted, and he held his fist in the air for a thousandth of a second, unsure whether to smash his face in or restrain the kinetic, hateful energy pulling on his arm from the pits of destruction. In the end he put the brake on and let his victim go, blood-streaming and splattered, but alive, bruised on the inside but still breathing. The orange-blossom-scented air the branches of Córdoba's orange trees spread through the air would soon have revived him, if destiny, that ever-vigilant serpent, hadn't flickered its tongue. Up to then, nobody had ever moved a single finger with such determination on my behalf, not even Scarface the miller had gone so far when rescuing me from the rage of toothless Santomás. My cause was that of the destitute, abused, and emaciated, the dispossessed, helpless, and needy on their uppers. A language is enriched by the disasters experienced by the people that speak it—their prolonged misfortunes. Language is an enigma of synonyms that come from the common weal of shared suffering, an alphabetic mirror of the dread circumstances men endure. The collection of symptoms of catastrophe articulated into a code shapes a single language: that of the wretched of this earth, that language I spoke so elegantly. How distant and yet how recent that world now seems. Nobody had ever bothered to wield on my behalf the brazen justice of bare fists, the kind that comes to the boil for all to see—noble, savage, powerful, and mighty. Never before had I seen someone else raise their hand to avenge me, and do believe me if I say that I enjoyed the feeling of being protected. Every time Gurruchaga's fist belted that Cordoban hooligan in the stomach, I smiled contentedly. The harder he punched, the more I relished it, until an ineffable smile of bliss almost lit up my face. Gurruchaga was the implacable avenger who appears in stories about helping the poor and needy, the fantastic hero who soothes pain and rights wrongs. That youth fled over the bridge like a rabbit, making huge leaps over the Guadalquivir, rapid leaps like the ones a river makes when poverty dwells on its banks. We watched him scarper under the crumbling ruins of the Puerta del Puente, beneath the cracked friezes of Samson and Delilah. He was a dead blob in the distance, a future corpse in the heat of the sun. Gurruchaga picked up the sack of tomatoes, and I slung the string of oxtails over my shoulders, and we made a triumphant entrance into the circus, two proud angels, two figures from the unfinished nativity scene of history.

As we entered the shadows of the big top, between the animal cages and past the troupe's covered wagons,

Gurruchaga proclaimed to all and sundry the dishes he was planning to cook for lunch: Cordoban *salmorejo* and oxtail stew. The circus people showed their surprise at the shit man's show of good spirits. Even the wild animals roared and grunted from the depths of their gullets. Being the prickly sod he was, his invitation to lunch sounded strange. "You'va cum troppo contenti della città. It's a rare evento to see youa lika thiss," said pudgy Di Battista, peering out of the door of his caravan, which doubled as his box office and bedroom. He was holding a glass of cognac on the rocks, and alcohol's eloquence thickened his speech. "Youa must 'avva known molta whora aroun' 'ere when youa woz an amico di la Reppublica Sppagnola. No é vero, Gurruchaga?" Di Battista threw out those insidious insinuations to sap his spirits and return him to the supine state of the oppressed. He was a dab hand at doing that and enjoyed preening over the people he humiliated. Perhaps it was his way of trying to keep his control of a domain that was in fact slipping from his hands; perhaps he did so to avoid confronting his disillusion with himself, and his evident bankruptcy. He was a posh bastard falling on hard times, a hapless fellow who finally met the bad end he was seeking. Gurruchaga looked down, frowned, and went quiet. Pudgy and his gripes had touched his Achilles heel of accounts he'd yet to settle. He still went around in fear of his life after twenty years. And with good reason, that's for sure. He said nothing and walked off to the lions' cage and, next to the bars daubed with excrement, started to redeem his guilt by preparing lunch. I knew nothing about Gurruchaga's previous life and thought Di Battista's spiel that had depressed him so was a prelude to disaster when it was simply an epilogue, an epilogue to the tremendous disaster of the war. I quickly went to sit by his side at the end of the esplanade where the circus—beautiful towers and a fantastic jumble of roofs—had been erected. The lions languorously whisked off the flies. Gurruchaga started skinning the tails. He inserted the thin point of his knife in the joint, opened a wide enough slit, and with one pull tore off strips of skin. Pink and naked, the tail now looked like a snake made of bare flesh. After a silent interlude when the only sound was of skin tearing, I plucked up the courage to speak. "I want to thank you for defending me. You are the first to do so. I don't know what more I can say." "Shut your trap, kid," he retorted, "I just did what had to be done. Foul behavior really riles me; foul behavior and the quantity of idiots who rule the roost over everyone else. Don't you ever let them harness you up. Nod and pretend if you have no choice, but the moment they're not looking, go for their jugulars and don't let up until they stink of death. There's a lot to be done, but this will change one day. You'll live to see it. I lose it every time people fucking try it on. We should have fought back better. If we'd have beaten them, they'd all be marinating six feet under and we wouldn't have to keep quiet. Times have to change. You'll live to see it, Goyito, you'll see it happen." Gurruchaga shut up, and the resentment he felt clotted in his throat again. He looked up at the sky and spat out slantways a green gob of spit to siphon off his anger. "Now go to the caravan," he said, "look among my bits and pieces for a tomato masher, and start taking out the pips. I'm going to make such a fucking great *salmorejo* it will sweep all our sorrows away." I went off to the caravan and spent a good long time rummaging for a masher among his clutter. I'd never seen one before. I'd never tried *salmorejo*, or oxtail, for that matter. I'd never shared hatred with anyone. I'd never tasted sweet sorrow with any other human being. It was all new to me, silent times, and new. In the bric-a-brac in the caravan, I found broken pick heads, frying pans that would fry no more, saucepans misshapen by the heat of stoves, door handles, sacks with rusty metal catches, candlesticks, lumps of marble, knives without handles, remnants of rags, lots of leftovers from demolitions and scrapyards, miserable junk collected together in a battered trunk of memories belonging to nobody in particular, odds and sods from nowhere in particular. All of a sudden while rummaging in that messy pile, I came across something quite unexpected that brought the golden glitter of surprise to my face: a book of poems, Federico's *Gypsy Ballads*. I held it for a moment, weighing up the nature of my find, and then opened it at random. *Stubborn guns ring shrill through the night. The Virgin heals with her starlight spittle. But the Civil Guard advances sowing bonfires where imagination, young and naked, burns.* Now that is what you call poetry, poetry with that charge you extract from coal-black veins of feeling. At the time, I knew nothing about Federico. I hadn't read his verse and wasn't aware of the circumstances of his early demise or the fact that he possessed an incorrupt arm stuffed with olives and shards of iris that glowed in the sockets of his skull. I later discovered he'd met a bad death, bitter as freshly brewed coffee at dawn on the sandpaper countryside of Andalusia, that four yokels killed him, and that with their outrage they unknowingly established a sanctuary now venerated like an apparition of the Virgin. I was fascinated as I leafed through the pages of the *Ballads*, petrified by poetry like the statue of salt in the Old Testament. It was a short book with a two-tone drawing on the cover of a pitcher on a kind of red cloth in the shape of Spain's bull-skin. Three black sunflowers seemed to sway under the title like tentacles of the night. The poet's name was written at the bottom in his own handwriting. I opened it. On the inside pages was a dedication, imprinted with old ink that looked like dry blood, signaling who the owner was: *For Gurru, my comrade in love and combat, with a French kiss for the moments we have shared. Mary Faith Oxen.* That book was the only thing I took with me the day I escaped from the circus. I never did find the masher.

When I left the caravan and got a whiff of the powder scattered in the skirmish, Gurruchaga the shit man had already been laid low by the Civil Guard. He was bleeding on the ground by the lion cages, his right hand on the wound from the bullet that had drilled through his thigh, his face a sorry picture of defeat. A civil guard's boot was treading on his neck, while his colleague squirmed in the pain from the knife jabs he'd received in the fight. Behind, a man in plain clothes looked on contentedly over a prominent paunch that was beginning to emphasize his waning youth. His name was Esteruelas, and he was in charge of the detail. "Kill the fucker," the wounded civil guard urged his colleague, "bash his face in," but the other was more measured in matters of delivering death and merely pressed the sole of his boot down on Gurru's Adam's apple. Their curiosity aroused, the circus people observed with the frightened meekness of the underclass. Pudgy Di Battista, in the meanwhile, was conversing with the man orchestrating the arrest, more worried about any repercussions it all might have on his business than on the dismal fate Gurruchaga was facing.

"Non só 'ow aquesta disgrazia canna 'ave 'appened, ma you 'avva to understan' that gentes siniestras down onnaze luck joinna the circus, that zey only 'avva to gnaw a bone to 'avva suficenti per soprevivere. Youa know we aren't preocupati about people's condizione ne do we investigari nel suo passato. Zey work 'ard in exchange for silence, bit by bit redeemin' zemselves con zi lavoro. Per la notte zey let off steam barkin' alla luna e esto é tutto. States tambene need lugari come aqueste dove keeppa la merda di la soccictá," he declared, exhaling huge amounts of breath in order to dilute as quickly as possible the impact of alcohol in his blood. I kept my distance, not daring to step forward. The vile shine of gunmetal paralyzed my will, and fear kept it that way. I was offering a master class in not giving help, but what else could I do but try and save my own skin?

Gurruchaga had been reported by the hooligans who came after us on Julius Caesar's bridge when we were walking back to the circus with our load of tomatoes and oxtails. The kid whose stomach he'd pummeled with his iron fists had bled from the brain after taking flight and dropped dead in front of the Caño Gordo gate, along one of the façades of the Mosque. Apparently he collapsed suddenly and, already dead, smashed his face on Córdoba's stony ground. A local poet would surely have praised the Roman whirls on the funeral wreaths if he'd ever gazed upon such a fine corpse. His mates carried him on their shoulders to the Civil Guard barracks and reported what had happened, taking no blame, exaggerating what had happened, creating a pantomime out of death. I tried to make an effort to come to his aid and tell those men it had been legitimate self-defense, but fear prevented me, and remorse still troubles my memory in that respect. I now know that my testimony would have served no purpose. My fate would have followed its preordained course, and I'd have reached this moment in time in exactly the same way. It *was* best for me to keep quiet.

Gurruchaga looked up at me from the ground. Tears glinted in his eyes, and petals of blood wreathed his forehead like carnations on a gravestone. They kicked him back on his feet and handcuffed his hands behind his back. He tried to say something to me, but cowardice made me look the other way and I couldn't read the words on his lips. "You lot, get on with your chores. Nothing happened here," ordered Esteruelas with the blocked flute of his nasal voice. "As for you and this absurd circus," he told Di Battista, "we shall investigate what this is all about and who is ultimately responsible." Before they took the prisoner away, that man scrutinized me, as if he were fascinated by my deformities, but then he walked off, and in the end I wasn't brought to account. We met up years later, there was even a time when I did some jobs for him, but he finally got his just desserts, not that I'd been wanting that. I watched Gurruchaga walk off for the last time. Red poppies streamed down his trouser leg. It was a stream of hope, that mirage he'd never believed in.

The dead don't speak, they simply rot away as the seasons come and go till they turn to dust or creepy-crawlies have their fill. The dead have little or no influence over their fates. They're sometimes called upon to test out the waters of transcendence with their own hand, but it's rarely a success. They say Jesus Christ was practiced in this kind of shadowy endeavor and that he brought Lazarus back into this world. He must have emerged from the grave pale and wan like someone returning from a catastrophe, and he surely trembled in fear and even found it difficult to control his sphincters. Resurrection did him no good—perhaps as a preamble to a fresh death, a second death, a dead man times two. For everyone else, it was perhaps a reason to cling to hope. You have invaded my home to relieve me of consciousness and snatch my life away. I knew that the second I felt your presence, and though I'd been warned about what was bound to happen, I never thought it would be like this. They do say that at the very instant of death, past time zooms past one's eyes at the speed of lightning and one relives every moment as if they were the frames of a film rolling to its end. Perhaps that's what's happening right now. Perhaps the deeds I've done, those that shaped my feelings and justified my transit through this world, are dizzily being reproduced before I vanish into the void.

I'd been planning to fly to London tomorrow to spend Christmas with my son Edén, but now that you're here, I realize that's not going to be possible. The boy suffered far too much as a child and was left a mute with an out-of-joint will because of something ghastly that happened to him. The doctors treating his autism in the W&S Institution say he is improving and in time will be able to come out of isolation and integrate fully into society. To tell you the truth, I don't know what will be worse, for him to remain an alien to this world, funneled into the unreality of his paradises, or for them to cure his illness and return him to the fold of normality. I sometimes tell him that when he's cured, I'll bring him back so he can take charge of my business, and he just stands and looks at me as if he doesn't understand the meaning of my words or would rather not speak his mind about the triteness of my trade. He really does understand, but he shows no interest whatsoever and simply becomes self-engrossed and puts on a deadpan expression. He doesn't know that I'm his father. I've never bothered to tell him that the corpse he saw swinging on a rope in time with the flight of the stone curlews didn't belong to his father. Nor do I know whether he could assimilate that. I just pay the costs of the specialist treatment he receives, go to see him now and then, and take him for walks in London's parks. I suppose that in the same way that he's not bothered about my companionship, he won't miss me in this grueling Christmas season. Maybe he's only one more bit part in the cartoon fable of my existence.

After Gurruchaga disappeared, the shit detail was mine alone. Nobody missed him, not even the animals he looked after. Those beasts just went on dying when their turn came, now without anyone to register their pain and suffering. I took over his bric-a-brac, that useless pile of junk, his herculean cleaning tasks, and the duty of finding food for the animals, which required great effort and dedication. Consequently, they became first-rate consumers of dog meat and other delicacies that disease and waifing and straying had left abandoned on Spanish steppes under the cellophane veneer of carrion. Pudgy Di Battista watched me from his caravan window, shielded by the specter of alcohol that was increasingly blurring his brain and blunting his desire to live. "Molto bene, lad," Di Battista would say, "'ard work dignify il uomo. Ma essere a divinna castigato earning ze pane with ze sudore della brow, in your case is ze case, the 'uge jobz youvva donna."

My silence made me an accomplice. My penance was the shame at having to remember Gurruchaga being seized and beaten. The most treasured of all that his disappearance bequeathed me was the copy of the *Gypsy Ballads* and its yellow pages peppered with metaphors that were completely useless in everyday circus life. I reread and reread his verse in a seething trance as soon I could dodge my duties, and all that one-track reading fired my brain and took a grip on my ideas. Knives, gypsies, and civil guards walked back into my life, and I was powerless to stop them. It was as if the resurgence of my memories took on a fresh life with that book, and I happily wallowed in the process, relishing each word as if it had in fact come from my lips. However, there was something with a degree of reality in that wealth of well-rhymed tales: the dedication that presided over the text, that *For Gurru, my comrade in love and combat, with a French kiss for the moments we have shared, Mary Faith Oxen.* It was tangible, oozed with life, and I found it really intriguing.

They called Dorotea Gómez "La Doris" because she gave herself Doris Day airs. She had the same bright, lively eyes and prissy hair. She seemed a spitting image even with her bronzed hips. She'd tell herself *she* was the one pirouetting on the trapeze when she went into the ring to swing and trigger that ebb and flow of flesh through the air in her perennial struggle against the forces of gravity. It was a pleasure to see Doris take flight, a rhythmic, musical pleasure. She'd push herself off with her legs, and when her intended flight reached its peak, she swooped into the void and spun around a few seconds until she met her partner's hands, his fingers padlocking firmly around hers to avoid a splattering fall. Doris rounded off her routine as a lithe beauty, ever flirtatious and provocative, spontaneously so. Gelo de los Ángeles, her high-wire companion, calmly watched her gravity-defying snaking and zigzagging and, at the slightest error in her takeoff or wrong turn in her flight, leapt quickly and expertly to safeguard her act, catching her like a flesh-and-blood feather afloat plunging down from the downy trampoline in the clouds. Nonetheless, I should say that both worked with a net, which perhaps detracted from their show, but it's true that while Doris didn't want to stake her equally supple limbs, youth, or life on hands that could easily slip, Gelo de los Ángeles was a feverish risk-taker, always pressuring her to heighten the spectacle with the threat of disaster. His lippy, dribbling mouth challenged her to perform at least once for real, wagering both their lives on that invisible precipice in the air. Gelo was intrepid because he wanted to stand out and was committed to the deceit of the circus; he knew that to keep roaming the world without thrills was a lethal waste of dreams. Doris didn't think of death, but whenever she couldn't help it, she could only ever imagine a stretch of ground closing in on her eyes, and that premonition scared her stiff. She still had the supple limbs of first youth and pliant bones, so flexibility was her forte. She wasn't afraid of heights. Though she didn't allow herself to be duped by Gelo de los Ángeles's old tricks, either. She wore a white leotard, and the gauze pressed tight against her body in a transparent display of her contours and sweat. It was wonderful to watch her climbing up the rope to the cusp of the tent. Her body shimmied and sashayed, and the second she reached the trapeze bar, she was transfigured into a gamboling figure of flesh, blood, and talc. The audience was dazzled by her movements through the air, their necks ached from looking up so long, their mouths gaping wide, the women incredulous and the men slavering like dogs. Fantastic pirouettes, svelte corkscrews, double and triple somersaults performed wonderfully show after show, and there was yet more to come; as the climax to her act, Doris gripped the trapeze bar between the backs of her knees and let the rest of her body hang down. Then she grasped a torch in each hand, which she lit on the small flame of a censer hanging from the mast that supported the platform. Blackish diesel-oil smoke then coiled to the top of the tent and begrimed the canvas. The ring lights went out, and she was left alone in the dome, half in shadow, half illumined by orange flames. Doris launched off, and when her zigzagging climaxed, she'd let herself fall, spinning, twizzling her own body around, keeping the torches apart on each side of her, twisting and sparking in free fall down the abyss of the ring until Gelo de los Ángeles swung his trapeze over and caught her heels in mid-descent. The spectators chorused an anxious "Ooh!" of delight and roared their applause, releasing the tension aroused by so much suspense. Doris finished her act by sliding down a thick rope into the arena, where she stood barefoot, throwing endless kisses to her audience, giving the horniest among them the opportunity to pleasure in measuring her breasts and even the soft half-moons of her buttocks, which, as one could appreciate from closeup, spilt their cream down both sides of her leotard. After the applause, after the public's regulation inspection, Gelo de los Ángeles descended, athletic and hieratic, from the heights of his trapeze, stood behind her, and wrapped the sweaty satin of his cape around her, as if consecrating the arcane mystery of her dizzy femininity with the concealment of her body.

Pudgy Di Battista drank the air that Doris breathed, which was hardly surprising, since when it came to drinking, he could knock back even the bad blood coursing through his veins. Essentially, the circus was a prison where he purged the accursed nature of his existence. It could have been worse. It can always be worse. He could have purged his accursed existence at a stroke with a eugenic bullet to the temple, which never happened, though several in the circus would have applauded heartily. Pudgy Di Battista's liver must have tasted of cognac, which he'd have willingly given up for a taste of

Doris, if he'd been able, but she was always on the alert and kept a diplomatic distance, though never entirely dodging a future commitment, emboldened by that kind of equivocal *yes but no* some women cultivate so artfully. Pudgy Di Battista would have squandered money he didn't have to savor the trapeze artiste's skin. He often suggested as much, and she'd reply the color of your money first, then full steam ahead, though at the moment of truth, I'm sure she'd have refused to allow even the fingertips of his shadow to touch her. Basically, she didn't lack a moral side and would only have tasted temptation to fulfill a pledge, to mortify herself, and maybe redeem some lost soul with her self-sacrifice, like an early Christian martyr. Doris was from a sleepy, bad-sounding village in Badajoz and spoke with its weary piggy snuffle. Words seeped slowly across her head from her fount of understanding and surfaced from her lips worse for wear, distorted by her accent, though she always kept quiet on the trapeze and let her contortions speak for her, which was what really mattered. Doris's skin still retained the veneer of youth but already showed a tendency to beget varicose veins and hemorrhoids, which betrayed the future her body was fermenting. She'd stand and look me in the eye when she walked past a cage I was cleaning out, and her broad smiles made me feel on top of the world. I didn't credit them to begin with, but then gradually recognized they were for real; the girl must have had a weak spot for me. "Gregorito, one day you should come with me and have a swing on the trapeze, you'll see what fun it is." She'd drawl slowly, relishing the words in her mouth before uttering any. I feel I can still hear them. I used to nod and hang out my tongue like a dog being offered a bone, and my eyes followed her as she walked away, staring at the cocktail of her swaying hips as they melded into the colorful spectacle of the circus. Gelo de los Ángeles, her partner on high, also desired her mentally, though he said nothing, in order to safeguard the smooth running of their act. He knew his strength was waning, but he gritted his teeth and kept silent, because all he was good for was swinging through space. In secret he coughed up sputum flecked with blood and drank lots of chicory coffee, bottomless wells of it that steeled his spirit and geared him up for their strenuous routines. "Hey, dwarf, look how I drink coffee to thicken my blood. I couldn't care a fig for anything else. I'm tired of wandering the atlas of the world and not taking root, but now I really couldn't care less." Athletic and stoic, Gelo de los Ángeles continued to perform and fill the breech in the program but kept quiet about the disease squirreling away his strength. He also kept quiet about how he was longing to let his desires loose on Doris's flesh, but all the males in the circus kept that to themselves, except for the elephants who signaled it with a retractable erection of their trunks the moment she and her female scent peered into their cages. Many spectators—and pudgy Di Battista made the most of her as bait—only came to the show to ogle at the curves that Doris funneled tightly into her leotard. The key aspects of her anatomy were thus put into relief, were marvelous to behold, and the success of her act was assured in advance in an upfront manner unusual for the times. It was an era of secrecy and darkness, an era when one could only sin in the mind amid feverish, filthy fantasies one could never confess.

Once there was a fracas with the Movement's provincial delegate in Zamora, who'd come to a show with his wife and seven children. The man was astounded, or so he said, to see her naked in the ring. Excitement coupled with the power of his position meant he began to clamor indignantly and proclaim like the troglodyte he was that it was outrageous and unworthy, an insult to the Christian faith and an attack on the fundamental principles of the Movement. There was no option but to suspend the show, and a writ was issued against the Stéfano circus in the person of Di Battista, whom the appalled bigwig wanted to deal with in the courts. Pudgy spent a month in offices and waiting rooms with lawyers, giving explanations, apologizing, and hyping his would-be past as a Blackshirt in Mussolini's Fascist Italy. Naturally, the incident with Gurruchaga again came to light, and the matter became more complicated than it should have. While Pudgy was sorting that business out with his fatuous, patriotic verbal diarrhea that stank of cognac, the Stéfano circus was sealed off by order of the government, and in the meantime we were all left without a damned crumb to feed our bellies, apart from our worries and the vagaries about our role in the legal procedures that were underway. The ones that really came out best in the interim were the animals; apart from enjoying a rest from the exhausting paces we forced them through, they were fed in abundance on the stray dogs wandering the city, an indigenous victual that hardly rivaled the fame of local cheeses but was decent enough to placate their desperate stomachs.

Any desire Pudgy cherished to assail and sack the tasty dish of Doris's body evaporated in the time he spent sorting out that business. In the end, with a couple of references, a bit of the old blind eye, and the occasional solemn statement before the Hispano-Olivetti of a rather dim-witted bureaucrat faithfully doing his duty, the issue was resolved with a small fine, and the Stéfano circus could continue to wander, offering hope of entertainment to the scabby towns and villages of the peninsular fatherland.

Whenever the opening of my sphincter is sore, poor Doris always comes to mind; what she was and how she ended up. Time sunders and sinks everything, and we can't repeal the law that says we must respect the outcome. Generally people try to hide this type of ache and pain, due to a misguided sense of shame. They keep silent, then burst. Doris suffered, too. They were big and granulated in the folds of her anus. Big, purple, and granulated, like blackberries in the thick of the brambles. Hemorrhoids in women betray blood circulation problems and in men, constipation. The reverse can also happen, but the predominant rule is the one I just outlined. Constipation in women is usually frowned upon and in popular wisdom is linked to a vicious temper and a disinclination to enjoy sex. The best cure for hemorrhoids is a French pomade made from polyethylene glycol. At least that's the view of Belinda Dixon, the European commissioner. It's sold with a pain-free applicator. You simply have to relax before applying it. It softens the hemorrhoids and immediately reduces them to a minimal fleshly presence. It gives immediate relief and doesn't leave sticky discharges. The commissioner spent the whole of the dinner singing the praises of that excellent pomade. In matters of protocol, affinity between guests is ultimately decided by those whose job it is to orchestrate the ceremonials; placing a dwarf is always tricky, so one can end up in any old seat. I'm not saying I attend these society bashes on a daily basis, but from time to time I'm certainly obliged to accept invitations I'm obsequiously sent by associations and public and private institutions. People generally believe that the talk at this kind of event doesn't center on key matters affecting the well-being of the body politic, and though that's true, it's even truer that talk will focus on the dirty linen and skeletons in the cupboard of both absent and present colleagues. At such gatherings, wine is drunk from brittle glasses that enhance its bouquet, and one chews exquisite food with a palate alert to subtle flavors, but when the time comes to converse, it's usually the same topics of gossip that are trotted out: personal grudges and bodily dysfunctions. Essentially, all humanity's feet smell cheesy and flesh rots identically. Money, power, fame, and renown can window-dress biology, but the same terminus always awaits at the end of the road: the terminus of death.

At the time, Spain didn't possess an adequate pharmaceutical product to relieve the pain of hemorrhoids. Doris had to treat them with xeroform powder. She snow-flaked the contents of a phial she kept in a cupboard in her caravan onto a piece of gauze and applied it to the crossroads of her butt by severely twisting her muscles and expertly contorting her extremities, standing up, leaning her hips forward, and raising her left hand behind her back until it brushed against the fated orifice. Such an action revealed a splendorous rump enhanced by that shifting, humiliating, erotic posture, an offering contemplated by whoever had the good fortune to be privy to such privacy. Providence granted me the opportunity, the result of a previous mishap that befell me; as popular wisdom has it, every cloud has its silver lining. Given the way I toiled in animal shit, I contracted an infectious fever that affected my brain. I was used to sleeping anywhere, anyhow, under the stars in summer months, in the winter crouching in a shelter of blankets I put up at the foot of the wild animals' cages so their breath kept me warm like a Baby Jesus in the manger. Life had showed me how hard it can be more than once, and I quickly learnt to resign myself, to fasten my heart tight to the hungry rope of my innards and drag myself along without more ado. However, when I fell ill that time, my spirit of resistance dissolved on the tongue like toffee, and my will and energy to live departed as quickly as a couple of farts. Nobody showed any interest in looking after poor me, streaming sweat, feverish, and prostrate—nobody except for Doris, who took pity on me and carried me to the shelter of her caravan, an austere, tidy, pretty place decorated with little bottles of half-used perfume. That space was the earthly seat of a paradise I didn't believe in. In a feverish haze, my eyes served up extraordinary, multi-scented visions that relaxed me then sent me crazy and led me into the wildest corners of my consciousness. Doris laid me on her merino wool bolster and over three days applied to my forehead cold cloths, herbal poultices, and towels soaked in therapeutic ointments until my feverish brow relented and saw off any possibility that I might perish. Delirious, half-awake, I gazed at her as I've just described: beautiful in her contortions, her enormous rump displaying to the whites of my sickly eyes the magnificent pomp of her private parts, crowned by the Morello cherries of her compacted arteries. Poor Doris. She was unlucky in life. Misfortune pursues some to the very threshold of the grave. I kept her secret forever, and even once it became evident, I kept my mouth shut and didn't betray her. She showed me affection, and I thanked her with my silence; though I was well rewarded by my lurid memories of her gruesome parts.

Doris sometimes killed time by knitting sweaters for her nephews and nieces back in her village. She wove them beautifully with Ancora perlé thread, a shiny, non-shrink yarn in solid colors that had only just put in an appearance on haberdashery shelves. "Look, Gregorito," she'd say, clasping her knitting needles under her armpits, "how do you like this? It's for Pedrito, my nephew, whose first tooth is just peeking through," and I nodded though I didn't understand a word of what she was saying, being quite unable to assimilate that remote world of happy families, loving childhoods, and knitted cardigans aired in the sun, light years away from the everyday shit that made up the circus world of my existence.

If it was the right kind of day, Gelo de los Ángeles paid Doris's caravan a visit after the show to share a spot of supper. Doris invited him to a plain omelet with ham, basically so the fellow, who was clearly very poorly, didn't have to start messing with pots and pans himself after using up all his energy holding her up on the trapeze. It was no trauma for Doris to sizzle another omelet with her own, and even an extra one for me when I hobnobbed with them late at night. Gelo de los Ángeles coughed when he chewed, drank chicory coffee, and spat out thick gobs of sputum. His illness was eating away his features to the point that they were completely glazed over with a film of mold. I took the *Gypsy Ballads*, that treasure which didn't belong to me, to Doris's caravan and after a meager supper, I'd insist on reciting aloud some of Federico's poems. It amused them both to watch how sweetly the words flowed in my passionate reading, it shocked them to hear a power that was so at odds with the contemptible, screwed-up figure I cut, they relished the paradox: a deformed

111

dwarf holding on his lips the tempered beauty of Federico's verse. *On the twenty-fifth of June they told the Bitter Man: You can now cut the oleanders in your patio, if you so wish. Paint a cross on the door and put your name beneath, because hemlock and nettles will rise from your ribs and needles of wet lime will sting your shoes.* That array of metaphors hit the rocky ground of Gelo de los Ángeles's mind like the sound of toads croaking. "All that word-spinning gets your tongue into a twist. Idle pursuits for females and fags," he'd say. "That's rich from you, a guy without the scrap of sensibility you deserve," retorted Doris as she counter-attacked. "Poetry requires sensibility the way you require muscles." Gelo shut up. He basically knew that was true, but at this stage in his life, he could do nothing to change the way he was. He'd continue to display muscle, and only muscle, muscle in his arms, muscle in his legs, a muscular, if sickly, scrotum that would never spill its lusting cum on Doris's skin. On the other hand, she was so feminine you entered her through the door to her heart, and I made the most of that weakness: *The moon turns in the sky over waterless lands while summer sows whispers of tigers and llamas. Sinews of metal rang out above the roofs. Woolen baa-ing curled on the breeze. The earth offers itself full of scarred wounds, or quivering with the piercing cautery of white lights.* "How lovely, Gregorito, why don't you ask Di Battista to let you read poems in the ring? They sound so beautiful when you say them. Come on, recite them again for me, you give me goose bumps," and savoring that victory in words, I reread the poem, as proud and preening as a Jack of Clubs who'd been proclaimed a King of Spades.

I always kept that yellowish, unbound book with me. My memory will always be marked by the magical rhythm of its verse, their incredible silken yet deeply mournful beauty. My memory always felt the impact of those bitter-sweet soirées, Gelo's gobs of spit, Doris's innermost feelings bubbling up after dessert, and that ever-present dedication like the spittle from a forgotten curse that was the prologue to my poetry recital: "For Gurru, my comrade in love and combat, with a French kiss for the moments we have shared, Mary Faith Oxen."

Nowadays nobody believes in circuses. In these times that augur the end of the world, when leisure is home-based and reality is reeled off in pixels, there's no place for wild animals, clowns, Chinese jugglers, or deformed dwarves who decimate their dignity on the ring's compacted sand to hilarious guffaws. It was different then. People came to split their sides over us, and nobody noticed the horrific poverty sustaining it all, the behind-the-stage scenes where all of us involved in that great family of freaks in the Stéfano circus struggled to survive. People applauded, exclaimed, were astonished, let out belly laughs like uncontrolled farts before returning home and continuing with the daily routines that comprised the inner workings of national unity: a job for life to sustain the family future, the vague presence of the catechism in everyone's behavior, Sunday mass as Saturday's still wouldn't do, hierarchical obedience, institutional conformity, the Generalísimo's Cup, and barbarian females from the north, those barbarians with low-slung breasts now beginning to sow seeds of fantasy or obscenity in the apocalyptic minds of Spanish machos: "Fuck, those bloody birds are what you call tasty, if only we could lay one!" and then they clicked their tongues and downed their glasses of Osborne, took a drag on their cheap cigarettes, and crossed their arms, lust prickling their skin.

We circus folk roamed the seven corners of the nation's geography and noticed the same damned lust frothing behind all the barriers in the arena of Iberia. "Iberia is like a bull-skin stretched from west to east, with its front limbs pointing eastwards and its bulk stretching from north to south." And that's how it was. Our endless wandering across that stretch of skin gave us a privileged perspective on the evolution of lifestyles, distorted only, as is natural, by the rootlessness of our own industry and our status as adepts of transhumance. I learned who I am in those Spartan times, observing, reflecting, and feeling the hard knocks from the logs of life on my battered ribs that caved inwards. I never went to school, they wouldn't let in the deformed, but I studied on my own from the open book of experience the only subjects that can validate human existence: love, rage, revenge, and the limitless passion to survive.

We reached a city, knocked on its doors with our clapped-out megaphones, and people came to our spectacle to see us celebrate the absurd. Children greeted our japes with vicious cruelty—there were times their fingers pinged pellets at us from elastic bands—adults scrutinized our faces, and their petty minds were struck with awe as we unleashed our unrivaled jumps, pirouettes, and other feats that configured our acrobatic existence. In their amazement, they lapped up those grotesque rituals, and the eager tongues of their fantasies licked every scrap of flesh Doris adroitly offered them. The spectacle unfurled like a freak show, which is what it was, in the end, and I went from strength to strength amid all that, with my few possessions, with my nothing at all, really, and with the ice-cool pride slavery grants those who hazily glimpse that one day they will cast off their chains and stand as the indisputable kings of creation. Children are soft-skinned troglodytes who enjoy the anger they see their elders repressing. Children are beasts who enjoy watching others suffer. It was obnoxious to watch them in the front row wishing a tightrope walker would fall and snap the cable on his groin, or that a wild animal would gnash his teeth and rip off its tamer's arm. The adults were more of the same, only with more elevated, not to say erect, thoughts. I crouched behind the big curtains that were the entrance to the ring and watched them from my hideout. They stared at the sand, and I looked into their eyes. They didn't know it, but they were my show, the greatest show on earth, I insist, the circus of this world.

Telekinesis doesn't exist, and I'm telling you that, and telling you convinced that it is a fact. Nor does the spontaneous combustion of people. If telekinesis existed, two-thirds of the audience at our shows in those years would have been struck in their seats by the devastating lightning of my thoughts. I wished they would be and raged in the attempt, but it wasn't to be. The desires we experience generally stay that way, mere desires that fade and disappear like the smoke of dreams in the air of the real world. Nevertheless, one day a miracle did take place during a performance. It was in a small town in Valencia where we went for its patron saint's feast day. It was insufferably hot and clammy in the big top. Doris was spinning through the air in looping pirouettes assisted by the hand of Gelo de los Ángeles. In one of my furtive inspections, I noticed someone in the audience following the impossible unfurling of her lightness of being through shabby, squint-eyed binoculars from the civil war. I witnessed that Peeping Tom from my little

115

hideout behind the curtains and immediately saw what his deal was. He was a horny bastard who rather than gaze at the art of the trapeze was weighing up the parabolic dimensions of Doris's butt and the centrifugal jiggling of her tits. He was an infantry officer in a garish uniform with a worm-like little moustache that emerged from his nostrils in a quite un-martial manner. His gesticulations betrayed the pleasuring he was after: feeding his libido and entertaining himself on the remote possibility that Doris might slip from those heights and split her head open on the sand below. He attentively followed the sequence of acts, scratching his groin on the sly, giving himself an undeserved thrill in the half-light of the tent and getting off on the risky business she was chancing up above. I wasn't sure whether to walk over and spit in his face, or to let him enjoy himself as he wanted, but Providence solved my dilemma. I looked up and noticed a red circle wetting the material of Doris's leotard right in the spot where it was drawn inward by her buttocks, like a virgin of yesteryear granted the gift of weeping blood, a virgin transfixed by the immense misery of humanity. Blood of the misery of a float-bearer in Holy Week, holy blood flowing from wellsprings of the suffering, dark, heavy blood of hemorrhoids soaking the Golgotha of this world drip by drip. I looked up at the sky and saw her anointed in ruby red, bedecked by a stain. Two twin drops then rained on him in unison, two drops that hit the wretched fellow ogling with such putrid lust plumb between the eyes. The brightest red was the last thing his retinas registered. The strident color of blindness.

The Culí-Culá brothers weren't brothers, weren't clowns, weren't anything but faggots. Theirs was a slick act that delighted the public, a string of farts and proverbially filthy chases around the ring that always engaged the spectators. Smooth-cheeked, soppy Frank Culá ran across the sand with a clumsiness he feigned as he dodged the attempts to catch him made by bearded Juan Culí, a huge prowling bear lumbering awkwardly after him with a gigantic club on his shoulder, desperate to bash his head or wherever with his outsized bludgeon. When Frank was on the point of being captured, he'd aim a sonorous fart at Juan, the stink of which knocked him for six. It was an absurd scene, a grotesque caricature of the struggle between David and Goliath that ended with the giant prostrate on the ground, the butt of zillions of farts, protracted, vegetable efforts his captor graciously directed up his nose. Such a tour de force could only come from a premeditated souring of the intestines that the spectators found a hoot. They all laughed their bellies off during the act and, when it finished, applauded, cracked jokes, belched, and even farted gleefully, a display of flatulence and foul air in keeping with the taste of the spectacle. Juan Culí and Frank

117

Culá made a stable item and, like the best of brothers, shared the intimate space of a caravan with an array of everyday gear for personal hygiene, leisure, and domestic life. Gillette blades, Lea shaving soap, a pockmarked set of dominoes, a depleted set of crockery, towels, bedroom linens and pajamas, and rusty cutlery that once belonged to Culá's mother made up the bulk of their possessions. Apart from their daily labors, they shared a bed that was on the low side and very plain but didn't blunt their diversions. The Culí-Culá brothers never showed off their homosexual condition in public, and their measured life, apart from the gross nature of their performance, did them credit and was even exemplary. They never bothered me. Nor am I trying to claim they respected me. Respect on the fringes of a life of disorder is a relative value and subject to non-codified, imprecise, changing criteria. Generally speaking, respect comes from the fear or admiration one has for others, almost never from a mere sense of the dignity that should be part and parcel of being human. In the circus, respect derived from the tried-and-tested strength and hardness of one's character and, in my case, in equal doses from the pity I inspired or the guffaws I provoked. Juan Culí, the manliest of the duo, perhaps aimed an occasional kick at me when I crossed his path, but apart from that routine reaction, the truth is we behaved as equals. Frank Culá was, however, much shiftier, with a hidden agenda, and probably as a result always looked so two-faced I'm amazed he didn't go cross-eyed. He'd spy on me doing my chores, I never did find out why, and now and then made lewd remarks, so hedged by warm tributes they were immediately swept away by his apologetic airs and appearance. Nevertheless, Frank Culá had the foulest of tempers, and rage coursed through his veins when he had a prey in his sights or an enemy in range. "Dwarfy, where've you left Snow White?" he'd ask, meaning Doris. "Haven't you let her taste your little red apples yet?" He guessed that I was devoted to her and simply wanted to find a way to ingratiate himself in my feelings. If he sounded so coarse, it was only because he wanted to define the boundaries of his domains, as animals do with their pee. We both knew on which side our bread was buttered and, in one way or another, enjoyed that complicity. I never thought their life as a married couple was at all obscene, and it never, ever occurred to me to play them a nasty trick as a form of retaliation for their devious ways. Quite the contrary, I secretly admired the sugary warmth with which they cohabited, a warmth they fenced in behind sharp spikes and barbed wire to protect it against the rigors of the social climate. I accepted in silence the tiny caresses they indulged in when walking by, the syrupy gazes caramelizing in their eyes, the slight brushes against each other—angel wings their fingertips, an archangel's their fluttering lashes— and at bottom they were grateful for that.

It isn't the sleep of reason but the unreason of Providence that finally engenders us monsters. Then it crosses our paths and abandons us to our luck, to our resilience. Frank Culá possessed the hidden strength of the weak and showed it in his use of contempt. He and I were to an extent similar, and so we tried not to cross paths beyond the necessary shoulder-rubbing that suited us both. In this way, year after year sped by for all of us who shared acts, because, things being what they are, I abandoned the shit in the cages and passed over to the ring with the wild animals; as Di Battista had ordained, one had to make the most of one's dwarves.

A hunchback climbed aboard in Cuenca; he was prepared to work for nothing, for the mere pleasure of seeing the world. He had no known name, and pudgy Di Battista decided to baptize him Mandarino, in memory of a cousin of his from Calabria who was shot down by the partisans. "Mandarino, go off dove li animali e aiuda titch with ze raka and ze forka so ze shit non li arrivi to 'iz neck."

Mandarino was built like a beanpole, and one of his legs was too short to touch the ground, so he made up for it with a thick, raised heel made of pinewood worn down by the pebbly paths he'd trod. He walked with a slight stoop in his right shoulder, and despite being so skinny, the plump cheeks that protruded under his eyes like a frog's were strangely fleshly. His whole body seemed lopsided as he walked, particularly if one kept an eye on his groin, which was quick to stir with an unheard-of thrust that gave a perpendicular aspect to his movements. He was amazingly well endowed. Mandarino started to help me with my chores. He spoke sparingly and initially seemed like a born mute, because he used gestures rather than his tongue when he wanted to communicate. As time passed, he started opening his mouth and even came out with bad-mannered patter, so we quickly concluded he was mad. I wasn't worried by that, so long as he gave me a hand and did it well. "If you hit the bear in the stomach with a stick, he soon feels like taking a piss. I like watching animals piss, because it takes my thirst away. Rain, rain, don't go away," and without more ado he'd start raking up poo that he piled into panniers. I'd look at him perplexed, and the most I saw would be golden piss streaming down his trouser leg while he sang. I don't know whether it was prompted by lunacy or biological necessity. Mandarino was always involved in one of two visible activities: pissing himself, or pleasuring himself with his hand. He'd do either and not blink an eyelid, and there was no mystery involved beyond the phenomenon he treasured between his legs and the unlikely nature of his behavior in public. It was hardly charitable to reproach him, given his dimwittedness and the fact he spent the whole blessed day sharing the degenerate habits of wild animals.

I've not eaten a hardboiled egg in twenty-five years. I soon became sick of the sight of them. On the other hand, that bastard Di Battista loved them. One sopping wet morning, he summoned me very early for a parley in his caravan. I'd not even drunk my breakfast glass of water. It was evident that he was in a big hurry. "Mandarino 'elpin' you bene with quello della merda degli animali?" he asked. "He does his tasks," I replied as calmly as I could. "Ascolta: I'vva pensato a nice nano like youa would bringga ze profitto megliore jumpin' aroun' ze ring zan pulendo la merda dell jaule. Don' youa agree, Gregorito?" "I don't know," I answered, shrugging my shoulders. "Ciai fame; non hai fatto collazzione?" he asked again.

Hunger always gives bad counsel, and it can be disastrous if you let yourself be guided by an empty stomach. My belly had suffered far too much. My guts had been wiped clean as a result of all that fasting with only a few bizarre snacks to eat; a slice of melon puréed in milk, or a hunk of dry bread with some red pepper rubbed over the top were sometimes tidbits enough to assuage a day's hunger. Nonetheless, such penury could turn to abundance overnight, and then we'd pay homage by stuffing ourselves and shaking off the harsh prescriptions of our usual wretchedness for a few hours.

I've never been short on hunger, and perhaps that's why Providence had the bright idea of inspiring me to set up a pizza delivery business, which is why I'm wallowing knee-deep in loot today. Pudgy Di Battista knew what he was doing and tempted me, given the starving state I was in, with the attractive prospect of having a full belly. I wasn't black, but I was hungry. Hear me out, and the comparisons I make won't seem gratuitous. The black children in Africa nurture a tarantula in their chests that nobody chases away, the tarantula of starvation. They eat air and die young and aren't even buried, and the cycle of catastrophes is thus continued. These are the times we live in, times to end time.

Pudgy Di Battista stirred from the chair where he was resting his buttocks and soon returned with a trayful of boiled eggs. He placed a bottle of cognac on the table, filled a glass to the brim, stared me in the eye, and asked me how many eggs I thought I could swallow in one sitting. And being, as I say, naturally hungry and not having eaten breakfast that morning, I gazed at the tray, didn't blink, and started chewing eggs nonstop while he gulped down his bottle just as quick. I can't remember if I downed ten or fifteen eggs, but the truth is in the end I was stuffed and satisfied as never before. "Molto bene, nano, molto que molto bene," said pudgy Di Battista, who was well and truly plastered. "Yourra belly nel future sera una fontana di riquezza per tutti noi. Fromma domani youlla perform in ze act with ze fratelli Culí-Culá and beforra ze pubblico youlla stuffa tutti le 'ard-boiled eggsa you can. Per te, 'unger ha acabatto. Go and dechirleso a elli from mi," and he burst out laughing like a madman from hell, oozing so much wine it even colored his tears, big teardrops he wept as he laughed so pathetically.

To begin with they just chased me around the ring, me clumsy and stumbling by nature, the Culí-Culás in hot pursuit, thrilled by the possibility I might bash my nose on the ground and spill my soul out, as had almost happened when I nearly knocked myself out tripping on one of the cables securing the safety net for the trapeze act. Then came the eggs and farts. In full view of the spectators, I ended my whole-day-long fast on hard-boiled eggs, gesticulating with gusto, and a chorus of guffaws from the audience, who surely thought it hilarious to see a dwarf like me dispatching a stack of what hens had laid. What's more, the banquet was accompanied by a concerto in C major of belches that had neither rhythm nor tune. Don't imagine that the general public hasn't always laughed at the same gross doings. Before, they used to do it in the big top, packed together and making the wild animals go crazy with the pong from their sweat, now they guffaw at them in their kitchen-diners, the scant three by six feet they generally inhabit, breathing in the stink of the family and greatly helped by the inestimable remote control, the real crook on which the whole woolly flock depends. The act we performed totally lacked imagination and hid no double meanings, although its cheeky barrel-scraping could have triggered the indignation of the righteous men who in every era cherish establishment thinking. That act was well below my capabilities, if only because of the silly way it was choreographed, so I had no choice but to come up with something within the range of the three of us. I pondered over it for three months and finally suggested it to Frank Culá. He looked thoughtful for a moment, then smiled in that sly way of his and accepted right away. "You've a good head on you, dwarfy, and that's why I find you interesting. You and I will do great things together, you just wait and see," he said, rushing off to tell his partner.

The new act was an attempt to hallow, if only in show-biz style, the actual marriage of the Culí-Culás. I suggested that Juan Culí should come into the ring disguised as a woman—huge, tawdry, with lots of lace, furbelows, and face paint—and that Frank Culá should pretend to be his husband. It was the reverse of real life, which added extra spice to the simulation. Juan Culí would display a grotesque twenty-month pregnancy in the manner of a female elephant, to which end he'd hang a barrel from his waist, inside of which I'd be hidden. After the usual chases around the sides of the ring, Juan Culí would exhibit his would-be labor pains to an amazed audience and the exaggerated histrionics of Frank Culá, who, to a rocket-launch countdown bawled out in English, would activate the spring, and, expelled amid sticky sheep entrails and a shower of fake gunge, I'd clatter out in a miscarriage every show, hitting the ground headfirst. "Faif, for, zri, tchu, wan, dwarfy!" and out I'd come, ridiculous and belittled, dirty and contemptible, the impossible son of a couple of deviants in a country under the cosh of repression and orthodoxy. Once I was born, my putative parents did all they could to feed me, and that's where the eggs came in, fed to me with the sweetest canings, loving bludgeons, pricked by knives and forks. I received all that fodder with resignation, more for the hilarity it sparked among the spectators than for the little good the eggs did me. Even so, replete and with no chance that I could increase my growth, due to the natural brake of my physique, I became heavier and happier, heavier because of what I was ingesting and happier because "laugh, and the whole world laughs with you." Hunger and punishment are always harnessed together by the rope of history. Punishment either kills or stirs to action. Hunger jolts the will and points it to the exact place where knives are being sunk into flesh. That's some road to get satisfaction.

I often receive invitations to go to galas, parties, launches, grand finales, homages, and other society events, but now I very rarely grace such occasions with my presence. Tonight was an exception. I'd not intended going to the dinner, then at the last minute I fancied dipping into a classy soirée that, for one reason or another, I suspected would satisfy my itch to feel in touch with the heartbeat of reality. Nobody in these circles knows anything about the circumstances of my past life, and I've always enjoyed the thrill of gratuitous deceit. Although I'd planned to fly to London to spend Christmas with my son Edén, closing out the social calendar by exhibiting my deformed body in an act of such a highfalutin' nature as this suddenly seemed to be what I felt like. The glossies would bear witness to my presence among the great and the good. Off-the-cuff decisions are the ones that generally generate most joy. Ordinary folk still believe that on such occasions there is never any talk of matters essential for the common good, and if that's true, it's even truer that what finally gets aired is the dirty linen of absent colleagues, and even that of those present. At such gatherings, wine is drunk from brittle glasses that emphasize bouquet, the excellence of the food is chewed by palates alert to subtle flavors, but when it's time to converse, it's always the gossip that surfaces: personal grudges and bodily dysfunctions. The European commissioner Belinda Dixon regaled me during the whole soirée with the delights of the anti-hemorrhoid cream she uses, to the point of obscenity in the minute detail she highlighted. She initiated her game plan by asking me upfront whether a man like myself, famous for creating a fast-food empire, considered that alcohol was damaging for varicose veins or if, on the contrary, I believed wine contributed to a well-balanced state of health. I sat and stared at her, perhaps intrigued by the unusual way she spoke. Her eyes were lovely, dense, deep, and always friendly. Her gaze bewitched, and her lips whispered words as if her vocal chords were made of silk. I replied that wine is the fount of truth, that humanity requires it to know itself without subterfuge, and that it is only by possessing truth that human beings can find genuine freedom. She smiled neither scornfully nor dutifully but rather malevolently. From that moment, our exchange took on a more risqué note. We made a toast with a long, intense clink of glasses that reverberated in the shocked tympana of the other diners. A photographer took a snapshot. The mayor looked at us askance and, ever smiling, nodded in our direction, quietly deferential. The commissioner had been asking me if my body's deformities extended to all its parts, in other words, whether my reproductive organ was affected by my dwarfishness. Simply out of curiosity, she confessed. I replied that it wasn't. I refilled her glass to the brim, and she gulped it down. Then I busied myself squeezing tasty morsels from my cocks' combs, far away, self-absorbed, as if that supper really was my last.

Initially I thought that Ms. Dixon's obscene verbal play was about probing my carnal appetites, and I can confess to you that it worked. She may very well turn up tonight, it's still not too late, and she promised she'd come. If she does, she'll be surprised to find a corpse, or better still, the vague shadow of a being who has ceased to exist. Although pity isn't a value that's much prized these days, I should recognize that I felt something similar for her this evening. That string of obscenities she unleashed on me dish after dish only hid a woman in turmoil ready to do anything to attain her stated goal, a goal she'd marked out, a victory she'd foreseen. Like so many others in this day and age who can only justify their existence through futile professional advancement, the European commissioner, if she could, would have mortgaged liters of her blood to lay her hands on an extra millimeter of power. Basically, beneath the big show of status, this kind of person hides only panic at the thought of failure, fear of themselves, and the consolation of ending it all with a single shot when the world turns against them and exposes their solitude. As pity isn't in any way at odds with the pleasures of the flesh, I think I did the right thing by accepting her offer, even if I fear it will be a great shame not to be able to enjoy hers.

I became tired of the applause from so many blank faces, so many sweaty palms clapping wildly after I emptied the platter of eggs the Culí-Culá duo offered me every show. That mockery of marriage that could have offended the susceptible or sparked indignation was on the contrary held to be a hilarious and healthy comic act, perhaps because it recreated scenes of domestic life only too familiar in the backyards of the commonalty, scenes never aired because of the predominant sense of prudery and the prurient nature of comportment in the public eye. The innate hunger that haunted me went in a flash, it was as if a pantry brimming with provisions had been stuffed in my belly to the eternal delight of my gastric juices; however, I soon reacted against the excesses of that fetal diet that became the cracked egg of a cross I had to bear in life. I quickly learned to perform acute peristalsis in the upper and lower reaches of my stomach in order to sick up or engineer less vaulted though equally effective motions that sluiced me out after each show. You can achieve anything in this life if you try, except beauty and height, which are both the attributes of angels. I became tired of all the applause that greeted our act; the plaudits were pathetic. The circus is the supreme spectacle of the grotesque, and the belly laughs often betray the unhappiness of those so reacting, of those in attendance, of that whole republic of idiotic children, hapless adults, and freak-seekers who in the end sustained us. I stared at their blank faces, their lidless eyes and mute mouths, and stuck to swallowing those eggs in order to survive. They came every day, circled the ring, hanging on the catastrophe that might shoot up their laughter levels, and on every string pulled in the show.

One afternoon, when we were performing on the Costa del Sol, I spotted a circular face amid the anodyne crowd that was scrutinizing me from the front row of the stalls. That mug had a pinkish hue, as if it belonged to a seventeenth-century English empiricist who was perhaps speculating over a translucent balloon of brandy about the planetary mechanics of heavenly bodies across the crepe of the firmament. His eyes watched our routine with a sense of ecstasy I found frightening. He returned the next day, the one after, and even the one after that. I used each performance to dissect the features of that individual. His gaze seemed at once balanced and tortured, conferring on his face a sorrow it wore lightly, like that of a child who has grown up prematurely and is fat to bursting he's been so indulged. He was broad, though not deformed, and plump, though not obese. On the fourth day of his presence, I spotted him in conversation with pudgy Di Battista. That very same night, after I'd had supper in Doris's caravan (lentils without insects or earth that peppered my belly with bubbles of gas), Stéfano di Battista came to speak to me. There was a starry sky, and the stars twinkled blue in the distance as if they'd escaped from a poem by Neruda. Poetry can sometimes be redeeming in the disastrous depths of daily life, but it was different that night. Pudgy Di Battista was well tipsy, and I don't say that because of the way he was tottering but because of his fermenting breath. He grabbed my shoulder and said that early the following morning, a car would come to pick me up, and I would spend the day in the house of a man who was interested in painting me. He insinuated he was an oddball who was filthy rich and that there was nothing to worry about; at the very worst, he might decide to give my bum a stroke. Then he handed me three thousand pesetas, the advance he claimed he'd received from that fellow for my services. Pudgy Di Battista was a posh bastard fallen on hard times, and death was his only cure, the one that duly wasted his insides.

I'd never seen the like of it. It was a Dodge Dart, and hearse-like it was so black, and so huge. The chauffeur was a guy they'd hired by the hour for the job and whose mouth sank into his cheeks; he didn't say a word on the whole journey. He drove me to the outskirts of Benalmádena, a built-up area with towering palm trees and houses with magnificent façades that ran down the slope of a cliff. We stopped outside one, the most precipitously poised of all. A man who'd just got up opened the door in a white cotton dressing gown. He asked me to accompany him, in a language with strange phonetics that occasionally sounded like Spanish. He ushered me into an immense lounge with a view of the steep cliff through a wall that was entirely glass. The rest of the room was built of stone ashlars that culminated in a lofty ceiling with two different heights, both furrowed by the veins in delicately carved wood that had surely survived from another century. Good taste and tranquility oozed everywhere in that silent lounge I felt to be inhospitable, a silence broken only by the lethargic crackle of a tree trunk that had been burning through the night and was now crumbling in the hearth. I inhaled the aroma of timber and opened my eyes wide, trying to anticipate what was about to happen. Dank with sweat, an unmade bed in the middle of the room displayed an epic range of sheets and bare pillows. Nearby, sitting on a plastic stool, the pinkish man I'd seen in the circus was waiting for me to come. He gripped a paintbrush in one hand, and the uneven outline of his face projected itself, black on white, onto the surface of a canvas, mounted on an easel, that brought a white sheen to his back. "Lie back and relax. I'm going to capture your best side for eternity, to my greater glory. In the meantime, would you like something to drink, Coca-Cola, perhaps?" he enquired in English, and using intuition rather than intellect, I went and reclined on the rippling sheets and spent the whole damned day there while he skillfully reproduced my portrait on canvas. He said not another word; nor did I. Neither did he stop for a bite to eat or to wet his lips. All he did was look at me, scrutinize my face, measure out the deformity of my body with his brush, and add color nonstop. Now and then, the man who opened the garden gate in the morning came and from the top of the stairs took a look at how the picture was progressing. He did so now stripped of his dressing gown, in no clothes at all; his soft, pappy flesh gave him an unusual air that made me avoid the glances he sent my way, deep, languid, wandering eyes I immediately put down to some incurable disease. I don't know if his sex was threatening or challenging, provocative or derisory, drooping heavily down his groin as it did, amid folds of flesh, like a clapped-out clapper. At the hour of the Angelus, another man, likewise naked, walked into the lounge. He embraced the first; they cuddled as they spent a while watching the representation of my image flower on the canvas. Generally speaking, artists are frantic people who spit out their arrogance with precision and beauty, beings fertilized by the accursed seed of sensibility, who like to cultivate the bloom of their own egotism. Impenetrable profiles characterize them, doubtful masks betray them; they are but false idealizations of themselves that, once understood, reveal their total defenselessness before the nagging round of existence. That man was no exception, save perhaps for his pinkish skin. As evening fell—twilight was sinking its twinkles into the sea—he decided he'd finished the task, and at last I could jump off the bed. I noted how numb my body was, like an ancient statue suddenly regaining movement. I bent and flexed, and yawned to stretch my ligaments. Prompted more by curiosity than by real interest, I walked over to the canvas to see what part of me had been recreated in oils, and I won't lie if I say that it wasn't surprise, admiration, or fear that dictated a squint-eyed reaction that must have made my slavering mouth snarl. It wasn't me in the picture, though I couldn't say it wasn't me on the inside, or that I might not be like that on the outside in a not-too-distant future. He'd pained my guts. There was no sense of shame in that painting; a series of thick, tempestuous brushstrokes had turned the most monstrous side of me into a magma of molten flesh. The end product of that painter's contemplation of my person now transcribed on canvas was simply a putrid effervescence of flesh transubstantiated into a bone structure in almost liturgical fashion. He'd painted me erect, like an untouchable idol, on the shameful pedestal of that bed, a deliberately disfigured idol sliding into the sewer of reality. I'd never have imagined anything like that could enter someone's head. That painting was a manifesto on the precarious nature of human existence, an extreme representation of the tragedy of life, as powerful and intriguing as that could be. They offered me another Coca-Cola and sent me back to the circus; I returned in time for the nighttime show. My chauffeur was as mute as ever. He now reeked of sardines and had an indefinable lump on his neck I'd not noticed in the morning. "I'd stay in bed every day for three thousand pesetas, what a great way to earn a living," I remarked. He looked in the rearview mirror and, without needing to open his mouth, I think he indicated that someone must have pocketed the difference, because twenty-five thousand had been paid for my pose. Some bastard, no doubt. I can't think why, but I started to think my chauffeur was a fish, a stinking fish that had escaped from a foul harbor, one equipped to drive, a smelly backbone of a fish, the kind hungry cats eat from trash cans. I took a closer look, and indeed he did have a protuberance on his neck that I felt looked like a gill. It's the first time a fish had given me a lead. Di Battista was the bastard; he spent the difference on cognac and left me howling at the moon. That very night, while the public split their sides and the Culí-Culá duo chased me wildly around the ring, I understood for the first time in my life that as in almost everything else, there were social classes even when it came to affectation, and that mine was way beneath the mediocre average that's the norm for most mortals.

Little Marisol was touring the world, singing that life was a tombola, which did her proud and got her happy little girlie smile on magazine front covers. That year, she was competing in the glossies with singer Raphael, Maricarmen Martínez Bordiú—Franco's granddaughter—with Julio Iglesias, bullfighter El Cordobés, and actress Amparito Muñoz, but the cream on the cake undoubtedly went to little Marisol—fresh, smiley, high-pitched, fizzy, dreamy-eyed, with the ye-ye innocence that comes with water-pitchers and *paso dobles*. Tom-tom-tombola: "The sweet actress is coming to the end of her holidays; a European honeymoon for Jane Fonda; Prince Charles of Romania has got into trouble with Scotland Yard; Eno Fruit Salts have restored my well-being and now I feel up for this wonderful party. Thanks to Eno, I don't have to sit out the afternoon."

Little Marisol was belting it out on high-society stages while the rest of Spain was still waiting for the true dawn to come. In time she'd bare the floppy cups of her breasts on the cover of *Interviú*, and all Spanish men would have to repent for the subterranean longing—pederasty, *par excellence*—that surged in their hearts. Binges, guitars, dry sherry and *tapas*, and the jingle of coins were all the fashion in that finite universe that was the indissoluble unity of the fatherland. Swedish women were beginning to dip their toes in the still-empty sands of Benidorm and quite unawares triggered multiple erections in building workers lacking a destiny and substance that on the other hand sentenced them to perpetual unease or real estate speculation. People spoke enviously of the sumptuous splendors of the Sha of Persia and the golden beauty of Farah Diba, his wife. Sara Montiel kissed Gary Cooper on the mouth in stills of *Veracruz,* while middle-class kids were fed on Cola Cao hot cocoa for breakfast and afternoon snack. The flushed glow of actresses, whether homegrown or foreign, aroused admiration in the sinews of dreams in the country's first dormitory cities; their fake monikers leapt by word of mouth from one end of the nation to the other, but when they reached mine, they slid straight off my skin, except for one: Marisol. Then one day when we were hard at it in the din and frenzy of the Costa del Sol, pudgy Di Battista came along, all sweaty and excited by the news he'd heard from Málaga that little Marisol would grace our show that evening. When I heard that, my pelvis flipped. I couldn't credit how elated I was and started jumping around like a lunatic. A jumping dwarf would have caused a stir elsewhere, but there we knew each other and nothing seemed as strange as normality. The whole circus plunged into a welter of preparations; it was all nerves, chatter, gossip, and finally that expectation bore fruit—little Marisol did in fact come. I will never forget that damp night, the very one that Gelo de Los Ángeles slipped off the trapeze and broke his neck on the compacted sand beneath. Everyone was astonished, but he was left paraplegic. He knew very well that he was ill, but perhaps wanting to display traces of agility stymied by raucous tubercular coughing, he had decided to do so without a net, in order to heighten the spectacle and make a greater impression on little Marisol and the whole retinue of hangers-on that followed her footsteps to every corner of the peninsula. Did he manage it? You bet he did. He was doing marvelously, until he had the misfortune to slip and hit the planet with his vertebra, which snapped like dry wood. It could have been worse, but wasn't. Things happen as things must, and there is little one can do to change their predetermined course. Little Marisol wept she was so scared, and that was my gain; my retina gathered up her tears like shards of translucent treasure, to be sipped away, secretion after secretion, in obsessive, untrammeled masturbation. The sound of a neck breaking is very peculiar, and once heard is never forgotten, like someone treading on a cockroach or cracking a dog's skull with a stick. They are precise sounds that, depending on when and how they happen, ensure you do or don't doubt the promised resurrection of the flesh. A bastard gremlin must have sliced Gelo de los Ángeles's wings at the root, because he fell vertically, the topknot of his skull aiming at the hole it would open up in the ring when it made contact. We were all struck dumb by the crack, and pudgy Di Battista, sitting next to little Marisol, sobered up as if he'd suddenly caught the plague. Out of inertia, Doris went on swinging from one side of the big top to the other, now abandoned by Gelo's muscles, while she incredulously contemplated the outcome of his fall. Some spectators shouted, and all of a sudden, someone started applauding. The clapping spread, and they all made the skin on their palms sore, not really understanding why. Some would be applauding the fall, others the catastrophe, but the truth is that the tragedy led to fun and games, which was little or no help to Gelo de los Ángeles, who lay there, transfixed on himself in a grotesque, agonizing posture, his bones shattered, anointing the sand as if he were the last drop of jam in the jar. It was a real pity the show had to be suspended; that made it impossible for me to go into the ring and pay my homage to Marisol by dedicating my act to her as I'd planned. I'd intended to put myself in the barrel around Juan Culí's belly with a bouquet of flowers, and when the cry went up—". . . wan, dwarfy!"—I'd fall out with the bouquet, which I'd run and exchange for a kiss from Marisol. It wasn't to be. That's often the fate of plans—tattered dreams shredded by fallow encephalic mass. A great pity. Little Marisol left the way she came and went on chirping in the midst of the tricky tombola of life, nurturing, meanwhile, the buxom breasts she'd then show us in *Interviú* to set us sinning. They swept Gelo de los Ángeles off in an ambulance to an operating theater where they didn't succeed in putting his bones back together. I never saw him again; I don't like rituals of fear or pity. Doris paid him a visit a few years later and told me about the ruin of a man he'd become, that man who used to shoot through the air, leaving in his wake whitish vapors like Milky Ways of talcum. She did so stooping down and sobbing on my shoulders, and I made the most of her sorrowful expression to brush her nipples with my fingertips and breathe in the sadness distilled by her sweat. Then she confessed she'd suffocated him to spare him further pain.

Out of the window, in through the door. Handsome Bustamante was one of those cheeky, thieving womanizers who're often up to their necks in fraud and filth, on the downhill slope to death. "See if you learn from me, Goyo, I'm a dab hand at doing it slowly—one hand on Paula's tits and the other on Tina's oyster," and he started laughing at his own joke as if his teeth would fall out they were so chuffed. Worst of all, it was true. He was really good-looking and fantastically agile. There you see the lunacy of Providence, some are born under an unlucky star, yet others come with a halo of the most luscious of dames, handsome, arrogant, and pampered like a fairy prince on a honeymoon far from the catastrophe.

Handsome Bustamante, so simple, supple, womanizing, and gorgeous, arrived as Gelo de los Ángeles's replacement on the trapeze, and while he was at it, he switched on a torrent of lust in the empty reservoir of the Stéfano circus. In a flash he laid any living flesh and still didn't find enough candidates to satisfy his wayward lusts. I don't know why he took to me, but the fact is I performed as the flag-bearer for his horny quests, scouting for his whims wherever we holed up, in the villages, steppes, or wastelands of Spain. There existed no place where I couldn't sniff out a brothel, the red light of a bordello, or the provincial reserve of a cat house concealed on the third floor, left-hand side of a mansion, with honor and gas in each room, but no lift. "Goyo, you don't disgust me, you make me lucky," the bastard would say, stroking my neck as if I were an animal he was fond of or felt sorry for. Although he didn't come with wings, he flew on the trapeze better than Gelo de los Ángeles, which was all to the good when it came to settling up with pudgy Di Battista. He coaxed Doris through the air with the Herculean strength of his hands and inspired her to try leaps, pirouettes, and corkscrews she'd never before attempted in the roof of the big top, quite self-confident with the precision afforded by her healthy new partner. At the end of their act, just like Gelo, Bustamante slid down the rope to the ring, where he'd give Doris the shivers with the black caress of his cloak as if it were the nocturnal garb of a vampire, the kind whose blood burns in eternal fire. The spectacle of that embrace was breathtaking, and, oblivious to any skullduggery, the audience clapped like crazy, as it was. The fleshy tentacles of his hands gripped the sides of her breasts till her eyelids fluttered, flirtatious and feminine, with a rush of adrenalin, and now and then even produced a gleaming bead of desire. If it was wondrous to watch them swirling through the air, it was even tastier to peer at them behind the mask of that embrace, a couple of Lucifers, or beasts from hell, slavering over each other's bodies for the pure thrill of it. I saw the dampness welling in the forks of their thighs and was distraught by all that frenzy that didn't involve me, simply out of envy and the desire to penetrate, once and for all, soft female places. Longing is longing and a void is a void, so it is written, and one can do nothing to overturn the enigmas of Providence. I can hardly invoke the ruins of my flesh, but I know what it's like to struggle up a steep slope. Nonetheless, over the years I've done things to open up the doors of desire so I can pleasure my whims: I've reduced life to merchandise. Now I buy everything, I sell everything, and, apart from giving worldly prestige, it sedates.

Handsome Bustamante tapped me on the neck, and I licked his hand with the tip of my tongue, at the ready like a docile dog. I counted more than a thousand fucks before I gave up. All full on, all satisfactory. I sometimes felt like sidling over to Mandarino to find his kind of consolation, but he gave off such a stench and his horniness was so *sui generis* I didn't try him once.

The Stéfano circus was increasingly dampening my energies with its fake routines. Stumbling alongside, I began to wonder what my life had turned into. It was a prison of wispy smoke where the bars only existed in the imaginations of the inmates, a prison in the form of a circus ring where wills were tamed by the lash of applause and the eruption of belly laughs. For how long would I have to purge my hapless deformity there? Would the rest of my life suffice to redeem the original sin of being born like that, or would I still toil at making the devils laugh in the great beyond misfortune would send my way after death? Handsome Bustamante, meanwhile, showed me that beauty—that illusion of the mind—can be accessed by fingers burning with desire, or the come on of a wad of notes. "Hey, Goyo, to go to bed with a woman, one of two things: you either spend your money or appeal to charity. That will be the cross you'll bear throughout life, so you just listen to what I say and start wheeler-dealing to get some dough if you want to get a bit of hole."

There are women who open the petals of their belly simply out of pity and give themselves up willingly like true martyrs. Others, however, use their secret crack as a piggy bank, and you put money in and they start working, the more notes, the better, until vice ravages them or they wither with age. I'd go on ahead to village brothels to announce that handsome Bustamante was on his way with his body in full bloom and his proud, gorgeous face. Doors swung open, and in I'd prance, and the limp folk in these whore houses laughed and applauded my strange embassy until Mr. Handsome arrived and stirred up the fug in the knocking shop with his cocky smile before selecting his women and stuffing them in bedrooms two at a time, as was his wont. Thanks to him, and often at his expense, on a more modest scale, I would bed a whore who entertained my rummaging, generally the ugliest and fullest at the hip, and exploring their flesh, my voracious lust sometimes had its way, but more usually it was a mere fancy of the moment. I'd never remember my mother, who was no doubt buried by oblivion in some crevice in my memory. A pity; later I regretted that. Handsome Bustamante was magnificent in those knocking shops, and then to work off his lust, he'd ride through the air with Doris, executing his routine with strict precision, and pleasuring in his own performance. I slavered pools of boundless admiration. I showed him respect and obedience, because he embodied what I could never hope to be, given the hand nature had dealt me. For his part, he cultivated my servility to suit himself and rewarded me with the crumbs I liked most, so he had me in his pocket. "Hey, Goyo, you should leave the circus at some point and seek out a life more in keeping with your ability. Here they've worn you down, and you'll never prosper. This world of ours is going to the dogs. The circus is dead. People want less in-your-face entertainment and find what we do boring. If you stay here, you'll melt down like those little candles old dears light for their dead." I nodded, though I didn't get his message, because all I knew was that world of wild animals and transhumance, and at best the lost world of my childhood buried under a mass of scar tissue. It's better forgotten. It's better not to know how to think and just climb into the lifeboat of Providence and drift with the tide. We'd go whoring, and he'd treat me; I got that from his generous side. The accounts pudgy Di Battista settled with me once in a blue moon didn't even cover the rags I wore or the few vices I indulged. "Molto moni mi paia la tua mamma forra youa. It was a badda deal, mi non sorri per que I luvva you como un figlio que sempere stara at mi side," said that bastard, tweaking my face, marinating his liver in cognac more by the day. He met a bad end, though I never wished one on him. Deformed, feeling sorry for myself, without papers, with a sick stomach, increasingly resenting my lot in life, my future certainly seemed less than secure. The only solace I could rely on in the circus was the applause I got, like communion wafers past their sell-by date. That still hurts when I recall it; that's my real patrimony, the memories of what I've been and my awareness of the fact that in life you can cry, just as easily as you can die, survive, and even laugh, and that's why it's important people never read your thoughts or penetrate your real state of mind.

During that season, the Stéfano circus performed in various places in Old Castile. Castilian folk are generally slow to laugh and never belly laugh unless it's over someone else's bad luck. We worked hard on our performances in Burgos, but the show never really took off. Perhaps the wild animals scared them, or maybe they recognized us for the bunch of idiots we really were. We didn't get a single clap in the ring, and a meager scattering of yawns hung in the air. We were down in the dumps, and my egg swallowing turned out badly; worryingly, my vomit started to trickle blood. Pudgy Di Battista, hard hit by the sullen audiences, shut himself up with his bottle in his covered wagon. Through the window, you could hear the sad songs from his land that he intoned with a slurp and a grieving heart, as if he were invoking the apocalypse. It was a dire night, and the bitter, bone-cold air slipped invisibly between our ribs. It's no fun contemplating failure, but the show we had on the road was out of sync with a changing Spain that was opening its legs to its own future. Handsome Bustamante, his back to the big top, was washing his armpits in icy water and generously splashing his naked torso in a battered tub he'd positioned on some stones. A few yards away, from the lit doorway of his caravan, Frank Culá was watching him, simmering with the kind of desire that really turned him on. Handsome Bustamante had been registering for some time Frank's rather morose looks in his direction. Now and then he'd give him rope, simply to spin his hopes along and get a free laugh from watching him suffer. To this end, he was now camping up his toilette and soaping with gestures that verged on the very vulgar. He rubbed his bare chest with eau de cologne and stretched his arms licentiously as if coming on to him unawares. Frank Culá had fallen into the trap and didn't know whether to go over or simply present a low profile and sneak away into his caravan. That was when I walked by, simply wanting to take shelter in my cot and sink into the hidden pleasures of a dream the nighttime might be so kind as to bring. "Goyo, where are you going so down in the mouth?" shouted Bustamante, only to trigger Frank Culá's burning jealousy. "This is no night to be alone in bed; come on, let's go whoring and see if that can stir our blood." I eagerly accepted his offer as I brought him his towel. Frank Culá gave us one last sly, resentful glance and shut himself in his caravan. He may have very well been looking forward to canoodling with Mr. Handsome, but then again perhaps he wasn't. Poor wretch, he only brought on the bad end that was lurking around the corner.

The whores of Burgos have ice-cold nipples, and their butts ooze the hoar frost they have to endure. It's no trade for that kind of terrain. Winds of death furrow their steppes, and their bones transfix the souls of their clients as if serrated by sorrow. We walked into the knocking shop on the Calle de San Juan that had been recommended to Mr. Handsome. A fat woman dressed in black and passing herself off as a respectable widow opened up. Her breath stank of garlic and the whiff of sweat she left in her wake, of curdled milk, as she ushered us into the small lounge where women waited in thick cardigans. Handsome Bustamente cloistered himself in a boudoir with two who claimed they were sisters, and a languid girl fell to me, the skinniest nude I'd ever seen. They called her Micaela, but her real Christian name was Angustias, which suited her much better. Her chest tasted of lard and her groin of dirty sheets. Penetrating her was painful and, like a piece of furniture, she didn't even whimper when I possessed her like an animal. She'd been properly broken in, that's for sure. My memories of her give me the shivers. We finished early, and Mr. Handsome handed Madame the stipulated rate and gave the girls a similar tip to spend on whatever they fancied. He liked to show off like that, and they thanked him from the bottom of their hearts while Madame merely scowled. "Fuck fatty," was his parting shot. When we got out into the street, a sharp, clean breeze rattled our lungs. "Cheer up, Goyo," chided Mr. Handsome, "shows are tricky things, one day they applaud, and the next they spit on the same spectacle. Stop turning that over and take a few deep breaths of this cold air that does you good; by the way, didn't your whore do you a bit of good, too?" In fact, I felt out of sorts. The cold always sets me thinking, and if I think, I explode. We were strolling down to the Plaza del Generalísimo when we suddenly walked by the crustacean windows of a seafood restaurant. The establishment went by the name of El Borde del Cantábrico, which was written in white paint and exquisite calligraphy on the window. Looking at us from the other side lay crayfish, small crabs, and lobsters, all lined up on a soft bed of ice and bay leaves. A pleasant light shone out that was perhaps too warm for the pernickety climate inside. "There are two kinds of oysters," Bustamante announced solemnly, "those you swallow and those you suck. As we've sucked, it's time we tried a little bit of the other, don't you reckon, Goyo? Have you ever eaten shellfish? Let's go inside. This is on me." Thanks to God, I'd already spewed up blood-flecked eggs and everything else, because if I hadn't, what was on the cards wouldn't have gone down well. The bastard maître d' didn't want to give us a table; he could clearly smell our class. I cowered there, crouching behind the legs of Mr. Handsome, who was arguing at the top of his voice with that shitty fellow. I mentally split my sides when I spotted a lobster with two disparate pincers, one tiny and the other gigantic, behind the aquarium's magnifying glass. The beast reminded me of the grotesque sight Mr. Handsome and I must have presented at that moment. Lording it around the restaurant, over-fifties with pencil mustaches, in gray suits, garnished by their tawdry wives—constipated to a woman judging by the stiffness of their perms—were gawping incredulously at the racket handsome Bustamante was creating on the small matter of whether his money wasn't worth as much as the loot paid by that pack of imbeciles who'd parked their buttocks there and were now stuffing their snouts with shellfish. Finally, in a gesture redolent of savoir faire and nous, Mr. Handsome solved the problem via a one-thousand-peseta tip he handed the maître d', all prickly

145

and powerful. Humiliated, but resigned to the dosh, the latter bowed his head like a donkey and without a whisper calmly led us to a table for two reserved in the best part of the restaurant. As we walked by, the other diners wanted to stare, but their good breeding deterred them. Such worthy politeness is cultivated by privileged social classes as if their very survival depended on it. They had to bring three big cushions so I could sit level with my knife and fork, and I settled down as best I could on my soft perch. Mr. Handsome ordered glasses of white wine to kick off, which they served in super-thin cut-crystal that looked as if our saliva would crack it. I noted the old woman at the next table was giving me the evil eye with her left. I registered that perfectly; such things often happen and cause untold personal damage. To ward off the spell, it's best to cut it dead with a quick belch, which is what I did, the loudest I could summon from my guts. The old woman repented when she heard it, had a spasm, and dropped her dentures in her shellfish soup where she'd been dipping her mustache; the rest of the restaurant quietly looked my way, and an extremely indignant gentleman in the corner had to soothe his good lady, who wanted to get up and go. There were no further incidents with the other guests, and dinner proceeded succulently. I engrossed myself in the crayfish, sucking the juice from their heads; I applied pincers to crack the necks of the small crabs, I pulled the legs off spider crabs, and used my teeth to extract the warmish slithers of meat from the goose barnacles. I chewed fistfuls of shrimps, diligently sucked the pink flesh of prawns like you suck a pink female body, and finally, keeping to his word, Mr. Handsome ordered a large tray of raw oysters—the briny kind, not the others—which we swallowed with lemon juice.

We devoured that sumptuous holocaust transubstantiated into crustaceans and with our dessert enjoyed the delicious smoke of Montecristo cigars apparently rolled by revolutionary women workers. For the first time, I took a deep drag on that miraculous tobacco, and my lungs expanded, relishing my new vice. "Dinner tastes better after a good fuck than when a hard-on is teasing your balls, right, Goyo?" Bustamante asked, a cigar stuffed in his mouth. I went on inhaling and said nothing. "What's wrong," continued Mr. Handsome, "did you have a bad lay with that rake of a whore?" "She was an icicle," I replied, "an icicle made of pumice stone." Handsome Bustamente guffawed like a flatulent cow and chattered on. "Whores are a world unto themselves, my lad, you never know what you're going to get. Some are long-faced but writhe like snakes in the sack, and others, who look every inch a whore, are a dead loss even in the dark, and the moment you touch them, they squeak. This life is all about luck; sometimes you get it and sometimes you don't. Don't you worry about the whores, they know what they're up to. You just choose wisely and have fun while you can, 'cause the Grim Reaper is always lurking round the corner. Besides, you're a dwarf, they're bound to like you for your oddity value if you give them a hard sell on your deformity, if not, you'll have to put up with the dregs in the whorehouse or will be condemned to rub off like that nitwit hornball Mandarino. I'm telling you what's what, and just take note, 'cause I know what I'm talking about; if you want to fuck, you've two choices: either you pay them plenty, or they'll do it out of charity 'cause they're sorry you're in such a rubbish state. Whores are a world unto themselves, and when you're least expecting it, they go all lovey-dovey, though I don't recommend trying it. I once went with a whore who pissed herself with pleasure if I chomped on her nipples. I was on my way to Valencia and had hitched a lift with a trucker, and we stopped off in a place where he'd heard you ate and fucked divinely for a good price. That woman's butt was like a mule's, without the flies or tail, and she offered it doggy style the second you were in bed. You should have seen her shaking it. The trucker and I laid her at the same time, and the more we went for it, the more the filthy bitch swung it, until she'd drained us dry after we'd done her from every angle. We had a great time, but just as we were leaving, she started to blubber big-time and asked us to take her a long way from there 'cause she couldn't stand life any longer in that spot. Then when she'd calmed down, she told us she'd given birth to an idiot and a dwarf and that was why she was a whore and would be till the day she cocked her toes up. As she'd been such a pain, she refused to charge us; I'd have gone for gratis, but the stupid trucker felt sorry and paid for both of us plus a tip—what a bloody waste of money. I thought her story about the idiot and dwarf sons was a hoot, but I didn't believe a word of it. You see how cunning women are, so clever at relieving you of your cash. There aren't that many dwarves, but even if it was true, she'd have been better served making up a more believable tale. Don't ever trust a whore or listen to their patter; now *that* is a good piece of advice."

The cigar smoke stuck in my gullet. Son of a whore— that was what I'd just been called by that real son of a whore who'd been gross enough to spell out how he'd fucked my mother. He met a bad end. He had to wait a number of years, but Providence dealt him that card, and it couldn't have turned out any differently. I never had any more news of my mother. Ages after, I went to the cemetery where her bones were rotting, the one next to the allotment where my brother was heading when the train engine sent his flesh and bone flying. I didn't pray for her, because I couldn't think of anything to say, and nothing struck the vocal chords of my emotions, either. I expect she's still there, unless they've turned her into fertilizer.

We left the restaurant stuffed with shellfish. I was also creased by rage, or sadness; I sometimes confuse the two. Alcohol sparked my desire to revenge myself on all fronts: my own existence, my wretched state, handsome Bustamante, and even old piss-pot Providence playing those jokes on me. Mr. Handsome was walking on in front of me as cool and carefree as a teenager when spring sap is rising; his blood was seething, but though he was quite unawares, the gray feathered wings of misfortune hovered over his every step, like a bird of ill omen preparing to pounce. We reached the wasteland on the outskirts of a city where the Stéfano circus had camped down. It was a moonless night and very late in the early hours, because we stopped to spit at some ducks who were snoozing on their waterproof plumage in a lake at a park. A tremulous light was flickering in the big top, and that was unusual for that time of day. Someone must have been up to no good. We approached stealthily. The contrast between that brightness and the dense, dark sky created an atmosphere of gloom. Everybody was asleep. I sometimes think that sleep sheathes the mysteries of this world, though it does no good to advertise the fact. Owls were screeching from the overgrown tops of the poplar trees, while other beasties were silent in their burrows. Suddenly a shot rang out. The blast came from the exact spot where the light was oscillating under the roof of the big top. We ran there, Mr. Handsome nimbly and me in fits and starts, falling ass-over-tit.

All corpses are the same: cold, blue, and repulsively definitive. The huge figure of Juan Culí stood motionless in the ring, haloed by the ghostly light of a candlestick. You'd have thought he was a statue made of flesh with that profile. His blank eyes were glued to the fresh corpse of Frank Culá, faceup on the sand. A fountain of blood welled up, glug, glug, glug, from a huge hole where his heart had been. Thirty bluebottles had already landed there and were sipping his lifeless blood like mini-vampires who'd not yet eaten supper. "What have you done, you wretch!" Bustamante shouted. "You've killed him; you've shot him dead," but Juan Culí didn't react. Silent, as if absent, perhaps struck dumb by the tragedy of the crime that had just been committed, Juan Culí loomed like a wardrobe and stayed that way until seven policemen arrived at dawn, seven in gray uniforms, seven jumping to the orders of the inspector in charge— Esteruelas once again, recently promoted to a position at police headquarters for being good at silencing what required silence.

A pistol lay on the ground next to the corpse. It had a shiny mother-of-pearl butt, and when it glinted, its feminine elegance made it eminently desirable. Handsome Bustamante had found it the moment he kneeled down to see if the dead man was still breathing, and then he held it in the palm of his hand as if trying to work out if it had shot the bullet that had finished off Frank Culá. "You killed him out of jealousy, you bloody fag!" he shouted for a second time. Given the tension in the air, and before the first onlookers from the circus, woken by the din, showed their faces, Mr. Handsome told me to take the pistol and make it vanish somewhere so Culí wouldn't be implicated in the death of Culá. The bastard still had a good side to him; a pity I was seething inside after the scene he'd described with my mother. I felt no mercy. I got rid of the pistol; nobody noticed. I took the barrel between two fingers and ran to the cages. The lions were waking up; the scent of blood had stirred their appetites. Mandarino was snoring, sprawled like a spineless pig, almost at their feet. The size of his member was gross even in repose. To his right, wrapped in damp rags, chunks of dog meat were queuing up to become the animals' breakfast. Without too much forethought, I unwrapped a strip of meat and rolled it tightly round the pistol. I jumped over Mandarino and threw the meat to the lions. They fought over it for a few seconds, but, like in the jungle, the law of the strongest rules in those cages, and the healthiest of the lot, one we called Perico, gobbled it down in one mouthful. I leapt back over Mandarino, aiming a kick at his face. "Wakey, wakey, somebody's killed Frank Culá."

The Stéfano circus was in turmoil in a matter of minutes. Nobody could understand what had happened; people were panicking and screaming. Pudgy Di Battista was cursing God in Italian, less upset by the sight of the corpse than by the fear he might lose everything by government decree. A pitiful fellow, he didn't realize that the most precious thing he had, his own life, was about to be thrown to the lions like the pistol that blasted the heart of Frank Culá to smithereens. Nobody ever found out it was a suicide over love, provoked by Bustamante's scorn, nobody, that is, except for Mr. Handsome. When the police arrived at dawn with Esteruelas at the helm and started interrogating in turns, everybody was shit-scared.

Nobody knew anything, and some wouldn't even testify that the Culí-Culás were part of the staff of the Stéfano circus, maintaining that they had only just joined up in a village in Badajoz. Fear has always free-wheeled, unlike meanness, which is a question of character. When it was my turn to be questioned, I spoke up loud and clear so everyone could hear me. Esteruelas's onion-scented questions helped me rush out my answers. "We'd just dined on shellfish," I declared, "and when we reached the circus, we saw the dead man, who'd been waiting for the murderer to ask him for a few explanations, because of the jealousy that existed between them; they're fags, did you know? And they behave in the way that crew does. As well as being a fag, the trapeze guy is a murderer. I stepped aside, because I didn't want to get involved in their quarrel, and when I was walking off to get some shut-eye, I heard the shot. Then I saw Bustamante run out holding a pistol and head toward the animal cages. He wrapped it in a chunk of meat and put it in the maw of Perico the lion. That's where it will be now, if he's not shat it out." They were all struck dumb by my account of events, to a man, nobody more so than Mr. Handsome. Juan Culí burst into tears.

Exercising the authority his position conferred upon him, Inspector Esteruelas ordered the lion be brought to the ring and disemboweled. "You, eyetie, don't worry about the expense you'll incur, police headquarters will look after that in due time," he told Di Battista to ward off his protests. He never saw a peseta for the sacrifice of the best of his lions, but the rest of us at least enjoyed the spectacle.

Esteruelas ordered one of the police to empty the barrel of his gun into the lion's head. A stink of sewers, rather

152

than death, spread through the air we were breathing when Mandarino ripped open the beast with the sharp edge of his knife. It was the stench from the rottenness of an era when passions were hidden and fear of freedom floated in the silence people kept as if it were some ancient creed. Ever ready to deal with entrails, Mandarino sank his arm up to his shoulder in the animal's guts and brought it out covered in slime, his fingers clasping the pistol that hadn't yet been digested.

When I'd finished snitching on handsome Bustamante, I felt good but deflated. I then remembered Gurruchaga and the time when they arrested him and took him away and I did nothing to help him. Justice is but the power to give everyone their just desserts; the dilemma is how to strike the right level. That morning I apportioned justice, at least as far as I was concerned. Handsome Bustamante turned pale when Mandarino extracted the pistol from Perico's still-warm entrails. He tried to throw himself on me and would have gouged out an eye if the police hadn't bludgeoned him until he was flat out next to the corpse of Frank Culá. He'd completely lost it, and that was his eternal downfall. "He killed him out of love," was the comment you heard in the Stéfano circus when he was carried off foaming with rage. Inspector Esteruelas also gave me a good once over. "You were the dwarf accompanying that commie we caught in Córdoba, aren't you, Snow White?" I denied that categorically. "We'll settle accounts one day, you and I," he threatened before leaving. I was right to lie, that divine right to go for the means required to achieve an end, and I was pleased as Punch, as I'd never been before. Emotion flooded my mind, and I enjoyed that moment as if I'd been reciting a poem by

Federico to a packed hall—*How horrific with the last / staves of shadow / Oh white wall of Spain! / Oh black bull of sorrow!* Federico, just like Perico the lion, was killed by a single shot for a spurious reason that had nothing to do with him. Before he was murdered, he toured the villages of Spain, performing for the peasants the lines by Calderón. *Violent hippogriff, running with the wind, ray without light, bird without hue, fish without scales, brute without natural instinct, in the confused labyrinth of these bare crags, where did you drag yourself and plunge down?* On that journey, he learned that the world was but a stage where everyone struggles to escape their role. Providence decided to grant him the role of victim. He was certainly dealt a bad end. I learned a little of the same at the Stéfano Circus, except rather than a stage, I perched on a cabinet of grotesqueries and stayed there, though now I enjoy better luck, controlling the fast-food market and banking disgusting amounts of money that have made a pillar of society of me. In any case, I had first to celebrate to the max my dwarfish condition by gobbling down hard-boiled eggs in the ring, surrounded by spectators, sick to the teeth of all that chicken nonsense, and with no way out, forced to carry on that way until I found a less outlandish way of life more in keeping with my age, which, year after year, was making my bones that much more brittle. Now that Frank Culá was dead on the altar of love—his heart sucked dry by flies—I was enthroned as king of the ring, and huge, uncoordinated Juan Culí had no option but to play a bit part in my routine. I completely revamped our act, which was now bereft of ghastly innuendo and piggish display, though it gained in comic vim thanks to my size and the astonishing contrast it created when exhibited next to Juan Culí's. Now it was my act alone, and that's how it was being advertised in the different places where we stopped and performed: *Gregorio the Great*, *Goyo the Dwarf*, and *Goyito the Bone-Cruncher* were a few of the names that cropped up on the posters; I was more up to my back teeth by the day, and the circus grew shabbier by the minute, left to its own fate, irrevocably damned by the ill-starred times and pudgy Di Battista's alcoholic downturn. "Pudgy's pissing blood," Mandarino told me one day in a nervous state as a result. That guy showed an irrepressible admiration for everything excreted, to the point that he hoarded certain dry turds that he rated highly; Providence alone knows why they were especially attractive to him. It was true. Stéfano Di Battista had been sick for some time, more as a result of life than his drinking, and still he felt he was secure in a stagnant, unchanging world packed with glory and great feats, elevated honors and official awards, when increasingly what ruled was the collapse of a dream, and a mass grave toward which we were all hurtling hell for leather.

Without a partner, Doris continued to whirl through the air by herself; increasingly overwhelmed by her solitude on the trapeze, she decided to call it a day and return to the village of her childhood for a spot of peace and quiet. Her departure was like a premonition of my own immediate future. The circus was grinding to a halt at the speed of light; the big top couldn't take more patches, and even its red fringes had turned the fungal green of putrefying meat. The few remaining animals were rheumatic and reluctant to perform their tricks and looked like beings marooned after a flood. Only the monkeys showed signs of life; when they were bored stiff, they masturbated without a flicker of lust, quite unlike Mandarino, who did it for consolation and pleasure. The artists kept leaving; some gave an excuse, some had a vital commitment, others took French leave. The Stéfano circus was the butt end of a guffaw, a broken shadow of itself, the stock perennial peering like a cypress over the damp slope of a cemetery. Doris left for Extremadura to thicken her thighs and hips on fruits of the pig and other innocent excesses. She soon married—badly. Poor girl, she found bad luck where she sought peace and quiet. The peremptory pressure of age, not love, pushed her into a relationship with a yokel whose stall sold pork, and cheese wheels from Casar de Cáceres; his stomach was a barrel and his tongue a black pudding, down to the excessive quantities of food he daily fed his body. She married him and misfortune. Riding on the one-way cart of passing years, Doris rushed to the altar dressed in pristine white with the obsolete virginity brought by disuse. He wasn't malicious in himself, just a dimwitted rustic, and that led him to rub shoulders with coarse fellows of his kind. Doris didn't love him, but that didn't make her suffer; she'd seen too many passions flow under her bridge. In the middle of the wedding reception, after slicing the chocolate cake and swallowing the dregs of his El Gaitero cider, he widowed her in the most ridiculous way imaginable. The crude yokels celebrating that bumpkin's wedlock, following a tradition rooted in barbarism, decided to auction off bits of the bride's white knickers and the bridegroom's starched tie, to which end they unfortunately employed a chainsaw rather than kitchen scissors, and a slip of the wrist sliced off his neck; he was beheaded like John the Baptist, only unshaven and flabbier around the gills. Dressing saints, weeping over the dead man's wretched fate, getting fat on the chorizos she inherited, and remembering, now in a widow's weeds, the excitement of the trapeze became the lot of withered Dorotea. The walking dead. She wasn't aware that history is a river sluicing us toward progress; that's why when it was finally time to go to the urns and see whether a new democratic creed could be fleshed out in a political constitution so many throats were chorusing, she went and voted no. Then she returned to her mother-in-law's house and continued the task she had undertaken: the creation of a new mantle for the Virgin, a riot of embroidery, lacework, and filigree, worthy in the final instance of being preserved in an out-of-the-way diocesan museum.

Time changes fashions, customs, people's politeness, peculi-
arities, partialities, and routine rituals. Folks were more into
Pedro Carrasco's boxing and the adventurous escapes of
El Lute the bandit from the prisons of Spain, than the arthritic
animals in the Stéfano circus. El Lute the bandit studied in jail
to become a lawyer, and a song with English lyrics was penned
about him: *The man they call El Lute*, it went. Fashions change,
just like the jail terms handed out, I can tell you, and the
Stéfano circus was caught in the time warp of a pre-television,
deflated world in which the show's exotica depended more on
the backwater bumpkins attending it than the wonders it
trumpeted over the megaphone—a *démodé* exotica of dingy
feathers and sequins on flaccid bodies, of seventy-year-old
animals with stomachs ruined by the ingestion of so much
rubbish on the road; an eccentric array of individuals deformed
on the inside or the outside who simply subsisted on the
inertia of the trail they tramped; an exotica of belches and
empty laughter that didn't even bite in the land of yokels. Folks
were focused elsewhere, on the Olympic gold hanging from
the neck of Paquito Fernández Ochoa, on Luis Ocaña's
pioneering pedaling as he climbed onto the Tour's podium—

and didn't he meet a bad end?—on the dream celebrations at the Venetian wedding of Natalia Figueroa and singer Raphael ("*I'm the one who pursues you through the night . . .*"), his hands clawing success out of the air, as if he were energetically pulling on Lady Luck's chain. Even the clowns had to seek out a mite of subsistence in television, that box for the creation of couch potatoes—what my pizzas did for palates. The country smelled differently, new longings, greater awareness of its own complexes. Pudgy Di Battista was bankrupt and entrenched himself in the glass bunker of his bottle of cognac. From inside it, a total alcoholic, he reminisced about glory days he probably never lived, mythical battles against the allied army when victory depended on valor and not bullets. He hummed imperial anthems about black shirts with flowery lyrics full of chimera, while banks, more merciless than his own ghosts, called in, one after another, the goods and mortgages he'd put up as collateral for loans that they'd dared, sometime in the past, to grant him. The future was uncertain, that was for sure. I'd wasted my adolescence on futile growth spurts, on beatings, whores, and hard boiled eggs and felt it was the moment to say goodbye to all that. In some part of the world, there must be a different way to live, and I wanted to find out. I wanted to reach for the skies, and, poor me, despite all I'd suffered, I'd yet to realize that the world isn't a bed of roses, or a comfy bed where you can sleep the sleep of the just; on the contrary, it is mud, chaos, and death, and only he who dares, wins.

The winds of early winter were beginning to blow in '73. We'd come to Alcalá de Henares to work Christmas hard, with two performances a day, three on Sundays and Saturdays, squeezing the most from our rickety potential. It was the nearest to the capital we'd ever been. I felt thrilled about visiting Madrid, walking its streets and riding in the metro. I'd heard about the colored lights that adorned its pavements with their garlands of kilowatts, and the consumerist ceremonials orchestrated by moneyed people in the Galerías Preciados department store. The rain washed the dirt off the caravans the whole night, and the next morning the circus encampment smelt of freezing cold. The animals were quiet, as if their nostrils had caught a sniff of the magnicide that was around the corner. These things do happen, the atmosphere turns electric with premonitions of evil, and animals inexplicably behave differently. It was Thursday. The sky was mottled by the bitter cold, and the air was so murky your lungs hurt when you breathed. There were five days to go till Christmas, and everyone was starting to enjoy all that sentimental shit in the family hearth.

Loneliness has never stopped me from doing anything. I was convinced that Madrid would quench my longing for change, and I was charged with desire. Adolescent things. It was early, very early, not yet 8:00 a.m. Some bailiffs turned up at the circus, to carry out a sentence decided in Sabadell to repossess whatever they could find. Their faces were the languid faces of men who walk the world with the foul constipation life brings. They asked for Stéfano di Battista, and I rushed over to his caravan to alert him. He was already up and awake; I expect he'd been watching over his bottle of cognac all night, the bottom of which he was stroking when I walked in. He stank of decomposing flesh. It was the stench of death. "Some guys are here from the court and want to talk to you." He stood and stared blankly and without a word stepped out to face his destiny. The bailiffs walked here and there, indicating, without a smidgen of pity, the goods to be impounded: the frame of the big top, the cages, animals included, the fences, the junk, the booths, and even the earthenware pots decorating the windows of some caravans.

I stayed out of it, watching them from the doorway of Pudgy's covered wagon. Everything inside was muck: the furniture, the utensils, the decorations on the walls, all throwbacks to other eras. Everything kept in place by inertia, from the toilet lid to the dining-room light, from the broken freezer buzzing beside the bed to a strong box that revealed the mortal remains of its antique trade like a profaned grave. "The safe," I told myself. I went over and started rummaging. Inside were dog-eared documents with mere nostalgia value, letters, maybe love letters, a cartridge belt and revolver with a rusty butt, and a polished dagger of the flashy kind Italian hit men wore strapped on the hip. A few thousand pesetas in an envelope perhaps bore witness to Di Battista's wretched luck. The rest was filth, unburied dust. I thought of grabbing that envelope as my just reward and clearing off from that circus for good without saying a word. Nothing was keeping me there now, not even the zeal of my owner. I decided it was no time to linger, and when I was about to pocket the cash, Pudgy appeared, flanked by the bailiffs. "Youa tambene hai decidido betrayya mi, nano?" he asked with a whimpering laugh as if he'd gone crazy. "Ahh, no youa, figlio mio, you belongga to mi and owa mi obedenezza. 'ere youa stay al mio sida tilla we rotta."

"Get out of my way, Pudgy, and out of that doorway; I'm off, and off for good," I announced, but he took no notice, grasped me by the neck, and kicked me with all his strength, buckling me over. "Porco animale. Feedda ze crows and zey'lla peck out i tuoi occhi. Migliore end la vita tua now so zi mondo don' havva to standda la tua compagnia," he croaked, pulling out the Fascist machete he kept in his safe. I jumped to the back of the caravan like a baby bunny and grabbed the first thing I found in his cubbyhole of a kitchen to defend myself—a pristine bottle of cognac. "Morire non fa male. Morire é dolce whenna don' bene; youa see," prattled a lunatic Di Battista to the amazement of the lawmen. Wanting to return the compliment, I threw the bottle at him with all my might and imprinted it on his face. The blow felled him amid a crashing of chairs and junk. Spittle and blood trickled from the corners of his mouth, and the bastard lapped it up with the tip of his tongue. My rage mounted, and to round off my heroic deed, I took the shattered bottom of the bottle and stuffed the shards into his mouth. He laughed with a bloodcurdling leer as if that were going to solve all his problems at a stroke. "Nano digraziato, I fuckka yourra motha per niente. An' ze shelta I gavva youa, the eggsa youa swallowed at mi expensa neither. Go if youa vuoi, but qualche giorno you'lla 'member mi and see 'ow tutti gli sforzi to getta on in life werra en vanno. Youa comma from niente and will rittornare to niente and I willa be waitin'."

More worried for their own safety than out of any respect for legality, the men of the law did nothing. I left that fool like a rag doll, within an inch of death, coughing his soul out, puking blood, defeated for eternity. Before I left, I indulged myself by perching on top of his body. The world from the vantage point of his entrails looked more beautiful and optimistic. Of course, that was a day with a difference, a day destined to pass into history; Providence had decreed it thus. That very same morning, as if devils were pulling him by his hair, Don Luis Carrero Blanco, President of the Spanish Government, was blown to bits. It was all fated. "Go fry your balls in hell," I rasped as my parting shot.

I broke the yoke and whiffed the scent of victory. Exactly like Spain's, my luck had just turned up a new path. A lone dwarf, undocumented, destitute, I faced an uncertain future, with no choice but to go for it.

THREE

A Scalextric loomed over Atocha, an eyesore of a monument erected in the name of the kind of progress that was revered then, a concrete and asphalt figure eight that has only bequeathed a few forlorn exhaust tubes to posterity. It immediately intrigued me. It's the first thing I ever remember when I recall that nasty morning when I shivered so much my bones rattled like the whitest icicles. I didn't hear the explosion, it had gone off by the time I arrived, but I did see the inhabitants of Madrid in a tremendous panic, terrified by the disaster like sheep abandoned by their shepherd. The savage wolf of destabilization had taken a surprise bite. Sirens were blaring everywhere, people walked out of work as the news of the admiral's death spread. Children were hurriedly taken out of their schools by mothers scared of rebellion; they were in a tizzy, and their little ones were overjoyed by an event that released them from the routine boredom of classes. As the morning proceeded, rumors about the terrorist attack filtered through by word of mouth. I roamed the streets going nowhere in particular, delighted by a situation that enabled me to contemplate an unusual, cowering Madrid. While rich old ladies and sanctimonious crybabies locked themselves in their air-conditioned apartments in the Salamanca district, I ambled down the backstreets happy as a sandboy, relishing the apocalyptic charms of the metropolis and finally savoring the pleasure of being able to stroll around unseen even though I was so different. It was a scenario of dire emergency and blank faces. Those crowing over that murder couldn't, however, show their bliss and had to be content with toasting the assassination like silent rats in their clandestine hideouts. Only denizens of the backstreets remained unfazed, as if they couldn't care a fig about what had happened—denizens of the backstreets, the fauna and flora of the ragamuffin underclass, the police apparatus summoned from the ends of the fatherland to uphold the almighty inertia of peace, and yours truly, a dwarf.

Carrero Blanco had risen toward the heavens like a saint levitating for the love of Jesus, except that he'd been elevated by plastic explosives that terrorists detonated as he drove down the Calle Claudio Coello on his way back from his usual morning mass. That was the morning I set foot in Madrid for the first time. I alighted from a down-at-heel van that had jolted its way from Alcalá de Henares, flitting through one dormitory town after another on the city periphery, where the modern life of those who'd migrated from their villages in search of a better life was fleshing out—a washing machine, a fridge, a ticket to see Atleti play in the Manzanares on Sunday, a down payment on the apartment, and a pay packet at the end of the month. They were people with tunnel vision, dazzled by the array of the latest electric goods. Over the years, they would feel disillusioned as they watched on powerlessly while the fangs of working-class unemployment sank into the carrion flesh of their children, emaciated by drugs and awakened for good from the welfare dream. I walked at random through city streets still reacting to the morning's terror. Like a Ulysses yet to drop anchor on his perpetual journey into the void, the wailing of sirens filled me with a strange spiritual peace I was experiencing for the first time. I'd never return to the circus. I'd never again taste a hard-boiled egg, even if I was starving to death. Those two thoughts encouraged me in my wanderings. When feelings of destruction can channel their flow, hatred thickens and sets, and the emulsion produced is at once bitter and splendid.

The admiral's car was reduced to a mass of twisted metal—a veritable potpourri of incinerated scrap. Special cranes had to be brought in to shift it from the ledge where it landed. For several months, Madrid people amused themselves by parodying the attack, and that involved folding a paper napkin of the kind you find in bars into a rectangular chimney shape. They'd stand it up on a table and set light to the top end. When the flame had burnt all the paper, ashes, as black as those of the incinerated car, spiraled through the air, reenacting the macabre trajectory of the admiral's car until it crashed in smithereens against the Jesuit monastery on the Calle Claudio Coello. That sarcastic jape went by the name of "The Slow-Motion Death of a President." People's cruelty has no bounds and thus becomes the common heritage of humanity

One-Eyed Slim demonstrated that gradual levitation of the paper napkin to me, that itinerant bum I met the day my luck changed and profited his. "Hey, dwarfy, look how Carrero Blanco's scrap metal ascended to the heavens," and he performed the parody on an old marble-top table in La Copa de Herrera, a low dive near Cascorro where he'd established

169

the center for his miscreant ways. That was a month after the assassination, a month into my new life, prelude to so many others still waiting in the wings.

One-Eyed Slim begged his way through life with a rare dignity seemingly inspired by some remotely noble blood in his veins. What's more, he prided himself on being one of the war-wounded, and that earned him the respect of the faithful who on Sunday went to the churches where he hung out. One would have readily gone along with such a ploy, if he hadn't been so keen to act spitefully, when the feeling took him, toward those who were his vassals in the mire. The socket of his left eye was a shining pit, a scoured-out hole that was home to the grit of sleep. He deliberately didn't wear a patch, in order to scare off men and arouse the sympathy of women so they'd dig deeper into their purses. Some reckoned it was a war wound, others, his rivals galore, said he'd been born one-eyed, and that if he didn't cover it, it was to make believe the reds had blown it out with a bullet and to display it for commercial ends in place of the medal of bravery in battle that, quite rightly, he was never awarded. "What's a dwarf doing scratching around underground?" he asked the first time he bumped into me.

With next to no money, no acquaintances in the city, and no means of identification to accredit my existence in that red-taped human zoo, I could really do very little to subsist in the inhospitable Madrid where I'd just fetched up. By midafternoon, the cold night air was already stirring, and the polyester sweater I'd been wearing since early morning felt totally inadequate. My bones cut into my flesh like so many nails, I was tired of wandering aimlessly, and I decided to descend into the heat of the metro. It wasn't such a bad idea, given that it saved me from freezing to death, and squatting amongst the rubbish in the passageways, Providence sprung a trap to set up one of the most crucial encounters in my life: I collided into Slim.

After a sequence of seven nonstop trips from one end of Line One to the other, I got off at José Antonio and decided to stretch out on one of the platforms. I curled up and fell fast asleep, axed by sheer exhaustion after the day's events. Irrational dreams invaded my head, and I began to see overripe blackberries hanging in bunches from Doris's secret folds. Huge and crystallized in chocolate, like fruit desserts in Aragon. Wintry ice swept down the tunnels, blown by subterranean currents of air. It was a freezing cold sewer, striated by shards of solitude. I must have been shivering for some time when the hot tip of something began to meander over my cheeks. Suddenly the blackberries in my dreams seemed juicier, rising to boiling point and starting to sting my palate. I woke with a start. The bastard was drawing the blue flame of his lighter across my cheeks. "Things must be really going to the dogs if dwarfs are going underground."

Late into the night, when the metro was finally closing its doors, One-Eyed Slim liked to wander through that network of subterranean labyrinths searching for leftovers daytime traffic had dropped. He rummaged and shuffled, and traveled hither and thither, from Atocha to Tribunal, from Palos de Moguer to Ventas, always well out of sight of the prying eyes above ground. He knew every nook and cranny in the old metro like the back of his hand and got in and out of the trapdoors in the ventilation shafts with sublime skill, like a suburban escape artist. I cuffed his lighter away; my skin smelled scorched. "What are you doing down here?" he asked. His face was frightening it was so ugly, one of nature's bogeymen, you might say, marooned in wasteland beneath the earth. Still sleepyheaded, and at a loss for words, I decided to tell him I'd run away from a circus. He must have thought the idea was hilarious, because he started splitting his sides with guffaws that showed what a buffoon he was. "You'll freeze to death here, dwarfy, you've not got a single rag to wrap round you. When the wind whistles down the tunnels in the early morning, it's icy, and you'll kick the bucket before very long without an overcoat. Come with me, if you like, to a place I've got. Outside the *grises* are stirring up shit, and it wouldn't be very clever if we got picked up by those cops. Come on, I'll get you some food and a good bed so you can have a decent night. Where I'm going to take you, the nuns will keep us warm with their farts."

Providence continually weaves together the loose knots of destiny, and we are mercilessly subject to its whims. I followed in that man's footsteps down pitch-black tunnels, not particularly thrilled by the idea he was guiding me, until we finally surfaced from a metal grille leading to a small garden in the Plaza de Jacinto Benavente, right opposite the Teatro Calderón. En route I did at least feel that, despite his horrific face, Slim was fashioned from rare, out-of-fashion noble stock, more akin to the proud and needy, and to noblemen without honor straight out of the selvage of some bygone century, that had little in common with the era of protest and agitprop beginning to make its presence felt in that sprawling human agglomeration Spain's capital was becoming.

From the very first, bastards had fancied attacking my body with sticks or stones and well-aimed kicks from the right or nasty trips from the left. It was a novelty for someone to burn my face with a lighter. There's always a first time for everything in this world, and it's hopeless to kick against the pricks. Generally speaking, if they are *comme il faut*, bastards derive huge pleasure from mistreating dwarves or upsetting the handicapped; these are mysteries unleashed on the universe by nature, enigmatic arcana that will remain a closed book to scientific knowledge and rational thought, as Gustavo Adolfo suggested in his poetic texts. Mistreating dwarves by deed, word, or sin of omission should warrant a clause or two in the penal codes of civilized countries and should be punished by sentences significantly higher than those decreed for individuals who insult heads of state or get their kicks buggering underage kids. There is no justice on this planet, and what happens is whatever Providence decides; each of us gets our lot, and nobody ever escapes their fate.

I was led by the hand of Slim, a true Virgil in the darkness of that icy-hearted Madrid I'm now describing, down the Calle de las Chinas to the so-called Old Convent of the Royal Trinitarians, a large, rambling building with a flaking façade and a roof beat up by centuries of leaks where the nuns, out of Christian charity, had established a shelter for beggars, the needy, the hapless, and everyone else manifestly on their uppers. We dwarves, as a matter of course, are greeted by an open door in such places, if only for the pity and sympathy we arouse in the great and the good, and although I'd yet to see any sign of that, Slim did a good job rubbing these facts of life in my face, and he funneled me into a métier that not only

173

guaranteed me minimal sustenance, but also produced profit to spare, which was usually put into the kitty for the general welfare of that guild of dubious snitches, motley tramps, and tricksters that made up the raggle-taggle brotherhood under his command. Little by little, almost unawares, I transformed my unproductive circus guffaw into the tear that can barely be contained, a moist glint setting the stage for the possible slippage that pity produces at the sublime moment when alms are placed in one's palm. Slim was the root cause of that, and I'm truly grateful for what he did for me; pity he met such a miserable end and couldn't later marvel at my wealth.

Those years in Madrid went by with a fantastic generation of fakery, bad faith, and bet-hedging, richly seasoned, of course, by sudden surges of energy as the Spanish awoke from their lysergic sleep to discover the many-headed hydra of ideology. Unparalleled years of leap-frogging, sprinting, and greasy-pole climbing, unrepeatable years when my apprenticeship in the new, frailer, less rigid realities craved the full attention of my intellect and the concentrated deployment of certain skills I'd probably rather not admit to. One-Eyed Slim put the last traces of his bygone dignity to good use, begging on Sundays at the entrances to Madrid's grandest churches: San Francisco el Grande, La Virgen de Atocha, La Virgen de la Paloma, Las Salesas, and Los Jerónimos Reales. He did so decked out in much-darned and mended suits that he donned on purpose, and he went about his work while wallowing in the pomp and ceremony of pauperdom. Sometimes, especially in the fair months of spring, he'd spruce himself up with a tatty dark-blue shirt he'd button to the collar to evoke a vaguely military air. He'd pin a crimson yoke and arrows badge on his right pocket to simulate a rank, or as a reminder of an aura or era that was being torn to shreds willy-nilly before our eyes. He was a counterfeiter, a one-eyed Judas, a hell of a swine who nevertheless put pride before hunger and appearance before desire. He exuded the magnetic attraction of the greatest or most sinister of men, and in times of yore, his cool aplomb or fierce demeanor would have brought entire continents to heel, he was such a cocky, confident bastard. I began to accompany him to churches, happy under his tutelage, and without more ado, I followed in his footsteps and began to beg. "Look sorry for yourself and make the most of your deformity, right, dwarfy? Don't be ashamed to stick your nose into the face of anyone who looks your way, make them pity you and feel guilty for your wretched state, let them be repelled and moved, and hold out your hand at the first opportunity, and don't let them get inside without dropping a few coppers into your palm. Watch me, and look and learn," and he sank his knees down on the well-worn steps up to Los Jerónimos, facing the sun, dramatically displaying his gaping eye socket to parishioners who still allayed their consciences with their Sunday prayers for the peace Franco had brought, before hiving off to a communion of *tapas*. "Spare a thought for a war-wounded down on his luck. Gimme your spare dimes, for the love of God." And small change rained down into the threadbare felt of the floppy-brimmed hat he held out to receive their alms. After three morning masses, we'd walk up the Calle Atocha through the haze of leaden car fumes to La Copa de Herrera, where Slim liked to knock his drink back in style. We'd hole up there most days and most weeks; it was a kind of office made up of tables that creaked under the weight of their marble tops and glistened with the cheap oil of fry ups, where we'd parley with petty criminals, the many hangers-on, customers, and grateful hoods that One-Eyed scattered around the neighborhood's street corners for his benefit and theirs, and the juicy sustenance of the general good. They were different, homespun times, devoid of cadaverous junkies or Chinese mafias and firmly closed to anything that might come from across the border. "There ain't no blacks in Madrid," One-Eyed used to say. "This city won' change as long as blacks don' come. Blacks is all that liberty and progress ever bring. One day, you'll see, dwarfy, and then you'll understand what I'm telling you now."

His monopoly over thievery had one purpose: to relieve people of excess from their bounty by pickpocketing, nicking, bag-snatching, and other less rigorously defined larceny that was equally effective, or by the simple practice of begging. In any case, it fulfilled an undeniable social function that everyone took on board and wasn't without a degree of rather inglorious prestige. Those guilds of the poor caused no greater ill than a brief upset for the victim of the moment, disgust soon swept away by the consolation of a random encounter with the purloined family jewel or filched Omega watch at a stall in the Rastro flea market on a Sunday morning. Those were times that were a-changing, when society at large was being hit by a disorderly avalanche of shocks to the system. After almost forty years of political freeze, the rotten, sclerotic foundations of the state were clearly beginning to shake. You only had to poke an ear out in the street to hear the cracking. People were muttering on all sides, some joyfully, others fearfully, most with high hopes. Ideas, new and old, clashed; fanfares of change trumpeted grandiosely, as troglodyte triggers were cocked and skulls bashed, longing to resonate with that patriotic music of violence Spain's out-of-tune choristers have always rendered so well. It was a fine scenario for those of us begging outside churches, relinquishing all shame and making the most of the ignorance of others. The National Catholicism that had welded institutions together closed ranks like a clam shutting its shell to avoid being gobbled up by the anticlerical lay thinking that was becoming so trendy. Places of worship increasingly seemed like sandbagged parapets or bunkers under siege. As clear-sighted as ever, Slim immediately grasped which way the wind was blowing and ratcheted up his histrionics so as not to miss out on the patriotic, Catholic self-affirmation of those inertia still kept in church. He didn't spare a single hallowed event that might bring forth alms; Corpus Christi, Saint Joseph the Worker, or the Epiphanies of Our Lord, and there were no special holy days, mandatory or not, when we could rest; we'd take our leisure when everyone else toiled, since there wasn't much unemployment yet. Generally, when social groups recognize some of their own are struggling, they'll rush to lend a helping hand, which was Slim's case on church steps, and handouts were many and benign. As I was saying, when I joined that guild, I was a rookie performing a pauper's duet by his side, but he soon saw that takings from the sympathy stakes would increase if I were to engage in a solo effort. Thus, within a few months of our meeting, thanks to my deformities, he sent me out to prospect the porches and atriums of other, less high falutin' churches than the aforementioned, not that they were any less edifying as edifices. There I had to fight for a pitch against other professional beggars, who eliminated all restrictive practices the second they heard who'd sent me and gave me full scope to beg to my heart's content, such was the respect, veneration, and fear that rabble felt toward One-Eyed. Seventy-five percent of all takings went straight into the pockets of One-Eyed; that was the price for his backing, a percentage he justified as a necessary minimum to meet the overall expenditure of the brotherhood, to keep lips sealed, buy favors, compensate for mishaps, and give every man jack exactly what he required to be happy.

In the matter of shelter and sustenance, I've already mentioned that we bedded down in the rambling old "Mansion" for the needy run by the Trinitarians, a place that was extraordinarily clean and exceptionally well ventilated where the broth ran like liquid gold. Slim signed me up the night we met, and with the paid agreement of the nuns, I set up in a nave on the upper floor where One-Eyed had a comfy boudoir for his own private use. When the rigors of icy winter turned the street into a freezer or the sun's brazier melted it down, the Trinitarian Mansion gave our carcasses the right shelter to keep our bones shipshape. True enough, the nuns saw to the elemental wants of the needy out of Christian charity, but it would be more to the point if we added that the princely treatment Slim and his supporters received from the Trinitarians was down to an accord of the flesh Slim had entered into with Sister Marta, the nun who was the one really shepherding that motley crew of chancers. For a bit of this and that on the side, she moved Rome and Santiago and even went to her hierarchy to soften attitudes, shape wills, and argue our corner way beyond the call of rules and regs that certainly made a case for giving shelter, though with the necessary restraint to ensure it didn't turn into a five-star hostelry for three hundred and sixty-five nights of the year. Apart from cultivating the joys of her vagina, Sister Marta extracted from Slim sufficient dosh for the good running of the institution, and, naturally, as the delicious food and spick-and-span shine of everything was there for all to see, the nun's mother superiors felt it wondrous she could offer such splendors for so little outlay, and they let her get on with it without poking their noses in too much, else they might have smelled something fishy, or worse still, the whiff of sperm emanating from her fake holiness. Like Slim, I loved the fact the place was comfy, but also that it was so central—four minutes from the Puerta del Sol, three from the Rastro, two from plazas Benavente and Tirso de Molina, and a mere gob of spit away from that hotbed of whoredom by the name of the Calle Espoz y Mina. I made that Mansion my home, and the respect I began to be shown there perhaps partly healed the sores suppurating within my sense of dignity, though it was true enough that the reverence I was held in wasn't prompted by myself but by fear of what Slim's fury might unleash, because, as everybody knew, apart from practicing the trades of fraudster, pickpocket, and bag-snatcher, he'd cemented profitable relationships with leading figures in several ministries, and thus, so it was said, he'd managed to cloak in silence his various operations in exchange for money or favors, and, consequently, if he wanted, he only had to ask to get a hit man to snuff out an enemy, a request that would be granted on the spot, via an "accident," bad luck, or police pressure. "We'll feel the pinch the day people stop offering Christian charity," sighed Slim. "The way the wind's blowing bodes no good for us, dwarfy, and it's a sure thing that all this is a dead duck. It's a real shame, because in the end we kept everything in the family. God knows who's going to take our place and what rules they'll make; look what they're

179

already saying," and he pointed to the front of a house where a Communist *groupuscule* had daubed a slogan on the wall— "The people's sovereignty is born in the struggle."

Slim had a very hierarchical, Manichean view of the world according to which any act or individual was judged in advance and slotted into one of the critical categories that, from his own experience, he'd stored on the shelves of his mind. This enabled him to reach decisions quickly when it was time to filch someone's wallet or tackle a more testing task. "That guy's a sucker, that one's got a screw loose, the one there's a weirdo, and the other, a prat," were his favorite turns of phrase when it came to labeling people. This perfect, harmonious system, almost on a par with the solar one, helped me no end to straighten out my thinking and stop being dragged aimlessly through life, as had been my wont. At the time, I'd yet to realize that Providence organizes everything and that we should justify the outcomes of our behavior in the light of its designs. The established order, or at least the one established by the Movement, had helped Slim to survive, and he wasn't prepared to let it go up in flames on any altar erected in the name of the fallacious progress of the people. Slim intuited that the Regime was near to collapse and would take his way of life with it to the drab kingdom of gray ash. He smelled it in his nostrils, savored it in his mouth. "When Franco hits the bucket, the reds will crawl out of their holes and make our balls itch with the shit from their doctrines. Just imagine a world run by workers, dwarfy. That's the best these buggers can come up with: do the same here as they do in Russia, everyone godless, drinking from the same glass and shitting in the same pan, and then, when you die, into a mass grave so your bones can rot alongside everyone else's," and so he'd harangue, anisette after anisette, in an alcoholic rant that was as rambling as it was depressing.

Bit by bit, like the late blooms of a cement springtime, slogans appeared on the most down-at-heel walls of the city. They were words of struggle or desire that clearly demonstrated how, beyond officially recognized reality, other clandestine ways of thinking existed and sooner or later were bound to surface. Quite wrongly, Slim was of the view that the leftwing ideology dissidents generally espoused automatically excluded charity as a valid means to redistribute wealth and dictated hard toil and the sweat of one's brow as the only route to perfecting humanity. He was by now of an age when he couldn't contemplate adapting to any new crap that life hadn't sent his way till now, so all those burgeoning freedoms made him see red. "I'd send these buggers off to another Valley of the Fallen to spend the rest of their lives breaking rocks rather than painting the walls with all that shit. The sov-er-eign-ty of the peo-ple comes from the strug-gle," he exclaimed, ridiculing the graffiti syllable by syllable. "Fuck you, the only sovereignty they're getting are the bullets that'll do them to death, and that's what we should be doing to that rabble now," and he'd spit at the wall in a real fury, and whenever he did so, the green gob would hit his target of the sickle, in the middle of the hammer. But the day-to-day side of our life wasn't simply sustained by charity. It was also about pickpocketing, taking loot from workers, or snatching stuff in big, mass public gatherings. It was a real joy to see One-Eyed snaffling wallets in the full light of day. With his guile and the luck that always came his way, I'd have sworn he'd never meet the bad end he did, but things happen as Providence decides, and one can do little or nothing to keep its whims at bay. We went to other pagan shrines for such ends: to the Santiago Bernabéu stadium, where people worshipped a ball in a distinctive display of white magic; to the Atocha station, a genuine sanctuary for the hapless flock from Hispanic territories; or to the Las Ventas bullring, cathedral *par excellence* of *toreros* and an exceptional place for thievery and other jiggery-pokery. There, when I'd slipped in through the dead bulls' corral, I saw Paco Camino cross himself on some of his best afternoons—fantastic flourishes with the first cape, rock-firm mettle at the moment of truth, the red cape to the fore to meet his fate, despondent as a god feeling sorry for himself, until he slowly completed the task with a single, pristine thrust of his sword. Any rally swarming with people, any flux of humanity sufficed for our presence to be felt: rush hour in the metro, the Three Kings Day parade, sales weeks in department stores, and later in the decade, when the transition—still not described as such—was creeping into the consciousness of the citizenry like a stupid, catchy hymn (freedom, freedom, no fury, keep your fear and fury to yourself, because now we've got freedom, and if not, we soon will have), political rallies and demonstrations authorized by the civil government. And no doubt there was, at least for me—just hear me out—not the cardboard, flimsy freedom that's so vaunted and that the man on the street mistakes for the line to the ballot box, but that other, absolute freedom, the one granted by that fine perennial truth known as money. Deny me that now with death, if you like.

Francisco Franco Bahamonde, Caudillo de España by the grace of God, was a corpse stricken by phlebitis who only breathed thanks to a ventilator, a paltry scrap of flesh with tubes everywhere and cables hanging from his nostrils like latter-day umbilical cords frantically attaching him to this life in a foiled bid for immortality. While he was dying, One-Eyed and I totted up the proceeds from our thieving and splashed it on a twilight drop of wine or anisette, as the mood took us, and, if that mood was the horny kind, on the ladies, too—never the pricey ones, only the sort who work with the tips of their fingers or the edges of their mouths; after sorting his setup with the nun, One-Eyed was always up for a little body-to-body contact—shady ladies on the Calle Jardines or Montera, frequently beset by gastrointestinal odors and itching with thrush. We were fond of various dirty dives for alcoholic pleasuring, where lovely gobs of wine stained the sawdust crimson; however, the haunt that Slim undoubtedly preferred was La Copa de Herrera, on the Calle Carnero. Señor Antonio, an easygoing old fellow with a gleaming baldpate and built like a farmer, poured us a crystalline anisette, when he was in the mood, one he received from the Sierra Morena in raffia-wrapped glass bottles. After a hard day's grind, we'd sit in front of the altar of our glasses, and when we felt like it, we'd take the plunge in that bitter alcohol that so loosened One-Eyed's tongue. While he was drinking, Slim did business with the locals who came there to give him his percentage or trade in tip-offs that he sold on to the highest bidder in the upper echelons. One day, he was tipsier than usual and told me about one of the latter. "Dwarfy, I've heard that Franco is dead and gone. They're only waiting for November 20 to tell the country, so the date coincides with the execution of José Antonio." Slim belched solemnly. "I'm kept in the know," he continued mysteriously, "by an important guy in the hierarchy of the Movement who I'm on good terms with, by the name of Esteruelas, and you'll soon get to know him. We're going to do a little job for him. I can't give you any details yet, but it's a tricky, dangerous business. We've got to work out a way to give him what he wants without anyone suspecting what we're doing. It would be better if I'm not implicated, especially with the storm that's about to hit us. You can be my messenger boy. Nobody notices you except to avert their gaze or give you alms. You're ideal for the job." When I heard that name, my body shivered and shook. Suddenly the memory bubbled up of the way Esteruelas had looked at me when he took Gurruchaga prisoner, and the same nasty scowl he rehearsed years later when he carted handsome Bustamante off to jug, knowing full well he was an innocent man. Slim registered my unease. "Something wrong, dwarfy?" he asked. "Aren't you interested in what I've got to offer?" "Maybe not," I replied, going cold on him. My attitude seemed to bother him. "If you don't want to come in on this," he said threateningly, "you'd better say so loud and clear." He stared deep into my eyes with the relentless confidence of a man who knows he wields power, as he held out his hand to shake on it. "Are we still comrades?" I replied that we were, simply so I didn't have to suffer the steely-sharp gaze from his single eye, although at the time I didn't realize that my survival was at stake. "Great, dwarfy, you're in; you just see how we'll disinfect the fatherland against the lice now infesting it. You keep your eyes open, watch what's happening, and take good note of everything. Difficult times lie ahead, but that's when the valiant show their mettle. Just do what I tell you, and you'll have no regrets." And so I decided to go along with him, at least as long as the fun and games brought me some cash; if not, I'd soon find a way to jump ship. In any case, if the job came from so high up, as One-Eyed had claimed, there'd be no harm in giving it a spin to see if I could get a leg up, even if only for a moment. I swallowed and looked at the wall. They'd just broken off the program on the black-and-white television hanging from La Copa's ceiling to broadcast the first official bulletin on the terminal condition of the Generalísimo. The headline breaking the news carried a black dot, as if mourning would very soon be in order.

All that mystery and big talk finally boiled down to Esteruelas having ordered One-Eyed to sniff out on street corners the movements of the leftist groups now beginning to spring up from the mud in the sewers and agitate in the shadow of the defining presence of the Spanish Communist Party. I began to understand that much as I got to grips with my spying assignment. Those at the Movement's headquarters knew only too well that most of these little groups were involved in harmless student intrigue that was of little or no matter, perhaps sponsored by some university teacher who wanted to wreak his revenge on the poor assessment the academic powers-that-be had made of his intellectual capacities; even so, they were obsessed with keeping control and had to be up to speed with every little development. They were anxiously beginning to detect unruly activity in the industrial belt on the city outskirts that was evidently connected to unrest in the dormitory towns most impoverished by unemployment and least favored by the easy life on offer from the now-obsolete benevolent paternalist system. Getafe, Alcorcón, and Móstoles were the champions when it came to poverty, but the communist activities they'd detected amounted to little more than folkloric carnival routines, perhaps initiated on the orders of old moles blinded by cataracts, performances that never went beyond the display of confused insignia and vague banners outside first communions, weddings, and christenings every Sunday in the month of May. In his excessive drive to assert control, Esteruelas couldn't ignore the fact that the anti-Regime rallies and demos were getting bigger and more frequent in the central areas of the city. He was afraid of street fighting and public disorder; if they weren't nipped violently in the bud, they might spread virulently throughout Madrid. It was urgent that the poisoned limb be amputated if the body politic were to be saved, and this was now a rotten society where the cry of "freedom" was being vilely puked up, black and sweet as honey and crawling with flies. Via One-Eyed's thousand eyes, Esteruela could keep his finger on the hidden pulse of society, anticipate movements, detect changes, and stymy agitation. The information Slim had agreed to deliver had to be a daily shot from the front line. The people really responsible for the subversive slogans spattered in acrylic on the façades of public buildings, or the political posters stuck with carpenter's glue on tiles in metro stations, could immediately be exposed if Slim felt like it, such was his hold over these sordid territories. In exchange for privileges, back-handers, and the proverbial blind eye, Slim had pinpointed informing and betrayal as the most efficient tools of his trade. Anything went, if it led to information that then helped the police brigades to carry out their repression. He ate humble pie and toadied to those who sought his services, however, because he knew how they needed him, when he looked at them, he would curse them, and when he nodded in their direction, he would scorn them. He was a complex individual and, what was worse, an unpredictable one, and though one-eyed, he weighed up everyone else's weak points to a tee. So in this kind of messianic project to rid the fatherland of undesirables, those of us on his payroll suddenly found ourselves working alongside others who weren't but had been drafted into his service and were in no position to tell him quietly and politely to go and get lost.

I know you're here to enjoy the spectacle of my death. I was warned from the start, but I always refused to take any notice and happily got on with making my fortune. We creatures of flesh and blood like to hide our heads in the day-to-day rather than courageously confront our awareness and the extent of chaos. Poets, fools, and dogs can intuit the worlds beyond and evoke them as best they can before the contemptuous gaze of ordinary mortals: the ones speak of fresh bouquets or funeral wreathes, the others slaver endlessly, and the poor animals howl at the moon on windswept nights until a local wakes up and hurls a stone at them to silence their whines. You may think you now understand the essential moments from my past, but you don't know the details that betray the keys to the here-and-now or the reason for your presence in my life. You still know nothing, not even the role you are playing in this farce. You aren't aware, say, that Providence decided on a whim to make me rich in a vulgar, if not ridiculous, manner: selling home delivery pizzas. It could have engineered my winning the lottery or inheriting a fortune from an aunt in South America, but it didn't do either. Things happen as they do, and we can do little or nothing to change their course.

Commissioner Belinda Dixon spent the whole of tonight hammering away at me with this scatological desire of hers for me to contemplate the swellings welling around her private parts. She refused to taste the cocks' combs, on the excuse that she found the texture repulsive, and when she saw me dispatching them wholesale, she whispered about risky backstreet butchers. "Offal ruins arteries and spawns pus. Better not eat anymore," she said, "you've had enough to last the rest of your life." I told her I'd not intended to go to the dinner, that I'd been planning to fly to London to spend Christmas with my son when an irresistible urge had changed my mind at the last minute and that was why I was sitting there next to her, enjoying her company at that gala banquet offered by the Meredith Brothers Foundation. She then asked me if I believed in fate; I had no choice but to answer that I did now.

I lost my appetite after so many cocks' combs. The wine didn't go down too well, either. The maître d' lost his cool when he saw course after course going by and me not taking a bite, and he came to enquire contritely whether I didn't like the dinner. I told him I did but not anymore.

The commissioner got embroiled in a long conversation with a brawny young second-rater sitting to her right. I heard her recounting her tale of wondrous pomades and arterial lesions. The guy, out of politeness, followed her spiel, perhaps rather worried that a leery woman like Madame Dixon might get mixed up in his promising career future. She saw straightaway that he was a greenhorn who could only offer the illusion of youth and resumed her onslaught on me: "Gregorio, when you defecate, do you note the color of your stools? Do you watch out for blood?"

I reflected for a few moments on the absurdity of my situation, then acted as accommodatingly as I could; that encounter must have been arranged in advance, it all fitted perfectly—the decision to defer my trip, the dinner venue, the cocks' combs, the commissioner and her scatological leanings. In the end I decided a good romp rewards the exercise of patience. All in all, it was my last night and my last supper. I realized that.

Though he was unaware of the significance of what he said, Gurruchaga reckoned that the meaning of transcendence was to be found in excrement. Slim, however, saw transcendence from a more commonplace point of view, with angels on the wing, heavenly clouds, and an almighty God who had undoubtedly helped us win the war. I expect you boast that you know yourself, but you do *not* know that you are simply one puppet more whose strings destiny is tweaking, and, immersed in the deepest darkness, you try to play at being free and imagine your life follows the dictates of your will. Perhaps you even gamble on the pools in the secret hope that chance, that euphemism for fate, will bring you a million so you can devote your life to doing whatever you please, freed from the sweat of toil. I thought along exactly the same lines until I began to receive the first anonymous messages. Then reality started to crumble around me—"We're going nowhere like this. I'm up to here with you. Either you keep to your own story line, or this will turn into an open-ended pastiche. Do you get what I'm saying, do you grasp what I'm planning?"

I tried hard to believe my commercial triumphs were solely the result of my own efforts. I tried to cling to the idea that the blight nature had brought to my physique would find compensation in the social success brought by wealth; I plunged frantically into the world of business, worshipping risk, loving profits, and idolizing the playthings of capital to my heart's content. This was a time when financial euphoria ran riot, aided and abetted civil-war-style economic tactics. I plunged in body and soul, scaled enviable peaks, reached magnificent glaciers on high, and settled down there. Only fleeting memories remained of Spain on its nerve edges, the Spain of protest songs and street fighting, like flatulence waiting to be expelled.

At dawn on November 20, 1975, the wailing of Trinitarian nuns dragged us naked from our beds, our sexes still erect, still swinging on the hinges of sleep like the mournful clappers beginning to clamor across Madrid's bell-bottomed sky. The Generalísimo had died. The screeching nuns airing the catastrophe in the passageways blew the sleep dust from our eyes and aroused us from our slumbers. We threw our thieves' rags on and dashed downstairs to the dining room, where breakfast was waiting. The nuns in the kitchen had prepared hot chocolate that wafted a comforting aroma up our nostrils. The paupers in the institution were already sitting at a table, with blank expressions, as if that solemn moment for the fatherland somehow involved them. Before he started devouring his breakfast, I noticed One-Eyed Slim's right hand draw a lingering In-the-Name-of-the-Father on his chest that I felt was sincere enough, even if it was one of his stock-in-trade tricks, and that led me to reflect that, despite everything, beyond creed and circumstance, death's august claws can make even the most wretched of this earth feel sorrow. Sister Marta came over to our table to give us the funeral chit-chat while we were busy dunking churros in our hot chocolate. "It happened in the early hours, from what they're saying on the radio. Poor little man. He was as wizened as a raisin. He is now with God in his Glory, but what will become of us without him?" Slim soothed her with a manly gesture, assuring her that while he was alive, the Trinitarian nuns had nothing to fear. Poor innocent. They didn't need him at all and gleefully went on with their business the day that a bad end brought him his final reckoning. A right mess—the pancakes with caramel syrup he was chewing suddenly mixed together with the gray matter in his head because of the explosion. It looked like a wasteland of limbs amputated by the wave of expansion, a higgledy-piggledy mess glazed by the fallout from the cafeteria. "Whoever they are, the dead deserve a reverence and a minute of prayer," Slim continued, "even more so if they were hated in their lifetime. Dwarfy, the day I die, you must do what's right and proper by my soul. Pray seven Credos, and remember how well I treated you."

The day I discovered that bits of his flesh had been splattered through the air, my first instinct was to call him a bastard, and though I'd never wished it on him when he was alive, I must confess I was overjoyed that death, that endemic scourge, had finally swept him away.

News of Franco's death immediately spread through the labyrinth of streets, and when the sharp cold of morning came, everyone was already joining in patriotic dirges. "Spaniards, when my time came to render my last homage to the Almighty . . ." There were people who uncorked champagne bottles for breakfast, and others, driven by a sense of honor, shirts a proud sea-blue, faces to the sun, dashed into the streets, arms aloft, to bid farewell to a sun as absent as the founder of the Falange. They shouted victory cries and chorused slogans now relegated to the dustbin by the material well-being heralded by Seat 600s and washing machines, which is what the Regime had now become. Such pride goes soft and limp when chewed in the mouth, doesn't taste the same, and when you've spat it out, you feel relieved and much happier. After he'd finished dunking in his hot chocolate, Slim detached the flask of anisette he carried strapped to his calf and emptied a small drop into the breakfast cups of all those present. "Let us all drink to the glory of the Caudillo," he exhorted those gathered in the dining room as he stood to his feet. I downed mine and stayed as I was—indifferent to death's victory and more concerned about what was going to happen from now on.

We left the Trinitarian Mansion after our toast and trotted off down the street to see what profit the day might bring us. We roamed around, keeping an eye on the situation as it developed, and rather than begging on the steps of a church or fleecing civil servants of their wallets in the metro as we usually did at that early hour, we decided to test the waters in the hotbed of rumors that was the Puerta del Sol. Midmorning news began to surface that they were going to put Franco's body on public display in the Royal Palace, and Slim's eye shed a tear at the mere thought of being able to go and see it. "Let's go, dwarfy, we can't miss this!" he said, pushing me in the back in the direction of the Calle Arenal. He was in a fantastic hurry and made me stumble, in the grip of soppy emotion that made me cringe, showing off his empty socket in classic style to emphasize his one-eyed mug, while I ran behind him like a dog under sentence rather than one following his master. People had already started queuing by the wrought-iron fence in the Plaza de la Armería in order to render tribute to the coffin in due course, sobbing, and hoarse from the "*Arriba Españas*" they'd been shouting. It soon became a long line that, as the clock ticked on, transformed into a vast horde of people extending round the palace perimeter and vanishing into the wastelands of the Campo del Moro, at the other end of the Plaza de Oriente. I'd not met such a crowd even on a Sunday when El Cordobés was fighting the bulls in Las Ventas; it was a crowd of loyal followers, addicts, and curious bystanders, and that's the honest truth. It was a fantastic ruckus as beset by mournful wails as seething with expectation, and Slim, who was no fool, immediately saw the potential for extracting filthy lucre from that heaving multitude and went for it. "Dwarfy," he ordered, "get into that line and act as if you're trying to push in. When they start moaning, just sit tight until I get there. Don't lose your nerve, and create a scene, if you have to, to keep your position." And that's just what I did. I walked over to the most packed section at the head of the line, a head combing its hair on the rusty fence round the Royal Palace where people were festering like lice. I tried to slip unnoticed under the skirts of a lady kitted out like a housewife on her way to the shops with her nylon string bag, gripping her purse tight and smelling unmistakably of vegetable broth. When she felt me around her hips, she looked down askance and in disgust but didn't dare say a thing, keeping a close lookout in case they finally opened the gate. I got more and more up her nose, cheekier and cheekier, until she could stand it no longer and walloped me with the corner of her purse. "Don't try to push in, dwarf," she hissed, shrill as a night watchman, in a cry that erupted indignantly from her lungs. "Shut your trap, you boiled cabbage," I retorted, strutting my stuff and stamping on her bunions. Then she began insulting me with phrases that simply described my appearance and started pummeling me with her clenched fists. "Deformed goblin," rasped the poor woman. I was delighted by her pathetic tantrum and scornfully answered back, "Shut your trap, you old beggar woman," not budging an inch from the spot I'd so cheekily squeezed into at the front of the line. People began to register what was happening and turned their nosy antennae toward the scene of the incident. "Nobody has a right to push in," protested a bald coot behind me. "Hey, I've been here since last night," I bellowed bitterly, trying to spread confusion. "You lying so-and-so," the woman rasped again, continuing to clout my head with her purse. "Don't hurt him, missus, can't you see he's handicapped?" interrupted a fellow wearing a jacket with elbow patches. "So what, handicapped he may be, but he's pushing in all the same. He's just trying it on." A welter of shouts, howls, and opinions went up for or against yours truly, getting ruder and ruder. Suddenly, with that assertive touch con merchants can sometimes bring to bear, Slim put in an appearance, shoving people aside. "Aren't you ashamed to be treating a poor dwarf like this when he only wants to offer a prayer to the Caudillo's body as it lies in state? Don't you have any feelings? I find it incredible that there's such a lack of consideration for the weak of this world; I hope your family's never unfortunate enough to have such a malformed member." Many changed their expressions and shut up after that harangue from One-Eyed; others, however, got even more indignant as a result of his play-acting appeal to their consciences and started insulting him, as well, telling him to clear off back to where he'd come from, and now both sides

locked into a flurry of flailing arms, punches, and shoves—
that, of course, being the whole point of the farce. From that
minute on, it was wondrous to watch Slim embark on a show
of thieving that called on every trick of the trade; his hands
flew over jacket lapels, his fingers slipped between pocket
linings at the speed of light, with scientific precision. I gaped
in awe at that master class; the guile of cunning angels was no
doubt guiding that guy in his deft fingering. I was bowled
over by his artfulness and threw myself into an imitation
game, starting with the coin purse that lady was using to bash
me on the head, though I was forced to bite it out of her
hand, not at all artfully. That hustle and bustle lasted a mere
four or five minutes, and in the midst of the uproar, at a wink
from Slim's good eye, we both scarpered along our own
routes. We replayed that ruckus and others in similar style
throughout the evening and into the long night of that wake,
and much to our advantage. We walked from one end to the
other of that line ever more thronged by devotees, gossips,
idle bystanders, out-and-out fans, and swarms of ordinary
folk drawn like flies by the political stench given off by the
corpse. In this way, by the good grace of our stratagems,
a host of ingenuous simpletons fell to our wiles: dental
technicians, neighborhood hairdressers, apartment block
concierges, Catholic lawyers, bus drivers, freelance fishermen,
rank-and-file sailors, pen-pushing wimps, parsons without a
post but hoping to find one, low-level civil servants, and even
a black man from the Cameroons who happened to be in
town trading in ivory. That disparate but single-minded
social galaxy fetching up at the farewell to the Generalísimo
in the incomparable setting of the Royal Palace would soon
disintegrate as it adopted the democratic creed that became

the rage, erasing the past at a stroke and signing up to a new account with the future. One by one, all fell foul of Slim's thievery, and his deft artistry was such that we were astounded by our large haul, so large that he even suggested we cross ourselves in an act of thanksgiving, thus acknowledging with restraint and humility the heavenly intervention in the catch we'd netted.

To end the day, in keeping with the solemnity the occasion demanded, we finally took our place in the line and waited for it to move forward until we emerged in the Palace's columned room of state, where the spectacle of the Caudillo's corpse on its bier was there for all to see. Dressed in a spanking new uniform, the cadaver revealed a rigor mortis that made one distinctly suspect his demise hadn't been as recent as we'd been made to believe. Could what someone had told Slim be true, that they'd wanted his death to coincide with Primo de Rivera's? It sounded quite esoteric, but anything is possible in the designs of Providence, and even politics needs it spot of goety. When it was our turn to walk past the coffin, Slim stopped abruptly, struggled to hold back a tear shed who knows whether from sorrow at the loss or gratitude for our takings, then stood to attention with a click of the heels, raised his right arm with renewed vigor, and, trembling with emotion, shouted a *"Viva Franco! Arriba España!"* that echoed dramatically round the palace vaults, to which those present responded with the inevitable *"Vivas"* and *"Arribas,"* bringing yet one more chapter in the history of Spain to a lovely, single-minded conclusion.

Sometimes smells help transport emotions through time and space. Haven't you ever been reminded of an unrequited love or scene from your past by a scent in the air or a piquant aroma? My sense of smell has always been as keen as that of a dog wandering the streets in search of a bone to gnaw. I expect it's because of my contact with those animals. When lions or tigers aren't washed or deloused, you can smell them a mile away, but once the smell has settled in your nostrils, you don't notice it, and happily coexist with the stench. Doris hoarded little flasks of eau de cologne in her caravan. She'd give them me to smell, and I'd shut my eyes tight in ecstasy and take a deep breath, as if trying to purge the fetid pit of my existence. Perhaps as a throwback to that habit, I now began to visit the perfume sections in the department stores in Madrid on Carretas and Carmen, where I'd go for free squirts of the colognes the manufacturers brought out every season. I'd go down Callao and into the Galerías Preciados, where they'd be lined up on the counters in small bottles. Aguasdeselvas, Floids, and Varondandis were practically a daily pleasure, but I didn't simply linger over male offerings, I often squirted the ones advertised for women. The shop assistants had me in their sights, but apart from the oddity of this custom I'd adopted, the times they were a-changing, and that sense of the absurd, which in another era would have been banned as a danger to public morality, was now something to relish, because it was so eccentric, quaint, and even grotesque. The structures that had sustained the Regime for so long suffered from the aluminosis brought on by longevity, and were beginning to implode as the mercury of a new politics ravaged arthritic joints. The people as such had yet to firm themselves up into trade unions or wondrous neighborhood associations, but they were now daring to stick their snouts out of the burrow of their new would-be freedom. "The people united will never be defeated," went up the anonymous cry in still-fearful streets, tempered by memories of tragedy. Outbursts of leafleting and fly-posting erupted in different spots in the city center like ephemeral gusts from a whirlwind struggle that was still being squashed by the brute force of the police. I'd see university students come up the Calle Preciados with their ideologies strapped on their backs, bent under the weight of leaflets carrying the fashionable slogans of the day—"Amnesty," "Freedom," "Release the Prisoners"—their clenched fists punching the swirling winds, long-haired with messy ideas, flared pants, and side-burns, and I wondered in my skeptical gray matter what that turmoil would ever come to. In the name of freedom, they were working the streets, airing the immemorial filth of the proletariat, oblivious to the fact that in other more plush confines, plans were being hatched for a less traumatic way forward for Spain within a conventionally bourgeois frame. They scattered their sputum and leaflets on the ground, to equal social effect, and both were swept up at nightfall by the municipal street cleaners. There was talk of people in high places being defenestrated, and the call for a general amnesty was gaining in strength. Time, not street fighting, was the name of the game.

One morning I was returning early from begging twenty-five peseta coins from pious old dears, tottering into the Barefoot Trinitarians', when I felt a sudden urge to dip into the perfume section of the Galerías Preciados. Very little time had passed since Franco's death, yet spring seemed to be smiling again—with the rictus of a corpse. The air smelt clean, and the morning was joyously slanting its sunbeams, apparently wanting to spotlight the detritus in the city. I took a shortcut down the Calle de Tudescos to the Plaza de Callao. Shops were opening their doors to passersby with brisk, business-like efficiency as late-rising shop assistants watched their sleep reflected in display windows. By the Callao cinema, a large group of youths was already making its presence felt, intent on demonstrating for their rights. One could discern placards sticking out from under their blousons, like tattered flags rescued from some imponderable defeat. Some had slung military-duty rucksacks over their shoulders, which were surely about to deliver up posters, pamphlets, leaflets, and other subversive material to be handed out at any minute. I glanced at them askance as I walked by but was much keener to give my nose the dose of scents it was craving than to inspect their behavior; I took little notice and pressed on toward the Galerías Preciados. As I was an avid visitor, they knew how I liked to squirt and sniff perfumes and, generally, let me get on with it, but that day, when a counter assistant saw me approaching, one suffering a bad bout of PMS, she dashed hysterically off to the floor security guard to inform him of my presence. I was in seventh heaven, trying a lemon-scented cologne that had just hit the market. Experienced in his job, the security guard crept up behind me, undeniably bent on doing me damage, and while I was swooning on that scent, he dealt me a cowardly blow that jolted me, with such bad luck that the bottle slipped from my grasp and smashed to smithereens on the floor. I lost my footing completely when he shoved me a second time, and I fell flat on my face and impregnated my cheeks with bits of glass. "Clear off, dwarf, and don't show your nose around here ever again," the guy dictated. Upset at my expulsion from paradise, and leaking blood like a slaughtered pig, I ran into the street, hiding my face in my hands. Blood is a spectacular red. Those who see it are either entranced or throw up. I felt really ashamed and let rip a series of curses against those stores and the lackey who'd attacked me so savagely though I'd not interfered with him or his floor; perhaps he was absurdly jealous because he was holding down such a mediocre job.

A few yards from the entrance to the establishment on the Calle Preciados, the head of a non-authorized demonstration, who was waving a banner with the slogan "Freedom Of Expression, Execute The Fascists" noticed but couldn't believe a proletarian dwarf was being mistreated, and, spurred on by his longing for social justice by my accusing shouts, he decided to change direction and march on the department store. Chaos, destruction, and wanton looting was the immediate fate of the Galerías Preciados. Rushing to fight my cause, the violent passions of those freedom-loving puppies shattered the brass and glass counters exhibiting the languid universe of fragrances created by Chanel, Dior, Loewe, and Balenciaga. I wondered at the scene, bubbled with satisfaction, then suddenly started to launch out at merchandise left, right, and center with all my might and the handle of an umbrella I'd half-inched, and I was so cock-a-hoop I totally forgot the deep gashes or glittering pearls of blood adorning my face like an ecce homo that's just be given a fresh lick of paint. Bottles of cologne, wall clocks, lace fans, and cans of lacquer flew through the air until the anti-riot cops piled in swinging their billy clubs, rubber bullets started bouncing off bodies, cans of tear gas suffocated throats, and, as best they could, everyone disappeared down their blessed clandestine burrows. Driven on by my forceful exhortations in the heat of battle, I wanted to teach the guard who'd assaulted me a lesson, breaking both his legs so he'd have something to remember me by and others could have a good laugh; that happened, care of a brawny, bushy-bearded fellow with a mop of matted hair, no doubt straight out of a coal mining nightmare. Not only was the establishment torn apart, its public image was sorely tarnished, and very soon it was expropriated by a democratic government elected with an absolute majority. Some of those who had fought that morning against the brutal ways of capitalism's lackeys must have contributed, of course, with their reluctant votes, but apart from surface ripples, that did nothing to help the cause of the people; in the long run, after an orchestrated orgy of asset-stripping in which everyone made a fortune, store and company were finally taken over by a rival. Apart from enjoying the heat of revenge, I decided that violence alone can legitimize the arguments of the weak; that all else is but wishful thinking and pacifist prattle—at the end of the day, a load of boloney.

Slim said he didn't have a dream, but you can bet he was lying. He was a great cynic, a Stoic of deceit encamped in the underworld. As the months went by, he got increasingly involved in politics. He was drawn in by the friendships he'd contrived in higher spheres. They had to have recourse to him, they were so at a loss confronting the changes underway. Slim traipsed the streets, knew what was cooking, and prided himself on being personally acquainted with even the pigeons in the eaves. The Regime's backwoodsmen and their draconic drive for démodé purges channeled him into a morass of political conspiracy. In exchange for his favors, they guaranteed he could continue exploiting the economic space of poverty and benefiting unpunished from extortion and thievery in the city. Pains in the ass, clinkers for the dustbin of history, tatters from the past. That way of life couldn't be sustained for any longer without a power structure to prop it up. I knew only too well that Esteruelas was behind this secretive maneuvering and that he was the one extracting the most from Slim's sneaking around in such a devious, rather than effective, manner. Nonetheless, One-Eyed hardly mentioned the inspector and, after Franco's demise, seemed to have dropped him off his radar. Public institutions were in a pickle, and everyone was waiting on the adjacent department to take up a definitive position in order to follow suit or criticize. Nobody lurking in the corridors of power dared make a move, raise a finger, or clear out files—just in case—not even those gathering dust and sleeping the sleep of the just in the Movement's catacombs. Esteruelas was the kind who turned a blind eye to an outrage simply for a chance to climb one step up the ladder, and who prevaricated with his eyes shut. After so many years squandering his youthful ambitions, wielding a billy club from one end of the country to the other, he'd now reached the center of power from which the juicy tidbits were handed out, and he could see the whole system collapsing before his eyes; his great expectations were increasingly going down the chute, and he was more scared than ashamed that he'd lose the little prestige he'd garnered in that swamp hole. I imagine it's possible he hoped deep down his efforts would shore up a hierarchical society whose orderliness derived from the principle of authority and respect instilled by a regime of repression that constituted the key elements in the manner of understanding society that the cane had inculcated into him from childhood. Achieving that was out of the question, and his concern for the fatherland only led him to a bad end. May God deal duly with his evil doings. As often happens in times of disarray when all that's rotten rises to prominence, Slim fished his biggest catches from the muddy waters of the Transition. That's why when a beggar stood up to him or an adversary wanted to pounce on a square inch of his power, a police van, at an order from on high, would turn up and the individual concerned would be beaten to pulp and invited by kicks galore to reside for a while in the Carabanchel jail for, say, endangering the domestic security of the State. Slim's field of influence was notorious, and, as his figurehead, I spread it thick on the four winds; subsequently, those in our guild looked on me warily, never stood in my way in the slightest, and always maintained a proper distance, for fear I might teach them a lesson they most probably deserved. I went scheming and thieving through the city with a domicile established in the Trinitarian stewpot and a permanent operational base in La Copa de Herrera. As a general rule, and except for the jerks whose wallets we nicked, we dealt with few people who weren't involved in the brotherhood, and that's why the mass action surrounding the perfumes and the indignation my mistreatment sparked in those young enthusiasts gave me food for thought for a good long while. Perhaps the world they wanted wasn't as bad as Slim prophesied. Perhaps the responsibility for oppression and injustice wasn't theirs or their cause's but rested in fact on the shoulders of those other guys who'd organized a rotten, bloated society for their own benighted benefit. Perhaps the solution would be to give Francoism the boot for good and start putting one's trust in the generous, gloved hand offered by democratic freedoms. What I'm telling you may sound infantile and small-minded, but just remember how people at the time were naïve, ill-informed, and had only just stopped believing in God. That Spain I'm describing was very different to the one today that's so coarse and consumerist and has pushed us into Europe for the bowl of lentils of the new welfarism. Madrid remained an insular city, stinking of miracles and ruffs. The grimy races had yet to hit its streets as Slim predicted they would. It was unusual to come across a Chinese person and even more unusual to stumble into any black people on the Avenida José Antonio.

Not even the Moors showed their heads, for fear of being deported back to the mosques of their ancestors in retaliation for the episode of the Green March. The political ban on anything foreign had stopped the mafias from setting up as they had in other latitudes, but South Americans would soon be here touting their cellophane-wrapped roses by night until the Chinese brought their syringes in and sent them packing, and then the heroin trade would transform the social tissue of street life and mess up the terrain for the glorious trade of small-time crooks. In the Madrid I've been describing, the guild monopolized the exploitation of all that shady business. Only riffraff who occasionally beheaded a housewife with a carving knife or took a hatchet to an old geezer to steal his wallet might perhaps unsettle the natural order of things now or then; such occurrences were bygone habits from an era doomed to die, and didn't abound. Slim claimed he had no dreams, but that's impossible. Everybody dreams, even the dead, who dream of the life that was truncated. A few days ago I had a dream, and you can bet it was a premonition. Let me tell you about it.

It was very light and warm. I could see myself strolling through an unknown hillside city similar to those lovely Italian Renaissance towns where houses cluster one above another to create strikingly beautiful urban mosaics. I was walking on a slope shaded by the crowns of huge magnolia trees when I suddenly found myself on the edge of a small plaza, three of whose sides formed a horizon of façades sheathed in green moss. These ramshackle, noble houses seemed to speak to each other in a language forged in an era when honor, dignity, or a man's word perhaps constituted the marks of identity of mortals. They were conversing, I imagine, about past glories or loves defeated by decrepitude brought on by the passage of time. On the side of the plaza that wasn't lined by houses, a huge wall kept the sea at bay. Waves surged tempestuously, crashed down on that supernatural parapet, and heaving waters sent foam eddying through the air to caress the edges of the flagstones on the opposite side of the plaza. Some men were enjoying a relaxed swim under the intense blue sun warming the sea. On the other side of the waves, in shadowy arcades, a few ancient shops were opening their doors to customers. A strange man with a book under his arm stood in the entrance to an elegant café, wearing a houndstooth check jacket. He looked vaguely familiar. I lumbered down to the plaza, striding toward where the man was waiting. I said something, I don't remember what, perhaps I asked him for the time of day, and then became fascinated by the sea extending behind me, not realizing it couldn't possibly exist. As absorbed as I was contemplating that wonder, I did still notice the way the foam the crashing waves created reshaped itself into eddies of words that threaded together on the parapet to form astounding texts that told the story of my life. Suddenly I wanted to plunge in; I was being dragged along by an irresistible force. Dazzled by the peaceful turbulence of the blue water, I stripped off my clothes, ready to dive in straight away and feeling extremely happy about the prospect. Then that man addressed me. "Don't swim," he said. "These are the Stygian waters that end men's existence, that give the final full stop to their words." I didn't understand his warning, or preferred to ignore him, and threw myself headfirst into the depths of the abyss. That was when I woke up. I could still taste the saltiness of that strange liquid on my tongue. Blue as ink, it nevertheless tasted of rust, like human blood.

Blue on white, his shirt cuffs spilt out onto a marble-topped table in La Copa de Herrera, covering hands that Esteruelas rubbed together against the cold while he waited for One-Eyed to come. I wasn't expecting to find him there; Slim hadn't tipped me off about his possible presence. It was an evening, one of those very nocturnal January evenings when the moon is so white it looks like pure ice. As ordained by habit, I'd dropped by La Copa to review the day's takings with Slim and to down a few shots of rough anisette before heading off to eat Trinitarian stew. When he saw me walk in, Esteruelas gave me an intrigued glance, as if dredging from the sewer of his memory a distant, lingering reminiscence of me. I went up to the bar and asked after Slim. "He's not come yet," Señor Antonio whispered in that hoarse tone cigarettes give a voice. "That fellow there has been waiting for him for at least half an hour and has smoked almost a whole packet of Ducados." Esteruelas was still rudely staring at me, nastily focusing on my misshapen protuberances, dwelling on them with relish; he kept that up a good while, until he couldn't resist it any longer and summoned me to his table with a contemptuous wave of his index finger, "Hey, dwarf, come here." I went over, not really afraid but wary of any danger proximity to him might put me in. "Don't I know you, Snow White?" he asked, arching his eyebrows in an unpleasant, know-all fashion. "I do know you, but you must tell me the wherefore and when." "I worked as a dwarf in the Stéfano circus," I answered honestly, my voice shaking in fear like a man who knows he is trapped, "you interrogated me seven or eight years ago in Burgos, but we'd met before that." Esteruelas snarled obtusely and took a last drag on his cigarette through a gap between his teeth. The smoke poured out from deep in his nostrils. Then he started remembering. He recalled aloud the far-off arrest of Gurruchaga, made special mention of how he stank like a pig, and didn't dally there but immediately went on to the more scabrous case of handsome Bustamente. Perhaps from the tone of his comments, I surmised that Esteruelas had known from the onset my betrayal was a fake, yet that hadn't prevented him from taking an innocent man prisoner. What's more, he'd derived great pleasure from not giving him the help he was due, because it allowed him to close down that murder case there and then, a feat you can bet brought him substantial kudos, and because he also enjoyed seeing others suffer unjustly. "It was brave of you to inform on him, Snow White, because that faggot swore he'd get you. He spent the whole night screaming at the cell walls that he'd live to see the day he'd kill you. It took a good beating to cool him down." He went on to tell me he'd got twenty years and had refused to say anything in self-defense. Esteruelas's statement was enough to ensure he was put away. He was abandoned to his fate, and that sounded strange, knowing Mr. Handsome, though it's true some people change their attitude as life repeatedly mistreats them, or he might have had some other good reason to keep quiet. "Twenty years is no proper sentence for a self-confessed murderer. In other times, they'd have slammed him up against a wall and peppered him with bullets. Twenty years pass quickly enough. The judges took into consideration the dead man's perversions, and that's why they reduced his time inside as much as they could. There's no God that can stop time, right, Snow White? It would have been better for you if they'd made a sieve out of him, because if twenty years fly by fast to begin with, you just wait and see what happens if they get the general amnesty everyone is calling for; as far as I'm concerned, the street will be flooded with rabble, and your skull will get the revenge bashing that faggot swore he'd give it."

I'm not sure whether Esteruelas was trying to have fun or scare me, but his words didn't dampen my spirits. Mr. Handsome was a distant memory, and I felt protected from any threats by the shadow of Slim. Esteruelas's lips dictated silence, he put a hand on his stomach, swallowed air, and, all of a sudden, let out a thunderous belch that echoed off the walls of La Copa before slipping up my nose. "Time simply flies," he resumed philosophically, "and I'm not as healthy as I was, or as nimble. I digest food slowly, and any upset builds up gases." He paused to think for a moment. "That other circus character, that hoity-toity bugger, who smelled sky high of shit, he was a friend of yours, too, wasn't he?" I can't think why, but the dedication to the book of poetry suddenly passed through my mind and I couldn't think what to say. Then I swallowed and said he wasn't.

That man, who'd spent his whole life sinisterly licking the backsides of the powerful, when he believed he'd finally seated his own butt on the best can in town, at the top of the political-social brigade, found himself threatened by times that were unstoppably a-changing. That bastard had never been very flexible; even as a youngster he'd been rocked by huge belches that left leaden dregs putrefying in the hollows of his mind. He was a piece of shit with a paunch who liked to generate unhappiness, a man who crippled himself and was forever dissatisfied because he thought himself better than everyone else; he buttered up the great and the good, played the tame poodle, went toadying and regaled their ears with praise, simply knee-jerking in his post, when in reality he hated their guts and would have royally stuffed them down the loo he'd just used and rubbed their faces in the feces they deserved. All people of that ilk are the same. Señor Antonio came over to the table with a fresh jug of wine he held by the neck. "Did anybody ask you for a drink, old man?" Esteruelas spat in his face in a ridiculous vaunting of authority. "No," replied Señor Antonio. "So get back to where you came from and leave us in peace." Señor Antonio cowered, turned round, didn't stand up for himself, walked back behind the bar, and busied himself with his chores. Once he was there, Esteruelas raised an insidious hand, snapped his fingers three times, and shouted to him to bring us a drink. The old guy obeyed without saying a word. The air one chewed in La Copa tasted staler and staler; outside it began to rain. Esteruelas enjoyed watching the old guy pour his drink out. Of course, a single stubborn man can sustain the structure of a political regime; on the other hand, his disappearance guarantees its collapse. When the admiral was blown sky-high, it was impossible the regime could continue. Nobody of any standing dared pick up the baton, and Franco was now a corpse. Perhaps the specter of old age or some figureheads' desire for a quiet life weighed heavily in the minds of those riding in the chariot of power. Never before had thrombo-phlebitis decapitated a state so definitively. People whose brains had stagnated, like Esteruelas himself, now drifted aimlessly down the byways of the bureaucracy, groping with their blind men's sticks, and they never grasped that the times were dancing to another tune. They sniffed the air like wild animals, then began to retch and didn't realize their own stench was the cause. In any case, Esteruelas hid all that under the strong smell of the black tobacco he chain-smoked, and rather than expelling the miasmas generated by his own putrefaction, he puffed out a potent, sweetish smoke that energized the brain. The bell over the door announcing customers tinkled. Slim had just walked in. Sopping wet, he was cursing under his breath the downpour that had caught him in the waste ground near Francisco el Grande. Initially, as he shook the water off, he didn't notice our presence, though he soon stopped scowling when he noticed Esteruelas sitting at one of the tables. "What a surprise to see you here, Señor Inspector, we weren't expecting you. Antonio, pour this gentleman a drop of the hard stuff." "Forget it, I've got all I require," retorted the other man. "Come and sit down, I need to speak to you, and don't call me Inspector again in public, you idiot." "Yes, Señor Inspector, whatever you command; it's force of habit that betrays me," replied Slim, flaunting the deferential bows with which he flattered those he reckoned were above him in rank. "Do you know *him*?" asked Esteruelas, pointing his fingertip at my face. "Yes," came back Slim, "Goyo works for me; he can be trusted. Goyo, say hello to Señor Inspector, Señor Inspector is a very important person in the Ministry of the Interior; I've

212

mentioned him to you before." Seeing how irritated Esteruelas was at *Señor Inspector* being shoved in his face, I simply looked down and shut up. He said nothing about our past encounters and ignored me until almost the end of the meeting. He was a past master at the game these bastards carry in their blood: hiding what the left hand does from the right and vice versa; I expect that's why he met a bad end. They talked for a quarter of an hour.

The presence of Esteruelas in Slim's holy of holies wasn't a routine exchange of data, nor was it a mere courtesy visit, on the contrary, it was down to a matter crucial for the future of Spain, or so he then thought, and as later seemed to transpire.

The eagle eyes, attentive ears, or silent lips we'd posted throughout the city over the last months had proved futile when it came to anticipating what was really lurking round the corner. We knew that some of the flats rented out in the area of Lavapiés, in one way or another, acted as a base for that motley, unwelcome rabble, as we saw when the time for the pact came. These activists frequently changed their hideouts, either because they were burnt out or flat-broke and couldn't pay the running expenses of rent, electricity, and telephone, though expenditure on water was never their problem. Night and their pitch-black habits sometimes reached us in dull, hesitant whispers, and, like a nightmare fading away, their visits left traces of their creeds on walls in the shape of hammers and sickles or letter As corseted in the enclosed circles of anarchism, though someone always recognized and observed them from a street corner, a doorway, or a night watchman's cubbyhole. We possessed loads of information about places, individuals, and slogans, but everything pointed to the fact that we'd not picked up on something really crucial.

A high-up in the Spanish embassy in Paris had been informed by third parties that Santiago Carrillo, no less, the *bête noire* of Paracuellos, was planning a secret trip to the Spanish capital. It seemed intolerable that Satan's most vile offspring should dare set foot in Madrid, and that profanation had to be aborted at any price, if only out of respect for the memory of the dead. If the message from Paris was correct, Santiago Carrillo was preparing a visit in spring. It seemed most likely he would use his presence to reinforce the hidden strength of the clandestine Spanish CP and try to endow it with strategies in keeping with those times that were a-changing, with a view to creating a flexible structure able to bring under its umbrella of influence every other communist *groupuscule* floating off the beaten track in the barren wastes of Leftyland. Only unity in struggle could guarantee success, and the establishing of a workers' republic was what they should all be aiming for. Esteruelas believed that the arrest of Carrillo, apart from being a legal obligation and moral duty, would be a hugely efficient symbolic deterrent and would bolster the Regime. On the other hand, if Carrillo managed to stroll freely around the Puerta del Sol and talk to the rabble awaiting him, it would be reported in the international press, echoes would career off the walls of the fatherland, and those same walls would be irrevocably fissured, the credibility of the system would be undermined, and, given the manifest bungling by the police, the scum would seize the streets and provoke the death rattle of forty years of peace like a knife slitting the throat of a whimpering roebuck. "That bastard won't have the balls to show up in Madrid, but if he does, we'll catch him for sure. So, One-Eyed, you must keep your eyes wide open and keep you ear to the chatter in the gutter and pick up on all the jabber. Stick your lugholes up that crew's asses if need be to find out what they're plotting. Don't spare any means, and risk your hide more than usual. I'll be hovering in the background in case you need anything. Any movement, any sign, any comment, however minute, may be of use. The moment you dig something up, let me know. Got that?" Slim excitedly ruffled my mop of hair, as if he were lovingly stroking a cuddly toy and calming his nerves. Esteruelas clapped a couple of times to order Señor Antonio to bring us the bill. "Two hundred and thirty-five," he mumbled from behind the bar. The inspector extracted from his wallet one of those green one-thousand-peseta bills where the faces of Ferdinand and Isabella occupied a fuzzy area between the excrescence of loot and the excellence of fame and glory, which he placed on the table like a snooty donation, or a tip delivered with contempt. Slim picked it up and handed it to Señor Antonio. "Give the Señor Inspector his change," he told the old guy in a rather sarcastic tone, emphasizing much to his own amusement his *Señor Inspector* to upset Esteruelas yet again and show him once and for all that wielding power was about style and not rank. "Keep the change, old man," Esteruelas insisted, "you'll need it when you've lost the strength to put water in your wine, and as for you, Snow White," he went on, addressing me, "you watch the witch doesn't get out of jug and come to return the poisoned apple you handed him. I wouldn't want to find you beaten to pulp on some street corner. We've got far too much scum to see to every day without having it spring up shaped like a dwarf." Slim stood and looked intrigued, not knowing what that warning was all about, but he said nothing. He simply accompanied Esteruelas to the door, and watched him walk off in the direction of the Plaza de Cascorro, that hero of the fatherland who, selflessly risking his own life, showed how valiant he was by burning Cubans alive with kerosene. It was still raining outside.

The twister of necessity triggered by political instability and the economic crisis attracted to the Trinitarians a mixed fauna of beggars, driven there from different ecosystems of poverty. Out of Christian charity, the nuns welcomed them with shocked horror. They planted mattresses in every nook and cranny of the Mansion, adapted areas set aside for the special activities of the closed order to give shelter to the needy, and with ant-like diligence supplied whatever the institution was lacking. The portions of grub diminished to a thin layer of gruel on the plate, and coexistence soon became unsustainable. The lines of the hungry began to form systematically outside the entrance day after day, several hours before lunchtime, and at night the dearth of cots meant people were packed together at close quarters in intolerably smelly conditions. Despite the effort made by a number of nuns, who took advantage of the situation to try to dislodge Slim from his privileged perch as a resident in perpetuity, neither the availability of his or my quarters was ever threatened, though that didn't mean we didn't face real inconvenience at mealtimes. One-Eyed had earned his commodious boudoir in the Trinitarian Mansion by flexing his scrotum, and nothing apart from death would ever snatch that away. Quite frankly, it wasn't only down to him; Sister Marta was equally keen to see his haven kept secure, though such requirements weren't that essential, for, as we all know, the tinder of carnal pleasure will spark wherever the land is most parched. Nonetheless, that procession of emaciated souls newly released from jail began to undermine Slim's authority and credibility in the Mansion in terms of the ragamuffin horde that constituted his original base, and there were mini-confrontations that augured nothing good. We'd enforced a decree of our making, namely that every newcomer should pay a contribution depending on their immediate travel plans: that is, a high amount if they were only en route elsewhere, or a small percentage if they were intending to settle and adopt thievery as their way of making ends meet. We maintained our established criteria and started to demand the usual tithe from the new sewer crop, but results were very disappointing, since they either took no notice or said yes and then didn't cough up. In the end, precedent began to rule the day, and most people exonerated themselves from any payment; when so many rebel against a set state of affairs, there's little one can do that doesn't involve bloodshed.

Among the rabble of ex-jailbirds that came knocking on the door of the Trinitarians was a man with skin as crinkly as pork crackling and matte eyes that harbored a harsh, metallic glint. He answered to the name of Ceferino Cambrón and knew how to see off people's stares. Everything about him was ashen gray—his hair, his hands, his words—and his was the icy demeanor of a statue erected to commemorate a thinker's most solemn thoughts. One night when we were dipping our bread in a bowl of juicy tripe, Slim ordered me to collect the levy from him. I left my bread to soak and sat down on the bench where Ceferino was eating, his eyes glued on his food, prickly, saying next to nothing to the people around him, who were busy washing the tasty tripe down with a drop of strong wine. "If you want to stay here, you must pay him the levy stipulated," I said, pointing a raised chin at Slim. He stabbed his fork into a piece of tripe that was dribbling orange goo and effortlessly lifted it to his lips. He chewed it unhurriedly, and when he'd finished, he deigned to reply. "And who might that be?" he asked disdainfully. "One-Eyed Slim," I replied, "he's the man who organizes this carry-on. If you don't pay up, he'll give you trouble." Both their gazes met at that point and sniffed a challenge in the air: Cambrón's was metallic, as if it were straight out of an iron foundry, and Slim's was fleshier, hence softer, but nothing happened apart from that electric charge from their eyes as they met in the pestilent atmosphere of the dining room. Ceferino went on chewing, not saying a word, with me at his side waiting like an idiot for his response. "What a shit life," the ex-jailbird exclaimed when he'd gobbled down what was on his plate. "Some seek a master they can serve without thinking, and others seek out freedom so they can think and not serve." Those words made my brain ripple in sympathy; they made me see how the human species, although it's a total lost cause, can entertain a thread of greatness that transcends mere daily survival—a hopeless longing to find a place where justice exists and is even practiced, a fallow desire to treat one's peers according to the mottoes of equality and fraternity that, as if by some subtle magic, had been watered down into simple self-interest. I'd just discovered the lay Franciscan creed of Marxists, a beautiful, impossible creed that would soon change the direction of my existence yet again and drive it, as if there were room for anymore, into wastelands of demagogy, farce, and self-seeking.

Drifting leaves, tell me, what became / of the princes of Aragon, Manuel Granero, the pavane for a princess / if Madrid glows like a slide show / if it's only in this district that seventy or seventy-five children jump, laugh, and scream as their mums show off Honolulu breasts, and girls walk by in fetching garb / micro-grooved skirts, shiny gloves, and glittering sandals, drifting, falling leaves / like Christ on the stony path, tell me, / who began this business of stopping, passing by, and dying, / who invented this game, this fearful solitaire / without a trick, that reduces you to cardboard, /if the Plaza de Oriente is a rose from Alexandria, / oh Madrid of Mesonero, Lope, Galdós, and Quevedo, / ineffable Madrid infested with diesel-oil, Yankees, and consumer society, / the city where Jorge Manrique would finally fuck up the lot of us. Blas was a man of reason, reason enlightened by darkness, the dense reason of a monk's sweaty, smelly habit. Blas had a Franciscan *je ne sais quoi* that endorsed his tolerance, his convivial spirit, and his non-metric verse. He was like Cambrón in his resonating consciousness; perhaps both passionately embodied the anguish of life. You could see the leanness of their bones in their eyes; fasting was their source of knowledge. I, on the other hand, had always suffered from hunger. Hunger had always bit into my guts with an urgent twist, and now I have grasped it was all a lie, invented sensation, stylistic artifice. Pizzas keep the wolf from the door with their crispy dough and shower of ingredients. Providence graciously decided I should devote my time to their home delivery, and in so doing, I stumbled upon a fortune. My Europizza has become one of the most solid investments in the country's entrepreneurial development. There's no doubting that it's an innovative line of business that has kept abreast of changes in habits, that gives me public recognition, not only in terms of sales numbers but also in the distinguished treatment I get from our institutions and the good vibrations I feel from so many contented customers. Five thousand direct jobs and another four thousand induced currently depend on the fact that I exist. Everybody orders them, everybody consumes them, but why? Mysteries are ineffable by their very nature, though one can't fail to note that their flavors are distinctive and appeal to the most plebeian tastes and straight away suit the gastronomic stereotypes of your average diner. Garlic, olives, olive oil, and tomato constitute in themselves an undeniable category of preferences shared by the communal palate. Greater sophistication is unnecessary. Perhaps that's the secret—simple food that comes to the table piping hot, a product suited to elemental IQs.

As well as being a construction worker on the dole, Ceferino Cambrón was also an elemental character. He never tried pizza; a bad end saw to him before the first of them hit the market. He did, however, possess dignity, the dignity of a scholastic creed one wears with a buttoned-up collar. He believed in social justice, in utopian socialism, in scientific communism, and in the poetry of Blas de Otero. Using the same criteria, he could have opted to believe in the resurrection of Christ, in the transfixion of the Virgin Mary, or in the poetry of Santa Teresa, but things are what they are and not perhaps as we would like them to be. I became increasingly intrigued by his standard patter; hearing him preach was pure bliss—what striking declarations, what clear concepts, what profound insights into people and their actions, all backed by analysis, reflection, and mature thought. He called a spade a spade, didn't beat about the bush, took the bull by the horns, and merely craved the respect of others, and the hapless fellow didn't even get that, so dismally was he damned. "Shut your trap, you shit-hole," they'd say, more for the fun sound than any strict semantic meaning, and he, unaware of the scope of those brotherhoods of penury, carried on with his preaching, upright, unflinching, exalting the grandeur of justice, the wonderful meaning of solidarity, or the pressing, irrevocable need to overthrow the bourgeoisie as the oppressing class. Ceferino Cambrón's frame had a haughty, Gothic aspect, which granted him a certain breadth from which to confront life emphatically from the flat peaks of his utopia. Besides, far from holding out his hand to beg for alms, though he didn't intend to abandon the gift of the Trinitarian stew, he started to earn money in the metro by selling banned books and dirty mags from Finland, where big breasts vied ebulliently with buxom busts to fill pages to the full. Marx, Engels, and Blas de Otero comprised the essential texts in the trade he hawked across the entire map of the metro, from Portazgo to José Antonio, from Ventas to Cuatro Caminos, and when the aches and pains of exhaustion sank their fangs into his thighs, he'd go to the hallway of one of the busiest stations in the network, spread his merchandise neatly on spit-ridden tiles, and launch willy-nilly into his sales spiel, using shocking phrases he'd fished out of the texts he was selling, which he seasoned with his solemn, pompous diction: "A specter is haunting Europe: the specter of communism. All the forces of old Europe have entered into a holy alliance to exorcize that specter . . ." At dawn on Sundays, he'd abandon the Trinitarian Mansion and go to the Rastro, where he continued to vaunt his products. He'd set up on a patch of pavement in the vicinity of Cascorrro and without more ado emulate Savonaralo in his denunciation of certain kinds of behavior and prophecies of catastrophe. People mostly bought his dirty mags, and as he bawled so much, they threw their coins at him. Slim ordered me to watch him from a distance and keep a close eye on the contacts who supplied the merchandise sustaining him in that poverty-stricken life, though it was hardly necessary, because I stuck to him like a limpet, and becoming aware I was stalking him, he transmuted my role, from spy to the meatier one of proselyte for his ideas, and he welcomed me into his shadow with a single proviso: that I should help him sell his goods. "Gregorio, you must recover the freedom to feel yourself a man and not allow anyone to appropriate your will. Use your handicap to bare the fangs of equality to the world and ensure at all costs that people don't pity you because of your appearance. Respect is earned by stubborn persistence; dignity is born within the self. Reject favors from the powerful on principle, and never feel sorry for your own fate." "Yes, Cambrón," I replied, "but do tell me again about the dialectic of the class struggle and the final demolition of the bourgeois state," and rather than injecting me with a dose of his doctrine, as I'd requested, he proudly began to recite the steely verse of Blas de Otero, as if wanting my consciousness to resonate with the artifice of his language. Like a proudly human angel, unleashed and pounding at the door, the verse flowed swiftly from his lips and hammered in my ear with inner, character-forging power.

One day Slim threatened Ceferino Cambrón with death. He grabbed him by his threadbare shirt collar and threateningly clicked his tongue in his face, clicks that sounded like bones breaking. "You're sinking deeper and deeper into that shit you keep preaching. It's people like you who are to blame for fucking up Spain. Keep an eye out, because I'll get you one of these days." "Right, the one you ain't got, you wretch," came the defiant reply.

Slim was dead sure that by ordering me to accompany Ceferino, he'd sooner or later introduce me to his circle of contacts and I'd be able to scrutinize at will their clandestine meetings, get to know his peers, their names, jot down their addresses, and find out what they were up to, and who knows, I might also track down information essential for breaking up their conspiracies, starting with that visit by Santiago Carrillo it was so urgent to nip in the bud. That's why he'd threatened him with grievous bodily harm; he'd hoped to arouse his ill will so he'd turn on me, a little wimp and butt of revenge he'd been handed on a tray and one entirely at his disposition. Snatching me from Slim's circle of influence was no doubt the most precious payback Ceferino could ever imagine; making me an adept of his creed and getting me to reject One-Eyed to his face, thus setting an example to the ragamuffins who were the minions in his dominions, would strengthen him, and he'd have no need to abandon his own terrain, could retain his generous convictions, illuminated once and for all by the sovereign triumph of reason. At the very least, all that was what was running through Slim's mind. "You take note of everything

224

he tells you, get him to trust you, let him persuade you to renege on all of us, and we'll settle our accounts with him when the time is ripe." Old age rather than any diabolical spirit is what allowed One-Eyed to sniff around the stamens of the human soul and sup on their hidden pollen, just like that thug Satan is said to be.

FOUR

The party locale was an old storeroom for kitchen and bath-room flooring and tiles. A bannisterless staircase connected the ground floor to the second floor of the building, a house with unrendered façades and a roof battered by the inclement weather winter inflicts on Madrid. It was situated on a side street behind Cuatro Caminos, very close to garages where the Municipal Transport Company parked its buses after midnight shutdown. In one corner of the locale, construction rubble was still gathering dust in a pile of boxes and plastic sacks; the rest was spick and span. It was lit up by various bulbs attached to cables hanging from the ceiling, and it was illumination worthy of the gallows; you'd have thought the members gathering there belonged to a creed from beyond the grave rather than any clandestine political party. Naturally warmer than that bleak waste you had to cross to reach it, the first floor was where the big names confabulated around three long tables swathed in a grimy, red cloth, its center decorated by the hammer and sickle. A dozen folding chairs scattered around were enjoyed by those attendees who managed to grab one and thus avoid standing during the interminable Friday-night meetings. Their exchanges were as dry as concrete and repeated ad nauseam by the privileged few who monopolized the right to speak. They talked of the strategy to follow to restore ownership of the means of production to the people, of revolution as the only viable method of political struggle, of the collectivization of agriculture, and the abolition of oppression through selective armed struggle—for every worker sacked, hang a boss. Then they chanted anthems, raised their fists, hugged and embraced, and off they went. I grasped little from the debates they engaged in, but, even so, one thing was clear enough: when the old crocks hogging the limelight started on about revolution, they did so full of nostalgia for their wasted youth, brows bristling in frustration that brimmed over into the wrinkles that furrowed their faces. They were simply phantoms from another era, at best lionized by a handful of ingenuous adolescents, people whose major achievement had been to survive. Another thing was clear: under that band of irascible old fogeys, Spain's future would inevitably remain in the usual hands; I didn't give a fuck.

I started going to the party locale, led by the hand of Cambrón, who, in his way, was happy with all that apocalyptic dissection of the way politics would be going. Demagoguery was basically his forte, stagnant thinking his bedrock, and communist doctrine his spiritual creed. All he lacked was the ability to levitate while brandishing a fist aloft. It was a different story out on the streets, where other energies were beginning to pulse, albeit slowly, with a very distinct take on the world. Past situations couldn't be extrapolated to forge conjectures about the future, at least not right then. A new reality had to be created and not the embalmed version proposed by those charlatans deformed by the dismal darkness of clandestine life—though *they* didn't realize that. Providence, meanwhile, had its own views on the matter, as we would soon see, including my future path, which is now drawing to a conclusion in your hands.

Nobody, not even those who attended the party meeting that evening, could fail to notice that the various political families sieving the dregs of power showed a latent interest in state reform. It was suspected that a deal was being done behind the backs of the people to shape the lines that would cement the framework of a new Regime that had yet to be built. Once final details had been signed, sealed, and duly orchestrated behind closed doors, the citizenry would be offered illusory powers of decision to endorse with its braying assent a process of transition that had been constituted beforehand. In fact, the government of the nation was secretly evaluating the political potential of an immediate referendum. The unknown factor was the stance the army might take when met with such a reduction in its authority, and the danger of insurgency its grievances might trigger. All in hock to the masters in Moscow, the orthodox communist groups that were then beginning to stick their snouts above the parapet of the sewer articulated a discourse around the keystone of a clean break. Their ranks openly galvanized to proclaim a third republic, this time of workers and toilers, rather than lawyers and orators like in the grisly version of '31 that set the stage for the definitive catastrophe of the left that was the bloodletting of the 1936 shooting party. Obscenities and trite jokes about the Bourbon proliferated, and the tricolor was advanced as a national symbol, not the red and yellow standard with the eagle nesting in the center. The supporters of the party whose mystic vision fired up Cambrón were totally opposed to reaching deals and

231

compromises, and light years away from the good-natured pacts and other petty-bourgeois tittle-tattle one heard round and about; all they proposed was the need to arm the people so that the pariahs of this earth and the hungry legions could finally seize the opportunity to express their desires with bullets.

That night, five men and one woman sat round the table with the hammer-and-sickle cloth. Between them, they must have racked up at least five hundred years. They had a big audience, as befitted the occasion. Rather than holding the session upstairs, as they usually did, they'd opted to use the much bigger ground floor. It had been swept, the dust chased away, and the remnants of flooring and tiles heaped into one corner. To give the scenario the right atmosphere, they'd taken party emblems, symbols, and posters printed in Argentina out of the trunks. The light was as dim as ever, but the many cigarette tips being smoked lit up the dreary darkness.

Cambrón, with me trailing in his wake, arrived just when the old crock chairing the session, a guy with a shiny skull that looked like he'd come straight out of a niche, was making a speech underlining the crucial importance of militant resistance in "these moments of open political struggle against the mummified perpetuation of the Caudillo's gang in naked connivance with the big banks to crush the dignity of the working people." It was strange to see such a big crowd in that space; something unusual was in the offing, no doubt, but Ceferino had told me nothing. We cut a path through the throng to be nearer to the table. I clung to his legs and twisted with his every movement while simultaneously avoiding like the plague being stamped upon or anyone stubbing their cigarette out in my hair. Huge conglomerations are generally an extra obstacle when it comes to dwarf mobility, and though I'd become something of an expert in the field, I still retained the odd memento in the shape of a broken bone, a finicky muscle, or scar. We sat in the front row. The atmosphere was extremely fuggy, and even at my height it was hard to inhale any real oxygen. The stench had never been so pungent in the Trinitarians' or reeked as vilely in the cages of the Stéfano circus. *That* was the scent blossoming from the proletariat. I leaned back on Cambrón's knees and prepared to swallow everything being said. Next to me, a little to my right, a woman with bulbous breasts and rotund hips was hanging on the raw-granite words issuing from the speakers' lips. That was my impression of Blond Juana the first time I saw her. I could tell you that she wore her hair cut short in the male fashion, that she wore jeans into which she'd tucked a collarless shirt, or that she'd wrapped an extravagantly flowery foulard round the firm flesh of her neck, though the flowers hadn't seen any water recently, judging by the smell. I could tell you how intently she listened or how young she looked, for all that stood out in such a geriatric gathering; but what can I really say, if the first thing I noticed were her bulbous breasts and the rotund expanse of her hips, which segued into a grandiose pair of spherical buttocks to boot?

Though she felt I was totally repulsive, over time I would be acquainted with her to an extent you'd never suspect. What's more, if it could ever be said that I was really in love, after my sad fluttering heartbeats for little Margarita, then Blond Juana was it. She'd have become a true daughter of the people, of the people and for the people, if her heroism hadn't been cut short in its prime. She came to Madrid as a girl, brought by migrant parents who ended up working as porters in a snobby building in the Salamanca district. She'd been educated in a nearby convent school after the astonishing efforts her mother made to secure her free enrolment. References, letters, and guarantors weren't enough, and a distant relative had to be called on, who was one of the hunting Caudillo's beaters, and he collected his commission in caresses. Rooted in the rural back of beyond and surrounded by so many straitlaced ninnies, Juana turned out on the wild side and learnt in her own flesh that the way this bitch of a world treats you depends on where you were born. She was coarse, coarse and wild, yet her cheeks reddened like poppies when anger or desire was driving her, or whenever she tired of shouting revolutionary slogans on street corners, was out of puff, and fell apart drinking wine in bars. I remember that first night, when I sidled up to her, how she smelt as bitter as an artichoke, yet I felt she was sweet, as if condensed milk, not blood, coursed through her veins; later, when I finally got a lick, it was no longer so thick or so sugary, that taste of bitterness I'd already divined was all there was left.

That old talking skull didn't stop evincing depths of dialectic that were difficult for a novice like me to digest, and rather than struggling to understand, I turned my head and, out of the corner of my eye, admired the strikingly female profile Juana used to promote her powerful presence. The rhetoric from the table went in one ear and out the other, didn't interest me at all—neither class conflict, the attractions of a clean break, nor victory in the final struggle—my concerns were limited to the carnal variety, and I'm not suggesting at this stage that such longings have deserted me forever, but simply that as you grow older, these desires

234

subside, before finally vanishing completely, I suppose, down the sewer of senility. Juana's body was warm, soft, and fresh and called to be relished the way bakers try out their bread—namely, with their mouths. I later discovered that following her creed, fancies, or convictions, it was an open secret that she willingly yielded to comrades who wanted it, something that fuelled my hopes, though where dwarves are concerned, promiscuity only goes so far, and my turn never seemed to come. I imagined her in her birthday suit the whole time that guy on the podium spouted his rock-hard doctrines. When he finally shut up, the corners of his mouth flecked with dry saliva, something totally unforeseen happened. Yet again, a preeminently sarcastic Providence erupted in the flow of my life.

I was caught off guard, engrossed, one might say, in Blond Juana's rough feminine ways, when, after the applause, the old crock chairing the session began to introduce the next speaker. He raised his voice and told us that the comrade about to speak had spent her youth fighting in the workers' movement, that she had struggled against fascism from a range of posts in the people's republican government and then greatly risked her life to defend her beliefs, in the mud of the trenches, shoulder to shoulder with Líster. She'd always excelled in her commitment to the revolution, and her energy had received manifold praise from her comrades, to the point that she inspired the pugnacious pen of the much lamented Blasco Castrillo to write those passionate lines in her honor: *You have faith and in the trench / springtime blossoms in your faith / and hoisted like a flag / your faith stirs and exalts you.* After the war, she had been obliged to go into exile in the Soviet Union and had held various posts in Moscow related to the spreading of communist thought to the countries of Latin America. She eventually moved to Havana, where she carried out equality of opportunity assignments in the Ministry of Education. Now, after thirty-seven years of exile, she'd returned to Spain in clandestine fashion to contribute with her presence to the cause of freedom. After his eulogy, the old crock proclaimed her name: Faith Oxen.

That woman was Faith Oxen. Emotion sparked and crackled in my imagination, linked to inner questioning that had never been resolved. The movements in my brain must have been intense, because by now Juana had registered my presence in the crowd and was simply staring at me, with a mixture of curiosity and repugnance. A whirlwind of reminiscences rattled the door to my memories, and when I went to open up, I found myself face-to-face with Gurruchaga and his devious silences; my first years in the Stéfano circus seeped through my perforated soul like a gas heavier than air, whose stench destroyed the will to forget. The lethargic animals, the turbid alcohol downed by pudgy Di Battista, that delicate dust in the noonday light of Córdoba where tragedy hovered in the air, the blows handed out, the book of poems discovered among the junk, with its dry, iron-specked pages, and that indecipherable dedication signed by someone also called "Faith Oxen," and Gurruchaga bleeding on the ground, later handcuffed and taken off to placate forever the insatiable larvae beyond the grave, were the tesserae that immediately contrived to shape that immense fragment in the mosaic of my life. I still possessed that copy of the *Gypsy Ballads*; it was perhaps the only thing to escape the debacle of the bailiffs the day I fled from the Stéfano circus. That item was the only thing left linking me to the events of my adolescence. I couldn't restrain myself a moment more and tugged on Cambrón's shirtsleeve to tell him of my anxiety. "Ceferino, I must talk to that old woman, whatever it costs." "Shut up, Gregorio, and just listen to what they're saying. If you like, we'll go over there when the meeting finishes."

I don't know whether the harangue is a genuine literary genre of the kind classified by academics in the black and white of their erudition, or if it is merely a fevered offshoot of oratory, but I can vouch for the fact that when it's born in the belly and blossoms virgin on the lips of the person spouting without deadening rhetorical frills or nonsense that could send it off track, a harangue can scare anyone, more because of the cataclysms predicted than any vehemence of tone. Even so, I assure you that political harangues have never disturbed me, and even less so in the period I'm now describing to you when the specter of done deals hovering over our heads meant that all that saliva expended in revolutionary-style pantomimes—as dead as the proverbial doornail the moment they were spat forth—was wasted. I don't remember a word of the harangue delivered by Faith Oxen that night. All I retain from that first encounter is the faded purple of an old woman's eyes embedded like raisins among her face's rococo wrinkles, and the resonant tone of her cavernous voice. After fists were raised—a forest of flesh and bone—and the seraphic lyrics of the Communist International chorused by that whole gathering, the event was concluded, naturally only after those assembled had been encouraged to continue demanding a revolutionary general strike and to maintain their cast-iron commitment to struggle against and defeat that species of "Francoist monarchy" imposed by the tyrant's urge to continue forever.

Almost all those present, their hearts fired up by that hot air, noisily began to leave the building, without a care in the world, as if it had been a nephew's christening party. A cold supper had been laid out on the upper floor for the speakers and bigger fish from party ranks. Those who'd been on the platform were already heading upstairs. At the end of the meeting, the people milling around Faith Oxen made it impossible to get near her, so I insisted to Ceferino that I must speak to her. Cambrón grabbed my shoulder and pulled me along until we reached the second floor. On the last step of the stairs, someone stopped us and refused us access, on the pretext that it was a closed-door meeting. Cambrón raised an arm and gestured to an individual who seemed to be bossing others around, whom he must have known, because we were immediately granted entry.

Generally people find dwarves to be repulsive. They immediately associate them with the world of the circus and a wretched life on the road; although there is some truth in that, the fact they may be right doesn't give them *carte blanche* to act with contempt. Faith Oxen stood and looked at me in amazement when I started telling her about Gurruchaga, about the dedication in the book of poems, his arrest in Córdoba, and as a diabetic tear sweetened the whites of her eyes, she came over and patted me on the head, not without a certain degree of reserve, as if she wanted to alleviate my suffering with her laying on of hands. That night, she told me how Gurruchaga had been executed after being taken to a northern prison and given a summary trial for high treason carried out under military jurisdiction. She'd found out, so she told me, from a British historian she'd hobnobbed with in Havana, one who'd been collecting eyewitness accounts of political executions in order to write a book about repression in Fascist Spain. I was really upset and deeply moved when I heard her repeat the last words he uttered before the execution squad: "More worms will eat *your* leftovers, you motherfuckers," a sentence of extraordinary beauty coming from a man who was usually so spare in what he said. It has to be a bad end when you see the bullet whizzing straight toward you to drill through your heart; it must be even worse when you don't see it because you're so terrified of dying. The tables were littered with Spanish omelets, chorizo and ham canapés, and plates of Manchego cheese and *jamón serrano* sliced into small morsels. Wine was a large demijohn of Valdepeñas whose only virtue was its high alcohol content. Some twenty or twenty-five people of those at the meeting must have stayed on and were now jabbering away with mouths full. I was struck by the huge array of political posters on the walls, with helmeted workers in overalls and peasants carrying scythes scandalously hogging the show as if they'd just finished an apocalyptic harvest. Perhaps in the end Esteruelas was right when he declared that everything now happening was the fruit of an international communist conspiracy against the unity of Spain. Cambrón was chomping on his food as I'd never seen him do with any meal at the Trinitarians', and it was obvious he placated his hunger here with his fellow believers, and I can tell you that the way the expression on his face changed indicated it was a blissful communion more than a mere meal. When I saw him crunching with such panache, as if he'd never enjoyed the vanities of this world so wholeheartedly, I was reminded of the lines by Blas he used to recite when he played the bereft victim in the metro—*like a wretched shipwrecked sailor*

239

moaning and swallowing sea as he swam—and I silently laughed myself silly, realizing that the foolish side of humanity isn't necessarily betrayed by bodily expression but by what is said or thought, and even felt or suffered. I don't know what moved her to do so, but Faith Oxen then introduced me to the rest of her party comrades as a companion skilled in the struggle against man's exploitation of man, interpreting my life story as she thought fit, recounting how I'd suffered humiliation, persecution, and ostracism galore, and she asked those present to show solidarity toward me as she tenderly patted my undersized skull as one might treat a dog that's been injured, a fool's ideas, or a poet's verses. For the first time in my life, apart from feeling humiliated, I felt exposed to people's hypocritical sympathy, and hatred burnished with a veneer of pride that went to my brain, and that's why when Blond Juana, coming on to me in public, loudly asked what my line of work might be, so everybody could hear, I brazenly retorted that I had two main lines, begging for alms in church doorways, and spending my earnings on whores, the pricey kind one finds on the Calle Doctor Fleming.

For months I attended classes on "theory" imparted in the party locale, not because I was hooked, as you'll see from what I'm telling you, but hoping that such close contact would give me leads that might be useful to One-Eyed in his campaign to cleanse the nation. I learned about their ideas, sniffed through the ashes of their lives, and ran their errands, too, whatever I was bid—from buying toilet paper in a drugstore to delivering messages, from finding a pharmacist on late-night duty in order to purchase sanitary towels for a disciple in a tizzy because she'd run out, to giving out leaflets, stickers, and pamphlets—even at some personal risk. Madrid was simmering in an amazing way not even Esteruelas could have anticipated a short time ago. Agitation was rife on the streets; workers, students, and motley activists were daubing sidewalks with anti-Fascist slogans in favor of freedom. Clandestine plotting, instability, and terrorist actions by Basques or far-right extremists meant the people remained silent, because they weren't sure what to say, rather than from any well-founded fear about losing their well-being. The people were ignorant, were used to being sidelined, cherished caution and mediocrity. A people sustained by a homely odor of fireside belches, a people with no critical awareness, no historical perspective, happy to slumber on in a frivolous life of routine and gossip. Their cowardly fear prevented them from seeing how the financial oligarchy and multinational capitalism, dismissing any decisions they might want to take and mocking any so-called popular sovereignty, had decided in advance how Spain would emerge as a democracy. I discovered things, heard rumors, mined nuggets of information I quickly passed on to One-Eyed when we agreed to meet in La Copa for a few shots of firewater before filling our gullets with the ever more dish-watery broth served up by the Trinitarians. "Dwarfy, you're doing a good job, keep it up, I've got it from a good source that one of ours, by the name of Suárez, is going to lead the government, and you just watch how we'll get rid of all this scum in one fell swoop," and then, each bunny ran back to its burrow in the oasis of the Mansion, he bedded down with his nun, and I between the sheets with my obsessions, dwelling on all kinds of rude thoughts stirred by none other than Blond Juana.

Every morning, as a rule, I'd set up on the steps up to Los Jerónimos before poking my nose into the political scene in Madrid. I'd hold out a hand and ask for alms in a fine, witty fashion, perhaps spurred on by the place's grandiose ambience. For a decent tip I gave a local, I was kept informed about the times of weddings, christenings, and the solemnest funerals, so that when a sacrament or a funeral mass was in the offing, I quickly covered myself in scabs and dirt to dupe the fools and rake it in with all those feelings of sympathy I aroused in others. Once, when a funeral was held at a tense political moment after some military officers had been massacred, I witnessed Fascists booing and jeering at Cardinal Tarancón, lambasting him as a red mason and worker priest, bawling at him, "Out! Out! Out!" and if he'd not cleverly beaten a retreat, they'd have made their point with fisticuffs and given him a drubbing there and then. I remember how I hauled in a good catch that day, it was like Jesus multiplying the fishes, if that doesn't sound irreverent in the context; the truth is that when emotion and feeling run riot, purses loosen and coins rain down like manna from heaven.

Now and then, rather than patiently waiting for these hallowed ceremonies in all weathers, I'd nip into the nearby Prado Museum, a famous warehouse for paintings like few others in the world, as I'd later discover, and wander through its rooms, marveling at portraits of saints and virgins, looking lingeringly at the food contained in still lives, and ecstatically enjoying landscapes imagined three centuries ago by the lunatic brush of an artist by the name of Bosch: cuddling pigs in nuns' wimples, stark naked men on all fours being sodomized with flageolets, amatory threesomes caught in the act behind the transparent cellophane of budding flowers, women practicing love with strange fauna, and a whole series of madcap acts the artistic beauty of which brought on my biggest ever erections. When I could stand it no longer, I shut myself in the gents, sat in the stench of those stalls, and jerked off joyfully, masturbations worthy of being put forth as irrefutable evidence at the Last Judgement. Much more so than *Las Meninas* or *Las Lanzas*, I loved to be riveted by Hieronymus's triptychs, savoring the art of that genius among the geniuses the Prado was so well stocked with, and I equally loved to while away my time staring incredulously at the portraits of dwarves and jesters. I was dazzled by the sly yet innocent expression on the mouth of *El niño de Vallecas*, a moron with the contented countenance of a mental defective, like a dog that's just been kicked up the backside and is thrown a bone to chew; I went on a high when I gazed at the gentlemanly aplomb of Don Diego de Acedo, the court jester, alias The Cousin, a high-placed functionary in Philip IV's castle whose job it was to imprint the monarch's signature on pages in books of state, an exalted task for one so ridiculously small and repellently misshapen. Why couldn't I be like that, in another epoch, in another monarchy? I asked myself disconsolately, and although the answer was self-evident, Providence deliberately kept quiet to ensure I ranted and raged. But of all the paintings of dwarves, freaks, and monsters hoarded in the Prado, the one I preferred, perhaps because of a striking physical similarity to me, was the *Portrait of Sebastián de Morra*, so beautiful in his crimsons and golds, in a smart green tunic worthy of a prince, a real Don Dwarf, who served Cardinal Infante in Flanders and immediately on his return to Spain, on the highest recommendation, entered the service of Prince Baltasar Carlos, whom he accompanied on hunting trips and whose will bequeathed him a silver dress sword on a leather strap, with matching sabre and dagger, together with another knife and two scallops with fleurs-de-lis. Deceased in 1649, that man gazed out at me from the painting, sitting just as I sat, sprawling woefully on the floor, bandy-legged, with an identically sad, cunning look, with that glint bad habits lends your eyes and necessity places on your lips. His breathing felt so close it seemed to escape from the depths of the canvas and crystallize in words within my inner ear, almost to the point of a whisper, and at some stage he may have even uttered in this vein: "I am you, learn to be dignified like me, establish your dominion in this world, arise and command, you oaf, or you'll never be more than an idealized version of yourself fashioned at your own expense by a word merchant." I didn't understand why that man's pose and aura seemed so strangely familiar. The intensity of his presence made me reflect on my own life and random, roaming condition, and also evoked in some way that visceral portrait of me painted in Benalmádena, as if such a paradox were a kind of gift I'd inherited from the past, a threatening specter of myself that never again abandoned me. Over time I discovered why. Providence was playing a joke on me. It was ever thus with geniuses; they immediately know where to find the inspiration they need to give material form to their own neurotic obsessions.

Events seemed to unfold at a headlong pace. Madrid dawned plastered in posters publicizing the imminent referendum in which the people were to be consulted about their longing for freedom; the Cortes had just passed a draft law for political reform. Summer had been a turbulent affair, with manifold ups and downs in the pigsties of power. Unable to keep pulling the rotten, ramshackle chariot of Francoism, Arias Navarro refused to continue, and the king of Spain, filling a gap with sly sleight of hand, had appointed Adolfo Suárez, an obscure bureaucrat with pretensions to fairness, to preside over the Council of Ministers. Every second, rumors of a military coup swamped the city center's gossip mill, simmering more than ever, from the hot air of so many vipers licking their lips in the hope of provoking destabilization. Even so, gambling with Spanish history in cavalier style, Suárez had used the summer months to prepare a draft law that, once approved by the Cortes, would precipitate the collective suicide of Francoism. The hara-kiri nature of the proposed reform stood out a mile, but only patriots of the old stripe displayed their dignity at such an insult and proudly exercised their right to resign. The Vice-President for Defense made angry public declarations in which he revealed that the government was preparing measures to authorize free trade unions, which, in his view, would lead to the legalization of the CNT and UGT trade-union organizations that had sparked the upheaval in the red zones during the Civil War. Then, pride smitten, he abandoned his post to the providential fate of the times. In the end, one September 19, the intrigues bore fruit, and the draft law was passed by 425 votes with 59 abstentions. Madrid dawned disguised in posters that hundreds of volunteers for freedom had stuck up overnight, cock-a-hoop with their buckets of paste, puerile patter, and packets of Ducados. "Speak, People, Speak," they said, "Seize The Time, Don't Let Them Decide For You," and all those who only a year ago had looked on, their hearts stricken, as the Caudillo entered the territory of Charon, people who'd never been perturbed by their own silences or the eager eloquence of others keen to decide on their behalf, suddenly emerged from their cubbyholes and dashed into the streets to participate feverishly in that novel puppet show they were being offered by the powers-that-be.

Such aspirations for freedom, expressed without anger, might seem banal or at the very least frivolous in the confusion at the twilight of a millennium when human beings are fully aware that they belong to a global tribe that worships statistics, monothematic thought, market profitability, and football the redeemer. Not then, when vehemence, spontaneous passion, verbal diarrhea, and inflammatory harangues were the craze. They wanted sovereignty to reside in the people, and the Spanish people, so they said, had come of age; they should express themselves, and so they did, just as they were asked to do. Not everybody wanted the same things, naturally, and while many hadn't a clue as to what was looming around the corner, others, the champions of wealth, longed to stake out positions, do deals, and weld minds together in order to seal the foundations of a new Spain that, apart from expounding freedom, equality, and political pluralism as the supreme values of its legal system, would also guarantee—and how!—their very own survival and perpetuation.

After a disconcerting morning when the habitués of Los Jerónimos gave fewer alms than usual, perhaps because of the unease felt by their purses after the announcing of the referendum, I met up with Ceferino, and we wended our way to the party locale. The dizzy pace of events probably meant there were new positions and opinions it was my duty to investigate. We'd not eaten, and my guts were in funeral-march mode. When we arrived, they treated us to a few shots of Anís del Mono, and after we'd knocked those back, a crowd began to assemble, desperate to receive the new party lines and slogans to fit the fresh circumstances. Faith Oxen arrived in midafternoon, looking well fed and digested after a siesta, though her manner reflected a good deal of despair. "There can be no voting without freedom," she clamored from the podium of her prestige. "Don't let's be deceived by this plebiscite fraud, by this insult to the people. Many comrades are still in exile, and others are risking their skins daily in clandestine activities; political parties are banned, the police persecute us, intent on repressing and jailing us, and now they summon you to a referendum. They're laughing in your faces. Their proposals are an insult. Say no to them, at the tops of your voices, tell them there can be no voting without freedom, no freedom without struggle, take to the streets, promote abstention, and call for a workers' republic where there'll be no place for them." The crowd gathered there applauded her diatribe, took good note of what had to be done, and left, looking forward to doing what was necessary. The few of us who stayed behind were invited to a snack at Faith Oxen's place so we could follow developments from there. "Gregori," which was how she addressed me now in her insufferable Russo-Caribbean accent, "go and buy some Cantimpalo chorizos and a few bottles of beer so the comrades have something to drink," she instructed me before I left the locale, and, of course, all of a piece with her proverbial meanness, she didn't give me a single five-peseta coin to pay for it.

From that day on, Faith Oxen decided to make me her errand boy and put me under her orders; I'm not sure whether she wanted to demean me even further, or take advantage of my meek, biddable disposition. I reacted angelically, as I was interested in being in close contact with her; I ran to obey her and adopted a submissive, humble attitude when it was time to get fruit for dessert, bread for lunch, or toilet paper for her backside, so we soon established a sickly relationship based on subservience, servitude, and deference. "Gregori," she'd say, "just realize you are a pariah on this earth, and rejoice, because soon you will have to rise up and topple the tyrants of this world," and I'd stand, look at her, and un-successfully try to detect a touch of conscious irony in her drift. Behind the façade of political commitment and the militant tenor of her past, she was simply someone who'd emancipated herself from humanity, a robotic offshoot she'd spawned to defend the monopoly of her own self-interest. One could have defined her attitude when I got to know her as senile and selfish; when she participated in the rallies or committee meetings she attended, the aura of her prestige convincingly fazed all those idiots who mistook revolution for arteriosclerosis and manic depression for the struggle. "We'll never accept a Spain whose flag isn't the tricolor, whose symbols aren't those of the workers and peasants. We'll never tolerate a nation of serfs who have to bow before a king. We'll never cease to battle until the wealth of the country is taken from the hands of the exploiters, and we'll never take a step backwards—not even to take a breather." And so she rattled on in a way she had learned in her youth, flourishing her cape in the most packed arenas of the nation's Left, where a few Stalinist geniuses and a similar clutch of geriatric internal exiles hung on her every word as if their lives depended on it, or at the very least the survival of their own memories. After the speeches, it was my job to accompany her home—a comfortable, bourgeois house rented for her in Alonso Martínez—and there I helped her undress, put on her slippers, and cooked any dish she asked for to cope with her hunger. Then I'd give Slim the list of names I jotted down and tell him in hushed whispers the things that happened both in the party meetings and the old girl's house. I sometimes exaggerated in order to keep him happy and continue as a spy, thus sparing myself the need to beg, an activity that was really starting to irk me now I was soaking up all that communist doctrine. He'd set up a meeting with Esteruelas to pass on my news, and he'd inflate what I'd told him, inciting the inspector to order beatings or shoot-outs performed by the wild men of the Far Right.

Faith Oxen, that fine female whose lips swelled when she spoke of the equality of human beings, treated her peers with an intolerable haughtiness worthy of medieval times. Generally

250

she reserved her blatant displays of arrogance for when she was humiliating an opponent or someone who simply dared to uphold contrary ideas. What's more, she would appeal straight away to the lives of those who had died defending the ideals she preached, and she made their self-sacrifice her irrefutable argument, which she systematically used to demolish the conflicting opinions of those who dared disagree. "Get up and be gone from this room, and remember, if you dare, those who fell in combat defending our ideas. They're the ones to whom you should be showing the respect you don't show me." Everybody went silent and looked remorseful, and nobody spoke again to contradict her. Her kingdom belonged to another world, and as times switched to a democratic path, she was gradually relegated to the junk room, kept well out of sight with other pains in the neck, and was only let out to be exhibited in party jamborees as a quaint relic from Spanish history. However, she preferred to ignore her new role as an occasional extra and turned up to rallies with her dignity wrapped in astrakhan, her greasy hair sleek against her skull, her nostrils thin and aquiline, and a contemptuous glint in her hazy eyes, as if she were plotting evil. I played the part of the obedient servant, and whenever the opportunity presented itself, I'd accompany her and flatter her ego by listening silently to the worn-out tales of struggle she told with all the digressions that come with old age. She'd sit in an armchair, and I'd curl up at her feet on the parquet. Propelled by the distant lilt of her verbal diarrhea into the ether of time, she liked to run her fingers through my curly hair. I've never been able to stand caresses received from a height different to mine. I sensed the hypocrisy in her gestures and her vital fluids calcifying in her whines. An old has-been. I can tell you I got used to running her errands and bringing her shopping home, and as I unpacked the bags, I could gauge the extent of the dementia leaking from her outsize ego. "Gregori, put the fruit in the fridge or it will get covered in moths. Fruit isn't what it used to be, there are no melons like the ones we got from Villaconejos before the war. My mother used to put them in the pantry, and our house would be flooded with sugar. The Fascists bombed them to smithereens."

I found myself a comfy corner in her house and wheedled from her tortuous chatter information I could pass on to One-Eyed in order to perpetuate my period of leave. Sometimes she'd go doe-eyed and nostalgic and talk about Gurruchaga and the many other lovers she proudly confessed to. She did so coldly, distantly, as if love for her were only the crystallization of desire. She detailed the stalactites and stalagmites of her amorous whims and languidly dwelt on the lost moments of her youth with that "oh, if I were only thirty years younger" you hear so often from individuals who find they've missed the train to the future. My impression was of someone with truncated emotions whose only links to humanity were her memories and her contempt. Apart from that, I can only point to how I began to cultivate an interest in delving into people's wily ways, how that shaped my attitude from then on, and how I liked to serve her faithfully as a dog does its master. She was a communist, but I was a beggar and as such awash with trash, remnants, and gifts that weren't helping me to prosper in life. I was sick of having to endure life in the Trinitarian Mansion, of tolerating the nuns' stinking boiled greens and the bad breath that always accompanied the fake goodness of their smiles. Living in Faith's plush pile at least comforted me with the thought that

I was under a different roof, away from God's charity and safe from the fleas harbored by all the bereft tramps now holed up in the city.

I spied on her with pleasure and a clear conscience. I enjoyed unscrupulously scrutinizing every hour she perpetrated in this world. When someone visited her, I'd put my ear to the sitting-room door that had been shut tight, and, keeping quiet, drawing on my seven senses, I'd catch the thrust of whatever was being debated. I loved lazing around the old girl's house, whiling away my time sniffing the sweetish aroma given off by mahogany furniture, or contemplating the paintings from every school that hung on the walls in flagrant contradiction to any claims to austerity. I put so much energy into my job, I soon found out a number of domestic matters. I discovered, for example, that the money to pay for that quite un-proletarian apartment came from a current account in a Paris bank that had been opened in the name of one Pierre Brouard, a putative son who clearly devoted himself to the real estate business and who, except for the financial side of his gratitude, displayed no emotional attachment at all, and that tore at her and creased her with sorrow for wasting those far-off maternal moments on politicking. In my guise as a cheap-jack spy, I also discovered the ins and outs of the promiscuity the old girl enjoyed in her good old days of fun in the sack, to the point that I began to see her as a class act in the crack rather than any champion of the virtues of universal communism; such was her passion for raw meat, I sometimes got the shivers when I felt the lusty breath powering her words, not because I was at all pernickety about the pleasures of the groin, rather I was afraid that if I yielded to her whims, she might pop a spring and die on the spot. I became aware of other facts that are irrelevant, which I won't pass on, so you can while away your time trying to imagine them; they all revealed a tortured, mean personality, an example of a life misspent in sterile activity. I'd spill most of these beans to Slim, but not the lot, and so, *piano piano*, I slowly honored our accord, and he, in turn, passed on the goods in doses to Esteruelas to cure the ills *he* seemed to be suffering much more than Spain; although ultimately there was no stopping all the hot-headedness and sooner or later the end had to come. In that whirlwind of anxiety, self-interest, and contradiction, everyone was quick to profess ignorance of any blame, and although we all bore the seeds of our own penitence, the future was overtaking us in a rush and entirely unpredictably. Only Providence, with its unerring desire to ignore man's freedom, had any previous knowledge of our sad, intense, inevitable finales: Esteruelas's and One-Eyed's—their brains smattered next to the whipped cream from atop a stack of pancakes in a upmarket cafeteria on the Calle Goya; that of poor Ceferino, lousily beaten to death like a dog; the demise, in great agony, at the mercy of my pleasure, of Faith Oxen; and now, suddenly, my very own, so ridiculous and small-scale, as couldn't be otherwise for someone my size.

One morning, as I arrived almost suffocated by the load of fruit and vegetables I'd had to hump up the stairs, my bones aching because the elevator engine was out of order, I was surprised to find Faith talking behind closed doors to a group of people who'd dropped by. I slipped into the room on the pretext that I had to tell her about my troubles on the stairs, but she was annoyed by my presence, and her withering look indicated I should make myself scarce. I'd never seen many of those present, and others I only recognized because I'd seen them in a clandestine meeting or two. I opened the kitchen door and left the door to the lobby half-open so I could try to hear what they were talking about. They were asking her to support the so-called Democratic Platform established under the auspices of the Spanish Communist Party. They wanted her to commit to a united Left that could manage a political transition based on democratic reform. A tall bearded man who said he'd just come from Rome announced that Santiago Carrillo was preparing a press conference in Madrid that would be attended by leading foreign journalists like Oriana Fallaci and Marcel Niedergang. They hoped that their presence would bring forward the legalization of the Communist Party and rally international support for the political option they had chosen. He also related how Enrique Líster and La Pasionaria had formally requested the Suárez Government issue them Spanish passports through a Spanish consulate in a city behind the Iron Curtain. More than ever, the Left needed to unite all its forces behind a common strategy for the future, not a single group should remain outside the front, and neither should Faith Oxen, because of her charisma and ideological standing, and also, it had to be said, because she'd had the courage to return to the country before anyone else, so she should feel duty-bound to support the position that would usher in an irrevocable expansion of freedoms. Ear on the alert, I took note of everything. I finally had concrete information that would enable me to bring my mission to a successful conclusion. I rubbed my hands together, though with a degree of lethargy I struggled to explain; I didn't want to fall back into the grubby ways symbolized by Slim, I'd accustomed myself too easily to my parasitic life with the old girl, and returning to life on the street didn't appeal one bit. Perhaps it was Providence who made the decision for me about such a change, for, though I wasn't in the know, it had lined up new territories of reality for me to explore. Faith Oxen got up from the armchair where she'd sat listening, the one where she'd stroked the curls on my skull, and, drily grandiloquent, she accused them all of being revisionists, self-interested delinquents, and traitors to the working-class. She said that the strategy for struggle could never encompass alliances with bourgeois parties or any others that weren't bourgeois but denied that the class struggle was the determining force in history. She then ran them out of her house, and they all left with their ears down, their tails between their legs, daring to say little or nothing to change the mind of that old fruitcake who must have smashed her pot of common sense to smithereens on the barricades of '36.

That very night the Trinitarians served up mussels boiled in dishwater and oxtail stew smelling of turnips for dinner. I sat next to Slim. I remember he hadn't trimmed his beard for two or three days. He'd been busy sorting out a couple of territorial disputes that, from what he said, were settled with knives in the quiet, early hours. The newspapers had blamed the murder on a Far Right that was out of control, and Esteruelas was annoyed by the unplanned complication Slim had triggered off his own bat. "I've got red-hot news, Slim," I said, sucking on a disgusting mussel. "Carrillo is planning to give a press conference in Madrid. The reds want to close ranks around him and secure the legalization of the Communist Party. Everyone but the old girl seems to be in agreement, but nobody takes any notice of her anymore." Slim stroked my skull, feigning friendship, and expressed his delight at the news I brought him rather offhandedly. "This is all very good, dwarfy, but now you must find out when and where. You can't string Esteruelas along with tittle-tattle. Get that old whore to tell you; trick her, do what it takes, get into her bed if necessary, but tell me something really useful. Things are well and truly fucked, and our survival depends on us having our wits about us. You understand me, don't you, dwarfy? You do know what will happen to us if we don't get what we're after? Just remember that you're doing what you're doing for your own good, and I should hardly have to add how upset I'd be if you had a mishap because you weren't doing your job properly." Slim went to his room early. When I walked past his door I didn't hear the nun shouting or a pig grunting. In the dense silence of those passageways, an acidic noise froze me inside; the hinges of my life were creaking badly.

Everything is written in the ineffable book of destiny, my life's a closed chapter, and it's your job to bring it to an end. The most hurtful violence that can be inflicted on a human being is the revelation of his lack of freedom, the predictability of his behavior, the exact outcome of his acts, even the exact date of his death. You have come here to amuse yourself with mine. You have intervened in my past purely to give it the endpoint it merits. Your presence in my story underlines how the savage reality of existence counts for naught, outplayed by the conviction that nothing, absolutely nothing, depends on individual will. We are simply spectators at our own tragedy, and we applaud and congratulate ourselves for our brilliant performances without registering the *deus ex machina* that guides our behavior according to a pre-established plan. The final applause is so much sarcasm or belly laughter; only when the curtain falls completely do we grasp what has happened.

Ceferino Cambrón paraded haughtily down metro passageways, hawking his trashy goods, as if by fulfilling some archangelic initiative, he'd thrive in a tramp's miserable guise. Charitable Trinitarian broth kept him alive, and the party catechism still nourished his spiritual appetite on the false creed of working-class equality. Poor Ceferino, he didn't ever manage to see that the earth would never become the paradise for humanity he dreamed of—not even at the moment of death. I'd spelt it out to him clearly enough just before. "Hey, Ceferino, leave me in peace with the old girl, and don't meddle in my affairs. If you hobble my business, you'll be the one to suffer." "Gregorio, you've no sense of dignity. You're a little swine only interested in your own gain, and I swear you'll never do that to the detriment of our ideals. I'll take your life first with my own hands." "You're a fool, Cambrón, you've let yourself be duped by a fantasy, you believe in things you can't see, you've wasted half your life on an illusory ideal and don't even realize that all the old girl is doing is leeching off the marrow in your bones, that you and your ilk are only of use to her as a pretext for staying alive. You chose the wrong world, and you'll die not understanding you're in the way here. Clear off, carry on fantasizing elsewhere, and leave me in peace. I'll say one last thing: don't ever threaten me again, or you'll regret it."

Ceferino Cambrón continued scraping a livelihood from his ideals until the night he lost his life. He met a bad end, a bad end very like what bastards get, though, if the truth be told, it might have been worse. I had no choice but to ask Slim to get rid of him. He was about to ruin my plans by telling Faith Oxen about my spurious behavior, even though I now reckon it wouldn't have changed my relationship with her one iota; on the contrary, she'd have been turned on by the idea of figuring large in a conspiracy. Sometimes I think that if Ceferino told anybody, it must have been Blond Juana. I never got round to asking her, and over the years I had opportunities to see her in different circumstances to those when her attitude toward me was one of hatred and violence to the point that whenever we coincided at an event, the only reason she didn't kick me in the mouth was her fear of besmirching her shoe on my sticky blood. Poor Ceferino, his poor damned life, on the ground, blood pouring everywhere and nobody coming to help. I don't deny that in another context and era, given his lean, willowy demeanor, he could have ended up heading some autonomous government body, the sort that come with a ready-made budget for their programs, but it wasn't to be. As I've said, things don't happen exactly as one wants but as they are ordained, and thirty-odd blows to the head, torso, and extremities well and truly did for him. "Take that, you piece of red shit, that will teach you; shout *arriba España!* Take that, you bastard, and stop fucking with us, shout *viva Franco, arriba España, viva Cristo Rey!*" He never kept back a peseta for himself. The little he earned selling his escapist garbage in metro passageways, he handed over to the party kitty. Other less inhibited comrades splashed out on lottery tickets and tasty midmorning breakfasts with big, greasy churros; that was the limit of it. He'd have been better off giving in and begging for One-Eyed, but, you know, that couldn't have worked. His corpse was so bashed to pulp, you could see through it. The trashmen found the bits next morning by some containers and almost mistook them for leftover scraps; at that time of day people are really sleepy, and it's hard to gauge what's in the rubbish. They took nine hours to ID him, he was so mashed up. "Ceferino's been beaten up, the *fachas* have beaten him to death!" Blondie shouted as she strode into the party locale. "Let's get after them; kill 'em all!" It was very tense, noisy, and uncertain; frightened and upset by the situation, I kept quiet and then suddenly realized I'd been the real cause of his death. "Fascist Murderers, Murderous Cops" is what they painted on walls the whole day long and well into the night, until a new day dawned, the sky turned blue, and, their desire for revenge poorly sated, they returned to their homes slightly less worse for wear; in the end it all came to nothing.

The following day, when I went to add the sourness of his death to the Trinitarians' broth, Slim sat down next to me, put his arm round my shoulder, stared into my eyes, and rasped, "Dwarfy, do you believe in hell?"

I collected the bundles of banned books and dirty mags that were Ceferino's stock-in-trade and, without giving them a glance, handed them over to one of the nuns to give out to the poor, all except for the one by Blas de Otero, the one where he was so fond of rediscovering himself. Rather than selling or giving them away, the nun burnt them with the coal for the boiler, creating a hotter flame than usual, which, like frustrated desire or lingering hunger, escaped with a sigh up the Mansion's chimneys. Nevertheless, I still read those lines when I am feeling desperate—*a generation with no other fate than to shore up the ruins*—and I am reminded of Cambrón's fate and don't feel a smidgeon of sorrow.

What's left at the end of a life? Very little, perhaps a small corner of one's memory to recall the pleasurable provinces of the flesh visited in one's youth, nostalgia for the tasty dishes enjoyed with gusto and digested at leisure in the uncertain shadows of the future, or the distant relish in one's mouth of cigar smoke smoked in the languor left by desire. (The scent of tobacco mixed with genital odors creates an unparalleled mass of morose aromas. The end result bewitches and fascinates. After copulating, nothing beats lighting up a good cigar, playing with the smoke in one's mouth, and exhaling the rings around the dampness of the other's sex; the heady blast curls through the air, annihilates the will, and justifies existence—and how!) What's left at the end of a life? The little things, the gestures, the details, the awareness that everything is preordained, even the universe's final big bang.

Santiago Carrillo didn't smoke cigars, he lit up cigarettes endlessly, one after another, as if daisy-chaining them. He once told me he couldn't help himself, when I asked him about it while we were waiting together before a radio chat show where, in one of those weird twists of fate, we'd coincided as guests. We discussed everything under the sun: the onset of dumbing down, the fall of the Wall, the growth of fast food, and the hunger ravaging the planet. Someone defended the impelling need to fairly distribute agro-food over-production stocks, and the rational control of waste products and emissions as perhaps the only valid ways to guarantee the sustainable survival of the species. To have fun and be polemical, I argued over the mike for the thesis that international organizations should act as vehicles to provide countries in need with fast food. Then I played the demagogue and spoke of the need to expropriate the territory of governments who were incapable of ensuring the survival of their inhabitants, and the need to exploit the riches—whether natural or otherwise—that they possessed through sales to multinational financial corporations and companies, and that provoked a flood of telephone protests that blocked the station's switchboard.

If I'd felt like it that day, I might have confessed to Carrillo that I'd participated in the plot cooked up at the end of 1976 that led to his arrest on December 22, seven days after the voice of the people backed with a massive yes vote the referendum for political reform in which it had been summoned to participate. I might have spelt out how it happened, chapter and verse, how, in the old girl's apartment, I'd found out when and where he was to put in an appearance and hold a clandestine press conference to announce his party's conciliatory positions, and that I rushed to the Interior Ministry to betray him. I might have told him about One-Eyed Slim, Inspector Esteruelas, and the snooping that went on at the time in Madrid, but Providence decided it didn't want me to. I might have let on about my sickly relationship with Faith, the way I discovered he was round and about in the Spanish capital sporting a wig, but he'd have stared at me, not really believing a word, in that sardonic manner that comes with maturity, and no doubt he'd have discounted the importance of my betrayal by declaring that half Madrid knew what he was up to, and that a return to normality for the Communist Party, and, likewise, for himself, was the only possible outcome Spanish history would have tolerated.

We shook hands when we said goodbye. I don't know if he liked what I said, or not. He was probably struck by the fact that such extremely free-market opinions about international relations should come from the mouth of a dwarf. I opted to tell him nothing about what I knew about the past; at the end of the day, amnesia was one of the cornerstones of national reconciliation. Besides, had I done so, I'm sure he'd have asked me what I'd earned from my squealing, and I'd then have confronted the moral dilemma of whether or not to answer *a night out with whores*, which wasn't totally untrue, given that One-Eyed turned up that day with a bunch of the pricey sort.

Because of Slim's daily exposure to the elements, a bout of pneumonia that wasn't properly treated penetrated his skin and bones, leaving his fingers limp, his mind twisted, and his pick-pocketing skills laid to waste, which meant his professional activities rather bit the dust. Already undermined by the quantity of ex-jailbirds now on the scene, his prestige hit rock bottom. Times called for a change of tactics, and the tricks that had always worked in the day-to-day flow were now consigned to the museum of has-beens, whilst delinquents and petty criminals sought fresh dubious practices. Slim finally had to resort to snooping for the police, a line that would die a death with the advent of democracy. The subterranean world of the opposition was starting to spring from the silt where it had been sidelined; over forty peaceful years, it had hawked its civil-war baggage through the network of sewers and other, possibly less pestilent, underground channels. Some of his perennial payers continued to pass on to Slim the tithe he collected for permitting them to beg in hallowed places or thieve in crowded spots, whether at bull fights or soccer matches, but they did so more out of tradition than respect and didn't realize there was no longer any reason to do so.

The tenor of the era, with its networks of well-organized international mafias without cultural affiliations, beliefs, or eccentricities that could bring to the pursuit of their activities a touch of honor or a spot of gentlemanly courtesy, was all about chasing a fast buck. That Madrid of bygone days, a uniform city with a single voice, where a foreigner would always stick out, was gradually filling up on different races, and overnight, the murky cosmopolitan style of the business they plied became what people smoked and injected.

"Blacks would be the last straw, dwarfy, I told you so some time ago," Slim grumbled at the start of 1978, still lolling back and languidly savoring firewater in the backrooms of La Copa de Herrera. "Fucking blacks, fucking our daughters and tainting our bloodlines," and Señor Antonio, oblivious to the maelstrom that would very soon convert his own establishment into a cheerful hamburger outlet, poured out at most a cold Coca-Cola to whoever ordered one, accompanied, naturally, by a small dish of roasted chickpeas or lupin beans.

In the mornings, I'd got into the habit of taking Faith Oxen a basket with the day's purchases—bread, fresh milk, meat, fish, cold sausage, and pastries—filling her pantry with my efforts in return for her caresses and crumbs. She had a crazy sweet tooth and shed tears galore when she poked the tip of her tongue into Chantilly cream or chewed one of the nuns' cakes. I left my cot in the Trinitarians' well before the dawn so I could beg for alms at the early morning masses at San Ginés and las Calatravas before I went shopping. With the money I got, I bought the supplies that I then charged up to Faith, in an endless flow of bills unpaid on the excuse that they corresponded to the kind of victuals I was actually taking her: always the best, naturally.

I wasn't Divine Providence. I was no Saint Francis of Assisi disguised as a dwarf. I did everything out of self-interest, to extract from the old girl the slice of loot she no doubt kept in some hidden spot on her person, to make the most of what her companionship might bring me in the mid-term, which was what happened, though I was forced to put up with a lot from her, certainly much more than what any human being should have to stoop to.

She ordered me to put the fruit on a porcelain tray on a sideboard, so it would perfume the house and prettify the air with its jolly, jesting colors—apple green, mandarin orange, strawberry pink, and peach flesh; though by this time, fruit was straight from cold storage, quickly rotted, and was soon crawling with flies and larvae—a real allegory to putrefaction. "Gregori, make me a cup of coffee and bring it to my bedroom with a croissant and an aspirin," she'd shout when she heard me come in. "Have you bought the cakes I ordered?" And Gregori obediently brought to her bed the breakfast she longed for, in the hope that the neurosis powering her headaches would prostrate her for the day and give me *carte blanche* to pilfer at my pleasure.

The old girl's bedroom stank of dirty clothes and leather parchment. I opened the shutters on purpose, and the polluted Madrid sunlight flooded in through the window and exposed to my eyes the stiff nightdress clinging to the wizened fruit of what were once her charms. My sympathetic smile brought solace to her decrepit old age, and, in exchange, she generously regaled me with words bathed in bad breath and with that look of somebody fresh from the cesspit she always wore when she got up. It was then most of all that I'd recall the moments in Doris's caravan when I started reading the magnificent verse from Federico's book that she, possibly in honor of an extraordinary lay, had decided to give to Gurruchaga, endorsed with her grateful dedication. I imagined him quickly and coarsely mapping her flesh with his tongue, and the hieratic, proud Faith letting herself give pleasure, if only out of a capricious wish to feel dominated for a few seconds. "I have never loved a man," she selfishly confessed, "though they'd come to blows over me, and more than one went crazy," and, waxing nostalgic, she'd slip down her nightdress until it was completely off. "Look at me, am I still desirable?" she'd ask, rubbing her jaded fingertips on the wrinkled parchment of her nipples. "Come here and lick them, tell me what they taste of," and, like a doltish donkey, I lay on the sheets and cooled her body with my saliva, behind and front, up and down, lingering with insane restraint until my phallus was on fire, burning for immediate release, then I'd use a hidden hump on her skeleton to come all over her. Old flesh brings to mind the antediluvian taste of tallow, makes the mouth sticky, and benumbs the palate. When I'd spent my desire on her, puking was the only way I could later unburden my conscience. By entering her flesh, I brought solace to her old bones, and she'd caress me warmly and let herself be served by my well-endowed size. As the months went by, my close scrutiny and charitable scrotum sank us into symbiosis. As the reform process gathered momentum on track to the creation of a lasting constitution and every sort of political tendency became as legal as another, her influence on party activists waned to the point of extinction. Now almost nobody counted on her to tease out strategies or reach agreements on common interests; she was only called upon when a figurehead was needed at some jamboree to vamp up the symbolism on behalf of the festive politics of the day. If it hadn't been for a bunch of youngsters led by Blondie who were swimming against the tide, emphatically pressing for a Nechayevian line, by virtue of which they visited her in order to share their legitimate aspirations as street-fighters, *guerrilleros* on behalf of the dictatorship of the proletariat, she'd have been relegated to sepia photographs, by far the best tint for the antechamber to oblivion. The occasional rookie journalist, one of those who were all for recovering unofficial historical memory, also dropped by from time to time and recorded conversations on a tape recorder, asking her about the behavior of the famous deceased comrades with who she'd shared communion in the faith. One in particular said he was called Señor Cherry or Señor Tree, or something of the sort, and he simply snooped obsessively into her culinary memories, as if the only interesting things to find out about the past were what Durruti had for breakfast or Stalin for afternoon tea; I wonder whatever became of that lad. Faith was still alive but was already imbued with the spectral dimension of a mausoleum.

Toward the end, the old girl's palate, like her blood, turned sticky and sugary, and she recklessly stuffed it with any cake, tart, tidbit, or chocolate her gums could mash. She made me tour the city's cake shops searching for homemade sponge cakes, crystallized flaky pastries, and fondant chocolates. At the time, it was unusual to find that kind of sweet offering, and I often had to work miracles to find any, to the point of being forced to humiliate myself in certain exclusive establishments. When they saw me walk into their hoity-toity shops with polished, gleaming windows that made them look like anterooms to paradise, they'd invite me to leave, afraid I'd scare off their clientele, and I only managed to avoid such a fate by the crude resort—being at the end of my tether— of flashing the bundles of thousand-peseta bills with which I'd pay for their products. Faith Oxen repaid these offerings with treats for me, and if I'd brought anything with merengue, cream, or icing, she'd first anoint my naked skin with a drop for me to try, just in case it had gone off; she was kinky like that, the old hag.

On balmy spring evenings when the swifts were mewling, Faith Oxen would fall asleep listening to the world go round beyond her balcony window. She snored like a trooper, and the house was filled with such a fearsome din, the walls seemed about to collapse. Gazing at her like that, as if she were the living dead, I'd get distressed and feel an ineffable wave of anguish bordering on the supernatural. At such moments of hopeless despair, I made the most of her sleep to make a stealthy exit and head to La Copa de Herrera, where I hoped I might connect with the throbbing pulse of the petty criminal underworld. "Hey, dwarfy, just been doing it with the old girl? See if you set her up so I can suck her off for once. I'm tired of all this waiting about, and you look ever dreamier-eyed, you're not in love by any chance?" Slim would guffaw and spit on the sawdust of La Copa's floor, which was filthy damp and on its rachitic last legs.

Every system tends toward chaos, every human being toward sclerosis. I was growing old in Madrid, and, likewise, Madrid within me. What must happen to a man in life in order for him to fall into the grip of happiness—an unexpected rush of emotion, a whim fulfilled, a dream become reality? Not any amount of gold or whatever gives the world its shine would have sufficed to bring me the beauty I might once have dreamed of. My short skull protrudes, my arms are skinny, the bones supporting my legs are tiny, yet even so I've survived my hostile environment and today meet with praise, congratulations, and laurels. My position is enviable, but perhaps the fact I did nothing to achieve it renders the merit null and void and the unease I can now feel is what made my village childhood miserable, what distressed my adolescence in the circus, and made my youth listless in the agitated, transitional Madrid I'm now describing to you. Nothing made life worth living, and I found no raison d'être in the feverish life of the underworld; the days still went by one after another, *to-day like yesterday, to-morrow like to-day, and always the same*, as Gustavo Adolfo wrote. Every system tends toward chaos—political, economic, social, biological, whatever. Chaos rules, and that's inevitable, because Providence wanted it that way. Every human being tends toward imbalance, sclerosis, and decrepitude. All that matters is to keep the imagination on fire, and maybe ascertain how one is going to fall apart, so as not to be duped by what fate has in store.

The fall of the Regime made life in the city harder. Those in power blamed the crisis on oil prices, the balance of payments, the foreign debt, even Satan's hairy cock, but the truth is that deprivation exhibited its suppurating sores out in the street, while working-class unemployment undermined the most vulnerable homes. Given the situation, indigence ceased to be a profession and became a way of life, pariahs spread and multiplied over the soil of public parks, and the starving legion of those bereft of welfare threw itself on charitable institutions more blatantly and wantonly than ever, as if wanting to guarantee sustenance at the expense of any remnants of personal dignity. The Trinitarian broth was reduced to a shadow of itself; the dishwater they dispensed turned into a metaphor for hot soup. Where once there'd been real chickens, now there were only lumps of chicken concentrate. Times change people's habits and even their way of eating. Cultural practices become standardized, and culinary idiosyncrasies, relegated to museums of anthropology. Hunger ushers in equality but predisposes people for disaster. Frugal diets preserve the organism, though everything has its limits. Vegetables create flatulence, meat accelerates the rotting of the digestive system, fish provokes emotional crises, and alcohol transfixes the brain to the point of drying out any intelligence. It is vital to ward off the inevitable erosion from what you ingest. If you want to survive, not merely my disaster but your very own, eat only boiled greens seasoned with a sprinkle of olive oil, drink only fresh spring water, eat loads of fruit, cleanse your intestines on whole-grain fiber, and show solidarity toward those who are starving on the planet. You'll feel better, you'll feel happier, you'll feel cleaner, and, most likely, you'll be prettier, although, in the end, that won't help you any, either.

Blond Juana would never have wasted a precious moment of her time beautifying an eyelash, bursting a zit in front of the mirror, or powdering her face, even with the cheap stuff. She was happy to dedicate day after day to fighting for her ideals at the cost of her health or bodily wear and tear. The spreading of her Nechayevian, dynamiting vein of revolutionary faith compelled her to do deals with the angels of her imagination, virile, brawny angels bristling with hand grenades, automatic pistols, assault rifles, and all the other tackle necessary for spreading subversion and total chaos throughout the mental breeding grounds of the bourgeoisie, the pastures of the oligarchy, and the capacious mangers of capitalism. Her intense female smell turned me on no end, and when I saw her, I swear to God I had to struggle not to scatter my seed in the immaculate shrine of her womb. To sustain the desire for devastation that was eating her alive, she combined a poorly paid job selling plastic food containers house to house with the distribution of revolutionary pamphlets and union magazines that carried grandiloquent headlines alluding to world-scale catastrophes and planetary-level disasters. She'd ask for a donation in exchange, but her lofty tone scared people, and it mostly boiled down to intimidation poorly camouflaged as buying and selling. She broadcast her material in people's faces at the top of her voice, and the shrill, metallic tone with which she shouted herself hoarse exposed her social pretensions. In truth, only a few purchased such propaganda, and at the end of the day, the newspapers hung over her arm, covered in sweat, their ink blurred. People looked the other way at her because she acted so prickly, and finally it made no difference whether she rang a doorbell or appealed to the conscience of a passerby, everyone tried to dodge her off-putting performances and would have given alms to a dwarf rather than hand over money to her. Nonetheless I felt attracted to her figure from the moment I saw her; it wasn't simply her ample, burly frame, the hint of flesh in her gaze, or the morbid come-on sheen of her fair locks. It's very likely that I lusted for her merely because I aroused so much disgust and contempt in her. In terms of both things and people, the more distant they seem, the more desperate we are to have them. When we bumped into each other at the party locale or a political event, or she visited the old girl in the unscathed privacy of her house, she went out of her way to avoid addressing me, and if compelled to do so, she directed her line of vision above my head, so I wouldn't see my reflection in the watery mirror of her eyes. What splendid twin windows they were, forever blurred by vague, impenetrable sadness, more suited to an abandoned animal than a full-blooded agitator after social justice! "Will you sell me one, Blondie?" I'd say, slavering my words out whenever I came across her in the vicinity of Tirso de Molina, on my way to La Copa de Herrera; she'd be preaching the gospel at full tilt at dusk, trying to offload her burden of libelous prose, but no way would she even deign to give me a reply. Contempt simmered on her lips, and she acted as if I were invisible. "The Voice of the People. For the Destruction of American Bases, an End to Yankee Imperialism on Spanish Soil," and her voice faded behind me, gilded and hollow like the tinkle of false gold.

The day finally came when the imperturbable powers that be, in a historic concession to the eloquence of democracy, decided that the legalization of communism was an evil it could take on board. As it surely had to, this departure materialized under the cover of the Holy Week holidays, when flounces from the bunker were arrayed across the fatherland swathed in the thick smoke of processional candles, backed by prayers and hallowed bursts of flamenco, and wrapped in the folkloric accoutrements of the National Catholicism that gave them their substance. It's worth highlighting that at the time, the official creed, among its many diverse mutilations of leisure, forbad the screening in cinemas of films that didn't exalt the passion and resurrection of Christ. Meanwhile, that other Spain, choked by its exclusion from public ludic zones, embarked on a frenzy of classic petting or feeling-up, or the private consumption of intoxicating resins that had begun to enter the Peninsula from neighboring Moorish lands up the anuses of pushers still rather wet behind the ears, though they did embrace the wayward illusions of youth. In exchange for the legalization of his party, Santiago Carrillo had just pledged to recognize the dynasty of the Bourbons and to adopt as his own the two-colored flag. Released from jail by a government that didn't know what else to do with such an uncomfortable figure, Carrillo showed off his now acceptable face by hosting Berlinguer and Marchais in the Meliá Castilla hotel on March 2. The end of furtive living was five weeks away. It was on April 9 that Adolfo Suárez took a run and a jump over the generals' moustaches and declared that the Movement was dissolved and the CP was legal. It was party time, and in the best bourgeois style, bottles were uncorked, flowers tossed, and virgins buttered. Each latent communist cell planned its own celebrations, so as not to pollute the purity of its hammers and sickles with the bastard tools of rival groups. In the locale of Faith Oxen's party, they improvised an open-house celebration in which neighbors, passersby, fellow travelers, and novices straight from the cradle participated alongside the autumnal staff of activists. The old girl and I showed up; she was choked by the emotions stirred, so she said, by the sight of communism out in the open once more in Spain, and I held her hand, a lapdog scared by the uncharted land the new circumstance had brought into my life. Clearly, Esteruelas had failed, and without his direct interest, I had few excuses to stay on with Faith that wouldn't betray my lack of enthusiasm for a return to One-Eyed's flock. By this time I had figured out how to reduce my subservience to the old girl while extracting as much profit as I could from her withered flesh. The truth is the locale was one big fiesta, lubricated by alcohol being poured out with no thought of tomorrow. It was all kisses, toasts, hugs, and bubbly, it was all ill-contained passion until Blond Juana appeared in the doorway and her scowling frown dampened the noisy partying. She was wearing her hair in a bun that was loose on the nape of her neck and threatening to spill down her back

278

like a waterfall. Her pose was even more statuesque than usual—if that's possible. Her breasts, her braless bosoms, loomed under the white T-shirt she wore, and it was noteworthy how her nipples stood out, and they were wonderful to behold, pert and bulbous like the enameled domes of a Byzantine church. She waltzed past my nose on her way to talk to the old girl and, turning her back on me, was quite unaware that her buttocks were quivering right by my tongue, which acted as a catharsis for my desire. She wasn't happy. The coming out of the CP, in her view, was no advance for the proletariat, it was yet another victory for a bourgeoisie that assimilated and digested everything. Soon only limp fragments of the party would survive, because, so she argued, acceptance of the rules of the capitalist game would lead irrevocably to sclerosis. Everyone, or at least most people, was now drunk on wine or cuba libres and lightly dismissed Blond Juana's spoilsport words at this point in their inebriation. It was time, so they believed, to enjoy the blessed resurgence of communism, after thirty-eight years of defeat—and in the middle of Holy Week, to boot. "Drink a bevvy or two, Juana, this Easter Saturday has been painted red!" But she was wiser and not so easy-going, and knew for certain that society isn't transformed by the sedative of the ballot box but by the impetuous throb of blood. I'd downed a few glasses of wine, wanting to still the anguish the new era was bringing to my steady routines, and felt sodden with contempt for that whole jamboree around me. Only Blondie aroused my interest, that is, my desire, and the mere fact we both breathed the same air was enough to send me into an insane dither. After a good while spent wining and jawing with this crowd, I watched her go up to the floor above. Suddenly, lust jabbed its sharp spur into my heels, compelling me to follow. Nobody was upstairs, and the room normally used for their debates and intrigue was now in darkness. The only physiological activity I glimpsed was in the lavatory; a ray of light under a stall door testified to an occupant. I put an eager ear and flushed cheek to the door. To my delirious delight, I heard a soft spurt splatter the majolica of the pan— Blondie's private music resounding like a heavenly symphony in my ears. Her melody triggered my lunacy, and, unable to curb my rashness, I seized the handle and eased the door open. The strangest things happen in lavatory stalls. The privacy allowed by these smelly places gains a new dimension when it is suddenly shared. Blond Juana, queen of her own seat, had enthroned her beauty with her jeans down to her feet and her knickers halfway down her calves. She was the Venus of the flesh no Botticelli ever imagined, a crystalline fount of a uric-acid Versailles in full working splendor. That sufficed for the adrenaline I'd suddenly released to have an impact on my organism. Boiling blood coursed rebelliously to my cheeks, and unable to tame the need I felt to touch her, I threw myself at her like a slavering, gasping troglodyte. My hands went after her breasts, and like a hugely clumsy animal, I tried to hop onto her, with no significant outcome. When she saw me suddenly open the door, she'd put the brake on the urine flow from her bladder, and the spurt stopped the moment I started feeling her up. It was a short-lived skirmish; wriggling free, she dug her elbow into my jaw and sent me sprawling. My eyes opened to a galaxy of pubic curls, screwed up toilet paper, dried up, blackened stains whose origins there's no need to detail. I turned round as best I could. I raised my head. The shock from that blow ran right through me, was deeply insulting to my dignity. My face hurt, but what hurt most, if that's possible, was the absolute ferocity with which she spat these words at me: "Not only do you enjoy your own deformity, you wallow in it like an animal," said she, slowly pulling up her knickers. I was dazzled by the glinting liquid still bathing the inside of a thigh I admired from the ground. Perhaps driven by my sudden blinding, I started to cry, desperately and disconsolately, like Mary Magdalene. I'd been hurt by her hostile rejection, though, of course, that wasn't enough to trigger such a River Jordan of snot and tears. As I blubbered, I started on a string of apologies in a sorrowful tone peppered by a spot of contrition from the toiletry bag of my heart. "I didn't want to offend you, Blondie, I'm sorry. I lost my head. I was very hot; I don't know what happened. I'm crazy about you, but I don't aspire to so very much; the most I wanted was to make love to you at some point. Please forgive me." Juana finished adjusting her jeans, not taking her eye off me for a second, as if she were afraid of another attack. When she'd finished, she went to walk out of the stall. She strode over my body, easily avoiding touching me, though not before she'd kicked me in the thinnest part of my ribs. "Pig," she said, "if you come near me again, I'll kill you." Without more ado, she disappeared into the crowd. That ingenuous soul didn't know Providence had preordained a painful moment for her, one that was intimately linked to the effusion of my liquids.

The streets were thronged with young Fascists flourishing their splendorous moth-eaten flags. A savage binge of violence was their favorite pastime. Baseball bats splintered by bludgeoning, bloodstained nunchakus, and octogenarian pistols none the less dangerous for their age would appear at nightfall in whatever seemed a suitable spot for a proper declaration of aspirations, display of intentions, and demarcation of territory. The pups of the still unburied Regime, desperately avenging the passivity of their elders, cruelly sank their milk-white fangs into tender flesh wherever their staves could inculcate the survival of ideals studded with obsolete metaphors. Most were posh little kids who eventually married pampered pussy, forgot airy-fairy bygone glories, and promoted profitable enterprises where they primed their paunches, went bald, and sensibly and civically drove their 4x4s packed with progeny. It was, for example, dangerous to roam dodgy avenues in the Retiro Park after twilight or to walk along the Calle Goya wearing distinctive badges indicating membership in the wrong gang. A punch in the face, the swipe of a machete, or a shot from a pistol could suddenly halt the traffic through the so-called "National Zone." Under orders from One-Eyed, I started to

282

ask for alms near the church of La Concepción de Nuestra Señora, halfway up the Calle Goya, a place whose congregation comprised the old-style faithful and military widows with their warts and their minks. Wide-eyed, I'd concentrate on displaying my poverty on my palm while keeping a look out for undesirable elements or agitators itching to be taught a lesson with a good beating. In the view of those parishioners, only the poor who bowed their heads deserved to commune with their aura and perhaps the pocket coins they threw them out of Christian charity. Esternelas had posted a contact at a street stall selling Fascist insignia and pennants that set up daily next to the Cafeteria California. He'd instructed me to go to the stall and alert them if I detected any leftists I knew ambling round the vicinity, so they could be taught an exemplary lesson, if the opportunity arose. Naturally enough, I didn't rush to snitch on every one I spotted; I only squealed on those I disliked, disapproved of, or detested for personal reasons. Luckily they tended not to show their faces in these neighborhoods unless they were roaring for a battle royal; so generally, when I went there, I simply worked at extracting alms in the role assigned to me as the spying beggar. At moments of stellar despair, I even prayed for Blond Juana to err and strut her stuff thereabouts. She never did, and I confess that if I had seen her around there, I don't know if my avenging mission would have overridden the desire to enjoy her there and then. The future never belongs to us, and though we'd like to shape our way and strive heartily to that end, it will never be given as we wanted.

When I completed my tasks after the final mass of the day, I'd walk around the area of the cafeteria, say hello to Amalio

Barrios, the man running the insignia stall, and tell him I was off, so he could activate the other systems of security alerts they had in place to keep it safe, which I won't reveal now. "Goodbye, kid," that hard man would say, "do you fancy a ciggy?" and when I held out a hand to take one, he'd smirk and snatch it away "No, 'cause you'd smoke it," would be his little punch line. He wasn't a bad fellow. His only problem was his intelligence never really came to the boil and he couldn't glimpse the future awaiting him through all those patriotic cobwebs. Basically it was no bad thing when he, too, was blasted through the air, otherwise God knows how the guy might have ended up. One-Eyed Slim sometimes dropped by the church to keep his eye on his interests and spend a while plotting with locals who were on the same wavelength. I know he met up with Esteruelas now and then in the cafeteria, and that they had dealings with other folk—in the sweet, rancid fug of a private room—about even murkier matters he never disclosed to me. Perhaps he already suspected loyalty is the bastion of the just or a necessity of the weak. The months that had flown by since the Caudillo's death had put paid to any likelihood he could ever redeem himself. Now he was a leftover man on a stage being dismantled by change, a cadaver adrift from the zeitgeist. There was no hope for them, only a final transit. Adultery and mistresses had just been legalized by the Cortes, and the Spanish, duly informed about the advantages of ballot boxes and cock-a-hoop with the reduction of the age of majority to the innocent age of eighteen, were eager to vote for a brand new constitution, by a margin of eighty-eight per cent. Less than a month before, a couple of high-ranking military officers had been caught plotting, breakfasting amid a galaxy of rampant nostalgia, a coup d'état that would have channeled the fatherland back along a pristine path of justice with public order reinstated and morality rearmed, which would have been no bad thing in terms of the sowing and perpetuation of our miscreant ways; it was not to be. That was the penultimate twist in Spain's history of darkness. The last would come several years later, complete with a grotesque operetta starring soldiers in period dress, as a newspaper across the pond was quick to point out. The world would once again have learned to speak Spanish.

Increasingly locked in the cul-de-sac of the future awaiting me if I remained marooned in those grimy territories, I preferred to focus my thoughts on plans to raid the riches of Faith Oxen. The idea of stripping her, while she was still alive, of the goods she'd shamelessly hid in her bedroom wardrobe, inside a safe embedded in the wall, seemed rather repugnant, not in terms of the larceny itself, but because afterward, I'd be forced to beat it with my booty, and that would deprive me for good of the close contact I so desired with Blondie. I'd still not discounted the remote, if crazy, possibility that I might bend her ear and claim her groin as my trophy. The idea of killing the old girl to steal the pearls and gold trinkets of hers from Moscow or wherever that made her cache so tasty seemed wildly attractive, but Slim would have immediately thought her violent death suspicious and come after a share of the spoils. In the event, trapped as I was between my filthy fantasies on hot nights at the temperate Trinitarians' and my days spent surviving the dizzy whirlwind of history, I concluded that the most sensible solution was to dance to the tempo of a death that looked increasingly imminent, awaiting the inevitable denouement, so that's what I did, although that didn't mean I just folded my arms; quite the reverse, I hastened the end on, sweetening the old girl's repose with tidbits, pastries, anisette, chocolate bars, and other succulent treats she downed in excess. She was diabetic and peed too much.

I've always mocked the recalcitrance of people who, when faced with the disastrous aftermath of their misfortunes, have been unable to grasp a transcendent sense of metaphysical inevitability. Though they call it bad luck, they don't see it as a set of circumstances prearranged by Providence where attempts to change or redirect are expressly forbidden. That's the self-deceit they endure. They believe they are champions of freedom but are puppets of destiny. One-Eyed Slim didn't know what the meaning of his life was but ploughed his furrow, on behalf of short-term gain, in rough-and-ready instant pleasures, drifting from day to day without worrying overly about the mysteries tomorrow might bring. That's why, when a bomb blew his life to smithereens, in that last second that must always exist, he didn't experience terror, pain, consternation, or fear—only disappointment. I should add that I was really lucky not to have accompanied him, as he'd intended, to the encounter where he'd been summoned by Esteruelas, along with three other individuals the newspapers never mentioned. My time wasn't yet up, and consequently, not imagining what the outcome might be, I didn't jump to his orders, and I let him go to his death, walking up the street to the cafeteria where GRAPO had placed a device that would blast them heavenward.

A drop of caramel syrup spreading over a dish of pancakes was the last thing Slim contemplated before the shock wave smashed his one-eyed view of the world. It could have been worse; his last snapshot might have been the dark circle at the end of a revolver barrel aimed at his watery eye, but that wasn't the case. Things happen as they do, however much we struggle to change them. Destiny is the text, and happenstance the calligraphy in the book where Providence lists the circumstances of our punishment. Slim concluded his odyssey sundered into a thousand pieces that would never be put back together. He would never have survived these chaotic times at the dawn of the millennium.

Nobody tries their patience today selling books in the metro. Times slough their skins, foreign customs are homogenized, and the masses finally temper their historical role as protagonists, except in the strictly sporting realm. Worship of football has totally replaced the interest in politics that was so much in vogue in Spain. Freedom has turned into a good to be bought and sold, and the people's anthem, the victory song of fans. It wasn't the case then. People then went hoarse proclaiming their ideals on the street, and sporting spectacles were restricted to more out-of-the-way locations, in the pigsties of the intellect. Apart from fools and rednecks, nobody ever read the sporting press in public, for fear of a reproachful glance or an irritated gesture from a passerby; now, you know, the opposite is the case, which guarantees rich pickings for all those who know how to derive profit from the general dumbing down. When you've done with me, I recommend you do what I did: make the most of the ignorance of others, sell them stickers, junk, or simply air wrapped in colorful cellophane. You just see how you won't regret it. The crux is to not worry about sabotaging human dignity and to camouflage your profits behind the drivel that is so popular about solidarity, social commitment, the sponsoring of children for a television marathon, or defense of the environment through advertising. Have yourself a ball. The grandiloquent spectacle of wealth basically stupefies the masses and predisposes them to do what they are told. Though the outlandish wealth of a minority demonstrates how shitty a social system that organizes individuals into units of consumption is, there lies the rub: it prospers, and nobody seems to be aware of the disaster. Let them eat trash and cheerfully share the incomparable experience, in the belief that they are free; let them teeter on, while others research new markets and explore unheard-of profit lines. Individual idiosyncrasies, the absurd dimension of people's presence in this world, are rooted in financial potential. Wealth dignifies, money extends horizons; if one has some, there's no limit to one's caprices and they are catered to on demand. The clouds clustered over existence can perhaps only be grasped from that deepest ennui wealth brings or by the extreme vicissitudes of poverty. The enigma of time can solely be perceived from this perspective; past, present, and future are uncoupled from the immediate moment and stand out as metaphors for everything. Only death unveils the cardinal truth hidden in life, what was once ordained and never ceases can only reach culmination in death: the universal diktat of Providence.

I know, I can tell you, that Faith Oxen hoarded the unknown riches she'd been gathering during her stint on earth in a safe embedded in one side of her bedroom cupboard. Might a watch incrusted with rubies right down to its innermost cogs be lurking in that enclosed, secretive darkness, or could a jewel of untold carats be sitting there silently, or was there a pile of American cash in wads of high-value greenbacks? That

289

treasure was a real riddle that I spent my time trying to unpick. I'd put my ear to the other side of the wall when Faith Oxen was opening it and hang on every sound her hands triggered. There were crick-cracks and metal tinkles my brain absorbed and distilled in its sickly imagination. It all fitted perfectly. The hypocritical old girl had devoted her life to haranguing the masses while behind their backs she espoused the cause of wealth and accumulated rather than distributed. In her heart of hearts, she was afraid of being abandoned, and no social system, not even the one she advocated to the world, would have treated her old age with the reverence she required on the final straight. Mental and physical incapacity reduce a human being to a passive scrap of skin and bone in the miscellaneous hands of third parties. She never revealed to anyone the existence of her hoard—not even notionally, although in the hours of repose after our amatory larks, she'd sometimes drop the names of lovers and the contents of the presents they'd lavished on her in return for her favors. Old age, among other things, confirmed the depths of her pettiness. "You're like me. You only believe in what you've suffered, and that's why you'll live on, Gregori. You don't have any scruples, and one day wealth will knock on your door," she said, her voice quivering in her throat, "but first the worms must lick my bones clean."

I've known many bastards in my lifetime and wished a good end on the lot. They reaped what was coming; some had it soft, others, rough, it depends. Esteruelas was blown to bits, and his belches and farts evaporated in unison, a veritable toll of doom. I knew he always knew that handsome Bustamante didn't kill Frank Culá, but he didn't give a toss who did; his only duty was to shut a case down as quickly as he could and carry on with life, never very clear as to why. Violent deaths sometimes provoke pity. However, sometimes violent, unjust deaths arouse more, and nonsensical or meaningless ones that suddenly spread disarray and panic even more so, if that's possible. They lived by plotting the deaths of others and for that reason probably didn't worry about their own, and that was to their advantage.

Now I feel myself under your own close scrutiny, I've been struck by a premonition of a darkness that's been distressing me ever since I became conscious of my tragedy. I have seen my longings, my feelings, my memories reflected one by one in your eyes and felt afraid of myself. Now I understand everything. I told psychiatrists of a bad dream I had, one that appeared to me in London when I visited my son Edén. I fooled myself into thinking it had been the fruit of the emotion I experienced on the day, that the end wasn't going to come so soon or in the dreadful way heralded, but here you are in this present moment that draws us together, listening to me rehearse my past, your very presence proving just how little time is left.

Dog dead, rabies sorted. To her eternal shame, Sister Marta identified the corpse by the protuberant mole of a birthmark at the point where his testicles joined, or so they claimed. The attack was splashed over all the front pages, and three days after the attack on the Cafeteria California, the Far Right, which was already bleeding to death, could do nothing to stymy the solemn ceremony held in the Cortes at which the king of Spain inaugurated the first legislature of the constitutional parliament. Rabies sorted, as I said, because without Slim's support, the chains binding me to the Trinitarians' broth were unlocked forever. In any case, it would have been madness to stay on any longer in a place where so many bore grudges against me. I cleared off with the sister who'd had carnal dealings with One-Eyed. She left her habits, which had been of no use to her, except perhaps to mop up the semen Slim liked to spurt over her, and I left another five years of my life impaled on the walls of that ineffable charitable institution. I was alone again, with nowhere in particular to go, but this time, unlike previously, the reins of my destiny were gripped by a voluptuous hankering after prosperity. As feral as a dog without a master, roaming the streets and sniffing trash bins, gnawing at any life left on bones it's randomly thrown, going this way or that, aimlessly, with no sense it might last another season more, baying impotently at the moon, I found myself out on a limb, scarcely imagining it was precisely in such a forlorn state that I was finally predestined to make it.

I sought shelter in Faith's house, and she, generous within the bounds of her tyrannical old age, let me sleep on a canvas mattress on her kitchen floor in exchange for my total slavery. I meekly accepted her offer. I woke up early, and after washing my sleep away with a couple of splashes of water, I'd go to the Maravillas market and do her shopping. I begged for alms, simply because I'd become so adept, or filched someone's billfold to buy the food so I could cook the items the old girl liked. I never came away without a bar of fondant chocolate or a tray of cakes to sweeten the corpuscles of her blood. I never put them out but hid them away so she'd properly appreciate them. She wolfed them down, ever more removed from reality, more volatile, more outrageous, and closer to the grave. It wasn't even worth strangling her. The exact words of Blas de Otero seemed to bring their two bits of gravel to that house's reinforced concrete: *Desolation and vertigo combine. We feel we're going to fall, that they're drowning us from the inside. We seem alone, and the shadow on the wall isn't ours, is a shadow that doesn't know, that cannot remember whose it is. Desolation and vertigo beat in our chest, wriggle away like a fish, our blood thins, we feel our feet give way.* And the more I read those lines, the more the atmosphere in which Faith was rotting day by day seemed to reek of the grave.

I survived in that putrid way for a few months more, months when barely anything happened in my life that I've not already described to you. I was bound to that house and

293

in its deep silences witnessed the decrepitude and decline of Faith Oxen. I fornicated with her to flatter her vanity, I fed her with my own hands and gave her succor in her solitude with the poisoned sting of my company. She mistreated me in word and deed, simply because she was aware that she depended on me, and in return I brought her lips the sugar of death. "You are my dog, Gregori, and you have to beat a dog so it will obey. You can't hoodwink me, you dog. I know you like to watch the way I'm dying, and that's why you don't scarper, because of that and the marrow you'll get from me when you chew on my bones. Do you think I don't notice what you're after? Come here and give my weary twat a lick," and I barked loudly, playing up to her words, vamping my desires in a grisly celebration of the absolute truth of her spiel. Outside, the world was endlessly churning, perhaps in quite another way, one I'd never perceived before, fresh and creamy, huge and juicy, and beautiful *malgré tout*, when one day somebody knocked on the door.

A sleety rain was falling, coating the city pavements in sticky, slippery Christmas gunge. It was Christmas Eve, at that in-between hour when people switch on electric cookers in their domestic heartlands to roast the dinner, that twilight hour of metallic shadows when trousseau tablecloths depart locked chests to spread an eternal smell of mothballs across languid drawing rooms, that tranquil Eve stalked by a prickly silence when hearts suffer such nostalgia. I was about to boil the old girl a line-fished hake to ensure a decent lay dinner, when the doorbell suddenly rang. Faith Oxen had been resting awhile with a bad headache. These headaches attested to the brittleness of her memory and often prostrated her on the black hole of her bed. In the kitchen, on an Aiwa transistor, the rim of its loudspeaker clogged with grease, the king of Spain's nasal voice was beginning to drone his traditional Christmas message: "The past twelve months, on the contrary, have witnessed the efforts made by all to accede to the levels of freedom and responsibility that the historical conjuncture demanded. On the matter of which, not too long ago, when I made a public evaluation of the culminating moments of the constitutional process, I expressed the opinion that the Spanish people, in an act of supreme collective freedom . . ." "Gregori, somebody's knocking on the door. Go and see who it is, and switch off that radio; all that speechifying is doing my head in, I can't stand it!" the old girl shouted from the depths of her dark cavern. I threw the rings of the onion I was uncoiling into the boiling water, jumped down from the bench where I was forced to stand to reach the hob, and went to open up. There stood Blond Juana on the doorstep, leaning her right shoulder on one of the jambs, eyes backstitched by a thread of hashish dilating her pupils, and she stared at me, I'm not sure whether in repulsion or astonishment. "What are you doing here, dwarfy?" she enquired matter-of-factly. "Making the old girl's supper," I retorted. Caulked in sweat, the keel of her body furiously fired my desire, and slaver foamed down my tongue as I told her about the job I'd acquired attending to the old girl at all hours, accompanying her solitude and enlivening her tedium. "You're a scavenger," she responded. "You're hoping to get something out of her." I ignored her insult and was in no mood to argue in those circumstances. She said she'd come to bid farewell to the old crock, and I ushered her toward the drawing room. It's strange, but just like the chauffeur in Benalmádena, she, too, reeked of boiled fish, of stagnant seawater, and from way off. Before I'd invited her to, she'd entered the drawing room and settled down on a corner of the sofa, shamelessly crossing her legs. They were packed into thick, faded lilac leotards, and as she went to sit down, she deliberately gave me an eyeful of the tasty sponge cake of her thighs. Or at least *I* thought she did

Wanting to give that encounter short shrift, I told her Faith Oxen was in bed with a headache and that I'd pass on the news of her visit so she could call her the following day. "She'll not get hold of me tomorrow," she replied emphatically, "tomorrow I'm leaving this shithole of a country and going to Nicaragua." Juana was torn between feelings of bliss and angst over the decision she'd taken, moved, she told me later, by her commitment to the revolutionary struggle. The Sandinistas were engaged in a bitter offensive against the Somoza dictatorship, and the West, with Yankee imperialism leading the way, was contemplating the country with the fear and suspicion one would expect from those who see that their own future is threatened. Blondie was convinced that the eventual triumph of the cause of freedom she was championing first had to pass through the hoop of her own self-sacrifice. That's how it turned out. With no encouragement from me, she launched into a harangue about how the harvests of tomorrow must be irrigated by the blood of peasants and workers if they were ever going to bear fruit. She spoke of the necessity of armed combat, of the ultimate dialectic of weapons, and the annihilation of the oppressor. The words flew from her mouth in a parabola as if they were grenades launched from a mortar-pad, but when they exploded in my ears, the only effect they had was to induce skepticism, so rather than interjecting, I simply decided to imagine her naked in the middle of the jungle, festooned with cartridge belts that crisscrossed her breasts in a big X, truly enhancing her beauty, a carnivorous beauty more akin to a wild animal's than a human being's, and perhaps rather ragged in the tropical humidity. The splendorous fantasy I concocted was immediately betrayed by the tent pole of my cock, which was less spurred on by the details of her close presence than by the pleasurable circumstances I was imagining and that had elevated her so. She noticed what happened and was probably astounded by the prolix nature of the item, and I immediately grasped the unmistakable scent of desire in the way she looked at me. The king of Spain was pursuing the gelatinous spiel of his speech on the radio in the kitchen. The echo of his voice wafted to us on the aroma from the stew simmering in the pot. In that gesture of abandonment that comes when the thing is unstoppable, Blondie suddenly unzipped her jersey and exposed the blouse underneath. Then, silently, without pausing, she undid every button, one by one, till she'd completely laid bare a flesh-colored bra that gave firm support to the baubles of her tepid breasts. "Come here," she ordered, not a tremor in her voice, "isn't this what you were after? Take from me what you will," and she bared the sweet expanse of her body, a honeycomb slurping with jelly where my member swarmed and eventually lodged. Aloof, like a red virgin set on self-sacrifice for God knows what outrageous theology, Blondie impassively yielded to my caresses. I went at it awkwardly. My tongue licked the hidden folds of her anatomy, I drank the juice from her flesh entire, and my mouth counted out the tiny moments when it was crystallizing her pleasure. She attended to my desires at every turn, was flexible, malleable, altogether consecrated to the dimension of her sacrifice, and struck dumb by the longing with which her will drove her on. "Gregori, dwarfy!" the old girl shouted from the stinking crypt of her bedroom. "What are you up to that's stopped you switching off that radio once and for all? That drivel is smashing my head in; I can't stand it!" I pushed Blondie a fraction of an inch away, sought confirmation in her eyes that if I left her, she'd stay riveted there, awaiting my next onslaught, that she wouldn't beat it, ashamed by her own abasement. As I scrutinized the *Yes I will, no I won't* in her pupils, those words of warning suddenly rushed to me from all those years ago, when handsome Bustamante had spat in my face: "Goyo, don't be under any illusions, women will only give themselves to someone deformed like you out of charity, or for money." However, times had changed, and out of the blue, a new way to accede to female flesh had emerged: the path of self-sacrificing solidarity. Concluding that my prey wouldn't escape me, elevated by my victory, the scepter of my cock hoisted in all its majesty, I unslurped myself completely from Blondie and ran to the kitchen to switch off the radio for Faith Oxen. "The monarchy I incarnate being committed to the fundamental aim of returning sovereignty to the Spanish people, and having achieved this objective set out when my task as king of Spain was inaugurated, I pledge to ensure it continues and to deepen solidarity with all Spaniards . . ." The king went on talking as the water simmered, and I don't why, but I instinctively felt like putting the radio, rather than the hake, in the pot, but the truth is the monarch's voice, soluble in the stock, instantly dissolved with a fish's oily, lippy slipperiness.

Some women don't try to hide it for one moment when they're freeing up the seams of their knickers from between their buttocks. They do so on purpose, cheekily, to arouse the dirty passions of the men looking on in amazement. Animal language takes on all forms. The striking—snap!—of elastic on thigh is a beautiful sound, which, apart from stimulating the imagination, courses through the veins with a licentiousness that is ever so fluid. Simply mental turmoil, you might say, and you wouldn't be deceiving yourself if you did. Some women feel no charity toward themselves and surrender their bodies to a tortuous calvary of restraint before immediately falling victim to the darkest putrefaction. Blind creepy-crawlies finish them off with gusto beneath the sod and without a single wail or hallelujah. Some women rise above the potential nature granted them and avoid the innocent exercise of fertility; conversely, others ignore their fate, and perhaps for that very reason end up confronting it with no holds barred. Faith Oxen was drifting off intermittently in the gaunt darkness of her room. Her erratic pulse, pounding blood, and staccato heartbeats were betrayed by the voice that croaked from the cavern of her larynx, summoning me to her side. "Give me your hand, Gregori, I'm on my way," she said, while cloying, childish whimpers stuttered from her nostrils, "I don't want to die, grip me tight, my breath's going." And it was true. The old girl was sinking, the blue tints of decay suffusing her cheeks, as if the circumstance of her death were one more testimony to its irrevocable summons. Her nightdress, which for one last time hid her withered flesh, bared an inextricable, labyrinthine trail of wrinkles on her neck, where old age was sliding her to the final exit. She found breathing difficult— short, stertorous, and ridiculous retches coughed up, inspiring terror. "Don't leave me, Gregori, don't leave me," she intoned, knowing full well that her time was up. I didn't feel pity or show any emotion. Nor did I feel at all distressed when I looked her in the face, a casual glance spliced with contempt, confirming to her that, in effect, she was dying, that she was so much dust in this world, and that she'd be dust in the next, too, given that the materialistic nature of her creed had ruled on the nonexistence of any possibility of life beyond this earth. "You're dying, old girl," I drawled, deliberately rubbing my words in her face, "very soon you'll lose consciousness and never recover it again. Keep faith with what you've always upheld, and ready yourself now on the banks of the void. It is unnerving, isn't it? Tell me, now you still can, what it feels like, share your last moments with me, tell me if it's true that you're aware of nothing on the last straight, no dark tunnels, and no distant lights switching on, tell me that you only feel terror on the edge of the pit." Anguish blocked her glottis; words fragmented in her mouth like pebbles hurtling down a bottomless ravine. With every second, it was harder to understand her, not because of death's weary tones but the anguish with which she was trying and failing to hang on to life. "So, was it worth it, wasting your life defending such claptrap?" I continued, joyfully sticking the knife in. "Or would you prefer to throw your past to the dogs for an instant's belief in a supreme being who could now bring relief from the terror tearing you apart? Where's that paradise you preached? Take a good look at me, old girl—do you reckon I look like a pariah on this earth? Do you want me to drop my pants to prove it? You're carrion now, and what was yours is mine, your furniture, your paintings, the jewels that the guys who fucked you paid out. You knew this was coming. Hang on in there awhile, you still have to thank me for putting up with you so long."

I took away the hand she was gripping so tight; at the cost of a nasty scratch, I prized myself free. I went over to the wardrobe, and, replaying in my memory the sounds of the safe's combination that I'd registered so often behind the wall, I opened it effortlessly. Inside, pearls and rings shared a shelf with watches and the bundles of bills that I'd imagined. I took out the contents, slipped on necklaces, put rings on my fingers, and spread the rest of the jewels on Faith Oxen's deathbed, so cool and casual, enjoying the spectacle of her gaze that was disappearing inexorably into nothingness. She expired in under ten minutes. Before doing so, she regained some of her waning strength, and was kind enough to grace me with the death rattle of a promise: "Your time will come, dwarfy". Then her hand flopped, her eyelids drooped, her nostrils closed, and it was over.

I stayed quiet for a moment, contemplating her corpse, not particularly wanting to surrender to the absurdity of the spectacle. I was absorbed by the coldness of the scene, engrossed by the heap of flesh being emptied of life before my very eyes, until gases erupted from the dead woman's mouth and hit me flush in the face. Then the penny dropped: if a world beyond existed, it, too, must be an abject place.

FIVE

Time passes at a dizzy rate, and we don't notice it eroding our expectations in the process. Fashions change, thinking diverges, and alliances break up and re-form behind the same scenes, ever marked by the movable feast of progress. The past recedes, the future looms, and nothing we represent endures. Look at me if you want proof; even I wonder at the way I have risen to the top—awash in an ocean of cash, treated obsequiously, buoyant in business, cossetted by life to the point of caressing immortality. Time flies, but in time kills.

The years of hunger are now distant memories, like the horrible cruelty I suffered in childhood, the hardships experienced in the Stéfano circus, the scavenging in a Madrid riding high on freedom. Who then would ever have believed I'd achieve what surrounds me now, the luxury, power, social standing, and public recognition?

For Ceferino Cambrón the meaning of life was forged in an impossible struggle for dignity. Gurruchaga reacted to life as a simple matter of survival. Conversely, pudgy Di Battista lived to drink, life being a bottle to swig until it was emptied. And what's life been for me apart from rambling memories and confused emotions? I feel it is all fantasy, a mere game, that I've been a puppet whose strings were brusquely pulled by Providence, a plaything in its hands. Can it be true that it's all a fraud—my name, my consciousness, my past? Can it be true its only purpose was to entertain you for a while, a while when my story achieved its one real dimension?

Philosophy is wrong when it tries to find meaning in human life. Philosophers only exist to get it wrong. Hobbes was wrong, though not because he was English or a liberal. He was wrong, though not like that pigeon in the poem which was so ingenuous it went soft in the head. Man wasn't a wolf to other men, but a market. "Man is a market to other men," Hobbes would have declared had he witnessed this era of ours. The pigeon is a trite creature of poetic convention; it would, of course, be much more interesting to use the image of a vulture or a bone crusher, birds of prey, to construct metaphors for high-flying humanity. The market. This is the calling that justifies man's presence in the world: the market as the single creed, profit as the supreme raison d'être. The market, I tell you. The market now stripped of pigeons and festering with hungry wolves. The market where dwarves jump and fight to consecrate their growth points.

I know you have come to be entertained by the spectacle of my death, if death is the word for what you've prepared as my end. My own story, the memories that weave the patchwork of my identity, my experiences, my most vital, least embittered hours, my emotions have been served up to you shamelessly, brazenly, for your amusement and delight. I am born again in your eyes, through you I endure and perhaps exemplify the paradoxes of the species, even the most terrible of all, an end that is a rendezvous with nothingness. Look at me. I'm still the fairground freak mercilessly displayed inside a circus tent, surviving on belly laughs. I can never escape myself. That is my sentence: to dance over an open grave above the slippery slope of the void. Gurruchaga didn't do transcendence but very wisely linked survival to excrement, even to the very last moment of death. He taught me to learn from my sense of smell. "Fear smells, so does anxiety," he'd say, "don't look into men's faces, first smell what they are about." You smell of nothing, not even of a drop of sweat. It's as if you don't exist, as if your presence were fake, as if you weren't there observing me, hanging on my every word. No matter. Your smell would never have changed the course of events.

Life became kinder after the death of Faith Oxen. I went off for a spot of sun, and success fed me the freshly baked bread of well-being. First I speculated on real estate; I bought, I sold, and I pocketed, though I soon switched to the hotel trade. There, Providence raised my stakes in life with an offering of fruit that went rotten before it was tasted. Anonymous messages followed, voices inside my head, doubts, anguished words, a string of random events, and finally now you're here to round off the disaster.

In other circumstances I'd have been happy to thank you for the interest you showed, by allowing you to share in all that is beautiful around me, but I'm afraid that's a caprice that can never be realized. Man isn't what he thinks, what he says, or even the projects he undertakes. Man is what he consumes.

In the advertising campaign we were planning to unleash on the market next month, we were going to use different notions extracted from various philosophical concepts to spotlight the attractiveness of my products: "You pizza, therefore you are. You are yourself and your pizzas. To pizza or not to pizza, that is the question. Nothing pizza-ish is alien to me," and so on.

You could have lent your face to the campaign, the anodyne face of any Tom, Dick, or Mary. You'd have been a success, no doubt about that, a success that would have brought you a share of the profits. A pity your presence augurs the imminent end and that what I've been saying is pure fantasy. In the last instance, you must decide whether it's in your hands to imagine a formula to carry it through. Try it out, test your luck, have a go, and discover once and for all that you're no equal player with Providence, but a mere facilitator of its caprices, one puppet more.

I could lie and tell you about the importance of will in the development of individuals. I could deceive you and tell you I am a self-made man, that I've come from nothing, that with all my physical defects, I decided one day to buckle down and prosper, that everything I have is down to graft, but I'm afraid I can't do that. The accepted dogma that every human being has success within his grasp and that it depends exclusively on the efforts each individual exerts is one of the fallacies propping up the foundations of society. Freedom of choice is another such. Fate rules the roost, and every one of our acts takes place in function of the measure of our own limitations. When humans sacrificed their gods, they thought they were sovereign subjects and set out to build their own paradise on earth, but it turned out to be a dung heap where they cheerfully still wallow, refusing to accept the real source of their contradictions. I could lie and indoctrinate you, in the spirit of the times, with some rigmarole identifying progress with the smug stats from the end-of-year figures, but you have come to witness my demise, and denying your rag-doll status isn't worth the candle, either. You'll see for yourself when it all runs its course.

Once, when Faith was alive, I went to buy a tray of honey-glazed pastries from one of those fancy cake shops that fascinated her so, and I chanced upon a terrible incident. A little girl was pressing her nose against the shop window. She was six or seven, a ragamuffin, and her fragile gaze led one to imagine the ravages of poverty she'd yet to accept. Someone took pity on her, went into the shop, and bought her one of those pastries she was coveting, a cream doughnut sprinkled with icing sugar. The girl was distraughtly happy, couldn't credit what she was holding between her hands, hardly dared to, but she *did* run her lips over the white surface, even caressed it with her tongue. "A pastry just for me," she hummed contentedly. I stood and watched in amazement, annoyed by the momentary reprieve such a gift had given her from her wretchedness, then walked over with a view to teaching her a lesson and grabbing the cake from her. She misread my intentions, thinking I envied her snack, and with all her childish tenderness she offered to share it with me, but I scorned her offer and angrily threw it to the ground. When I did that, she burst into tears.

It's blatantly obvious that the world is plagued with contradictions that make one appreciate the need for a pre-established order to fix them in a righteous harmony. Wealth, poverty, love, and suffering are only aspects of that ferocious whole driving us on and swallowing us up; and if free will doesn't exist, nor does there exist any guilt to excuse. Unlike animals, the only grandeur human beings can cherish is the ability to acknowledge the extent of their own disaster; all else is deceit, a soporific fug deadening thought.

Little Margarita never let herself show a scrap of pity toward me, and didn't even show any warmth when she eyed up my handicaps. Her arrogance made her powerful, though it's true they were different, more iron-clad, times when people often acted brutishly. Fools, dogs, poets, the deformed, and pure bastards were generally denigrated, that being our daily bread.

Although One-Eyed Slim was a poor wretch, he idolized order held in place by discipline. Once when walking down the Cuesta de la Vega, I remember we came across the corpse of a dog that had been run over. It stank to high heaven, and its guts made ours turn over. He waxed serious and began telling me how members of US army elite units used to be given a newborn pup each to feed and look after until it grew into an adult. Once they were fully grown, they had to grab them by the snout and cut their throats on the sharp blades of their machetes. The aim of the exercise was to eradicate compassion from their behavior. They had to face the enemy with mercilessness etched on their muscles if they wanted to emerge with their limbs intact and their vital organs unscathed. Those were the rules of survival. He seemed to enjoy relating the details of such a practice, but I was shocked, not by the sacrifice of the animal as such, but by the ability to bend and shape people's feelings that way.

Little Margarita lacked compassion toward the weak and enjoyed seeing others suffer. She didn't even cry when her father was hacked to pieces. I've often recalled her from the loneliness of my office and tried to imagine what must have become of her, always with a residue of bitter memories in the pit of my stomach. The callous of this world always get their just desserts. That's the way it has to be, otherwise the social order would collapse and paradoxes would infect the collective consciousness. However, the people are not in control of their fate, that's why hunger and injustice sometimes wield the allure of power exemplified by history. What do you expect me to say? I'm proud I don't believe in the norms of society. It's some time since I suffered hunger or justice placated my thirst for revenge. Power, luxury, wealth, and social status hoist one onto an ivory tower of pride from which one observes the passing of time with surprising lucidity, almost on a par with what humiliation and poverty foster. Basically, maturity has enabled me to understand intolerance and fanaticism, which is why they don't frighten me. I've never got used to the excrescences of this world, perhaps because I've never been anything but a runt, a puppet whimsically fashioned by Providence. What saves me now in the eyes of others is my wealth, just as my poverty or belly laughs did previously, and that's the only difference. Intolerance is simply the boundless assertion of one's own self, something that is very obvious in children and that, nonetheless, is tempered by the hypocritical way society is organized. The humble fawn before the powerful, the weak before the strong, the ignorant before the cultured, and that's our way of sharing the supernatural fact of existence with each other.

What I experienced in my own flesh taught me to scorn those who revered me not for what I *was*, but for what I *possessed* in their eyes. The times were a-changing, and suddenly height brought vertigo, the sickly vertigo of ripe figs. I've known a host of bastards and always wished them a good end, not that they necessarily got one—but that's neither here nor there. Soon pleasure became a caprice; prickly behavior quickly changed to velveteen manners. In people's eyes I began to seem someone worthy of attention. I gradually climbed the steps of the social pyramid, till one fine day I found praise raining down on me, alongside bloodcurdling deference. Everything is written in the unknown pages of destiny and sometimes in blank verse. Everything is set in concrete, and all those sentences simmering with the semantics of individual effort, freedom, or work are but vases for the fallacies used to bedeck the suffering of the poor. My good fortune came ready-made; I did little to deserve it. I spent the jewels and money I stole from the dead woman bronzing like crazy under the sun on the Costa, well seasoned by amenable females, the kind that charge a rate for their friendship, and well oiled by the endless pampering siestas that sign off *les grandes bouffes*. For several years I simply did what I fancied. Marbella was in vogue, and the most select items of Mediterranean high society grazed there, doing what they willed. A dwarf can hardly pass unperceived in such a milieu, and the mounds of cash I carried meant I was soon admitted to the sumptuous fiestas and late-night bashes sponsored by idle aristocrats or bourgeois plutocrats. My free-spending ways attracted clusters of beautiful hangers-on I cultivated with profuse gratitude and purchased with the increasing acquisitive power of my bank balance. I'd put behind me the clandestine movements, the weary rallies in the shadow of the class struggle, and the vague horrors of tramping from the far-off political Spain of my misspent youth. Everything was different now; hip couturiers even came to blows over my deformed body, upon which they wanted to exhibit their extravagant creations at the gala banquets of the day. I'd become fashionable in a matter of two years, and my seed money suddenly multiplied in astonishing, if not yet boundless, ways. Helped by some of those so-called men of means, I gained entry to the world of easy, prosperous enterprise, generally of a speculative nature, which soon gave me the chance to initiate projects of my own. On the advice of one of these characters, I acquired a bakery on the cheap, and rather than selling it on at a profit, as was my wont, I had the bright idea of turning it into a fast-food sanctuary. Tourism requires food on the spot and spiced up for foreign tastes, and I managed to take advantage of the old, arthritic infrastructure of a catering industry in decline to meet the needs blown in from abroad by the winds of the free market. It was the early eighties, and the big change was going to come any minute now. Ideological Spain was giving way to economic-free-for-all Spain, and no holds barred. Diego Armando Maradona had just been signed by Barcelona Football Club for almost a billion pesetas, and hardly anyone could credit such a showering of capital. The spectacle of the coup d'état performed by a lieutenant colonel of the Civil Guard had been broadcast on television screens across the planet to the stupefaction of the international community. Everybody threw themselves into the street, united behind posters for peace; democracy passed the pistol-firing re-sit with top marks. The Rumasa conglomerate had just been expropriated in a political decision taken by democratic socialists, voted into power at the ballot box in the autumn of '82, and José Luis Garci was about to show that something Spanish could, rivaling feats from other eras, attain the impossible dream of an Oscar. In Spain, in that Spain nobody would soon recognize—not even the fucking founding fathers—a world of money was beginning to dawn.

No merit accrues to me in what I'm recounting, take that as read, it's simply the spinning mill of destiny. After a whole day spent between the sheets, with a clammy mouth and drowsy head, I strolled down the streets dotted with cheap fry-ups that lead to the Plaza del Chopito, in the heart of Marbella. I amused myself by looking at the knickknacks in the souvenir shops for penny-pinching tourists: flamenco-dancer dolls; garish postcards of girls on the beach, windswept hair, bare asses; inflatable mattresses; fuchsia thongs; and a pile of cheap trash. It was seven in the evening. I'd been invited to a cocktail party in the Nautical Club at eleven, one of those ineffable soirées where the vanity of the beautiful people is venerated amid champagne toasts and trays brimming with canapés. I had plenty of time and suddenly felt like going into a movie house where they were showing the then voguish film *E. T. the Extra-Terrestrial*, a charming tale of intergalactic deformity. Why so? Yet again, the invisible hand of Providence was whimsically guiding my hesitant steps. I've sometimes even thought that Steven Spielberg only filmed that story so I alone could watch it. Seeing that film, I was blessed by a revelation that in recent years has guided my steps along the path of plenty. Employing the mechanisms of the world for one's own ends is an attractive concept that in no way contradicts the rigors of the established order. At the very least, conjuring up the idea affords pleasure, and just as I said that your sudden appearance in my life augurs the end point of my wanderings, I'll also underline the benefit of the supernatural side to my sitting in that seat snowed under with popcorn, blinded by the revelation of a stunning idea that would grant me economic good health: the home-delivery pizza.

On the screen, some American children were playing a board game in a very homely kitchen scene. They were talking, joking, and airing their childish differences. Outside it was nighttime, and a UFO had just taken off, abandoning an extraterrestrial babe on the planet. Suddenly one of the kids expressed the bright idea of calling for a pizza, and they all heartily went for it. "Bring us a Papa Oom Mow Mow," they said, and very shortly, the Papa Oom Mow Mow pizza was delivered to their door. Couldn't I perhaps do likewise, and take pizzas to people's doors on the basis of a telephone call?

The four seasons is the pizza that synthesizes above all others the four ages of man, from conception in the uterus to immersion in the grave; the four seasons is by far the best pizza representation of man's wanderings across this world, soft as a cheese melt, slippery as a mushroom coulis. We devour the cycle of life in its circumference, as if communing with our own anguish. And it was a vein that had yet to be mined.

After eating dinner, I hardly care how things might end. People generally run shy from any mention of funeral matters and prefer to waste their time shutting the sphincters of transcendence rather than striving to investigate what might very well be awaiting them, hence the sidelining of poetry. It's at such extreme moments that humanity plumbs its innermost depths and prays, and, if passionate enough, it might even get lucky and see an extraterrestrial being. E.T. the extraterrestrial, though fictitious, was a repulsive character, deformed in every way, his unsightly proportions greased in fecal hues—the crowning glory to a disgusting sight. Nonetheless, children loved him, and parents bought thousands of E.T. dolls that had been mass-marketed. His secret wasn't novelty, or sentiment, but the mental level of the society amid which he landed. In exchange, the film recorded out-of-this-world profits. It's a fallacy to state that people shouldn't envy wealth, even if fraud or crime are involved. Wealth accumulation is the coat of arms that sets human beings apart from all other zoological species. It ushers them into a state worthy of flattery, adulation, honors, and all kinds of favorable treatment. Wealth is a tool

Providence has in its gift to present to whoever it chooses. After my youthful years swallowing eggs to survive, after rocky times begging, and shameful years spent in petty crime and fraud, I found myself to be a privileged plutocrat, without ever going out of my way to become one, and that made me suspect something supernatural ruled my steps; in the course of time, I confirmed that, when the specter of Faith Oxen did herself proud by appearing to me in a London hotel.

Life as a businessman absorbed me in mercantile spheres of life, and for over a decade I endeavored to raise the empire that has brought me renown. I acquired the lease on a down-at-heel, antiquated bakery on the outskirts of Marbella and transformed it into my alchemist's bubbling crucible. I pulled down partitions, demolished walls, installed lighting visible from the coastline, contracted a number of employees to stir dough with poles, and imported a couple of auto-ignition Murdoch & Panelli ovens from the United States to cook the products of their sweat. The first premises of the Europizza chain had just been born. Everything else came swimmingly. It all happened very quickly: limitless amounts of money spent on nights when vulvas sprouted, my reputation as a dwarf growing by virtue of my social success, and the splendid profits from my investment in pizzas. Overnight, I became a celebrity in the catering trade, was inundated with commercial opportunities, riding high and ringing up the zeros. Everyone was vying to contact me, to suggest new projects and count on my financial support. The same guys who in other circumstances would have spat in my face now deferentially shook my hand, and I extracted a slice of profit from every squeeze. Faith Oxen would have enjoyed the rich pickings I gained from the money I'd thieved from her; she'd have had a nasty turn in the grave seeing me so rampant. I later discovered she had, because she returned from the dead to disturb my life with her pitying words. You don't know this yet, but people go hungry in the next world, and it's a hunger devoid of hope that nothing can ever satisfy.

I still find it very odd that at the gala dinner organized by a charitable foundation they should serve cocks' combs in batter, and even odder, if that's possible, that the whole evening, someone should be recommending fellow diners an anti-hemorrhoid cream. As you can imagine, affinity between guests in terms of protocol is ultimately decided by those whose job it is to orchestrate the ceremonials, and it's always a tricky business deciding where to place a dwarf. Besides, the organizers weren't expecting me (I'd not confirmed I'd go), and they'd had to find me a niche at top speed and under pressure. In the end, I was parked next to the commissioner and across the table from the mayor, thus in a place where I was equidistant from the diplomats. I reckoned it was a decent spot. The photographers thought so, too.

I should add that I'm not trying to suggest I make a habit of rushing to the tables of this country's pillars of public life, though I am often duty-bound to respectfully accept the invitations sent to me by the most diverse entities. People generally continue to believe that nobody at this type of event talks about issues that are vital for the common good, and though that's true enough, it's even truer that at the end of the day what they do air is the dirty linen of those present and absent. On such occasions, wine is drunk from brittle glasses that enhance its bouquet, and people chew excellent food while paying close attention to subtle shades of flavor, but in the accompanying chitchat, it's the gossip that's prized: personal grudges and bodily malfunctions. Tonight Commissioner Belinda Dixon decided either to provoke or defer to me by revealing the cure she'd been using for her intimate hygiene problems. She didn't try the cocks' combs, for moral reasons, she alleged, yet she had no compunction when coming on to me repeatedly in the course of the evening. I acted politely and kept trying to stop her rehearsing out loud the details of how to apply the pomade. Some women's libidos make their brains simmer most strangely, and they'd happily lose a limb for a night between the sheets with whoever takes their fancy. She left me no alternative than to try to dissuade her by talking about a different kind of scatology, though she didn't desist, and I had to join in her game. Basically, a uterine rage of the kind suffered by Ms. Dixon either points to emotional deprivation or is evidence of Providence's intervention in the day-to-day of life, which doesn't dampen my libido at all; on the contrary, it stimulates it. Besides, I've come from the mire and have learned to keep up appearances. Cynicism is a beautiful creature, a way of relating to people that finds its most majestic manifestation in contempt. It's an exhilarating activity, and to acknowledge that is bliss. The state in which one anticipates darkness is similar to the perception of lucidity; opposites rub their opposite sides, and that's why pleasure only gives way to restlessness. Poetry is an instrument of transcendence, a system of signs through which men construct their intuitions

321

of the supernatural. I decided to speak about all that during the dinner, but the commissioner hardly let me get a word in edgewise, she was so busy pestering me with the ins and outs of her anal bulbs. The fact is we formed a pairing as extreme as it was eccentric, as admirable as it was divergent; perhaps that explains why we were the center of attention that night. Everybody was watching us suspiciously; it was obvious from the watery glint in people's eyes. Cocks' combs don't crackle when chewed; the cartilage comes apart in the mouth like communion wafers. A pizza made with cocks' combs might be very original, but it wouldn't appeal to the mass market. Man is a market to other men, a market ruled by the blind hand of fate. On a piece of paper where I'd hastily scrawled during the desserts, I jotted down my address for the commissioner in a rounded hand that replicated the circumferences of her breasts; she's an exuberant woman, but her skin looks sad, like a woman who cries every night when she gets into bed. She assured me she would immediately dispatch a previous engagement and then rush to my place to give me a private viewing of the miraculous results of the pomade. And here I am, still waiting.

Something unexpected happened before I got home. My chauffeur was chatting to the valet by the restaurant entrance. They were leaning against the trunk of a magnolia and smoking. It was cold, and hot air melded into the smoke. Their body sizes were different. My chauffeur isn't exactly small, but the other guy was an example of a body that seemed simply huge by his side. He was wearing a peaked hat, as if trying to invest himself with an authoritarian style that was past its shelf life or had been ill served by history. When that guy saw me walk out, he stood and stared quite rudely, then threw himself upon me with open arms as if he'd had an attack of cramp, smiling limply, a smile I immediately recognized—"Goyito, Goyito, it can't possibly be." It was Juan Culí, or his specter returning from the shadows of the past disguised as a scarecrow, with a whistle and bargain-counter uniform that betrayed his precarious lifestyle. "Goyito, for God's sake, it *is* you, let me give you a hug." Standing in the background, my chauffeur was astonished by this peculiar encounter. I extricated myself as best I could from Juan Culí's embrace. "Don't lick me, please, can't you see you're slavering all over me?" I pleaded, knocking drops of his saliva off my suit. "I can't believe it, Goyito," he went on, quite beside himself, "you look really great, you even look like a VIP. Don't tell me you were inside with all those big names," and he waved the palm of his hand in the direction of the restaurant. "You were always special; I knew that from the very first day you worked with us. Do you remember? You don't know how much I miss the good times we had in the circus."

Juan Culí continued graphically recalling the past, while I, given the situation, had no choice but to stand and listen. Could I have possibly experienced all that, had we really shared freezing nights in the towns of Spain, the fetid breath of wild animals, the relief their panting brought when we were out of sorts, the modest meals by moonlight, or the despair on the road when the silt of love sometimes bore fruit?

The world is in itself an unnerving spectacle where one performance follows another. Enjoyment comes with a price that's almost always high. I felt no sympathy toward Juan Culí. I could have rescued him from wretched poverty, but I didn't.

I could have made him a lucky man, he could have been fired by love of the flesh if that was what he craved, all that and much more one word from my lips could have granted him, but they didn't. Sentiment doesn't change the direction of fate. I told him I was in a hurry, we could meet up some other time; I got into the car. He opened the door servilely, drooping his eyes in farewell. Then I remembered pudgy Di Battista and that morning when I splattered him on the floor of his trailer, giving him a whiff of the disaster that would be his eventual demise. "What happened to Pudgy?" I asked before he shut the car door. At that point the commissioner left the restaurant on the arm of a bodyguard. She gestured to me, clenching the fingers of her left hand as if wanting to ratify our agreed rendezvous. I winked back in accord. "It was dreadful, he went mad soon after you left." Juan Culí told me the banks cleaned out the little he had; they left him sod all and even confiscated his passport photo. His face went blank, then alcohol soaked his chops and left him with a lunatic rictus. He began proclaiming that the Virgin of Fátima had appeared to him: "*We shoudda coronata the imagine de la nostra signora*," he kept ranting, totally out of his mind, "*we shoudda makka eet to il Carmelo de Coimbra and wash zee feet of sorella Lucia, we shoudda tell of the terzo of the message, we shoudda holify les festes.*" His body was disintegrating internally, and his breath stank. It was impossible to look him in the face. One morning he swigged Conejo-brand bleach instead of cognac and disinfected his guts for good. His *was* a bad end: he bled and convulsed, writhed round like the severed tail of a lizard. "He didn't deserve that," concluded Juan Culí, "we'd had a happy life with him, they were basically good times, weren't they, Goyito? Good times. Now we suffer other pains."

324

A past can be constructed to fit the exact needs of the person involved. Fakery is, after all, one of the best-loved tools of humankind. Right then I'd have preferred to have no past to remember, but that was impossible, and Juan Culí was living proof of that. "Do you still like getting it doggy style?" I asked him obscenely before I drove off. He didn't reply. I took my billfold out of my jacket, commiserated, and gave him a tip, "Here you are, get yourself a good time." The note fell crisply between his hands in a symbolic farewell. As I returned home, my spirits were dowsed in sorrow, or nostalgia. As I sank into the firm leather of the car's rear seat, the hand Pudgy placed on my forehead the day he purchased me from my mother started to sear my memory. I tried not to remember but couldn't stop myself, until I suddenly realized I wasn't that youngster anymore and that all I had in common with my former self was the embittered circumstance of my solitude.

Beetles that have four knuckles on the tarsi of their back pair of legs and five on all the others, like the dung beetle, are a kind of scarab and cram their natural filth in holes dug out of the mud. Providence could have gifted them a life in a luxury mansion, like the one I own here, isolated from prying eyes, closely guarded by complex electronic systems, with lovely lawns and beautiful architecture, but it wasn't to be, and that's why they spend every cycle of their lives frolicking in the mud. Insects don't protest about their filthy environment, and that's really virtuous of them. Then something stamps on them unawares, and their senseless lives are squelched flat. Everybody should have the right to a reasonable abode, a decent roof beneath which to drop dead, a roof of their own and not the universal one of the stars, but it's not the case, and that's the difference that ensures that we who do have one delight in the pleasure of possession.

My brother Tranquilino, may he rest in peace, set fire to the ants' homes with no malice aforethought. The flashes of light given off by burning phosphorus illuminated their tragedy, and they were singed in a second. The iron express swept my brother Tranquilino off. He met a bad end, but had he survived, you bet he'd have threatened the whole Spanish ant population with extinction. Those who pass away early find that the exercise of their will, assuming they ever had such a thing, is axed at a stroke, and if not, no matter, they can just fertilize history. The bathroom where I defecate every morning has a set of mirrors with a hanging shelf where fifteen bottles of scent give the utmost joy to my sense of smell. I sit on the pan, look at myself, and wallow in the teratology that gives me substance. Then I open the bottles one by one and breathe in the perfume. Apart from calming my anxious brow, I register the fact that contradiction is the foundation stone of the universe, and perhaps that's why harmony can only arise from antagonism. My truncated silhouette stands out against the wall of mirrors and reflects a chimera of myself that's the real me. If you could smell my insides, you'd be surprised that far from stinking, my aroma is simply expectorant. If one could sniff people's pristine insides, Western civilization as we know it would, however, choke to death on its own vomit.

Early one morning I was having a shower and witnessed an extraordinary event that shocked me to whatever marrow is in my bones. Water was splashing off my body, and the steam it generated gradually coalesced on the bathroom mirrors. Some drops liquefied on the surface, and instead of dripping down onto the perfume shelf, I could see they were scrawling signs that were initially undecipherable. I stared at the spectacle and noticed that the steam was changing into a written word. I stayed stock still until it finished. An emphatic *bastard* appeared in perfectly shaped letters on the mirror. That happening stayed with me for a considerable time. Initially, I thought a member of my domestic staff, a maid or my butler, must have inscribed the word on the mirror so it would stand out when dampened by the steam, and although I concluded it was not at all likely, I sacked the lot. I felt it was intolerable that someone could, on the sly, profane the holy of holies of my defecations. Normality was restored, until a few months later a new message materialized before my eyes, and this time without recourse to steam. No doubt about it—my life was under threat.

The pizzas produced in my premises are aromatized with fragrances that consumers immediately recognize. They are elemental smells, capable of transporting them to a would-be childhood of wood fires, freshly reaped corn, and damp grass at dawn. One has to exploit everything in the free enterprise jungle, from recourse to clichés to the cultivation of customers' trite sentimentality. Profit is the goal; a good return, the way to go. Wealth expansion can only be assured through sustained growth. It's no use having a sales boom if tastes move on and one is unable to keep up with society and adapt one's products to the volatile whims of the people's palate. A hundred years ago, chicken was a dish reserved for the jaws of the rich, and look how that's changed. If one wants the sustained development of fast food, there's no choice but to respond to consumer preferences at every turn. Quality levels and excellent products can only be achieved by paying close attention to the idiosyncrasies of the people destined to eat them. A proper monitoring of products underpins launches of other riskier, more innovative items that guarantee our brands remain the consuming public's favorites. The business context in which my Europizza outlets strive to trade is framed by aggression and originality that outdoes the competition. These are free-market times in which man is but a customer to man, and that, it seems, is how it is written that it should be. That's the gift with which Providence regales men on the make, those whose true stature thrives on big challenges, those whose brilliant drive and energy shape societal behavior, and also those who quantify morality in statistics.

The analysis and study of customer prototypes is, I can tell you, an essential exercise to guarantee the survival of any enterprise. Who eats my pizzas? That's the question we in Europizza constantly ask ourselves. Statistics give us our answers. Midweek it's married couples with small children, and eighty percent order our more classic products, while a similar proportion of young singles of either sex eat our pizzas with the most exotically sounding toppings. The Mazzo pizza is the most popular item from our entire menu—surimi with a base of green garlic, capers, mushrooms, and a savory dressing of yogurt and basil. Weekend demand, however, is dominated by family sizes; the Half-Yard Magnus, the DeLuxe Big'un, and the Maxi-Mix with triple cheese are our star-rated specials. Thousands of families with average purchasing power just love to consume them in the privacy of their homes while watching a game of football nicely served up on the box. The added value our products bring to the well-being of society is the undeniable guarantee of our commitment to the future. Apart from securing a proper return on capital invested, we try to ensure that the communities in which we have a presence accept us as one more element in their diets and leisure pursuits. Consequently we take care to decorate our premises in step with the individual characteristics of the different places where they are sited; we make a real effort to adapt to local customs and traditions and even grant communities the social cohesion they lacked. In our outlets, customers receive a friendly, casual, attentive welcome, which at the same time is always respectful, warm, and polite; our employees look youthful and are biologically tested to avoid any possible spread of undesirable diseases. To keep abreast of the times, we take pride throughout our chain of production in a transparent commitment to the environment, so every piece of our packaging is recyclable, and all the packaging we use carries a green statement endorsing the obligations we recognize we have toward society. Solidarity guarantees our future. That's the image we want to promote.

My brother Tranquilino, though a simpleton, understood little of such nonsense. He never tried a pizza, a train swept him up in the dawn of youth. A great pity. He never tasted a pizza, though he would have hated the flavors; he was happy setting light to ants and sucking on his fingers and nails, which were always full of dirt. He also took out snot when it was clogging up his nostrils. If I was nearby, he'd stick it on my face and laugh, though never maliciously. Once, I remember, he put a fat blob in my mouth, and it tasted of cooking salt. If he had lived, he'd have envied me my fortune, and I'd have had no choice but to pay his bills—down to what they call blood bonding. The dead sometimes yearn after the life of the living and put in an appearance in order to disturb their peace and quiet. Faith Oxen would have cursed my success if she'd lived another twenty years, but nature is wise and sensible and took her off in good time to that other shore of nothingness, where food, so it seems, is in short supply.

I know you have come to be entertained by the spectacle of my death. Night is coming to an end, and the birds' hungry squawks are beginning to echo against the metallic dawn sky. I'll soon lose this illusion of consciousness with which I still think I remember past time, and I will enter a territory of oblivion I should never have left. All those who saw fit to know me will participate unawares in the ritual of my destruction, and although they, like you, will end up realizing they are guilty, it will be through them that my life assumes the meaning for which it was created. That is the paradox, Providence's sarcastic grin my way: whoever kills me also gives me life; whoever resurrects me, condemns me. I knew it would happen, but I didn't think it would happen so ridiculously. I was forewarned. First there were the insults written in my bathroom, then the anonymous messages. I started receiving them by phone. I'd get calls at an untimely hour on private numbers that only my trusted circle had access to, and that alarmed me. "We're going nowhere like this. I'm up to here with you. Either you keep to your own storyline, or this will turn into an endless pastiche. Do you get what I'm saying? Do you grasp what I'm after?"

"Tell me who you are, you wretch," I rasped angrily, but nobody answered at the other end of the line.

Over time the messages began to appear in strange places that were completely inaccessible for people who didn't belong to my entourage—words painted in lipstick on my car's white leather upholstery, notes inserted in my billfold, missives under my pillow, and even strange voices buzzing around my head, as if, in addition to myself, a voice-over from someone else's consciousness were shouting inside my brain. Then came the apparition, and everything began to fall into place.

Human beings find it hard to accept proof of their own precariousness, and that's why they cling to the minutiae of day-to-day life to try to gain strength in routine; as soon as they drop their guard, however, fear surges, defeats, and annihilates them. Of the four evils that claw into man's so-called freedom—impotence, fear, neglect, and nostalgia—nostalgia is the worst to experience at night, when consciousness is least alert and words scrape the throat as they are silenced in desperation. One can bite the jugular of fear and it will fade like the phantom of the self it is, one can fight impotence plastered on alcohol and it will be forgotten till the next restless night, and one can hold neglect at bay with the saturnine sauces of pleasures of the flesh; conversely, it is dangerous to resist nostalgia, because it returns with renewed energy and is then quite unforgiving.

If not Providence, it was perhaps nostalgia that compelled me after all those years to track down the whereabouts of little Margarita. Private eyes do their job the best they can, and given the right economic wherewithal, they can come up with astonishing results. It took hardly a week for a report to appear on my desk detailing her abode. She lived in Ciudad Real, she was a widow, childless, ran a small haberdashery stocked full with extra-large knickers for fat ladies, and on a Saturday night she liked to go to a flea-pit of a bingo hall called The Eldorado Palace, which she sometimes left on the arm of a handyman. For private eyes, life is reduced to aseptic dossiers, surreptitious photos, and brief notes, totally lacking any meat or passion. That's their work, and that's why they get paid. "She is a completely uninteresting woman," that skinny, anodyne fellow told me when I handed him a check with his honorarium. "And what exactly would not being 'completely uninteresting' mean in your book?" I asked brusquely, annoyed by his inopportune suggestion. "I don't know, having a secret, hidden side, some criminal intent to investigate," he replied, his eyes glued to the scrawl of my signature. "Would you perhaps find me interesting?" I decided to enquire. "Yes, of course. You are a wealthy man."

The flaking façades of the houses that light up the Ciudad Real ring road looked like tiny drawers in the cupboard of life. There, everyday shortages must impregnate the minds of the inhabitants with the reek of boiled greens given off by disillusion. I gave my chauffeur the address from the report, and we soon found the spot. I got out of the car and stealthily walked over. I looked dispiritedly through the shop window at the way time, that sidekick of putrefaction, had mistreated the impossible love of my childhood. The kilos tumbled off little Margarita like chewy strings of cold sausage, and the whole mass of her body came to rest on the powerful seat of her buttocks. The goddess of my dreams was only recognizable in the sneering mouth and lengthy eyelids that as an ingenuous child I'd mistaken for beautiful features. It was there, standing by that window, chagrined at being stripped so suddenly of the great white hope from my past, when, God knows why, the idea of killing her suddenly sprang to mind. It was a viscous feeling, as if excreted from the sphincter of a supreme being rather than being born within me.

Ordinary people's hands aren't usually stained with blood. Ordinary people don't realize they are playing bit parts in the tragicomic farce of existence. Poets often gloss the paradoxes of human drama in graphic fashion, by simply letting the ink flow freely, without subterfuges or palliatives. When ordinary people stain their hands with blood, they never think that the act they've committed hasn't depended strictly on the exercise of their own individual will and that it might, on the contrary, be a decision taken by an unknowable supreme entity; they assume their guilt and at most purge it. Taking little Margarita's life wasn't in my hands. Nor do I think it was in yours to come here and entertain yourself with my vicissitudes. Just like me, you are part of destiny's cunning game, and we're both made to believe we are in control of our own decisions, when we are only bit parts in a pre-orchestrated show; some are dancers, others, actors, and most, acrobats, or the distinguished public that at best is stunningly grateful for the truce brought by the interval as they gradually realize everything is empty, hollow, and made of cardboard.

Thrust lock, stock, and barrel into that farce I'm recounting, I began increasingly to wonder how I could take life away from little Margarita. A mere thought became an obsession, a wish, a necessity, as if by committing such an act, I could put aside the bloody chalice of my past for once and for all. I only imposed a single condition to purge my consciousness completely: she should be fully aware I was the one sending her the ultimate gift of death.

Even if every inch of my behavior was investigated, it could never be said that I'm a criminal, or, conversely, that

I display the usual conventional prejudices against crime. Men's painful acts are predetermined, that's why they commit them. Likewise their playful forays. Destiny is a book beset by meaningless replies. I hardly had to rack my brains to concoct the means; Providence deemed fit to mete out its sarcastic punishment by having it come to me while I was having a pee in my office toilet. I could have paid the rate and hired a local thug to get rid of her, but it was out of my hands. I could have ordered my chauffeur to knock her over any Saturday I wished as she left her bingo hall, and, for the right price, he'd have obeyed my orders and not argued, but I didn't do that, either.

Events developed apace a few days after that trip to Ciudad Real, and everything happened within the bounds of my own office. Because of my blight, I have to perch on the pan when peeing, just like a female, though in reverse, with my torso always facing the wall. How he tricked the security systems controlling access to the building and managed to overcome the restricted entry to my floor is something I'm in no position to explain. One enjoys a beautiful view of Madrid from high up in my bathroom. The tops of the highest buildings are within my purview, sometimes hidden in smoky mists of cloud, and nothing vitally important seems to happen in the labyrinth of streets, the same streets where I tanned the leather of my youthful hide in a life of petty crime. Right opposite, in the distance, one can see the top of the aerial of the Telefónica building on the Gran Vía and, slightly to the right, the flat roofs of the westward-facing Edificio España. The city is unreal from so high up; there should be a ban on constructing into the heavens.

Perhaps he gained entry by swinging off one of those platforms used for cleaning skyscraper windows out in the elements, but I didn't ask. While I was peeing, and recreating in my mind's eye the voluminous spectacle of little Margarita, a brutal shove suddenly bashed my face against the lavatory cistern. My lower lip split as it hit the lid, and a streak of ruby-red blood stained the icy-white porcelain. Still not grasping what was happening, I felt a nasty kick in the ribs that really hurt my insides. I remembered Blond Juana and the time I accosted her in the lavatory in the party locale, but these blows were more accurate and more vicious. I looked up, and the first thing I saw was the slanting scar starting on the right cheek that split his face in two. "You must have stolen one hell of a lot, dwarfy, to get so high, and you didn't remember your friends one little bit, did you?" Years of suffering had slimmed him down, with the help of a rapacious infirmity; he was half bald, missing teeth, and, above all, was no longer handsome. "Hey, Handsome, don't trample on me, take your foot off, I can't breathe." Handsome Bustamante laughed over me, the holey sole of his trainer pressing down on my chest, on the point of bursting my lungs. "Well, well, Goyo, you're not the clown you were, you don't laugh at your friends' little pranks no more, the good life means you're not as humble as you used to be. Pity your luck's run out." Bustamante thrust his right knee into my stomach and ran the edge of his knife along my lower jaw. "I've been after you for years," he said, splattering me with gobs of saliva. "Prison is a good place to work out revenge, there's a lot of time in the pipeline and not much to do. When the lights went down, the sound of your disgusting squealing echoed round my head night after night, and my blood would start to boil; only a hit of horse could dull my desire to kill you, but to get those I had to sell my ass to the dealers. Look what's left. I'm no good even for buggery anymore, and now you're going to pay for all the damage."

The merciless, heartless, impious prison air had implanted its shadows over handsome Bustamante's body. From prison to prison, from cell to cell, like a pilgrim of the holy bars, Handsome had learnt to put up with life with a mixture of resignation and scorn, seasoned with the oil of revenge. After the great amnesty release, he'd pursued me for weeks, then tired of enquiring on street corners and opted to inject china white into his veins, beating people up, stealing, living poorly off whores—the kind that bring neither profit nor pleasure, who'll suck you off with a mouth full of chewing gum—working the streets to the limits of what's healthy, till he fell in with two other guys and snuffed out a queer jeweler who traded in bits and pieces, little knickknacks. Beatings, sexual favors, and the meanest squealing, such exemplary behavior thus earning him over the years the third degree treatment, and the big scar that sailed across his face bore witness to his private little hell. Infectious gawkiness had replaced the agile, angelic movements that once made him so admired on the high wire. He was like a mortally wounded animal that might still have clung to a lingering beauty, an animal caught in a rusty trap that destiny had laid with its eyes shut. Time hadn't showed him one iota of pity, and his lordly, youthful arrogance had shrunk to a frightful bellow, and the last straw, his stinking breath spread manure over every word he uttered. "Have the guts to not kill me and get the most out of me, Handsome," I said with no conviction. Right then nobody would have bet a counterfeit coin on my life, and yet Handsome, perhaps out of nostalgia for the past, stood and looked at me thoughtfully while the point of his knife gently stroked the wall of my jugular. "What do you mean 'get the most out of you'?" he asked, intrigued. "The most I'd like from you is to see you dead." I implored him to go easy with the pressure of his knee on my chest. I knew that if I could offer him a credible way out of these desperate acts, I might be able to save my skin, at least for a day. I sweet-talked him all I could and calmly went about persuading him. "There's nothing we can do to change the past, Handsome," I drawled, "forget it and try to enjoy what you can get out of life, for as long as you can, if you use your wits. Let me give you the means. Look at me, don't you see how I live in a land of milk and honey. I'm no use to you dead; alive you can have my money." Handsome Bustamante's eyelids drooped, he removed his knife, and, with obvious reluctance, listened to the offer I made, which he accepted, without a qualm. A pity. It cost him his life.

What won't a man do for money—swindle the innocent, defecate in public, renege on his religious convictions? Money is the measure of all things in this world, those that are what they are, and those that aren't what they aren't. Money relaxes the sphincters and relieves stress; whoever's got some knows so, whoever handles the stuff guesses it's so. What wouldn't you do for money—bear false witness, eat worms straight from a corpse, murder whoever you were told to? I was telling handsome Bustamante about my plan to end little Margarita's life, and he thought it a wonderful idea, provided the reward was substantial. "You name the price you want. Half now, the rest when you've done." Handsome Bustamante accepted the deal; one death in exchange for another wasn't a bad fix if rich pickings were on offer—for the two more days of life the syndrome would have granted him, that is. I insisted on only one thing: that before ending little Margarita's life, he should recite to her on my behalf a few lines from Gustavo Adolfo Bécquer, so she could be under no doubt that however much we struggle on, the past always comes back to defeat us. I wrote them on a piece of paper while we waited for a small suitcase to arrive with half of the amount in cash Handsome had agreed to as his price. "Is everything all right, Don Gregorio?" asked the security guard who'd been told to bring the money when he saw that hoodlum by my side. "Yes, Jimmy, everything's fine, leave us alone, please." (Security men are yet another symbol of the uncertain times we live in—if you can pay for them, that is, if not, you'll simply be on the receiving end.) When Handsome finally left my office, he looked and stared at me as if something strange were troubling him inside. "What did I ever do to hurt you, Goyo?" he asked. "Nothing you'd ever accept as an explanation." "Why did you pin the death on me, you bastard?" he asked again nervously. Nobody had insulted me like that in a long time, and coming from Handsome on this occasion, it inevitably reminded me of the night when Frank Culá died for love. "I don't remember, Handsome," I lied, "time erases everything. The only thing I can say in my defense is that it wasn't me, it was the justice system that clapped a life sentence on you. What's more, you already had problems with the law. Blame Lady Justice and not me, take it out on her apparatus if you're still so angry,

341

and if you do, remove the blindfold over her eyes for me, will you, and stuff it up her cunt, like a sanitary towel, so when it blows up it doesn't spatter the world. I've just bought you oblivion. Now, in exchange, try doing what I've paid you to do. When you're done, we'll be quits. Nothing else matters, Handsome; can't you see nothing else matters anymore?"

I have known countless bastards in my lifetime and never wished a bad end on any; if that's what they got, it was down to something else. Providence likes to sketch out the designs of men spitefully, that's its sarcastic bent. Little Margarita told the police that a rook, black as the center of hell, flew cawing out of Handsome's skull, but they didn't believe her. Police take only facts as proof and discount any possible supernatural intervention. In my lifetime I have watched several rapid-action scenes that were preludes to death and have studied the faces of certain individuals and discerned a motive for betrayal, or at least the name of the culprit. In every case, I've sensed the lyrics of destiny hysterically weighing in. Poetry sometimes resolves problems of transcendence; at others, however, it makes them worse.

The judge lifted up Handsome's still-fresh corpse, with an expression of repugnance. His head had been sliced in two by the bullet fired by little Margarita right between his temples. "It was self-defense," she said, quite without remorse. She was telling the civil guards how he'd forced his way in and was intending to inject her with a syringe full of AIDS-infected blood. "The gun belonged to my father, and

343

he was one of yours, you know. He threw himself at me like a wild animal. I had no choice but to shoot him. He must have been jonesing like crazy, because all he did was say that the swallows would come back and hang their nests on my balcony and other such nonsense."

The bullet split his skull in two like an Easter egg, out of which a crow flew out cawing rather than any child's treat. It must have been Handsome's thoughts. "It flew out of the window, I swear to you. It was this big, a disgustingly big bird that wouldn't stop squawking."

I saved on the other half of my outlay, but little Margarita saved herself from a bad end and is still around wallowing in the mire; that was the source of my discontent, and now nobody will ever bring me relief on that front. There are people who swear blind about the everyday nature of paranormal events, and would never question the hypothesis that a rook had flown out of Handsome's brain, just as little Margarita claimed. However, daily duties block our perception of what is beyond comprehension and atrophy our minds like crazy. Having a family, worrying about it, and striving to make it a success diminishes our ability to appreciate the extraordinary. Every family has its smell, just as every animal has its stench. Some conceal it under fragrances purchased at perfume shops, but even so they don't eradicate it entirely. A good nose can be a rare nasal skill, but it helps the economic standing of its owner very little, or not at all. I sweated out my youth under the patched tent of the Stéfano circus, a veritable perfume lamp of pestilence. It was there I learned to guess an animal's illness simply from a whiff of the vapor rising from its excrement, to calibrate a man's fear by smelling the sweat of his brow, and to assess the appetites of a female from the aromas when she was in heat. Gurruchaga taught me. Smell reveals the identity of the species and determines individual traits. Bastards carry a dense smell of vintage semen or cerumen; you can tell their condition a long ways off. Little Margarita always smelled of rotting flesh, though I never noticed till the day Handsome didn't deliver the goods. Gelo de los Ángeles smelled of sweaty talcum and slippery disasters. He slid off the trapeze and was confined to a wheelchair for the few years left to him in this world. "If I'd known I'd be reduced to an invertebrate, I'd have been better off killing myself when I fell." Doris did the charitable thing and brought him death on the sly. She suffocated him by putting a dry cloth in his mouth and soaking it till she blocked his trachea. She shed one tear after another while she did so. She only ever told me. Then she paid for a couple of masses, to see whether his soul might make it up to the skies as nimbly as he used to when he was young. On the other hand, I never did find out whether they consummated the love they never confessed to. Doris smelled of a bunch of fruit, of black grapes macerated in the oblique light that's the death rattle of a dying summer. I still remember her with her back to me, treating her swollen rectal veins with Xeroform while, prostrated by a temperature, I inhaled the spectral effluvia of the disinfectant, though quite unintentionally. I've only ever smelled anything like it on one other occasion. It was in a London hotel. I'd taken a few days off to visit my son Edén in the institution where he was receiving medical treatment. We went for a walk in the meadows in Kew Gardens, we lunched on cheddar and cucumber sandwiches in Fortnum and Mason's and then paid the Tate Gallery a visit to kill time. It was showing a retrospective of the painter

Francis Bacon. They say that art eases the understanding of autistic children and can have surprising therapeutic outcomes. I excitedly told the doctors what had happened in the museum on our return to the sanatorium, but they gave it no clinical importance. They simply shook my hand and assured me that the cure for his illness was a slow and complex business and, as we know, what's slow and complex is always expensive.

I'd still not taken my clothes off. I was waiting for room service to bring up the selection of cinnamon and ginger cookies with the warm glass of milk I'd ordered. Although my stomach still felt upset after the day's ups and downs, I felt like eating something sweet before going to bed and comforting my mind with a pill or two. Someone knocked on the door, and a uniformed waitress trundled in the sweets trolley and parked it under the large damask curtains framing a window that looked over Regent Street. Outside, a whispering drizzle dampened the murky streetlights. The gloom filtered through the windowpanes, and its brushstrokes darkened my spirits. I've always thought that extravagant bedrooms in grand hotels were pantheons to vanity; the comfort is funereal, and their ostentation shrouded in meaninglessness. The waitress withdrew from the small drawing room but not before giving a small reverential curtsey and bowing her head, though rage flashed in her eyes at having to perform such a pantomime before a dwarf; one notices such things. I remained deep in thought for a few seconds. Suddenly, an incandescent glow began to surge in a corner of the room. It was a streak of shadow tinged with a phantom gleam, a somber wraith of frozen light that gradually set into a figure with a human aspect and recognizable features. It smelled of aldehyde, asepsis, and the infinite. I didn't budge; neither was I especially shocked when I recognized her. Before my astounded gaze, Faith Oxen had returned from the land of sepulchers. "I'm hungry, Gregori," the dead woman told me, "there's a lot of hunger in this novel, chew a sweet for me." I obeyed. I put a bun in my mouth, biting into it reluctantly as I eyed the ectoplasm's movements. The specter gave a satisfied smirk and went on talking. Its silhouette shook in the air like the blown wick of a candle, and that made it difficult to anticipate how it would move. It assured me that in the world beyond, from which it had just returned, food and drink didn't exist, nor did any feeling that might recall the sensuous joys of conscious life; there was only equivocation. "I'm creased with hunger, give me more food before you, too, disappear," the scarecrow droned. I swallowed and concentrated my nerves in my Adam's apple, not daring to utter a word. "You were deceiving yourself when you said it all ended with death," it continued. "You were deceiving yourself when you thought I'd leave you in peace if you stuffed me with sweet pastries. You wanted me to die inconsolably, and now I've come to ask for solace."

Clearly, that thingy had come to criticize my behavior, wielding all the authority its supernatural dimension granted. I didn't respond to a single one of its needling provocations; I simply tried to relax while watching what was happening. For a whole ten minutes, long as fragments of eternity, the apparition continued its speech from beyond the grave, a speech shot through with vagaries and imprecision that nevertheless contrasted with the surprising exactness with which it displayed its knowledge of certain unspeakable incidents from my past. The scarecrow laughed, and with every guffaw exhumed, it undermined my sangfroid. The hermetic nature of its language meant I didn't grasp the entire disquisition, but at one specific moment, I thought I did see it was making fun of anything to do with my wealth and treated me as a simpleton, a puppet, a fictional being. Past, present, and future seemed to issue from its mouth, and it made no difference whether it dredged up a memory or sketched out a prediction when it came to appreciating the unreal mush permeating its words. Listening, I was reminded of forgotten incidents and learned of others that had yet to happen, like the unforgivable one here and now when you, on the other side of this book, are reading what happened and realize you are my interlocutor, the person in whose presence my existence must run its course. "We the characters don't belong to the universe of the living, nor do we commune with the detritus of the dead. That's our sentence, Gregori," Faith told me. "We have no options, criteria, or will. We just play out our roles in the farce we are called to inhabit. We jump to the orders of whoever granted us this pretense to consciousness and are in debt to the imagination of those who read us. Our blight is that we're created; our challenge is to be credible. Please chew another sweet for me, the juicy kind that can bring a tingle of pleasure back to my palate. In this life without life where I roam, one can't even enjoy the sensation of being nibbled by insects. Man's struggle is futile, Gregori, a dwarf's struggle against fate; abandon them to their second-guessing and come and enjoy me while you can. Why don't you answer me? Come on, give me the solace you denied me; I beg you, drop those trousers, I'm famished."

I didn't budge or say a word. I wasn't upset and didn't make a run for it. I didn't shout or spit in the air to vaporize the nightmare swaying before my eyes. I picked up the sugar bowl and hurled it at the specter, hit it on the head so unluckily it went clean through its nonexistence and crashed into a genuine Chinese vase I'd placed on a marble-topped chiffonier, unleashing a calamitous din of broken porcelain that dissolved the apparition without more ado. With a dramatic flop, that entire structure of antimatter ceased to exist, leaving only traces of the disturbing odor I've described and the enigmatic echo of its words buzzing round my head like so many burst bubbles of unreality. Later, over time, I preferred to believe that that scarecrow wasn't really Faith Oxen, that the apparition I'd gazed at had only existed in my imagination, that it was all the product of a bad dream, perhaps provoked by the horrific upset I suffered when I heard for the first time in the Tate Gallery the accusations leveled at me by my son Edén. However, I've gradually come to realize it was quite the contrary, until I finally managed to decipher the message that bastard Faith Oxen had decided to reveal from her fantastic world beyond in order to make me suffer. I've become increasingly convinced and demoralized as I've been forced to accept that it really was Providence whimsically tracing my steps across this world, which may or may not be real, where the story of my life was forged, one story locked into another, one that's more generic but no less phantasmagoric: the general story of Spain that unites us both.

There was a knock on the gate that morning. The sun was spreading springtime, chirruping across the sky, and I was in time, breakfasting on a pippin apple. They came to inform me. A beggar woman was down in the street shouting that she would slice open her veins if they didn't let her see me immediately. She was accompanied by a silent child who gazed blankly at a nonexistent horizon. I ordered my butler to call the police, and he replied that he'd already taken the liberty to do so, but the situation remained extremely compromising, and the mad woman's life was surely in danger. I peered at the security monitor that records images of the entrance and identified her at once. On that black-and-white screen, she looked like driftwood cast onto the shore of life by the tide of time. I ordered them to let her in. She'd aged, and she burst into tears when she saw me, and that made me reflect on how much she must have suffered to humiliate herself before me in that manner. My brother Tranquilino burnt ants' nests as a form of amusement and never worried about the insects' suffering. It wasn't in his nature to feel or not to feel compassion; he did what he did and didn't think about the consequences, he never regretted doing it—that, at least, was in his favor. "Why are you paying me a visit after all these years, Blondie? It doesn't seem your enthusiasm for revolution worked for you." Blond Juana, in rags, gripped her son's wrist. Hard times had prematurely aged her; her flesh looked soft and puffy, as if kneaded by a bludgeon. Nobody would have been surprised to see her selling paper hankies by a traffic light. "This boy carries your blood," she said drily, "he was your farewell present. I can't provide for him anymore, and he needs medical attention. He's ill." The true victory in my life had come by surprise, like those sudden deaths that dishearten the enemy and suddenly frustrate their battle strategy.

I could tell you that man's fate is written by the angels in semen on passion's damp pages, but I won't, just in case that, too, is true. Blondie's memory had disintegrated, and now she only believed in reasons to survive and in the peace of mind brought by not thinking. She told me of terrible things, worse even than burning ants for pleasure or bludgeoning dogs in the teeth for the fun of hearing them howl. My son was absent and stupefied, and though he looked at me, he kept his thoughts to himself, supposing he had any. "What's your name?" I asked. "Edén, like Comandante Cero," he replied without a glimmer of pride.

She told me of terrible things. She'd killed men and women with her own hands. She'd sliced through their necks with a blunt knife when they were still gasping their last; she showed no pity to her enemies. She endured five of the nine months of her pregnancy shooting it out in the sierras, then rage won out, and she fell in with a traitor. It was like a little girl's crush, and softly, softly she saddled him with her offspring. They abandoned the hue and cry of pistols and settled in a little village to the east of Matagalpa.

They ran a bar where the troops drank rum to let off steam. Her man drank a lot and then took it out on her with a club. After he'd given her a good beating, he'd switch tack to make a quick buck from her flesh, which he sold on to Sandinista officers for two notes per ride. Whatever they found out from chitchat, they'd pass on to the Contras, in order to sustain life between two lines of fire, and they carried on until, for a handful of coins, the barman finally squealed to the military all they could possibly want to know about their enemy's positions, plans, and matériel. My son grew up at his mother's side, bereft of intellect, detached from any upbringing that wasn't what you learn from the behavior of animals. He'd sulk and spend the whole day sitting by the entrance to the bar, telling the time by the frequency of the customers' bouts of drunkenness, his mind frazzled by the sun that poured down. Blondie wasn't aware of the barman's treachery, and that saved her life. First they beat her in the face with the butt of a revolver, then they thrust the barrel in her mouth and fired it without a bullet, to give her a fright, or perhaps it just failed to fire. One of the *guerrilleros* wanted to slice off a nipple as a souvenir with a huge curved dagger, but by that time, they'd calmed down, after having fun executing the traitorous barman. When they tired of beating her, they buggered her unenthusiastically. They did it right there in front of the boy, while flies, those angelic insects, buzzed over his little head with proboscises smeared in lizard shit. Before that, as I said, they'd leisurely taken out their anger on the squealer. They put a hood over his head, a rope round his neck, and after breaking every bone in his body, they swung the little life left in him from a tamarind tree soured by toucan piss.

353

What wouldn't you do for love—provoke a natural catastrophe, undergo genetic alterations, even participate in sporting events? When it comes to love, the will is hallowed, and one goes into absolute self-denial to the point of annihilation. Blondie's body was covered in the scars from the blows meted out by the barman when he possessed her. Bastards sometimes sing from the same hymn sheet, and at others not so much, one can never know. When it comes to love, one would go round the world in rope sandals, or selflessly allow one's every other finger to be amputated. Blondie's skin was still marked by the gashes the barman's belt buckle left when he dowsed her desire to up and leave that tropical inferno. For a moment I imagined her naked on the earth floor of the bar, laid low by a soporific siesta, sniffing the shadows with her dilated nostrils, perhaps with the other guy next to her, crooning cheap, dirty lyrics in her ear and letting his hand wander whimsically over the ravaged geography of her thighs. I imagined her yet again feeling in her flesh the simmering crack of the whiplashes, and I was reminded of the rage with which little Santomás tore off strips of my skin that night, and then I glimpsed three or four drops of blood dripping down his side and, in a shocking fusion of pain and desire, melting into his sweat. My son later saw his putative father dead, swinging from one side to another, his head half-severed by the knife that was the rope. Croaking stone curlews flew close to his danse macabre. The scene must have drained his neurons, because the boy didn't burst into tears, he peed himself and became mute forever.

Humiliation is a visual expression of defeat. The humiliated adversary secretes defenselessness and generates pleasure in the executioner. I humiliated Blond Juana twofold, first by sinking the seed of my descendent in her flesh, and then by purchasing at the age of nine the life it engendered. "I'll look after the boy on condition that you never claim him and never see him again. At the same time, I'll rescue you from poverty and pay you a pension so you can get back on your feet, if that's what you want, in a life without a past, where neither he nor I exist." She accepted. I was also sold on as a child. They say history repeats itself. I never told my son of the circumstances that brought him to me, nor did I bother to inform him that a dwarf was his real father. I was resigned to seeing him remain locked in the hermetic box of his memories and sent him to London, to a renowned, highly recommended institution where he'd get the best treatment possible, which is the sort that one pays for quickly, without any wrangling. He didn't react when his mother bid him farewell forever with a kiss poisoned by remorse. He is stolid, impenetrable, and blank. He inhabits inner universes and only very occasionally shows remote interest in trivial or ephemeral matters. It's a sorry business to walk by his side. His companionship is pure ice, and I often wonder whether the grave wouldn't at least relieve him of that lethargy to which his autism condemns him. However, perhaps it is his fate to live in imagined worlds where the rules of logic don't exist and passions don't unleash their designs. Perhaps that world is truer than my own, the one where I find myself now, alone, empty, scrutinized by you, waiting for nothing else but the endpoint of my own consummation.

Pizzas are made from flour dough, baked in special chambers, strewn with tasty dressings, chewed with quiet relish, and, once digested, are expelled from the anal sphincter, transubstantiated into excrement. Levels of reality can be multiple and don't necessarily have to pass through the digestive tube of what is explicable. Dogs, fools, and poets intuit the worlds beyond what surrounds them and behave accordingly: the first howl, the second slaver, and the third make rhymes of passionate non sequiturs nobody appreciates in the slightest. I told the doctors; they mainly ignored me. My fool of a son spent the morning apparently engrossed in a painting hanging in a room at the Tate Gallery. We'd just lunched at Fortnum and Mason's on cheddar and cucumber sandwiches, which Edén barely touched. He was still too accustomed to eating the quasi-rotten food seasoned with chili his mother offered him. For a long time he made no sound that gave proof of thought or an intelligible expression of will. Whenever I go to London, I take him for a stroll along Oxford Street, or have fun accompanying him to see the caged animals in the Regent's Park Zoo. We also pop into the odd big department store, where I usually spend vast amounts on toys I send to the sanatorium with a view to bringing some relief to the inner solitude that fences in the brains of the children shut up there. I often take him to museums, to familiarize him with genuine parameters of beauty. He doesn't flinch or get upset; he follows me and says nothing. That morning in the Tate Gallery, he sat absorbed in that painting and didn't make a single gesture or murmur, he only let out a fart that flooded the room with an intolerable stink. The people looking at pictures around us turned their heads and eyed us, visibly annoyed by the bad odor—perhaps they were concluding that the stench originated from me and my deformities—when suddenly my son, as if struck by an epileptic fit, went into a purple frenzy of verbal diarrhea and began shouting out gutturally, as he pointed his index finger at the painting he was looking at. "It's you! It's you!" he cried frantically. I didn't react right away, I was so surprised to hear his voice, and it took me a few seconds to cotton on to what was happening. I had to stifle the boy's hysteria with a couple of slaps, which appalled the public there. "You are that dwarf," the child under sentence kept repeating, and in fact he was right, because that mess of floating entrails hanging on a wall of the Francis Bacon retrospective was yours truly, or rather, yours truly thirty years ago; that handicapped youth whose decomposing guts the pink-cheeked artist had felt like painting in the twilight brine of the Costa del Sol.

Fools, dogs, and poets are generally the ones who best intuit other worlds beyond. The first do so with slaver, the second with howls, and the third in verse. The fact that my son broke his word fast in such an explosive way put me in a sad mood for the rest of that day. Then the appearance of the specter

357

of Faith Oxen sewed the last stitches in the shroud of my anxiety. At the time, I didn't altogether understand what it said, but I gradually teased out the meaning of its sentences, until I grasped that scarecrow had learned all it uttered in the completed novel of my life, the seemingly trivial object your hands are holding at this very minute.

Disquiet unnerves me, predictions turn out to be true, and grief shoots through me like an electric shock, more and more by the day. Previously, I've never confronted the certainty of nonexistence, and yet the inevitable inspires no fear in me. I foresaw it simply looking you in the eye. I know your intentions aren't entirely to blame, that perhaps you don't even enjoy the irrelevant act of my disappearance, but I can do nothing to forestall what's written. I'd been advised previously about what was coming, but I didn't think it would be like this. It's hard having you here, intrigued by the last flourishes of my life, meanly longing to reach the moment of the finale that's now very near. However, it's Providence, not you, that decided the outcome in advance; you will merely acknowledge it when my words lurch to a final full stop. The imminence of the disaster gives me the strength I need to keep talking without cursing you. I need one last gasp of breath to distil in your face the few tremors of consciousness I have left, and to clear away, as that poet pointed out, circumstances referring to yesterday, to past time, which complete the scenario by relating things that might be of use to you in the struggle humans wage against destiny, a struggle they are fated to lose.

Listen to my death rattle, as you read, if it gives you pleasure. Birth comes on a warm, tender breeze that carries in its folds a completely enigmatic scent of a genome. Then the furious winds of life gust away and snatch whatever they can from each of us—a heart, or a soul. Poets, like fools and dogs, are privileged with a vision of the death agony of the time that belongs to humanity, its fleeting eras and futile endeavors. Doesn't death alone drive consciousness? Today, mine comes led by your hand, but it will be your turn one day, and you, too, will be forced to confront the murderer's ghastly silence.

I'd have preferred not to know that nothing is as fake as our own memories, that all is premeditated sarcasm, and that what we think are our experiences, hopes, or innermost fears are only the paltry manifestations of the uncertainty spawned by our attempts to believe we are alive. You, at least, exist for me at this very second. You are the only certainty left to me, and I know it will be in your hands that I must commend myself to my destiny at the turn of the page. Cocks' combs fall apart in the mouth like communion wafers, and as they slip down, they release an early morning cock-a-doodle-doo flavor. There is always a last supper. Sometimes one is aware of it, sometimes not. That's the only variation. I should have ignored Providence's orders and turned down the invitation it issued. Right now I'd be flying to London to spend the New Year with my son, and my life would follow its orderly path, but fate decided everything should take this ridiculous path—you waiting on tenterhooks, and me, sentenced to make my exit, still expecting to see Commissioner Dixon, panting to see the exceptional results produced by her pomade.

Dirt only anticipates the end that awaits us, in a trial run of the final shakedown that precedes the grave. Gurruchaga liked to contemplate the steaming excrement of the wild animals; he said it smelled of life, and he celebrated the stink. Conversely, Mandarino was happy with much less; lust ruled him, it was written in his nature. I had no news of him for a long time afterward, until on one of those restless nights when nervousness disrupted my sleep and television supplied company in the early hours and I saw him performing in a pornographic film. He was shown between two women whose nakedness was so much plastic. Mandarino sniffed their hidden corners with his grand schnozzle, whimpering from deep in his throat like a grateful dog. Their hands, meanwhile, toyed with his cock, using their hands, mouths, and sexes in an extraordinary outburst of animal activity, until he finally came in an avalanche of liquid snow that spoke of progeny.

It's strange to see how each individual incorporates their own behavior into the general unfurling of events to the point of self-redemption or self-annihilation. My brother Tranquilino failed early on because he crossed a railway track. He never kissed a woman or tried a slice of pizza, nor did he have time to meditate on his impending doom, and that was his stroke of good fortune. Without your mediation, I might have kept treading the illusory furrow of wealth, or become more renowned, if that were possible, in the choppy waters of the times, but a flash of intuition sufficed for me to understand the end was nigh, that my days would peter out in your hands. Hours, like pages, follow each other apace in a helter-skelter maelstrom. My hours were your pages, my pages your hours, and that's why I'm exhausted. You are my executioner, my hangman, the garrotter by appointment to Providence. Be aware of that. Finish my words, read the void on my face, for the last time close the book you are holding, then the consummation will be complete.

There's a knock at the door. Commissioner Belinda Dixon assured me she would come tonight to satisfy her most out-of-the-ordinary appetites, though I rather fear she won't arrive in time to save me from the end. A pity. I'd have liked to enjoy the electric thrills of the flesh for one last time. After all, the moment of desire is when a human being simmers most intensely, to the point of feeling immortal, but that's impossible now, all that's possible is a return to the inhospitable chaos of our departure point, which is where we come back to in the end.

In my lifetime I have known many bastards and wished a bad end on none, but perhaps you are one of the few I feel heartfelt gratitude toward; you've whiled away your time nosing around in my existence, recreating my world in your fantasy, gleaning from my sentences touches of reality not too distant from your own, even possessing the integrity to reach this crossroads in the fable where, by dint of peculiar arrangements you and I can't fathom, everything will now be consummated.

There's a knock at the door. Leave before it opens. Nobody's keeping you here, and I've no more spiel to spin to detain you any longer. The end moment is often much less horrific than people think, and you've had enough of the spectacle by now. The second you leave, my life will have attained its full meaning; what will linger on will be the frugal eternity of words and the curious way feelings are perpetuated across generations.

Nonetheless, two things will remain on my wish list: first, my inability to give little Margarita the bad end a bastard merits, and the knowledge that she's still dancing around out there somewhere, pickling in her own putrefaction; and secondly, dying without discovering what the hell the tomato masher looks like that Gurruchaga ordered me to fetch the day they took him prisoner on the merciless path to an execution squad. All down to Providence and its guiltily swishing tail.

Otherwise, after discounting luck and abandoning all hope, the only thing left to me is to ask that when your feigned pain becomes real and your heart beats restlessly, you recall yet again the poem which affirms that in the end, nothing can be done, that our orchestrated finale is imminent, that the adventure must end as it must, as it is written, as it is inevitably going to be.

ABOUT THE AUTHOR

Fernando Royuela is a Spanish lawyer and fiction writer who lives in Madrid. He has published six novels as well as several short stories and books of poetry. The success of the Spanish edition of *A Bad End* confirmed his place among the most talented writers of his generation and earned him the prestigious Ojo Crítico Award for the best novel of the year.

ABOUT THE TRANSLATOR

PETER BUSH is an award-winning translator who lives in Barcelona. His translations from Spanish include Valle-Inclán's *Tyrant Banderas*, García Lorca's *Sketches of Spain: Impressions and Landscapes*, and García Ortega's *Desolation Island*. His translation of Quim Monzó's *A Thousand Morons* is just out and other fiction from Catalan will soon follow: his wife Teresa Solana's *The Sound of One Hand Killing* and Mercè Rodoreda's *In Diamond Square*. His first translation was Juan Goytisolo's *Forbidden Territory*. He has translated a dozen books by Goytisolo.

Lightning Source UK Ltd.
Milton Keynes UK
UKOW01f0840140216

268285UK00002B/2/P